633 SQUA

OPERATION DEFIANT

By the same author

Novels in the same series:

633 Squadron: Operation Rhine Maiden
633 Squadron: Operation Crucible
633 Squadron: Operation Valkyrie
633 Squadron: Operation Cobra
633 Squadron: Operation Titan
633 Squadron: Operation Crisis
633 Squadron: Operation Thor

Rage of the Innocent
In Presence of My Foes
Years of the Fury

Saffron's War
Saffron's Army

A Meeting of Stars
A Clash of Stars

The Persuaders: Books 1, 2 and 3

Other novels:

Of Masks and Minds
Laws Be Their Enemy
Lydia Trendennis
The Sin and the Sinners
The Grotto of Tiberius
The Devil Behind Me
The Storm Knight
Waterloo
The Wider Sea of Love
The War God
A Killing for the Hawks (Mark Twain Literary Award)
The Tormented
The Obsession

Non-fiction:

Write a Successful Novel (in conjunction with Moe Sherrard Smith)

Novels under the pseudonym David Farrell:

Temptation Isle
Strange Enemy
Valley of Conflict
Two Loves
The Other Cousin
Mullion Rock

633 SQUADRON: OPERATION DEFIANT

Frederick E Smith

SEVERN HOUSE

This first world edition published in Great Britain 1995 by
SEVERN HOUSE PUBLISHERS LTD of
9–15 High Street, Sutton, Surrey SM1 1DF.
This edition published in the USA 1995 by
SEVERN HOUSE PUBLISHERS INC of
595 Madison Avenue, New York, NY 10022.

British Library Cataloguing in Publication Data
Smith, Frederick E.
633 Squadron. – Operation Defiant
I. Title
823.914 [F]

ISBN 0-7278-4774-0

All situations in this publication are fictitious and
any resemblance to living persons is purely coincidental.

Typeset by Palimpsest Book Production Limited,
Polmont, Stirlingshire.
Printed and bound in Great Britain by
Hartnolls Ltd, Bodmin, Cornwall.

Dedicated with love and affection to Barry, Rita, Vincent, Barry and to Liza who was so kind and helpful to my wife during her stay in England and who helped me to prepare the manuscript of this novel.

Acknowledgements

The author wishes to acknowledge his debt to the authors of the following works of reference:

Edward Bishop, *Mosquito Wooden Wonder*, Pan/ Ballantine.

M. S. Hardy, *The de Havilland Mosquito*, David & Charles.

M. Clarke, *De Havilland Mosquito Portfolio*, A Brookland Book in conjunction with Aeroplane.

Bekker, the Luftwaffe War Diaries, Macdonald.

Adolf Galland, the First and the Last, Methuen.

Richards and Saunders, *Royal Air Force 1939–1945*, HMSO.

Sir C. Webster and N. Frankland, *The Strategic Air Offensive against Germany, 1939–1945*, HMSO.

Chapter 1

The Me 262 jets came out of the sun like as many meteors and tore through the boxes of B17s almost before their crews could react to their danger. Unable to lay their Brownings on the dazzling jets, beam-gunners stared at one another in amazement. As half a dozen huge Fortresses, hit by the massive firepower of 30mm cannon, reeled from the formations and began spinning earthwards, startled pilots caught glimpses of streamlined bodies soaring up like rockets to make another attack. Startled voices and curses filled the airwaves.

'Sonofabitch, what the hell are they?'

'They've no props, Mac. You see that? They've no godammed propellers.'

'Look out, you guys. The bastards are coming again.'

The section leader was right. Swooping out of the sun again, the 262s picked their targets. Equipped with the latest R4M 5cm rockets beneath their wings, their pilots had no need to dive within the 800 yards range of the Fortresses' Browning guns. Instead each pilot released his salvo of 24 rockets and peeled away, leaving the tracer from the B17s arching impotently away into the empty sky.

The effect of each salvo was deadly. Giving a spreading cone of fire like a huge shotgun, the rockets swept down on each box of B17s like a murderous net. With a single hit sufficient to destroy an aircraft, Fortress after Fortress either exploded in midair or went reeling down with wings severed or engines aflame.

Nor did the B17s' escort of P51s fare any better. With the Me 262s at least 150mph faster, the Mustangs had suddenly become outmoded aircraft and their efforts to drive off the attackers only resulted in heavy losses themselves.

The sky was like a sea in which tiger sharks were darting among a bunch of ponderous turtles and tearing them to pieces. Showing great courage the B17 crews closed up their formations as bomber after bomber went down and continued on their mission. Relief only came when their attackers ran out of ammunition and were compelled to dive triumphantly away.

As shaken crews attended to their damaged aircraft and their wounded comrades, one thought was in everyone's mind. If the Germans had many more of this wonder aircraft, the Allies' hard-won supremacy in the air could no longer be taken for granted.

Hearing the sound of a car outside, Brigadier Simms glanced from the french windows of his library and nodded at Davies' question.

'Yes, it's the general. He's usually on time.'

Air Commodore Davies, small in stature but dynamic in personality, was wondering yet again why Staines wanted to see him. He had only received Simms' message that morning and in the hope that the American general had some important interservice operation in mind, he had driven straight over to High Elms.

Expecting Simms would have some idea what Staines wanted, he had been disappointed to find the SOE officer was as ignorant as himself. Since then Davies' mercurial nature had begun to show impatience as he waited for the American to arrive.

The library door opened half a minute later and a young Army captain appeared. 'General Staines is here, sir.'

Simms moved forward to meet the man who pushed past the captain. Staines, known by his American aircrews as Old Scratchy or Thunderass, was a big man in every sense of the word and his greatcoat added to his size. In his fifties, weighing 220 pound of bone and muscle, he had spiky hair and the face and body of an ex-boxer, although in fact American football had been his game. His gravelly voice had a Texan accent.

'Hiya, Simms. Good to see you again. How're you keeping?'

No contrast could have been greater than the one provided by Simms, the SOE officer. Slim in build, always courteous, distinguished in appearance with iron-grey hair and a small trimmed moustache, he was the archetypal English officer as imagined by Americans. His quiet, clipped voice matched his appearance.

'Good morning, General. Welcome again to High Elms. As you will see, Air Commodore Davies is here, as you requested.'

Staines grinned across the library at Davies, who gave him a salute. 'Hiya, Davies. Good of you to come at such short notice. How's that ace squadron of yours?'

'They're fine, thank you, sir.'

'I hear they did a damn fine job in Norway just before Christmas.'

'Thank you, sir. We think they did too.'

Staines's grin spread. 'I understood that maverick of yours, Harvey, led 'em. Who did he knock cold this time?'

Davies was unsure whether to smile or to defend his choice of leader. He decided on the latter.

'As he'd recovered from his wound, I decided to use him again.'

Staines moved over to the fireplace where three huge logs were burning. 'Yeah, so I gathered. Well, the guy did a great job at Buchansee. There's no denying that.'

The American held two big hands out to the fire. 'Jeez, it's cold this morning. I guess I'll never get used to your English winters.'

Simms was never slow to take a hint. 'Would you like coffee, General? With a dash of brandy perhaps?'

Staines gave his broad grin. 'You'll lead me into temptation, Simms. OK. Why not?'

As Simms pressed a button on the long mahogany table, Staines turned again to Davies. 'I expect you're wondering why I asked for this chinwag this morning, Davies?'

Davies, impatient as always when he believed his squadron might be involved, nodded. 'Yes, sir. I had wondered.'

Before enlightening him any further, Staines fumbled inside his greatcoat and drew out a cigar-case. Extracting a cigar that looked as big as a toy airship, he offered the case to the two men. As both declined, Davies watched Staines bite off the end of his cigar and light it. As the American inhaled, Davies had difficulty in hiding a shudder as memories flooded back to the time when, rather than play chicken, he had dared to accept one. As Staines gave a throaty chuckle, Davies knew the American had read his mind.

'What is it, Davies? Are you thinking about the time you smoked one of my stronger ones?'

'Yes, sir, I was.'

'It didn't do you any harm, did it?'

'I lived through it, sir, if that's what you mean.'

Staines grinned and blew out an expansive blue cloud.

'They grow on you, Davies. And, as I told you the last time, they're good for your libido.'

'They didn't do anything for my libido, sir. I couldn't look a woman in the eye for over a week.'

Staines grinned again. 'I guess it proves the old saying: What's one man's meat is another man's poison.'

'Yes, sir. I'm sure you're right.'

Feeling he had done his part in the courtesy foreplay, Davies felt it was time the serious business began. To his relief the American's change of tone suggested he felt the same.

'All right, gentlemen. Let's get down to the nitty gritty. I asked to see you both this morning because I wanted to know what information you have about these new fighters the Krauts are using.'

Simms was the first to answer. 'I take it you mean these Messerschmidtt 262 fighters?'

Staines gave a grunt. 'So you've heard about them?'

'Indeed we have. Are you finding them a threat to your bombers?'

'You can say that again. We sent ninety B17s out two days ago and the sons-of-bitches shot down sixteen of them.'

Davies gave a low whistle. 'Were your men escorted, sir?'

'Yeah. With a wing of Mustangs. And they couldn't get near them. Major Dent, the wing leader, reckons they were at least 150mph faster than his ships. Have you run into them yet, Davies?'

'No, but we've heard plenty of rumours. You don't think that plant we destroyed at Buchansee is in production again? Or that there's another one somewhere else?'

Staines shook his head. 'No. This isn't an adaptation from an old design. From all my boys say, it's an entirely new aircraft. And it's sensational.'

'They don't have propellers, I understand. What are they? Rocket-propelled?'

'No. My guys couldn't see any exhaust gases. Our Intelligence tells us they have an entirely new method of propulsion. Something about a mixture of gas and air that explodes and shoots them forward.'

Staines turned back to Simms. 'I'd like to hear what your people have found out, Simms.'

While the two Air Force officers had been conversing, Simms had been speaking quietly into a desk telephone. As Staines turned to him the door opened and a uniformed girl appeared. Saluting Staines, she handed a folder to Simms before saluting again and leaving the library.

Staines was eyeing the folder curiously. 'What's that? Your Intelligence report?'

Simms nodded and opened the folder. 'London sent us this information a few months ago. I'm afraid it's a bit like the curate's egg. Very detailed in places and sketchy in others. The enemy has been keeping very close security on these new aircraft. Just the same, London has done remarkably well to put all this together. It seems this new aircraft has been under development for the last four years.'

Staines raised an eyebrow. 'Four years?'

'Yes, but as you'll know an entirely new concept does take time to develop. The original plan was to produce a super bomber, which had Hitler's full approval. Apparently he wouldn't allow the word "fighter" to be used when discussing the aircraft, although when they saw its potential the Luftwaffe begged for a fighter version. It seems it has taken the massive Allied raids of the last nine months to get his agreement that some fighters should be built, although rumour has it he gave that permission very reluctantly.'

'It doesn't sound as if Hitler can be all that bad,' Staines muttered.

With a half smile, Simms turned back to the folder. 'From all we can gather the technical problems were formidable. It seems the first experimental unit was formed at Lechfeld, near Augsberg, under a Captain Thierfelder. It wasn't an entire success because he crashed in flames during one of the first trial operation sorties. He was succeeded by Major Walter Nowotny—'

'Nowotny,' Staines broke in. 'He had a hell of a record in Russia, didn't he?'

'Yes. He was an ace many times over. His conclusion was that his ground crews and pilots would need intensive training on such a revolutionary aircraft before they could become operational with any success but the Luftwaffe Command demanded immediate operations. So in October last year Nowotny and his Geschwader were posted to Achmer and Hesepe airfields which, as you know General, lie right across your main American bomber route. Nowotny could only put up three or four 262s at one time and yet in a month his unit knocked out over twenty aircraft.'

'Yeah, that's right,' Staines confessed. 'They weren't B17s from my unit but we got news of it.' His gravelly voice turned curious. 'You've got a hell of a lot of information there, Simms. How come? New aircraft designs don't come into your brief, do they?'

Simms, who was known by Davies to keep his cards close to his chest when matters of Intelligence were discussed, gave his gentle half smile again.

'Don't forget that for years we've been flying agents behind enemy lines. So we have needed to know what dangers they face.'

Staines gave a grunt. 'Maybe, but the stuff you've got there sounds as if it's come from the Kraut High Command itself. You got a man planted in there, Simms?'

The brigadier's smile gave nothing away. 'It's mostly come from London. Probably gathered from hundreds of sources and put together like a jigsaw. London is very adept at this kind of thing.'

At that moment a girl brought in a coffee tray and bottle of brandy. As she left the library, Simms picked up the brandy bottle and poised it over one of the filled cups.

'You'll say when, General?'

A perceptible pause followed before the American lifted a tobacco-stained hand.

Simms turned. 'What about you, Davies?'

Seeing Davies shake his head, Simms poured a spoonful into his own cup and then raised it.

'Your good health, General.'

Staines nodded, then continued where he had left off. 'You were talking about problems relating to the 262s, Simms. Do you know anything about the technical ones?'

Simms glanced down at his file again. 'London assumes most of them were caused by the 262 being such a revolutionary design. It's believed there was trouble with the engines overheating and with their positioning along the wings. Another problem appears to have been the 262s' armament. It originally carried either 20mm or 30mm cannon and although the latter shells were deadly if they struck, to fire them the 262 pilots had to close within the range of your B17's Brownings. So, lightning fast though the 262s were, it was possible for them to be hit when they flew through a box of Fortresses.

'The answer came when a new weapon was devised. It's a 5cm rocket carried on wooden rails beneath the 262's wings. They have a much longer range than the Browning guns and so can be fired at a box of Fortresses when outside their firing range. As a 262 can carry twenty-four and they can all be fired at once, the effect is like that of a huge shotgun. The rockets spread out and so increase the chances of a hit.'

Staines, who had been listening intently, nodded. 'According to my boys that's what happened two days ago. The goddamned rockets were coming at them like a swarm of bees. But what about the metal the fuselage and wings are made of? Is it a new alloy?'

Simms shook his head. 'For a long time London believed it must be to withstand the heat of high-speed flight. But recently that theory has been eliminated.'

Staines frowned. 'Why?'

'It seems our boffins did some experiments in wind tunnels and came to the conclusion the same metals used in standard fighters would suffice. In many ways this came as a relief to us. Until then, knowing Germany buys alloys from Sweden, our only hope of finding the 262 centres had been to follow a shipment from its docking in Germany to its ultimate destination. But because alloys are used for many high-speed weapons, including V2 rockets, we knew that our agents, even if they discovered the smelting centres, might still be led along dozens of red herrings before they found a 262 manufacturing plant.'

Davies was looking puzzled. 'But if it isn't necessary to buy alloys from Sweden, doesn't that eliminate one way of tracing a 262 centre?'

Simms nodded his appreciation at the question. 'Just the opposite, Davies. It cuts down the odds. Our boffins are pretty certain that the 262 parts are prefabricated before their final assembly. We also know that because of our heavy air attacks the enemy is having to work in protected environments such as railway tunnels and old coal mines. So, as the enemy buys steel and other products in Sweden, we checked with our military attachés there and they discovered the Swedes are also supplying some prefabricated parts. So it would seem reasonable to assume they are destined for 262 production.'

Staines's tough face had turned dark with resentment. 'If our people know this, why the hell hasn't anything been done about it?'

Simms shrugged. 'What could be done, sir? We can't

stop Sweden trading with Germany and these are Swedish ships sailing under a neutral flag. And even if we flouted the Geneva Convention and tried to sink them, it is well nigh impossible to get our submarines into the Baltic today.'

'OK. I give you that. But once in Germany the parts have to be transported by road or rail. Why hasn't a trace been put on them?'

'I suspect the answer your people and mine would give is a simple one, General. To date it hasn't been thought worthwhile.'

A cord was standing out on Staines's thick neck. 'Not worth while! When my boys are being killed by these 262s?'

'I appreciate how you feel, General. But it can't be denied that until now the 262s' effect on the air war has been minimal. And as our armies are on the German frontiers, I suppose the Powers That Be have decided other things take priority.'

Staines muttered an oath. 'For Christ's sake, these ships are lethal. If the Krauts had had 'em in service a year ago we wouldn't be flying in thousands over their Fatherland today. Has anyone any idea how many they're likely to build?'

Simms shook his head. 'I suppose that depends on too many factors: whether Hitler has changed his mind about putting defence before attack; what assembly lines have been put aside to build them; whether we can find and bomb these assembly lines, and so on. However the general consensus from both your Intelligence and ours is that it's now too late for the enemy to produce enough to change the course of the war.'

Staines gave another grunt. 'Yeah, that's what they keep telling me. Only it's not much consolation to my boys and their wives and sweethearts when my ships are shot down in flames as they were two days ago. I want to hit the bastards, Simms. The war could go on for months, may be another year, and if they aren't stopped I could lose hundreds more boys. So what can you do to help me?'

'We know where their new engines are manufactured. At Nordhausenn.'

As Staines gave a start of anticipation, Simms shook his head again. 'No, that's no use to you, General. The plant is quite secure against air attack.'

'Why? We can fly almost anywhere in Germany these days.'

'The engines are being manufactured alongside the V1 rockets and the entire complex lies underground in forty miles of tunnels.'

Staines's scowl returned. 'Then we're back to those prefabricated parts and their assembly points. Haven't you any idea where those points are?'

'No, General. But you can be certain of one thing. They'll be so cleverly sited or camouflaged that we'll never spot them from the air.'

'Yeah. That's what our Intelligence guys tell me. Then what about these shipments? Can't we have them followed?'

Simms hesitated. 'I could ask London but I'm afraid I know their answer.'

'Then what about using your own agents? They've done some great jobs for you in the past.'

Neither man noticed the slight start Davies gave at the mention of using the brigadier's SOE agents.

'I might get permission for that,' Simms said. 'But even if I do, don't expect too much. The enemy security will be rock-solid, as you can imagine.'

Davies broke in before Staines could reply. 'I'll ask if Moore has any ideas. After all, he told us there was talk among the German aircrews that a new fighter was on the stocks when he was in that German military hospital last year. We were only concerned at the time about the adapted aircraft that could be produced in thousands, so we didn't take much notice about the new one, possibly because the German crews themselves doubted it would be ready in time to affect the war.'

Staines's tough face lightened for a moment. 'Yeah. I remember that. So you'll have a word with Moore?'

Davies nodded. 'I'll also ask Anna Reinhardt if she has any ideas. After all, she did meet and talk to Von Haldenberg, who was working on the Buchansee project. He might have mentioned something to her about this new fighter.'

'OK, Davies. I'll appreciate any information you guys can get for me. And if you can get your agents working on it, Simms, I'll be grateful.'

Simms inclined his head. 'I'll do my best, sir.'

'Good man. My boys have had heavy losses since '42. I don't want it all to start again.'

Staines picked up his greatcoat, then paused and glanced at the Brigadier. 'Where did you say the bastards first appeared?'

Simms consulted his notes again. 'At Lechfeld, near Augsburg.'

Staines showed immediate interest. 'Augsburg? If this fine weather holds I've got orders to send my guys there to hit a diesel factory. I think I'll go with 'em. The 262s might turn up again and I want a look at 'em first hand. I might take a photographer with me.'

He glanced at Davies, then gave a grin. 'You don't feel like a bus ride in a B17, do you, Davies?'

Davies gave a start. 'You mean go with you?'

'Yeah. It might be real educational.'

Caught by surprise, Davies hesitated, then took a deep breath. 'Yes, I'll go. Why not?'

'OK. I'll transmit the details to your Group when we've gotten everything finalised.'

Simms broke in hastily. 'You don't need to go yourself, sir. We've got photographs of a 262. A Mosquito was attacked by one in July last year when doing a reconnaissance near Munich. His navigator got a few photographs before his pilot dived into clouds and escaped.'

Staines nodded. 'I know. I've seen 'em. But they don't give much detail. I want a close look myself.' His eyes turned back to Davies. 'Still want to come?'

Davies hoped his face was expressionless. 'Yes, why not? Just send me the details and – orders permitting – I'll be there.'

Nodding, Staines went to the door, where he turned and grinned again. 'Keep working on those cigars, Davies. They're a hundred per cent better than monkey glands.'

Leaving a trail of blue cigar smoke behind him, he acknowledged the two men's salutes, then shouldered his way out of the library.

'He loves his damned cigars, doesn't he?' Davies muttered when the American's footsteps died away.

Simms was showing concern. 'Why on earth did you agree to go with him? Don't you realise how dangerous it could be?'

Davies realised it all too well. 'I could hardly say no, could I, when he's going himself.'

'Of course you could. You're too important an officer to risk your life on a mere surveillance mission.'

Davies shrugged. 'Staines is a general and he's going.'

'Totally unnecessarily, in my opinion. A photographer is all he need send.'

Davies had never seen Simms so curt and critical before. As for himself, he couldn't decide whether his resentment was due to Staines's challenge or to Simms' disapproval. He climbed into his greatcoat before replying. 'Perhaps Staines is right. Perhaps we should all be reminded now and then what our boys have to put up with.'

This time Simms' reply was less curt than rueful. 'Let's just hope it isn't too expensive a reminder, Davies.'

Realising now there was personal as well as professional concern behind the SOE officer's disapproval, Davies relaxed and gave a wry grin. 'I'll second that, sir. In the meantime I'll have a talk to Anna and Moore.'

'It would be helpful. London likes us to do all we can for our Allies.'

As Davies saluted and made for the door, Simms forgot his stiff-upper-lip professionalism for a moment. 'Good luck, Davies. Don't forget to contact me when you get back.'

Chapter 2

The military transport halted at the roadside opposite Sutton Craddock airfield. Thanking the driver, Adams jumped out, took the suitcase handed down to him, and then helped his woman companion to descend. As the 25cwt truck turned and made for the airfield entrance, Adams motioned at an old building half hidden by two crabapple trees. 'Here it is, The Black Swan.'

His blonde Norwegian companion was a shapely, supple woman in her early thirties. Wearing a coat and fur-lined cape, she moved along the pavement to gain a better look at the old inn and then clapped her hands in delight. 'It's charming, *kjaere*. Just as you described it.'

Adams smiled. 'So you think you'll be able to live there for a while? I'm afraid it hasn't many modern conveniences and the bedrooms can be very cold this time of the year.'

Helga laughed. 'Frank, have you forgotten who you're talking to? I'm a Norwegian and lately I've been living in snow-covered mountain huts. So how am I going to perish in England?'

'True,' Adams admitted. 'But I'd have liked you to have some comfort now you're over here. It's just a pity there aren't any rooms vacant in Highgate at the moment.'

She leaned forward and put a hand over his mouth. 'I don't want to live in Highgate. I want to be near you so that you can come over from the airfield when you are free.' Turning, she glanced across the road where two aircraft hangars could be seen towering over a perimeter fence. 'Or won't they let you live out with me?'

Adams' hesitation was barely noticeable. 'No, I think I can get permission. But let's take a look at your room first.'

An icy January wind was stirring the bare branches of the crabapples as he carried her suitcase down a gravel path to the private quarters of the inn. As he swung down a heavy knocker on the thick oaken door, Helga hugged his arm excitedly. 'It's so good to be here, Frank. I was beginning to think they'd never release me.'

Adams frowned. 'So was I. It's ridiculous the time they took.'

'I suppose they have to make sure we're not spies. But it was so lonely in that London hotel.'

Adams was thinking caution had been carried to excess this time. After Steen Jensen's trick after Operation Thor, which had resulted in Helga sailing to England with Adams, he had believed she would be allowed to proceed with him to Sutton Craddock before being subjected to interrogation. Instead he had been ordered to take her to London where she had been kept nearly three weeks until an interrogation team had been satisfied with her credentials.

Adams had wanted to stay with her during this time but had been ordered to return at once to his squadron. Although Davies, delighted at the success of his mission, had put his name forward for a decoration, that had been the end of Adams' rewards for the moment. With 633 Squadron now playing a supporting role to the Allied armies in Europe, he had been posted to France two days later.

Yet Davies had not forgotten his debt. When news had reached him that Helga's credentials were accepted, he had had Adams flown back to England, so giving him the opportunity to collect Helga from London and bring her up to the squadron's base in Yorkshire.

As Adams rapped on the door again, he heard hurried footsteps approaching it. A moment later it swung open and Maisie, wearing a sweater and an apron, appeared. Her eyes brightened at the sight of Adams. 'Hello, Frank. We were wondering what time you'd get here.'

'Hello, Maisie. Meet Helga. Helga, this is Maisie. My friend and a friend of the entire squadron.'

Maisie, a dark-haired and handsome girl, whose sense of humour matched her well-endowed figure, gave a giggle as she held out a hand to Helga. 'What a way to put it! Whatever will the lady think?'

Adams almost blushed. 'Sorry, Maisie. You know what I meant.'

''Course I do. Come out of the cold, both of you.' Turning, Maisie gave a shout. 'Joe, Frank's here. And brought the Norwegian lady with him.'

Joe Kearns, the innkeeper, called out from the bar. 'Hello, Frank. So you've got the lady here at last.' As he came bustling out into the hall, a stoutly built man with thinning white hair and a countryman's ruddy face, he paused, clearly impressed by the Norwegian girl's bearing and blonde good looks. 'Good afternoon, Miss. Have you had a good journey?'

Helga stepped forward, her hand outstretched. 'Hello, Mr Kearns. I've heard a lot about you from Frank.'

It was a remark that clearly pleased Kearns. 'You have? Aye, Frank and I have been sharing our baccy ever since his squadron moved up here.'

Helga turned to Adams. 'Baccy?'

'Tobacco,' Adams said. 'Joe and I share the same brand. Three Nuns.'

She gave a laugh. 'Oh, yes, I see. You are both pipe smokers, are you, Mr Kearns?'

'Aye, that we are, Miss. Mind you, I wouldn't have

been smoking Three Nuns these last two years if it wasn't for Frank. He brings me some from the Mess now and then, you see. He's a generous feller, is Frank.'

A dimple appeared in Helga's cheeks as she glanced back at Adams. 'I shouldn't be hearing these secrets, should I?'

'No, you shouldn't,' Adams said. 'Let's take a look at your bedroom before Joe gives any more away.'

At a nod from Kearns, Maisie led the two of them through the oak-panelled hall with its mullioned windows and blackened beams to a staircase. Through an open door Helga could see into the popular bar of the old inn. Wooden tables, the cross-cuts of some huge and ancient tree, stood around its white-washed walls. Like the counter that stretched almost the full length of the room, the tables and beams that supported the ceiling were blackened from centuries of wood and tobacco smoke. A wide stone hearth was littered with copper ornaments and recent photographs of young airmen. As she reached the staircase Helga glanced back at Kearns. 'I know I am going to love your inn, Mr Kearns. I love old buildings and this must have many memories.'

'Aye that it has, Miss. And a lot of memories from the last few years as well. But I'll bet Frank has told you about them.'

Helga laughed as she followed Maisie up the stairs. 'If he hasn't I'll soon see that he does.'

Adams followed the two women into the bedroom that overlooked the airfield. Sparely furnished, it contained little more than a double bed, a chair, a mahogany wardrobe and dressing table and an ancient wash cabinet with water jug and basin. Maisie gave Helga a doubtful look. 'Are you goin' to be comfortable here, Miss?'

Helga glanced at Adams and laughed. 'Oh, yes. I'm going to be very comfortable, thank you.'

'Then I'll leave you to unpack. But if there's anything you want, just give me a call.'

As the girl left the room, Adams turned to Helga. 'Joe doesn't usually take guests because he has trouble getting maids or housekeepers. But he's let Anna use it when Harvey's on operations.'

'Anna is the German girl you have spoken about?'

'Yes. The girl who's now Harvey's wife.'

'But why is the room free? Isn't Harvey your squadron commander?'

'Not any more. He was given the rank for Operation Thor but to Anna's relief Davies has let him go back to the Operational Training Unit where he's an instructor. The two of them have a bungalow in a small village near the OTU called Hasilton. So we're lucky the room's free. I don't think Joe could have managed with two guests.'

Throwing off her coat, Helga gave a sigh of contentment. 'Then we are lucky. After that London hotel, I couldn't ask for anything better.'

Adams frowned. 'They took far too long interrogating you. For God's sake, you couldn't have had better credentials than being a member of Steen's partisans. I'd have thought Simms' word alone would have been enough to clear you.'

'Never mind. I suppose they have to be careful.' Helga's blue eyes twinkled mischievously. 'Who knows, *kjaere*. You might have brought a spy back with you.'

Adams, used to the eternal carping of his wife, Valerie, was finding it difficult to adjust to a woman who took adversities in her stride. 'One thing is certain, Maisie and Joe will look after you.'

'I know they will. But what did you mean about Maisie being the friend of the squadron?'

Adams gave an embarrassed laugh. 'I didn't put that very well, did I? It's just that Maisie never fails to run outside to the gate and wave when the squadron returns from a mission. It's become a tradition here and the boys like it. I think it assures them in some way that they're safely home.'

'Didn't you once tell me she'd been engaged to someone on the squadron?'

'You mean Gillibrand, the big Canadian? I don't know about engaged. I don't think Gillibrand knew what the word meant. But she was in love with him and was broken-hearted when he was killed defending the airfield.'

She gave a faint shudder. 'I was right about the inn having memories, wasn't I?'

For a moment Adams' sentimentality and hatred of war came to the surface. 'Wait until you go into the bar and see the photographs there. Bergman, Teddy Young, Gillibrand, Hopkinson . . . dozens and dozens of faces and I knew them all. I sometimes think it's a bad dream I'm having and one day I'll wake up and find they're all alive again.'

She crossed to the mullioned window and gazed at the airfield. 'Yet it looks very quiet and peaceful over there.'

Adams joined her. 'That's because they've been over in France since Christmas. There's only a skeleton staff on duty at the moment.' Adams took a quick look at his watch. 'But they'll be flying in soon and I'll have to be there to debrief them.'

'Why are they coming back?'

'They've been flying on maximum effort and their aircraft need refitting. Also the boys badly need a rest. I suppose it could all have been done in France but Davies likes to keep an eye on his squadron.'

'From all you've said about Davies, I'm amazed he let you fly back to England to meet me.'

'He owed it to you,' Adams said. 'He knows what you and Steen did to help us destroy that molybdenum mine.

I'm sure he was embarrassed at the time London took to clear you and he's tried to make it up.

She laughed. 'You never change, do you, Frank? You're the one he's rewarding. For all the danger and pain you suffered over there.' The girl paused. 'But to do that he must have known about our relationship. How would he know that?'

'There's only one way,' Adams said. 'Steen must have said something in one of his coded messages.'

She smiled. 'So you had the same thought. I'm sure we're right. It's typical of Steen to break all the rules.'

'Unless Davies noticed something when we were over on Operation Valkyrie,' Adams suggested.

'No, it's Steen. He'd want to be sure I was well looked after.' Helga's tone changed. 'I hope they're all safe and well over there.'

Knowing she would never have left her friends from choice, Adams tried to sound confident. 'Steen can take care of himself. I've never met a better soldier.'

'But he takes such risks, *kjaere*. Sometimes it frightens me.'

Unable to deny it, Adams was glad when she changed the subject. 'You've hardly mentioned Valerie today, Frank. What is going to happen there?'

Adams sighed. 'All I know is that she went back to London after the squadron was posted to France. I suppose that without Richardson she was bored to death. As soon as I get a moment I'm going to write and ask her for a divorce. But whether she'll give me one is another matter.'

'Surely she will if you tell her about me.'

Adams started. 'I can't do that.'

'Why not?'

'I can't drag you into a sordid divorce. It's out of the question.'

She laughed. 'Sometimes you can be so funny, Frank.

Tell me something. Do you intend to sleep with me now I am in England or did that stop once we left Norway?'

Seeing Adams' embarrassment, she laughed again and kissed him. 'You can't say it, can you, so I will say it for you. Of course you are going to sleep with me. You are going to sleep with me at every opportunity you get. I'll be very disappointed if you don't. So doesn't that make me your mistress and won't that help your divorce?'

Adams frowned. 'No, of course it won't. I'm not letting people think that.'

Her blue eyes gently mocked him. 'You won't let people think I'm your mistress? Then what other word will you use? If there is another, I was never taught it at school.'

Adams was still looking shocked. 'No one's going to call you that. It's unthinkable.'

'But they will, Frank. Because that's what I will be.'

Adams' face set. 'Then we won't sleep together. Not until I get my divorce.'

She pulled a comical face. 'You mean we are going to miss all those wonderful nights together?' As Adams frowned again, she laughed and flung her arms around him. 'You silly man. I don't mind being called your mistress. Why should I be ashamed of being in love with you and of showing it? I want the world to know that I'm your lover.'

Not for the first time Adams wondered what he had done to deserve a woman like this. 'I can't let people think that. Nor must you.'

'You mean I mustn't be so shameless?' Before he could answer, her lips pressed hard on his mouth. 'I've missed you so much, *kjaere*. I've wanted you every night you've been away. Do you have to go straight over to the airfield? Can't you stay with me just for an hour or two?'

With her supple, shapely body pressing against him, Adams felt the situation was fast running away from him. 'The boys will be flying in before it gets dark. And I must have my office ready when they arrive.'

'Does that take long?'

'No. But—'

'Then close the door. Let the war wait just a few minutes more.'

Knowing he was lost, Adams was crossing to the door when he heard the downstairs telephone ringing. A moment more and there was a shout from Maisie. 'Frank, there's a call for you from the airfield duty officer. He wants to know if you've arrived yet. What shall I tell him?'

For a moment Adams was gravely tempted. Then he hurried downstairs. 'Yes. It's I, Adams. What is it?' A pause followed before Adams' resigned reply. 'Yes, all right. I'll be over in ten minutes.'

Replacing the receiver, he slowly returned to the bedroom. 'I'm sorry but the duty officer's got word the boys have crossed the coast. I'll have to go and open up my office right away.'

She gave a shrug of resignation. 'Never mind, my love. These things happen. Will you be able to come over this evening?'

'I shall try,' Adams said, reluctantly climbing into his greatcoat. 'You can be sure of that. But I might be late.'

She held out her hands to him. 'It doesn't matter how late you are. I shall be waiting for you. Now give me a kiss before you go.'

A minute later Adams was crossing the road and entering the airfield gates. As the sentry drew to attention and slapped his rifle in a salute, Adams gave him a cheery good afternoon. Leaving the sentry gazing after him in astonishment, Adams found himself humming as he strode past the guardroom and made his way towards his Intelligence Office. War or no war, Adams decided, life was still worth living.

* * *

Helga heard the howl of the airfield siren as she was unpacking her suitcase. Running to the bedroom window she saw three trucks moving into position on the airfield perimeter. Half a minute later a deep humming began to rattle the windows of the inn. As the sound grew louder, the runway lights came dazzlingly on, glistening on the damp tarmac and giving a yellow glow to the winter evening.

Fascinated, Helga saw a large twin-engined aircraft swoop over the inn and settle down on the runway. It was followed fifteen seconds later by another. As they grew smaller at the end of the luminous runway, the first of the squadron's Mosquitoes passed overhead and waggled its wings. Glancing down, Helga saw Maisie standing at the gate and waving a scarf.

One by one the Mosquitoes kept coming in, some so low that Helga could see patches on their wings and the oxide emissions from their exhaust stacks. Every pilot in turn waggled his wings at the waving girl. When the last plane landed and swung off the runway towards its hard standing, the brilliant yellow lights switched off, leaving the airfield to the grey anonymity of the winter evening. Watching from her window, Helga saw Maisie turn and somewhat reluctantly walk back into the inn. As Adams had confidently predicted, Maisie had once again welcomed her boys home.

Chapter 3

Adams' Intelligence room, which every crewman from the latest 'fresher' to the squadron commander called The Confessional, was crowded that early evening. Still wearing their thick flying suits, men stood in animated groups, smoking cigarettes and drinking tea brought in by Waafs after their debriefing by Adams and his assistant, Sue Spencer. With the hut's windows closed against the winter cold and almost every man smoking, the models of German aircraft dangling from the ceiling looked like bandits taking cover in high-level cloud. With the odour of combat still clinging to well-worn flying suits, the Nissen hut stank of sweat, smoke, oil and cordite, for the squadron had been in action only that morning.

Adams, installed at a long table covered with maps and photographs, was at present talking to Tommy Millburn, one of the few men present not wearing flying clothes. Millburn, a tall, well-built man with a shock of dark unruly hair, was an American who had crossed over to Canada before his country had entered the war and volunteered for the RAF. Since America's entry, the USAAF had shown keenness to enlist such an experienced pilot but Millburn had refused the many offers made to him. His excuse (for Millburn had a great sense of humour) was that, as the British had fed him and paid him a pittance of a salary all these years, it would be both unkind and unfair to deprive them of his services in their hour of need. In fact, although he would have died rather than admit it, Millburn was more British than the British in his pride of his élite squadron and it would have taken a direct order from Eisenhower to drag him from it.

Evidence of this attachment showed in his presence in the Nissen hut that afternoon. Having been wounded in the arm during 633 Squadron's pre-Christmas attack on the molybdenum mine at Rosvik, he had missed going over to France with the squadron. Not due for hospital release for another week but hearing about the squadron's return, he had sought and obtained permission to be present that afternoon.

He was accompanied by a small wiry Welshman with sharp features and somewhat prominent ears. Nicknamed Gabby the Gremlin because of his appearance, Johnny Gabriel had been Millburn's navigator since the American had joined the squadron. With Millburn hospitalised after the Rosvik raid, Gabby had missed the squadron's sojourn in France and been forced to spend the recent weeks doing general duties on the airfield. Possessing the pre-war British belief that France was populated by hosts of beautiful lascivious women, Gabby had not borne his loss lightly and tended to put the blame on his wounded pilot.

He was wearing a scowl now as Adams asked Millburn when he expected to leave hospital. The American flexed his left arm. 'I guess I could leave now.' Millburn's accent was southern: he came from El Paso. 'The arm's nearly OK. But I've gotta stay until next week when they're giving me a final medical.'

'Then you'll get convalescent leave, won't you?' Adams asked.

Millburn grinned at Gabby. 'Yeah. Two weeks. Maybe four because they owe me two from last year.'

Gabby scowled. 'You've just had five of 'em, sitting

on your arse and chatting up those nurses. How much leave do you want?'

Millburn grinned again. 'What's wrong with you, shortass? You jealous?'

Gabby sniffed. 'Jealous of a bloody colonial. That'll be the day, Millburn.'

'Don't give me that, you randy little tom-cat. You looked as green as duck weed when you saw all those nurses round my bed.' Millburn turned to the amused Adams. 'You know what's wrong with him, Frank? He's blaming me because he couldn't get over to France and get his hot little hands on those French women. The guy needs seeing to. I think I'll have a talk with the MO.'

Sue Spencer, Adam's attractive Waaf assistant, taking notes from one of the pilots, glanced over her shoulder and smiled at Adams as she overheard the two men's conversation. Although in reality inseparable friends, they were notorious throughout the squadron for their quarrelling and scathing banter.

Gabby was in full flood now. 'Listen to whose talking. He meets that woman ferry pilot who delivered our high-altitude Mossie here and he's been smelling roses ever since. You're the one who needs doctoring, Millburn. For your own bloody good.'

Seeing Millburn's expression and knowing there was truth in the Welshman's assertion, Adams broke into the argument. 'You'll have heard that Davies took Harvey off active service after Operation Thor and posted him back to his OTU, Tommy?'

Millburn nodded. 'Yeah. And I was glad to hear it. The guy's done far too many ops: it's time he had a real rest.' The American glanced at the chattering groups of aircrews. 'Have you finished debriefing them?'

Adams nodded. 'Yes. They're waiting here because the CO wants to see them.'

'I believe they lost four kites while in France.'

'Yes. Three of them over Bastogne. Johnson, McArthur, Jones and a new pilot and navigator who joined us after you were wounded?'

'How?'

'Ground fire. They think LMGs got Johnson and the two new men. McArthur and Jones bought it when they attacked a column of tanks.'

Millburn's wince said it all to Adams. Aircrews felt they had a chance when engaging enemy aircraft because skill could sometimes play a part in the outcome. But when attacking ground objectives, they might be the target of a hundred invisible guns and then only luck could see them through. 'What the hell were they doing attacking tanks?' the American asked. 'That's a job for Typhoons, isn't it?'

Adams shrugged. 'That's what I thought. But everything was being thrown in during the Battle of the Bulge. Davies didn't like it, of course, but I think he lost some control over them while they were over in France.'

Millburn's tone changed as he glanced at Gabby. 'You see what I saved you from. You might have had a few shells up your arse if I hadn't been wounded.'

Gabby scowled. 'The way you fly, that's more than bloody likely.' Before he could say more, there was a shout as the door opened. 'Attention!'

The call came from the Adjutant who entered the Nissen hut with Henderson, the Station CO. A moment more and Henderson walked towards the long table. Tall, middle-aged and broad-shouldered, unlike most of his young aircrews Henderson was a professional airman. Benign in manner, a Scot by birth, he was popular with his men. Conscious his crews had been on maximum effort since Christmas and nerves were frayed, he had decided beforehand to keep the meeting informal. After a quick word with Adams, he turned to the attentive crews, his voice carrying a faint trace of Highland brogue.

'All right, men, don't look so worried. Air Commodore Davies hasn't another mission for you yet.'

A relieved sigh sounded and someone breathed 'Thank God.' Acknowledging the benediction with a grin, Henderson went on: 'Just the opposite, in fact. You're going to stand down for a week. Maybe two.' As excited voices sounded, the Scot held up a hand. 'Don't let it go to your heads. It doesn't mean you're going on leave. Your ground crews will need you around while they're re-fitting your kites. But other than that you can put your feet up during the day, have a lunchtime drink in the Black Swan, and go and see your popsies in Highgate in the evenings. You might even get a late-night pass or two if you behave yourselves.'

An Irish voice broke in. 'What about beer, sur? Is that goin' to be plentiful?'

'From what the Mess Officer says, it will be, Machin. But that doesn't mean you're going to wash your feet in it. I don't want you pie-eyed and paralytic when your ground crew needs you.'

Machin, one of the squadron's old sweats and a volunteer from Eire, could always be relied on to enter the mood of the moment. 'Then that's all right, sur. I never wash me feet in me beer. It'd be a wanton waste, wouldn't it, sur?'

Taking courage from the general bonhomie, a voice shouted from the rear of the assembly. 'You're a liar, Paddy. That's why it's got such a bloody awful taste these days.'

Adams half expected the Adjutant to call the assembly to order but Henderson, aware of his crews' need to relax, only grinned. 'I'll remember that the next time I feel like a pint, Peters.' His tone changed. 'All right, you can slope off now and relax for a few days. But keep in touch with your ground crews and stay near the airfield during the daytime.'

As the Adjutant called 'Dismiss' and the crews began filing from the hut, Henderson turned to Adams. 'I want you in my office in half an hour, Frank. I've got Davies coming.'

Adams looked surprised and not a little apprehensive. 'Davies? What does he want, sir?'

Henderson, only too aware how Davies' visits were connoted with complex and dangerous missions, gave a shrug. 'He said he wanted some advice. He's bringing Moore with him and he's sent for Anna.'

Adams looked puzzled as well as concerned. 'Anna and Moore? After he's given permission for the Squadron to stand down? He's not fattening us up for something, is he, sir?'

Clearly not pleased that his own secret fears were shared by the Intelligence Officer, Henderson gave a grunt of impatience. 'Don't be a Cassandra, Frank. He says he's only coming for advice, so let's take him at his word.' Before Adams could reply, the Scot turned to the American. 'How's that arm coming along, Millburn?'

Millburn flexed his arm again. 'Almost as good as new, sir.'

'You mean you can lift a pint of beer again?'

Millburn grinned. 'I guess I could if someone bought me one, sir.'

'Then you'll be back with us soon?'

'Yes, sir. After my leave, that is.'

'You mean convalescent leave?'

'No, sir. I've two weeks due from last year.'

The Scot grimaced. 'Then let's hope Davies isn't coming with some new scheme for us. Or you might have to wait for that leave.'

For once in his life Milburn looked shaken. 'That's not likely, is it?'

Henderson picked up his cap from the table. 'Not according to what he said but Davies can keep his cards close to his chest. I'll know more after he's been.' He turned to Adams. 'See you in my office in half an hour, Frank.'

As he disappeared from the hut, Gabby turned to Millburn like a wicked goblin. 'That shook you, didn't it? Maybe you're not going to have your wicked way with Carol Manning after all.'

Millburn gave him a look of dislike. 'I'm having that leave if I have to throw my brevet and gongs into the trash bin and join a real outfit.'

'You mean those part-timers, the Yanks?'

Millburn glared at him. 'Yeah. I mean the Yanks.'

Gabby, who was missing the sexual escapades he and Millburn had shared before the American had fallen for the ferry pilot, chortled. 'I told you not to put all your eggs into one basket, didn't I? Now you see what it can do to you.'

Chapter 4

Henderson reached out for the ringing telephone. 'Yes, what is it?' He listened for a moment, then turned to Davies. 'It's the guardroom, sir. They say Anna's car's here.' He lifted the mouthpiece again. 'Tell the driver to bring it round to my office right away.'

As he replaced the receiver, Davies gave a grunt. 'That's a relief. I thought that husband of hers might have stopped her coming.'

Henderson hid a grin. 'I can't see Harvey doing that, sir.'

Davies glanced at Moore who was seated alongside Henderson. 'If the bugger can knock out my Squadron Commander and take his place on an operation, he can do anything. You should have heard him arguing when I phoned his bungalow and asked to speak to Anna. The cheeky sod asked what I wanted with her. Can you believe it?'

Moore, the good-looking, highly decorated pilot who had once been the unit's Squadron Commander, was smiling. The bad feeling between the mercurial Air Commodore and the tough, rebellious Yorkshireman was legend in the squadron. 'You can't blame him being suspicious, sir. You've talked to her before and look at the dangerous jobs your talks led to.'

Davies scowled. 'This is different. I told him I only wanted her advice and he still acted like a dog sniffing at a rat hole. You're the last one who should defend him,

Moore. You haven't forgotten how he nearly broke your jaw, have you?'

Moore's lips quirked. 'No, sir, I haven't forgotten. But I couldn't fault his motives, could I? And what about his behaviour during Operation Thor after Millburn was wounded? It might have cost him his life to stay behind and escort Millburn back.'

Davies scowled. 'You mean it might have cost another aircraft and another crew. That's just the point I'm making. The man's a born rebel.'

Seated by the window, Adams, the fourth man in the office, was thinking that only Moore could have argued this way with the irascible Air Commodore. 'The boys value his leadership, sir,' the young Wing Commander said. 'There's no denying that.'

'I'm not talking about his leadership, Moore. I'm talking about the way he disobeys orders and generally acts like a Bolshie.' As a car engine sounded outside, Davies rose to his feet, his voice irritable. 'Anyway, it's all irrelevant now. I can't use him again after my promises to Anna.'

Moore showed relief. 'You've decided that, have you, sir?'

Davies glared at him. 'With people like you around, I haven't much choice, have I?' Without waiting for Moore to reply, he stalked out of the office like an angry bantamcock. As the sound of his footsteps died away down the corridor, Henderson grinned at Moore. 'I thought after the Thor affair he'd had a change of heart.'

Adams shook his head before Moore could reply. 'It's an act, sir. Underneath he has enormous respect for Harvey.'

Moore nodded. 'You're right, Frank. Harvey's much the same. They both respect one another but they'd face torture rather than admit it.' His tone changed.

'Has Davies told you yet that he's going on a bombing mission with Staines in the next day or two.'

Both men gave a start. 'A bombing mission?' Henderson asked, 'In B17s? Why?'

Moore told him. 'I don't think he felt he had any option when Staines invited him. We'd probably have felt the same.'

Henderson was looking shocked. 'For Christ's sake. Has Staines gone out of his mind?'

Equally shocked, Adams was quick to point out the hidden dangers. 'Don't they realise the risks they are taking as staff officers? If they are shot down and captured, the enemy will have a field day finding out all they know about the two Air Forces.'

'Try telling him,' Moore said. 'I have and he nearly bit my head off. As long as Staines goes, he'll go with him. And Staines is going.'

Henderson motioned for them to be quiet as footsteps sounded down the corridor. As they drew nearer Adams heard Anna's voice. Although her English was excellent, it contained a faint accent that Adams had always found attractive. 'I'm sorry I'm a little late, Arthur, but we ran into an Army convoy and they wouldn't let us pass for a while.'

A moment more and Davies led her into the office. As the three officers rose, Davies, full of amity again, waved a hand at them. 'I think you know everyone here, Anna. We're all grateful you've agreed to come.'

Adams, unnoticed as yet by the girl because of his position near the window, watched Davies help her remove her coat. A German girl who hated Nazism, Anna Reinhardt, now Harvey's wife, had several times been landed behind enemy lines to locate targets for the Allies, knowing all the time that if she were captured the Gestapo would take a terrible toll for her defection. Tall, slim, dark-haired, graceful in movement, she possessed the kind of serene beauty that all men could admire. Even Adams, longing to get the conference over so that he could return to Helga, felt her spell reach out to him.

As she turned so that Davies could draw off her coat, she noticed Adams. A cry of delight broke from her and she ran towards him. 'Frank! Oh, Frank, how lovely to see you again. We were so worried when we heard you were captured. But you were so brave. And here you are, safe and sound. Ach, it is wonderful.'

Adams knew his cheeks were glowing pink as she kissed him. 'Hello, Anna. I intended to come and see you both. But I only got back from London today.'

She laughed again. 'With your Norwegian friend! I know all about her, you see. Frank has told me everything.'

The embarrassed Adams kept his eyes averted from Davies. 'Yes. She's here. She has your old room at the inn.'

'Then I must meet her. Oh, Frank, it is so good to see you again. There was a time when we never thought we would.'

There was a subdued cough from Davies. Adams pressed her hand and then fumbled with the words to bring the conference back to its agenda. 'I'll bring her over to Hesilton when I get the chance. In the meantime the Air Commodore's wondering if you can help us with a problem he's got.'

Taking the hint, she turned to face Davies. 'What is it, Arthur? You know I'll help if I can.'

Looking relieved the situation was back on the rails again, Davies told her about Staines's request. 'At the moment it seems an American problem. We've no report of our heavies being attacked and it might be the Germans haven't found a way of flying these new fighters at night. But High Command likes us to keep our allies sweet, and in any case Staines has been a good friend to us in the past. So if you've got any ideas, I'd be grateful.'

'Do you know how long they have been working on this project?' she asked.

'According to Brigadier Simms, at least four years. So we wondered if Von Haldenberg mentioned anything about it to you when you dined with him in Austria.'

She paused a moment, then shook her head. 'No. All he talked about was the adapted fighter they were building.'

Davies showed his disappointment. 'As he is one of their leading aircraft designers, we were hoping he might have had a hand in it.'

'It's quite possible he had. But he said nothing to me. He'll be in disgrace now, of course, after the Gestapo discovered him consorting with an Allied agent. I'd be surprised if he isn't in a concentration camp.'

Davies had little sentiment where the enemy was concerned. 'Let's hope he is. It'll be one German designer less to worry about.' His tone changed. 'So you haven't any idea where these planes might be manufactured?'

She shook her head. 'I doubt if there'll be a single centre. As you will know, for a couple of years they've been dispersing aircraft factories into smaller units and siting them within forests, railway tunnels and even old coal mines to escape your bombing.'

'Even below lakes,' Henderson said, referring to Operation Crisis.

Anna threw him a smile. 'That's right. My friends over there told me forests alongside the autobahns and railways are sometimes used so that the finished products can be easily moved away. They've even used the autobahns as makeshift airfields.'

Davies, who was looking disappointed, nodded. 'We know their fighters sometimes use them. So you're saying these 262s could be manufactured on dozens of different sites?'

'They could be but on the other hand as this is a very specialised aircraft, there might be only a few technicians qualified to construct it. So it's just possible there might be one main centre even if smaller ones exist.' She glanced round the office. 'Do you have a map I could look at?'

Henderson fished into a drawer of his desk and unfolded a large map of Europe. As Anna stood over it, the four men gathered round her and watched her slim hand tracing out the possibilities she was offering them. 'If I'm right, the centre will be as far away from your bomber bases as possible. This means it might be over here, in Bavaria or Austria, but on the other hand it could be here, somewhere approaching the old Polish frontier.'

Davies gave a start. 'Poland?'

She turned to him. 'It might be, particularly as you are now reaching Bavaria and Austria. I know you can reach the Polish frontier too but you have to cross far more heavily defended cities and enemy fighter bases on the way. Of course the Russians will soon be threatening them from that side but when they were siting the centre they might have believed they could hold the Russians. If there is a main centre, of course. Please understand these are only guesses of mine.'

Davies glanced at Adams. 'Are they good guesses?'

Adams nodded. 'Yes, I think they are. A revolutionary project like this must require specialists and Anna's point that we would have to fly over hundreds of miles of heavily defended territory makes sense to me.'

Davies turned back to the girl. 'I suppose you can't hazard a guess where a centre could be in those parts?'

'No. Only that it would need to be somewhere where the rail and road communications are good and the countryside provides plenty of cover. That might narrow down the choice a little.'

Davies was silent a moment, then straightened. 'Well, at least it's something and the best we can do. I'll get in touch with Simms and leave the rest to him. As he wants to help Staines, he'll probably tell his German agents to get working on it.'

Adams, standing close to the girl, saw her give a sudden start. For a moment he thought she was going to make a protest but instead she recovered herself. 'I'm sorry I can't be more help, Arthur. Do you want anything further or can I start back home now?'

Davies helped her into her coat. 'No, you've done all you can and I'm grateful to you for coming.' As the girl buttoned up her coat, he turned to the other three officers. 'This is all hush-hush, so not a word to anyone. All right?'

As the officers nodded, Davies led Anna out into the corridor. Moore followed and after a word with Davies he took Anna's arm. Believing he was going to escort the girl to her waiting car, Adams was surprised when Anna excused herself and hurried back to him. 'Can you spare a moment, Frank?'

Seeing Davies and Moore glancing back, Adams hesitated. 'Yes. Of course.'

The girl spoke rapidly but quietly. 'Can you arrange for me to see Brigadier Simms? As soon as possible?'

Adams showed surprise. 'Yes, I suppose I could. But can you give me a reason? He might want one.'

'I can't explain now, Frank. But it is very important. Will you try?'

Seeing Davies' impatience, Adams hurried his answer. 'I'll ring him in the morning. Phone me after 10.00 hours and I'll let you know what he says.'

Reaching up, she kissed his cheek, then ran after Moore and Davies. Behind Adams, Henderson, locking up his office, gave a chuckle of envy. 'What was all that about, Frank?' Does she fancy you after all your Norwegian exploits?'

Adams hoped his lie sounded plausible. 'She wanted to know when I was going to introduce her to Helga?'

Henderson chuckled again. 'You'd better get over there before some other girl waylays you. Don't you know that since Norway you're the new station pin-up?'

Sensitive about his new fame, Adams said goodnight to the Scot and hurried from the Administration Block. Outside he saw Davies was standing impatiently beside his staff car while Moore was having a few last words with Anna. Knowing the young Wing Commander was secretly in love with the girl, Adams felt a twinge of sympathy until he remembered Helga was waiting for him in the Black Swan. Instantly every other thought in Adams' mind took flight as he hurried towards the station gates.

Chapter 5

Adams phoned Simms at High Elms the following morning. After a short delay he heard the officer's courteous voice. 'Good morning, Squadron Leader. What can I do for you?'

Adams told him of Anna's request. 'I can't tell you what she wants, sir, but she sounded urgent. Can you fit her in some time?'

A pause followed, then Simms returned to the phone. 'I can see her this afternoon. At 14.00 hours. Do you think that'll be convenient?'

'I would think so, sir. She's phoning me in half an hour, so I'll soon know. Do you want me to ring you back?'

'Only if she can't come, Adams. Otherwise I will expect her.'

Knowing the SOE officer's many commitments, Adams was thinking there could be no better evidence of the high respect held for the German girl in military quarters than Simms' willingness to see her so promptly. As he replaced the receiver, Sue Spencer raised her head from a pile of photographs she was examining. 'How is Helga finding the Black Swan, Frank? Does she like it there?'

From anyone else, Adams would have found the question nosey and meddlesome but from Sue Spencer he knew it came only from her interest in his well-being. 'She's loving it. I was a bit worried at first that she might find it chilly after her London hotel but not a bit of it.

She says she's never been more comfortable. Mind you, she loves old English pubs, so that's a great help.'

'I'm so glad. I'd like to meet her some time.'

'You shall.' With the Norwegian girl his favourite topic, Adams found it easy to be carried away. 'She's quite amazing, Sue. You should have seen her drawing sketches of those bluffs in Norway with the wind cold enough to freeze her fingers off. And living with the partisans in conditions not fit for a pack of huskies. I couldn't have done my job without her help and yet she dismisses it all as if it were nothing.'

Although he was unaware of it, Adams' expression was matching the enthusiasm of his words. Sue gave a laugh of pleasure. 'You're happy at last, aren't you, Frank?'

Adams gave a start, then smiled sheepishly. 'Does it show that much?'

'It shines out like a light. And I'm so happy for you.'

Adams made the confession he would have made to no one else. 'But what am I going to do? She wants me to live over there with her but if I do that, everyone on the airfield will know.'

'Does it matter? Valerie's gone back to London, hasn't she?'

'Yes, but it's not Valerie I'm thinking about. It's the talk there'll be on the station. I can't make her look like my mistress.'

'What does Helga say?'

'She doesn't seem to care less. But that's not the point, is it?'

'I'd say it was exactly the point. She loves you and doesn't care who knows it. That's how some women behave when they're in love, Frank. You should be happy you've found one of them.'

Adams frowned. 'I'll never understand women in a thousand years.'

Sue laughed again. 'We're very easy to understand, Frank. It's you men who bring up all the problems.'

'So you think I should billet over there?'

'I think you'll be crazy if you don't. And callous. She'll be lonely out of her country and she'll need you. So stop being a gentleman and be a lover instead.'

Adams showed surprise as well as gratitude. 'I never expected you to talk that way.'

'Why not? I'm a woman, aren't I? Do you think I'd mind what people thought about me if Tony were nearby? I'd go on the Tannoy and tell the entire station I was living with him.'

As Adams took a deep breath his phone rang. Picking it up he heard the duty telephonist. 'There's a Mrs Harvey to speak to you, sir. Shall I put her through?'

'Please,' Adams said.

Anna's voice sounded a few seconds later. 'Hello, Frank. Have you spoken to the Brigadier?'

'Yes, and he'll see you at 14.00 hours. How will you get there?'

The girl's voice betrayed her relief. 'I'll come by train and take a bus or taxi to High Elms.'

'Wait a minute,' Adams said. He had a quick word with Sue and then lifted the receiver again. 'I'll come to Hasilton and pick you up. I can borrow a car. With the boys standing down we're not busy at the moment and in any case Sue says she'll stand in for me.'

'No, it's too far. Wait a minute, please, while I look at a timetable.'

She returned to the phone a minute later. 'If I hurry, I can take a train that gets me into Highgate at 12.20. If you have the time and can borrow a car, would it be too much trouble to pick me up there?'

'No trouble at all. I'll be there and take you on to High Elms.'

'This is very kind of you, Frank. I'm very grateful.'

'I'll see you at 12.20 or thereabouts,' Adams told her.

Sue's voice interrupted his thoughts as he replaced the receiver. 'She still didn't say why she wanted to speak to the Brigadier?'

Adams shook his head. 'No. But she gives the impression it's urgent. Perhaps she'll tell me more this afternoon.'

Although a pale sun was shining, frost was holding High Elms in an iron grip that afternoon when Adams' borrowed car was halted at the entrance by a half-frozen sentry. After showing his credentials and waiting while the armed MP phoned back to his duty officer, Adams was finally allowd to drive through the imposing gateway. As they approached the huge house and its wide frosted lawns lay on either side of them, Adams gave an involuntary shudder. 'I wonder how long this cold spell's going to last.'

Anna gave him an amused look. 'You should be used to it.'

Adams, whose mind was on her meeting with Simms, showed surprise. 'Me? I hate cold weather.'

She laughed. 'Is that why you volunteered to go to Norway?'

Adams gave a groan. 'Not Norway again. When am I going to live that down?'

Anna laughed. 'You aren't. You came back a hero. That's why Davies and everyone else has such respect for you. If you want to remain anonymous, you shouldn't do such brave things.'

'Now you tell me,' Adams grumbled. 'Don't worry. It's not likely to happen again.'

Her laughter pleased him. He had sensed a certain tension in her since picking her up at Highgate station but she had offered him no reason and he had respected her silence. Nevertheless his curiosity peaked when, as he drove into the car park and switched off the engine, she turned to him. 'Frank, do you mind if I see the Brigadier alone? I promise I won't be long.'

'No, of course not. In any case I didn't ask an audience for myself. Off you go. It's almost two o'clock.'

'But it'll be cold out here. Won't you come inside the house? Someone will surely give you a cup of tea.'

Adams snuggled deeper into his greatcoat. 'No, I'd rather wait here. Truly.'

By this time an Army officer had descended the house steps and was approaching the car. Adams exchanged a few words with him, then turned to Anna. 'The captain will take you to Brigadier Simms, Anna. Off you go.'

Puzzled, he watched the officer and the slim figure of the girl disappear into the house. Twenty minutes passed before she appeared again and hurried towards the car. Jumping out, Adams opened the door for her. 'How did it go? Is everything all right.'

Half-expecting her to be non-committal, he was surprised by her reply. 'I'll tell you about it on our way back.'

Feeling it was better she set the pace, he said no more as he drove from the grounds and took the road back to Highgate. A full two minutes passed before she turned to him. 'As you've gone to all this trouble for me, you have a right to know.'

He made an immediate protest. 'No, that's silly. I've no right at all. If it's something you don't want to talk about, don't. I'm perfectly happy as things are.'

Her tone changed. 'No, Frank. I want to talk now. I'd like your views before I return home.'

She paused then as if to gather her words. With little traffic using the lane, Adams could hear ice crunching beneath his tyres. As he approached a leafless oak, a crow flew from it as if to escape the keening wind and took shelter in the frosted hedgerows. As he changed gear, her voice was almost drowned by the higher engine note. 'It's the investigation about this new German fighter, Frank. Thinking it would be carried out by London's agents, I wasn't concerned until Davies said Simms was involved. Then I suddenly realised it was likely he would call on the Germans who saved my life at Nurnbach.'

Adams thought he was beginning to understand. 'There were two of them, weren't there?'

'Three in all although only two were involved when I was captured. I've worked with them before and they've become my friends.' She turned towards him as if an explanation were necessary, and Adams thought again how lovely she was, 'You know how it is on the squadron, Frank. When men risk their lives for one another, they become closer than brothers. That's how these men have become to me.'

'And you feel Simms will be putting them in danger?' Adams said.

'If he asks for their help, yes. Terrible danger. They killed two Gestapo agents to rescue me. If the Gestapo ever catch them, I daren't think what revenge they'll take.'

With Adams' own experience of the Gestapo only a few weeks away, the point needed no emphasis. 'So you went to ask Simms not to use them?' When the girl jerked her head, he went on: 'What happened?'

'He was sympathetic and listened to everything I had to say. You know what a courteous man he is. But—'

'But he didn't promise anything?' 'Adams finished.

She bit her lip. 'No. He said he'd bear in mind everything I'd said but good agents were few and far between and if we don't destroy or at least cripple this centre, hundreds more Americans might lose their lives.'

The vile mathematics of war, Adams was thinking. The statistic that bears no argument, that the sparing of a few lives cannot equate the deaths of many. Adams tried to comfort her. 'Perhaps he will use other agents.'

'He probably will but I still feel Hausmann and Meyer will be among them. The Brigadier knows what good men they are. I think he'll use them even though I said their Bavarian accents might make them more conspicuous.'

'But the factory might be in Bavaria,' Adams said. 'You said it was possible.'

'Possible, yes, but I believe the eastern borders of Germany are far more likely.'

'But surely Simms knows about the Gestapo agents they killed. He won't want to risk losing them any more than you do.'

She seemed about to speak, then shook her head and turned away. A wheel sank into an ice-covered pot hole, jolting the old Hillman on her springs. Frustrated by his failure to comfort her, Adams inwardly cursed roads that the war was allowing no one to repair. Unable to find any other words of comfort, knowing he would feel the same if his own friends were involved, Adams made one of the impulsive gestures he was inclined to make when his sympathy was aroused. 'Would you like me to speak to Davies about it? He might have some influence on Simms.'

She stirred. 'Yes, if you will. I suppose it can't do any harm.'

'Then I will. But in the meantime you must stop worrying. They haven't been used yet and perhaps won't be.' Adams glanced at his watch. 'Look. We've an hour and a half before your train leaves. So why don't we go to the Black Swan? You'd like to meet Helga, wouldn't you?'

Her beautiful face lit up. 'Yes, I'd love to.'

'Good. Then that's what we'll do.'

The dog jumped to his feet, gave a loud bark, and

ran to the front door of the bungalow. As footsteps sounded outside, he barked again, his tail wagging furiously. As the door opened, he leapt up at the tall, powerfully built man in uniform who entered, jumping and barking in a frenzy of welcome. Behind him Anna was laughing. 'Anyone would think Sam hadn't seen you for months.'

Harvey, wearing no greatcoat in spite of the cold, grinned down at the excited dog. 'Shut up, you daft old mutt. Settle down.' As the dog quietened, he turned to the girl. 'Sorry I'm so late, love, but the cold's been causing problems today.'

'I know,' she said. 'I guessed it would.'

He caught hold of her and gave her a kiss. Then he stood back and gazed at her. 'You're looking very posh today. What've you been up to?'

She laughed. 'So you noticed?'

'What've you been up to?'

'I've been to Sutton Craddock.'

Harvey's craggy face suddenly looked puzzled and apprehensive. 'Again? Why?'

'I went to see Frank Adams.'

'Frank? But didn't you see him last night?'

She hesitated. On the train back she had decided not to tell him about her concern for her two German friends. She knew he had not fully recovered from his Norwegian experiences and her talk with Adams had made her wonder if her fears were somewhat neurotic. Accordingly, although she hated lying to him, she had decided that a white lie or two might be prudent. She motioned to the settee. 'Sit down and I'll tell you all about it.'

He was frowning heavily now. 'Davies hasn't been getting at you again, has he? He hasn't asked you do to another job for him?'

'No, of course he hasn't?' She tried to push him towards the settee. 'Just keep calm and listen.'

For a moment he resisted her. Then he dropped on the settee. 'How did you get to Sutton Craddock? Did Davies send a car again?'

She sank down beside him. 'I've told you, it had nothing to do with Davies. I took the train there and Frank met me at the station. He wanted me to meet Helga.'

He gave a start of surprise. 'Helga!'

'Yes. That's all I went for. He invited me last night.'

'Then why didn't you tell me last night? I could have organised a transport to take you to the station.'

'Frank wasn't sure she'd be at home today,' she lied. 'I had to phone him this morning to find out. So I took the train and he met me at the station.'

His big frame was beginning to relax. 'And that's all you went for? Davies wasn't there?'

'Of course he wasn't? Why would he be? Frank took me to the Black Swan and the three of us had lunch there. That's all that's happened.'

His face cleared. Lighting a cigarette, he leaned forward and patted the dog who had settled down at his feet. 'What's she like, Helga?'

'Oh, *Leibling*, she's lovely. So warm and friendly. I liked her from the moment we met. I think Frank is a very lucky man.'

'Is she pretty?'

She punched his arm. 'Trust a man to ask that. No, she's not pretty in the way you mean. She's a woman, not a silly child. She's tall and blonde with a lovely figure and has a face that's strong but very attractive.'

Harvey grinned. 'Like you?'

'I'm not blonde, you silly man.'

'No but you're strong. And obstinate.'

'Listen who's talking. Davies thinks you're the most obstinate officer he's ever known.'

Harvey grinned. 'Did he say so last night?'

'Not in front of me, but I know he thinks it.' Her lovely

grey eyes twinkled. 'You know something, *Leibling*. I think he is right.'

He grabbed her and crushed her against his hard body. 'What did you say?'

She pretended to fight him. 'I said I think you are an obstinate man.'

At their feet the dog began to bark. 'You see,' she said. 'Even Sam thinks I'm right.'

He kissed her, then drew on his cigarette. 'I've been thinking about that discussion you had in Henderson's office last night. And something about it doesn't fit.'

She drew back. 'What do you mean?'

'It's Davies. I can't see him taking all that trouble to do a favour for Staines without some other reason.'

'Why not? He said himself that High Command likes us to keep the Americans sweet, as he put it. So why shouldn't he go to a bit of trouble for them?'

'Because he's Davies, that's why. He's never happy unless he can find a big job for the squadron that'll put him in good odour with the Brass Hats. That doesn't mean doing small favours for Americans.'

'Is that quite fair, *Leibling*? You've said yourself and so has Frank that his fellow officers are jealous of his squadron and there's nothing they'd like better than to see it taken from him and returned to routine duties. So isn't it natural he wants to keep it occupied?'

Harvey reached out and flicked his cigarette over an ashtray. 'I'm not saying he doesn't want to keep the squadron. What I bellyache about are his reasons. He doesn't do it for the war effort. He does it for his own ambitions. And that's another ball game altogether.'

'How can you be sure of this? How can anyone be certain what's in another man's heart? He was kind enough to visit me at Christmas when we all thought you were dead.'

Without Harvey knowing it, his voice was turning hard and gritty. 'You forget I've had to work with the little bastard for nearly two years. He's never alive unless he's plotting some filthy job for the lads. What was he like last night? Off-hand, curt, bored? Or was he full of beans and enthusiasm?'

'He was energetic,' she admitted. 'But I've always found him a vigorous and enthusiastic man.'

Harvey's craggy face, slightly shadowed by a day's growth, gave a grimace of dislike. 'Aye, he's enthusiastic all right. A real little eagerbeaver. Never happier than when he's sending young lads out to die for King and Country.'

About to argue further, she changed her mind and ran a gentle hand down the Yorkshireman's rough cheek. 'You know your problem, don't you, my love? You've always cared too much about the men you've led.'

It is doubtful if anyone else in the world could have made such a statement to the tough Yorkshireman without causing an explosion. Instead Harvey only scowled and fell into using the service language he usually kept from her. 'Don't talk bullshit, love. I just hate ambitious officers who climb up on the bodies of dead kids. Is there anything wrong in that?'

She laughed to lighten his mood. 'You hate the class system in general, *Leibling*, and you see Davies as belonging to the privileged classes. But he isn't, is he? He's just another officer like yourself.'

Harvey shook his head. 'I know what Davies is and I'll lay odds of ten to one that he's agreed to help the Yanks in the hope he'll get a job for the squadron. Want to take me on?'

She hid the faint shudder that ran through her by snuggling closer to him. 'Let's stop talking about Davies.

Whatever he does you won't be involved this time. You've promised me and so has Davies. So, whatever happens, you'll keep your word, won't you?'

For a moment she felt him hesitate. Then he drew her towards him. 'Aye, lass. You needn't worry. I'll keep my word.'

Chapter 6

As the truck jolted over a crack in the perimeter track, Staines, looking enormous in his thick flying suit, slapped Davies across the shoulders. 'This is better than flying a desk, isn't it, Davies?'

Davies, similarly dressed, hoped his answer was adequate. 'I'll let you know in a couple of hours, sir.'

Staines grinned. 'You're as excited as I am. It's like old times. No paper and no bullshit. Just us and the Krauts.' His tone changed. 'I hope those sonsofbitches don't let us down today or the weather doesn't foul things up over the target. The Old Man nearly threw a fit when I asked permission. He'll never let me go a second time.'

Davies knew the Old Man was the Commanding General of the American V111 Bomber Command. 'I'm amazed he gave you permission this time. Generals know too much how the system works to fly over Germany and they aren't exactly thick on the ground either.'

Staines chuckled. 'I shot him a line saying how our crews would love to hear that staff officers are prepared to share their dangers. And how good it would go down in the papers back home. You know something? He fell for it.'

'Let's hope the idea doesn't spread too far,' Davies said dryly. 'Or my boys might be briefing me on our next operation.'

As Staines gave his big, infectious laugh, Davies glanced through the windshield at the long row of B17s that stood on the frosted grass alongside the perimeter track. Along with Staines and the driver, he was sharing the front seats of a 15cwt truck that was taking the two officers to their waiting aircraft. It was 07.50 and bitterly cold. Davies had arrived at the American airfield the previous evening but although a billet had been set aside for him there had been no chance to sleep. Staines had been fretting that the weather might change and as he clearly had no intention of resting until a final decision was made, Davies had felt obliged to keep him company.

It had been 03.20 when the teletape had informed the station to continue its preparation until further notice. With Staines still edgy, Davies had discovered to his dismay that he was to be shown all the major procedures taken before an American bombing mission.

He was first taken to the Intelligence Room where the station's Duty Officer had traced out the outward and incoming routes on a wall map. Next came the Operations Room where the Watch Officer had checked the crews' list with the Squadron commander and the Chief Navigation Officer had marked on a wall map a convergence point over the North Sea.

Next he had been introduced to the Group Commander who arrived at 04.27. Then, for all the world like an enthusiastic headmaster showing a visitor around his school, Staines had led him to the crew rooms where the pilots, co-pilots, navigators, bombardiers and gunners were climbing into their flying outfits: the heavy underwear, the electrically-heated 'zoot' suits, the fleece lined leather pants and the sheepskin jackets. Seeing the resentful looks thrown their way and guessing the reason, Davies had found this visit embarrassing.

After an early breakfast, Staines had taken him to the Flying Control Officer whose task was to plot the position of his B17s on the perimeter track so that each could take off at thirty second intervals and be in its right place when the aircraft made formation at 6000 feet.

Finally Davies had found himself at the crews' briefing where pilots, navigators and bombardiers occupied the front benches and the sergeant gunners sat at the rear. Here Davies had felt at home, seeing in the Americans the same youthful anxious faces he had seen so often when conducting his own briefings at Sutton Craddock.

There had been the same low gasps and nervous whispers when the crews were given their target for the day. The MAN diesel engine plant at Augsburg! With his own throat turning dry at the prospect, Davies could understand only too well the looks the crews gave one another. Augsburg was a long, long run and its defences were formidable, as a Flak Officer endorsed when he gave the crews precise details where the enemy heavy batteries were sited.

The weather report had come next. An unusual spell of good weather was favouring the British Isles and Europe (this had brought sardonic laughs from the young Americans) and weather planes reported skies clear over Bavaria, although there might be some alto-stratus at 20,000. Freezing level was at zero feet.

The general briefing had ended when the crews were told about the 'spoof' operations that would be carried out to divert enemy fighters and the seven squadrons of Mustangs who would arrive and escort them home. Afterwards the pilots, navigators, bombardiers and radio operators remained behind to lay out their plots, study the target pictures, and receive the call signs of the day while the gunners were dismissed to carry out a final check on their weapons. At this point Staines had led Davies into an office that had been set aside for him and produced a half bottle of Bourbon. 'What do you say, Davies? Old sonsofbitches like us deserve a shot don't we?'

Davies, who seldom drank during the day, had hesitated, then decided there were moments when a wise man put aside his prejudices. As he was sipping at his glass an orderly entered and handed Staines a piece of paper. A moment later Staines gave a deep grunt of relief. 'The last weather report, Davies, and it's still OK. The mission's on.'

Davies' reflections on the long night were scattered as Staines prodded his arm again. 'Listen. They sound sweet, don't they?'

Davies realised he meant the ragged roars of sound as around the field mechanics tested B17 engines. He was saved from a reply when the driver halted the truck. 'This is your ship, sir.'

A B17 was standing on its dispersal point alongside them. As the 15cwt sped away, Staines led Davies towards it. 'C'mon, Davies. Let's meet the crew.'

Davies' first impression of the B17 was relief that its exterior carried no evidence of the high-ranking cargo it would soon be carrying. Its only emblem was a large sweater girl painted on its nose but that made it no more conspicuous than any of the other decorated Fortresses lined up on either side. Although half-frozen line mechanics were still working on the plane, he saw no evidence of the crew and realised they were inside taking cover from the bitter cold.

Staines's bulk needed Davies' help and a mechanic's to squeeze the general inside the B17. Following him, Davies discovered three extra bench seats had been bolted to the floor just ahead of the side gunners' positions. Before being strapped into them, Staines insisted on introducing Davies to all ten crewmen plus the cameraman he had brought with him.

With all the men wearing their high flying equipment, Davies would have had difficulty in identifying any of them later even if his mind had not been occupied by the mission ahead. Because of their close proximity, however, he did take greater notice of the cameraman, whose bench seat faced them, and the two waist gunners.

The cameraman, who had not flown on a combat mission before, was named Allison. He was a thin-faced man in his mid-thirties who claimed he had once worked for *Time* and *Life* and *National Geographic*. His talk and generally assertive demeanour found little favour with Davies who preferred understatement to over-confidence and he let Staines do all the talking to the man.

The gunners were veterans of twelve missions. One, Jackson, was a short, stocky man with a freckled face who disarmingly told Staines he had been unemployed before the war. His companion, Perez, was a swarthy man of medium height who seemed embarrassed by the presence of the two officers and said little to either of them.

When the pilot and co-pilot had finished their checks an order came back for Staines and his two companions to be strapped to their seats. In spite of Staines's complaints, the B17 captain then ordered all three men to wear flak armour. After intercom and oxygen leads were connected to their face masks, Davies began to feel a trussed-up chicken would have had more freedom of movement.

Ten tense minutes followed. Outside ambulances and a fire wagon had congregated at the end of the runway. On the balcony that ran round the Control Room, the Operational staff of the airfield had gathered. The Flying Control Officer glanced for the sixth time at his watch, then nodded at a sergeant. A second later a red flare arched over the centre of the field.

The ragged blast of engines from all twenty B17s rattled the windows in billets and offices. For a moment no movement could be seen. Then the first Fortress emitting a cloud of blue smoke, was seen moving along the perimeter track. It was followed by another and then another, nose to tail, brakes squealing as the twin line stopped and started again. When both lines converged at the far end of the runway, all movement ceased as the pilots consulted their watches. When 08.20 arrived, the leading Fortress's engines roared into life. Swinging her 30 tons on to the runway, she began heading along it at ever-increasing speed. Faster and faster, frost and spray hurling back from her tyres, she bounced and bounced again until at last she tore away from the ground and passed with a relieved roar over the Control Tower.

'Sweater Girl' was the twelfth to go. Davies could hear the rumble of her tyres beneath the roar of her straining engines. As her speed increased, Allison, the cameraman, furtively crossed himself. Catching sight of the gesture, Davies felt a moment of gratified malice.

The Fortresses were forming triangular elements of three. As each moved on another element formed in its place. On the distant horizon tiny specks could be seen as other Combat Wings from other airfields prepared to join the mission. In less than half an hour a huge box of Fortresses, with each element flying higher or lower than its neighbour, was spread out over miles of English sky.

As the entire formation steadily climbed, the navigator in the leading B17 was kept busy computing the drift. With radio silence strictly enforced he was unable to signal his findings back but with the box of B17s following his every move communication was not necessary. At the same time every veteran crewman in the box, and that included Davies, knew that the German monitoring service would already have detected the heavy activity over American airfields and from their assembly point have guessed that the operation was aimed at central or southern Europe. As a consequence fighter squadrons would already be moving to airfields west of Rheims. Once there pilots would wait in their cockpits until their controllers could give a reasonable estimate of the

Americans' target. Once it came they would scramble and launch their attack.

Although there were a few cumulus clouds up to 10,000 feet visibility was good and when the English coast disappeared on the horizon, orders came for battle stations. Alongside Staines and Davies, the two waist gunners took up their positions, looking like spacemen in their thick flying clothes, flak jackets, masks and helmets. As an order rasped through the intercom, Jackson leaned apologetically down to Staines and indicated his oxygen lead. Davies caught the text of his shout. All men must go on oxygen. Strapping his mask in position, Davies caught the taste of metal and rubber as he turned on the tap.

The two gunners, alert now by the Brownings, looked even more bizarre as the bladders from their masks dilated to their breathing. As the long minutes passed and the B17s reached 20,000 feet, Davies wondered when the first attack would come. In the old days, if bombers had gone out unescorted, the attack would have come soon after they crossed the enemy coast. But as the air war had swung in the Allies' favour and the enemy losses had mounted, the Germans could no longer afford to disperse their fighters over occupied Europe. They were now kept for homeland defence only, although ironically, because they were defending their cities, their pilots now fought with the same desperate courage as the British pilots had fought over England four years earlier.

Hearing a shout in his ear, Davies lifted the side flap of his helmet. Staines was jabbing a finger at the clear space below. 'If this weather lasts all the way to the target, we're in clover. Keep your fingers crossed, Davies.'

Davies was about to reply when a vicious crack sounded and the B17 gave a shudder. Glancing through the opposite aperture, Davies saw ugly black mushrooms bursting among the Fortresses. The debit side of good weather, Davies thought. The enemy didn't need predictor controlled guns to latch on to his targets.

AT 25,000 feet the winter sunlight was brilliant. All the B17s were giving off contrails now, white streams that reached back for miles and made a path for fighters to follow.

The flak came at varying intervals and in vicious clusters as the formation passed over heavily defended areas. Sweater Girl's waist gunners reported seeing two B17s hit and destroyed and a third crippled Fortress had been forced to turn for home. Although no one made the comment, with marauding fighters about every man knew its chances of survival were no greater than a crippled reindeer pursued by hungry wolves.

The flak came again and this time Sweater Girl reeled as a shell burst below her starboard wingtip. When she recovered and Davies' own heart resumed its beating, he saw with satisfaction that Allison's thin face had turned a palish green. When Davies peered out of the side aperture half a minute later he saw that a full three feet of wingtip had been blown away.

For a few minutes the flak died away, reminding Davies how intense the cold was. In spite of his protective clothing he had lost feeling in his legs and feet. As he stamped on the metal floor to restore circulation, Perez leaned over him and told him to turn up his oxygen tap.

With every crewman searching the dazzling sky for bandits, the minutes seemed endless. But although flak rocked and jolted the B17s at varying intervals and one Fortress blew up and fell in an inferno of flame, no fighter alarms were raised in the hour that followed.

With every crewman dreading the onset of fighters Davies saw the irony as Staines bellowed in his ear. 'Where's the goddammed air defence? Why don't they come up and fight?'

Davies could only hope his shouted reply didn't sound too gratified. 'I shouldn't worry. They'll be here soon enough.'

The flak was growing even fiercer now, a blizzard of red-cored explosions hurling shards of vicious steel in all directions. As the pilot's voice came over the intercom, the reason became clear, Augsburg had been reached and the B17s were tracking to their target.

With radio silence no longer necessary, Davies could hear the comments of the leading crews as the target slid into their bombsights and they dropped their bombs. When Sweater Girl's turn came, Davies felt his muscles tighten. For the endless seconds that a bomber had to fly level and straight while the bombardier lined up his bombsight, his aircraft was a sitting target for flak gunners.

As murderous shells burst around her, Davies heard the bombardier's instructions over the intercom. 'Bombardier to Radio, start your camera. Bombardier to pilot, left left. Steady. Left, left. Steady . . . steady. Bombs away!'

As the final command came, Sweater Girl rose buoyantly at the release of her load. Elated shouts sounded over the intercom and someone shouted: 'Let's get the hell out of here.' As Sweater Girl banked steeply, Staines tried to see where the bombs fell. Failing, he turned to Davies. 'How did we do?'

Davies shook his head. 'I couldn't see either. There's a hell of a lot of smoke down there.'

The flak was still intense, rocking Sweater Girl like a ship in a storm. Clinging on their gun positions, Jackson and Perez looked almost relaxed and Davies knew why. While the guns were firing, the fighters would stay away. But when they stopped . . .

They stopped quite abruptly and seconds later an urgent shout came over the airwaves. 'Enemy aircraft at one o'clock high. I think they're 190s.'

Davies winced. With their performance and heavy

weaponry they were his own squadron's deadliest enemy. Alongside him Sweater Girl's waist gunners were suddenly alert, peering at the dazzling sky through their smoked goggles.

The Focke Wulfs belonged to 26/JG1, a highly experienced unit, and seeing that the Fortresses all had 'chin' turrets, they made their attack from the rear, sweeping down on the formation like a horde of gannets. Opening fire with their cannon at 800 yards, firing until the last minute before collision, they rolled away and dived to avoid the fire of the bombers' ventral and waist gunners.

Staines and Davies could hear Sweater Girl's rear gunner firing and feel the jolt of his heavy Brownings. Jackson could not line his sights on the attackers but Perez opened fire as they dived beneath him and shell cases spewed out on the metal deck below Davies' bench. Knowing he must not interfere with the waist gunners' movements, Davies remained in his seat but Staines found his excitement too much to contain. Unfastening his straps, he climbed to his feet and tried to peer over Perez's shoulder while the man was firing.

As the first wave of fighters climbed back for another pass, a second wave came plunging down. A burst of shells struck a B17 full in its forward hatch and the effect was horrifying. Flesh, bone and metal were literally fused together as the cockpit became an inferno of flames. With its controls locked, the Fortress reeled from the formation like a blinded animal before it slowly turned over and began the long plunge to earth. Only three parachutes blossomed out in the tracer streaked sky. As the machine-gun fire ceased for a moment, Davies heard Staines's angry shout. 'Where the hell's our goddamed escort?'

Opposite Davies, Allison was frozen to his seat by the ferocity of the battle. Although two more B17s were destroyed, one blowing apart as its gas tanks exploded, the battle was not one-sided. Hit by at least twenty heavy machine guns, a Focke Wolf disintegrated in mid air. Another had both wings blown away and went spinning down like a featherless dart. Another collided with a B17 and the two planes, locked together, sank down in a welter of fire and oily smoke.

Shouts of relief a moment later signalled the arrival of the Mustang escort. As the fighters clashed above and below the formation, a breathless Staines sank down alongside Davies. 'You think that's it?'

With no idea, Davies shook his head. Staines glared at the frozen Allison in his frustation. 'Where are those goddamed 262s, for Christ's sake. We're on their route, aren't we?'

The jets came when they were least expected. An attack by Me 109s ten minutes later, which destroyed another B17, had just been beaten off by the Mustangs when an alarmed shout came over the airwaves. 'It's those new ships, skipper. Six o'clock high.'

Staines was off his bench in a flash and Davies' own curiosity got the better of him. As both officers peered over the tense gunners' shoulders, they saw a single twin-engined monoplane diving from the dazzling sky above. Cutting through the escorting Mustangs like a knife through butter it settled on the tail of an adjacent B17 and opened fire. The next moment the Fortress blew up as if a bomb had exploded within it. Staines let out a curse. 'What the hell are they using? Rockets?'

Before anyone could venture an explanation, four more 262s sliced through the alarmed Mustangs and picked on individual B17s. As one swooped down towards Sweater Girl, Davies had a blurred head-on glimpse of a slim body, tapered wings and a triangular nose pumping out shells. As the 262 swung away at dazzling speed, Jackson tried in vain to follow it with his .5 Browning. As his elbow collided with Staines, he gave the general a look of reproach.

Davies tried to draw the intent Staines away but the American was too busy trying to get the frightened Allison to take photographs. His bellow sounded above the clatter of machine guns and the scream of the airflow. 'C'mon, you sonofabitch. Get those pictures taken.'

The frantic Mustang escort was doing its best to guard its charge and for a few moments, while the B17s were unmolested, Allison was persuaded to take film of the swooping darting 262s. Then Perez pushed the photographer aside as the jets broke through the cordon and attacked again.

This time they dived on the centre of the formation. A B17 above and to the left of Sweater Girl staggered like a hamstrung horse and then began sliding away. With the gap opened, another 262 came at Sweater Girl in a semi-beam attack. Alongside Davies Perez stood his ground and hosed bullets at the oncoming jet but its speed and firepower made it an uneven contest. A shell smashed diagonally through the waist of Sweater Girl and hurled Perez like a smashed doll to the floor. Another shell exploded near the tail and a third made the B17 swerve violently before the pilot could correct her. As fumes and fire filled the fuselage and urgent shouts came over the intercom. Staines grabbed a fire extinguisher and made his unsteady way towards the flames.

Davies was to remember little of what happened next. The entire world seemed comprised of the clatter of guns, the banshee howl of air, and the scream of overworked engines. Tripping over the body of Perez and slipping on blood and hundreds of shell cases, Davies grabbed the stricken man's gun and tried to find a target. Seeing a lightning-fast shape darting past he tried to sight on it but his stream of tracer fell well behind. Nevertheless he kept on firing intermittently until a hand gripped his arm and he saw Jackson shaking his head. Realising the jets had gone and the Mustangs were driving off the 109s, Davies released the trigger and clung somewhat shamefacedly to the mounting.

As he turned he saw Staines was bending over Perez's body. Releasing the gun mounting, Davies knelt beside him. 'Is it bad?'

Staines made no comment and Davies understood why a moment later. The explosive shell had smashed into Perez's stomach and left a bloody carcase hardly recognisable as once belonging to a man. Allison, who had been shoved back into his seat by Staines after the 262s' second attack, had recently vomited into his face mask and dribbles of it were staining his flying clothes.

With the jets gone and the 109s driven away, the Mustang pilots returned to their stations above and below the formation. The flak began again and followed the B17s all the way to the Dutch coast. Over the home airfield, responding to the red flare her pilot sent down, Sweater Girl was given a priority landing. With half her rudder missing, her approach was unsteady but although she bounced heavily a couple of times, she made a reasonable landing. As she drove off the runway towards a waiting ambulance, Staines let out his breath and turned to Davies. 'We made it.'

'Just about,' Davies said hoarsely.

Staines unfastened his straps and tried to rise, only for his legs to fail him. As he tried again and succeeded, he gave Davies a rueful grin. 'I was right. We are too old for this kind of job.'

'Now you tell me,' Davies said, his own legs unsteady.

Staines glanced at Allison who seemed unable to believe he was still alive. 'Never mind, we did see the sonsofbitches. And if we're lucky we might have gotten a few pictures.'

The ambulance crews were now removing Perez's

body and the body of Sweater Girl's rear gunner who had been killed in the last jet attack. Staines glanced at Davies as the two bodies were carried into the ambulance but for once the tough American seemed lost for words. Instead he shook his head and allowed a couple of mechanics to help him to the ground. As Davies followed him, he nodded across the airfield. 'I guess we'd better join the boys at the de-briefing. Or are you in a hurry to get back to your Group?'

'No,' Davies said. 'I'll come with you. We might learn something from the other crews we didn't see ourselves.'

Nodding, Staines turned towards a transport that had driven up for them and walked wearily towards it. As Davies handed his parachute to a mechanic and followed him, he realised for the first time that he too was desperately tired.

Chapter 7

Gabby paused in the cafe doorway and shivered at the icy wind that was keening down the promenade. 'Look at it. Three days and it's still colder than Siberia. Why can't we get one of those Mediterranean postings like other squadrons get?'

Millburn grinned. 'Sure. Flying every day. You'd like that, wouldn't you?'

Gabby glanced back at the cafe. 'At least we wouldn't get spam all the time. Do you realise that's all we get every time we come into Scarborough? What's happened to all the fish they catch here? I suppose it goes to the bloody Army or the Navy.'

Millburn clapped him across the shoulders. 'You're in a great mood today, aren't you, boyo? The original sunshine boy. Why don't you climb that big cliff over there and jump off? Then it would all be over. No more spam and no more English winters. Just old Nick's fire to stoke every day. I don't know what holds you back.'

Gabby glowered again. 'It's all right for you, Millburn. You've got that ferry pilot woman to see next week. What am I supposed to do while you're having your nookie?'

'You've got leave too, haven't you? So what's your problem?'

'What use is leave to me? All I can do is go home to Swansea.'

'So what? Don't you always tell us you've got the greatest girls in the country in Swansea?'

'What if we have? They're on my doorstep, aren't they? If I get any of them in trouble, everyone'll find out. And what then? What about my Mum and Dad? There's no mercy among chapel people, Millburn.'

Millburn grinned. 'Yeah, they tell me chapel in Wales is really something. You ought to take it up, kiddo. Three times a day on Sundays. That'll straighten you out and put hairs on your chest.'

Gabby's Celtic mood would not be lightened by humour. 'Stop talking out of your trousers, Millburn, and let's get to your car before I turn into a bloody brass monkey.'

Hurrying down the frozen pavement, the two men jumped into Millburn's tiny Austin Seven. As Gabby sank into his seat, a gust of wind sent an icy draught into his face. 'Do you know you've got a leak in this window?'

Millburn nodded. 'Yeah. I keep it that way to stop a certain little pisspot borrowing it for his popsies.'

'I wouldn't put it past you,' Gabby muttered. He stared down the long promenade where a lone figure, muffled up to the eyebrows, could be seen walking his dog. 'What the hell are we going to do, Millburn? It'll be dark soon and we can't waste an afternoon's pass.'

'I thought we were going to the movies.'

Gabby grimaced. 'I'm sick of the movies. Why can't we go looking for women like we used to?'

'Because we're officers and gentlemen, that's why. His Majesty the King doesn't approve of his officers picking up loose women.'

'It's never stopped you before, Millburn. Why don't you admit the truth. You've gone soft on this woman ferry pilot and the rest of us have to suffer for it.'

Millburn motioned at the Welshman's door. 'No one's stopping you getting out, boyo. You can always play that old act of yours, that you're a wounded fighter pilot who's just lost his girlfriend. Some dumb woman might fall for it and take pity on you.'

Gabby scowled. 'How can a man pick up a woman in this weather? Let's go to a dance, Millburn. There's sure to be one on somewhere.'

'You mean a WVS dance?'

'Any dance as long as there are women there.'

'They won't let you in. They're for enlisted men only.'

'There must be dances for officers somewhere.'

Millburn shrugged. 'Where?'

A silence fell, relieved only by the muffled sound of the waves. It was broken by Gabby's tentative voice. 'Of course we could go to Hull again.'

Millburn stared at him. 'You mean Hessle Road?'

'Why not? It wouldn't take long for Sandra to call up a couple of girls.'

'Are you out of your mind? Have you forgotten what happened the last time?'

'Yes, but that was a frame-up. Sammy wouldn't know we were going this time.'

'He wouldn't need to know. The Navy hate us so much they've probably put a watch on the house.'

'That's silly, Millburn, and you know it. You weren't scared to take such chances before.'

'Well, I'm scared now, boyo. A dozen big hairy matelots scared. Which means we're not going to Hessle Road. OK?'

There was a Welsh sniff, silence, and then Gabby tried again. 'What about your lot?'

'What do you mean – my lot?'

'Our Allies. The Yanks. They must have some arrangements. Yanks can't live without their nookie.'

Millburn grinned. 'Listen whose talking.'

'It's true, Millburn. I'll bet Swartz has set up secret brothels to stop 'em going out of their minds.'

As Millburn gave him a glance, the Welshman went on: 'Everyone knows it. Randy Yanks who can't keep their pants up. They've got bases in Yorkshire, so they must have set up clubs somewhere.'

Millburn was looking reflective. 'You might have a point there. When I got that packet of Lucky Strike from the Yank airfield, someone told me they'd a club in Scarborough. Yeah, I remember now. In Sefton Street. They can get drinks there when those crazy licensing laws of yours keep pubs closed.'

Gabby was brightening fast. 'What about women?'

Millburn gave him a look of disgust. 'It's a club, not a brothel. Do you want to try it or not?'

'I suppose it'll be better than the flicks,' Gabby muttered. 'But I'd rather go to one with women.'

'You'll have to take what you can get, boyo. Anyway,' and Millburn paused maliciously, 'there's no guarantee they'll let you in. You are a foreigner, after all.'

Gabby nearly shot out of his seat. 'A foreigner! In my own country? To a bunch of sex-craved Yanks! That'll be the day, Millburn.'

Grinning, Millburn reached for the starter. 'I guess we can try. If I say you're a midget I found abandoned from a circus they might give you a Coke.' Before Gabby could frame his indignant reply, Millburn switched on the engine. 'OK. Let's go and see what Uncle Sam can do for us.'

The doorkeeper looked dubious. 'I don't know I can, sir. This is a club for the American Air Force only.'

'You mean it's for Americans,' Millburn said. 'Well, I'm an American.'

'I can tell that, sir, but you're in the Royal Air Force.'

'So what? We're fighting the same war, aren't we?'

'I suppose we are, sir, but rules are rules.'

With the icy wind stinging his face, Millburn decided the situation called for more devious measures. 'You haven't got it, have you? I'm an American on loan to the RAF. They make me wear their uniform while I'm with them but I'm still a serving American. And that entitles me to the same privileges. Right?'

The middle-aged doorkeeper hesitated. 'But your friend isn't an American, sir, is he?'

Millburn slapped the back of the scowling Gabby. 'He's the next best thing. He's our liaison man. Our translator. Some of our ground crew speak Welsh, so the RAF lent him to us.'

The doorkeeper was looking more confused by the minute. 'I think I had better speak to our manager, sir. If you'll wait just one moment.'

Millburn gave a simulated shiver. 'Can we come inside? It's forty below out here.'

The doorkeeper sighed. 'Dear me, this is difficult. Very well, sir. You can wait in here while I see the manager.'

The two officers found themselves in a spacious hall. As the doorkeeper hurried up a flight of stairs, Gabby scowled at Millburn. 'You're wasting time. The Yanks have got it all sewn up. We can't have a drink in our own bloody country.'

As he spoke, laughter and singing could be heard from behind a closed door. Millburn turned to the Welshman. 'We're inside, aren't we?'

'Only until the manager comes down,' Gabby complained.

Millburn pushed him towards the door. 'We're not waiting for the manager. Come on. In for a penny, in for a pound.'

A couple of seconds later the decibel count shot up as he pushed the door open. Inside a cocktail bar ten or more uniformed Americans were either clustered around a piano or lined up at the bar. For a moment no one noticed the two RAF officers and then a shout went up. 'Hey, you guys. Look over there. Someones let a couple of Limies in.'

The singing at the piano ceased as everyone turned to stare at the two men. As a humorous catcall or two broke out, a stocky captain pushed himself from the bar and made towards them. 'Hiya! What can I do for you guys?'

Millburn gave him a grin. 'You can start by giving us a drink?'

The captain hesitated. 'I'd sure like to, squadron leader. But this is a club the guys have set up and the rules say only American can use it.'

'Then that's OK,' Millburn told him. 'I am an American.'

The Captain had now recognised his accent. 'Say, so you are. But how come the uniform?'

'You've heard of the Eagle Squadron, haven't you? Yanks who joined the RAF before Uncle Sam came into the war?'

By this time half a dozen other men were crowding round. One of them, a tall and burly lieutenant, pushed forward. 'Those guys came back to us when we entered the war. So whose leg are you pulling?'

Millburn turned to him. 'I didn't say I was in the Eagle Squadron, lieutenant. I was telling the captain I'm a Yank who joined up the same way.'

'You mean in Canada?'

'That's right.'

The burly lieutenant nodded at Gabby. 'This one do the same?'

Millburn grinned. 'No, he belongs here. He's my navigator.'

'Well, he can't drink in here, buster. This is for Yanks only.'

A voice came from the back of the group. 'Hell, Simpson, who's going to know if we give the guys a drink? We fly with the guys, don't we?'

Simpson turned. 'We fly with 'em because we have to. That doesn't mean we have to live with 'em.'

'You're a really friendly feller, aren't you?' Millburn said. He turned back to the stocky American. 'You feel the same way, Captain?'

The American looked uncomfortable. 'Hell, no. Not at all. It's just that we've been told we mustn't entertain other servicemen or women or we could lose the club.'

The aggressive Simpson was gazing round at the curious faces to judge the general reaction. Hospitable by nature, the Americans were showing indecision and embarrassment. Simpson took their silence for approval. 'That's the way of it,' he told Millburn. 'And we sure aren't losing our club for two gatecrashers. Right, guys?'

Although nobody answered him, Simpson turned to Gabby. 'As you're a real Limie, that means you're taking a walk, buster. Through the door and into the street. OK?'

Gabby, who had not spoken as yet, took umbrage as only Gabby could. 'You're full of wind and piss, Lieutenant. More piss than wind. You think I want to drink your bloody bourbon? Squirt it up your arse.'

There was a gasp of surprise, then a roar of laughter from the onlookers. Looking stunned for a moment by the attack, Simpson stepped in front of the diminutive Welshman as he turned for the door. 'Who the hell do you think you are, you little flying asshole?'

Knowing that Gabby was capable of throwing a punch at anyone from King Kong downwards, Millburn stepped between the two men. 'I told you who he is. He's my navigator. And that means he and I fight the same war. You object to that, Lieutenant?'

For a moment, eyeball to eyeball, the two men glared at one another. The tension was broken by an authoritative shout from the captain. 'That's enough, Lieutenant. Back off! Back off or you're out in the street yourself. Now!'

Simpson gave Millburn a last glare and then drew back. Millburn grinned at the embarrassed captain. 'You've got a friendly character there, Captain. What beer does he drink? Steinfurt or Kronenburg?'

The captain winced. 'Don't get us wrong, Squadron Leader. This isn't our club. It's been loaned to us for our use, and so we don't want to do anything to spoil it for the other guys. But, hell, there can't be anything wrong in giving a couple of guests a drink. Come over to the bar.' As Millburn hesitated, he held out his hand. 'I'm Newcombe. Harry Newcombe.'

Millburn relaxed. 'Tommy Millburn and Johnnie Gabriel. Only we call him Gabby for short.' As the still smouldering Gabby scowled, Millburn dug him in the ribs. 'The captain's offering you a drink, boyo. Be a little gentleman and accept it.' As Gabby growled something, Millburn turned to Newcombe. 'He'll have a bourbon with me, Newcombe. And I promise he won't squirt it up anyone's arse.'

With the exception of Simpson, everyone in the room burst out laughing. As Newcombe ordered two bourbons from the bar, he glanced at Millburn. 'What's your outfit, Millburn?'

'We're at Sutton Craddock, near Highgate,' Millburn told him. 'The unit's 633 Squadron.'

Newcombe gave a start and his eyes opened wide. '633 Squadron! No kidding.' When Millburn nodded, he turned to the rest of the officers who were now crowding round the bar. 'You hear that, you guys? These two are from 633 Squadron. The outfit that got the Congressional

Medal of Honor. And we weren't going to give 'em a drink!'

A buzz of surprise galvanised the room and in seconds the two RAF officers were surrounded. As excited men threw questions at them, Newcombe held up a hand. 'Hold it, you guys. Hold it a moment.' As the voices died down, Newcombe turned to Millburn. 'Have you heard of Major Dent?'

'Yeah. He leads a wing of Mustangs. They've escorted us on a few missions. They're a great bunch of guys. Why?'

As a cheer went up, Newcombe grinned at the men around him. 'That's our outfit, Millburn. Dent's our squadron commander. He'll be sorry he's not here tonight to meet you.'

It was Millburn's turn to show surprise. 'Dent's guys? But I thought you were stationed further south.'

'We are. But we've been sent up here for some low-level practice in mountains. We go up to Scotland nearly every day.'

Millburn turned to Gabby who had already finished his large glass of bourbon. 'You getting all this, kiddo? These are the guys who escorted us to Bavaria and Copenhagen.'

Excited American voices drowned Gabby's reply as Copenhagen was mentioned. A tall pilot pushed forward. 'That was Hitler's birthday party, wasn't it, sir?'

'That's right. We were sent over to wreck the celebrations.'

Another eager voice broke in. 'Yeah. Your Mosquitoes dropped pisspots and toilet rolls on the Krauts. They shit themselves thinking they were bombs.'

Yet another pilot brought a gale of laughter from his colleagues. 'You remember how that Kraut band of musicians ran? And the way the Danes took the piss out of them. Geez, that was some mission.'

Bonhomie was fully established as more memories of combined missions were exchanged, Gabby, fully integrated into the party after two more bourbons, waved a cigarette at the empty chairs. 'Why can't you have women in here?'

A fresh-faced American, barely out of his teens, answered him. 'It's a rule of the manager. We can only use the club ourselves. I guess he's scared we might run a brothel here or something.'

Gabby, with his libido inflamed by bourbon, looked shocked. 'No women at all! That's terrible. You guys have transport, haven't you?'

'Sure we have. But what's the connection?'

Gabby put a finger to his nose and lowered his voice. 'I know where there are plenty of women.'

Hearing the Welshman's voice drop and seeing half a dozen Americans drawing into a huddle around him, Millburn crossed over suspiciously. 'What are you up to, Gabby?'

Well oiled by this time, Gabby gave him a defiant look. 'It's nothing to do with you, Millburn. Not now that ferry pilot has tamed you.'

Glaring at him, Millburn turned to one of the young, eager Americans. 'What's he been telling you?'

'He says he knows where there are lots of women, sir. Plenty for us all.'

Millburn turned back to the Welshman. 'You're not telling 'em about Hessle Road, are you?'

Gabby's voice was slightly slurred. 'No, I'm not. I'm telling 'em about a place in Scarborough where there are dozens of women. And it's not far from here.'

'You mean the Old Ladies Home?'

'No, I bloody don't. I'm talking about the Hotel Imperial. You didn't know the Army train female wireless operators there, did you?'

Millburn looked unconvinced. 'How do you know that?'

Gabby put a finger to his nose again. 'Because I keep my eyes and ears open, Millburn.'

'All right. What if there are? They'll all need liberty passes to get out. How do you get round that?'

Gabby held out a hand and rubbed his palm. 'Money, Millburn. Something these guys have and we haven't. We'll bribe the guards and whoever's in charge of them.'

'You're drunk,' Millburn said. 'As drunk as a fart.' He turned to the grinning Americans. 'He gets this way after a few drinks. Thinks he's Houdini or Casanova. Don't take any notice of him.'

'You're just jealous you haven't thought of it yourself, Millburn.'

'Jealous of a crazy scheme like that? You haven't a hope in hell of getting away with it.'

'Want a bet, Millburn?' Gabby turned to the circle of amused Americans. 'Are you guys prepared to put up ten quid each?' When every man nodded, Gabby smirked. 'That's a lot of money, Millburn. You still sure it can't be done?'

'You can't bribe guards. And what if there's a battleaxe matron in charge of them. She'd probably have you put inside for bribing His Majesty's Armed Forces. You could end up in the Tower, buster.'

Gabby smirked again. 'You're not so sure of yourself now, are you? What about it, you guys? Are you coming with me?' As a cheer went up, the Welshman pointed at the bar. 'Buy some bottles to take with us. Plenty of 'em. Then let's go.'

A single voice, more sober than the rest, halted Gabby as he was turning towards the door. 'Where are we going to take dames if you do get them out? We can't bring them back here.'

Millburn grinned at the question. 'A good point, you little pisspot. Where will you take them?'

Gabby was too far gone to allow such minor matters to deflect him. 'It's a big town. We'll find somewhere. And if we don't, there are always the transports. Come on!'

As a cheering group of men followed the Welshman to the door, Newcombe grinned at Millburn. 'You've got quite a navigator there. Is he always like this after a few drinks?'

'Mostly worse,' Millburn told him. 'It does something to his libido.' He eyed the laughing, chattering group filing out into the hall and then sighed. 'I guess someone has to get him back to camp after he's made a fool of himself. You coming or staying?'

Newcombe draining his glass and then collected his coat. 'I think I'll join you. I've got a gut feeling this might be worth watching.'

Chapter 8

The man standing beneath a tree at the edge of the wood could hear the night wind approaching as it rustled the tall branches of the firs. When it reached him he felt an icy tingle on the nape of his neck as a sprinkle of snow fell from a branch above. Brushing it away, he continued examining the village below him.

Bathed in the light of a waning moon it lay on the foot of the shallow hillside, a cluster of picturesque cottages bisected by a narrow road that ran on through the valley and disappeared round another wooded hill. With no artificial light visible, the entire village appeared to be sleeping. Although most of its chalets and the road had been cleared of snow, the virgin white hillsides gave evidence that winter still held sway in the Bavarian highlands.

Satisfied the village was clear of military traffic, the man moved out from the shadow of the trees. Tall and lean, he was wearing a thick coat, breeches and mountain boots. Although snow impeded his descent to the road, once he reached it he made better time, walking with quick, hurried strides. As he reached the village a dog began barking, followed by another a few seconds later. As a curtain was drawn back from a chalet and a dim light appeared, the man cursed and hurried on.

A moment later he ran up the steps of a chalet and tapped on the front door. As a woman's voice sounded, he gave a quiet reply. 'It's all right, Freda. It's me, Horst Meyer.'

Bolts were withdrawn and the door opened, revealing a stout, motherly-looking woman in her early fifties. Without a word, she drew him inside and closed the door before asking her anxious question. 'What is it? Has something happened?'

Although the man had gaunt, sardonic features, his smile was reassuring. 'Stop looking so worried, Freda. Everything's fine. I just want a talk with Gunter, that's all. Is he home?'

As the woman relaxed, a voice sounded from the rear of the chalet. 'Who is it, Freda?'

'It's Horst,' the woman called back. 'He wants to see you.'

Heavy footsteps sounded and a moment later a burly, middle-aged man appeared. 'Hello, Horst. Come inside.'

Meyer shrugged off his thick coat. 'I've just a few things I thought you'd like to hear about. You're not doing anything important, are you?'

Catching Meyer's surreptitious glance at Freda, Hausmann took the hint. 'No. I was just sitting on my backside reading. I suppose you haven't had dinner tonight?' As Meyer grinned and shook his head, Hausmann turned to his wife. 'What about fixing something up for him? These bachelors are all the same. They put their drink and their womanising before their bellies. That's why they're all so gaunt and skinny.'

Freda was not so easily diverted. She turned to Meyer. 'I hope you haven't come with some news from Anton.'

Before Meyer could reply, Hausmann scowled. 'For God's sake, woman, when will you learn to mind your own business? Go and get some food for the man. Can't you see he's half starved.'

Freda sniffed. 'If you ask me, he deserves all he gets.'

Meyer gave her a mocking bow. 'I stand chastised, Frau Hausmann.'

Fighting back a smile, Freda gave another sniff instead. 'Oh, be off with you. Go and get drunk with that stupid husband of mine.' Giving Hausmann a glare, she turned and made for the kitchen. Grimacing at Meyer, Hausmann led him into the sitting room. 'Come in and have a schnapps.'

As he followed, Meyer noticed the burly Bavarian was favouring his left leg. 'What's wrong. Is your arthritis playing up again?'

Hausmann nodded as he limped towards a cabinet. 'Yes, damn it. I can't wait for summer to come.'

He poured two glasses of schnapps and gave one to Meyer. Then he sank with relief into a chair. 'That's better. Proust!' As Meyer acknowledged his toast, Hausmann's voice dropped. 'Well, what is it? Has Anton had some good news for us?'

Meyer lifted an amused eyebrow. 'Good news? From Anton?'

'Hitler might be dead,' Hausmann suggested. 'Or the Allies might have reached Berlin. No? Then I don't think I want to hear Anton's news.'

Meyer gave his sardonic grin. 'You're going to hear it just the same.' His voice lowered. 'He says SOE is suddenly anxious to find out where these 262s aircraft are built.'

Hausmann's weatherbeaten face frowned. 'You mean these new fighters? They could be built anywhere. Probably in a dozen different places.'

'They don't think so. They believe there's a main assembly centre because they know some 262 parts are pre-fabricated in Sweden.'

Hausmann gave a slight start. 'Sweden?'

'That's right. The tip off came from one of London's military attachés there. It seems that because of the Allied bombing, the 262 airframe manufacturers, Junkers and Messerschmidtt, were given permission by the *Technische Amt* to have some pre-fabricated parts made in Sweden. Then they're shipped over to Rostock.'

Hausmann gave a grunt of appreciation. 'You've got to admit it: the Nazi bastards are smart. So what does London do now? Bomb the Swedes?'

Meyer grinned. 'I don't think that's in their minds. But they are thinking the Rostock trains that carry the parts might be traced to their destination.'

Hausmann frowned. 'How could that be done? Docks are guarded better than virgins in a nunnery. So how could anyone know which trains were which?'

'They could know if London had men over in Sweden to tip them off when a ship carrying the parts is about to sail. And another agent who's an official in Rostock's marshalling yards. He could let London know when a consignment of parts arrives and be able to find out the destination of the train from its timetables and schedules.'

'Are you saying London has an official in Rostock?'

'So it seems. He was planted there years ago when it became known that Sweden was providing Germany with quality steel, ball bearings and the rest. He's now the ideal man to tell London which train is carrying the 262 parts and where it's going.'

Hausmann shrugged. 'So what's London's problem? They get the train's destination from him and so get a fix. The Yanks then send a hundred daylight bombers over and bingo. No more 262s.'

Meyer shook his head. 'It isn't that simple. London doesn't know how many steps there are in a 262's construction. The parts might go to intermediate plants for drilling or checking before they're sent to a final assembly plant. In which case raids might be costly and futile.'

'You're saying someone has to follow these trains and report back?'

'Can you think of any other way it can be done?'

Hausmann's weatherbeaten face was full of suspicion now. 'Why is London telling us all this?'

'It isn't London who's provided the information,' Meyer told him. 'SOE have taken on the job, although God knows why. Anton thinks they've persuaded London to instruct their agents in Sweden and Rostock to help them.' He paused. 'You can guess the rest, can't you?'

Hausmann's low, explosive curse told that he could guess it only too well. 'The bastards! Haven't they had enough out of us already?'

Meyer grinned wryly. 'We're still alive, aren't we?' So while we are, they'll use us.'

Hausmann leaned forward, his voice low but intense. 'Horst, the war's nearly over. Germany can't last much longer, certainly not beyond the end of the year. So why is this new aircraft so important?'

'Because it's knocking hell out of the American daylight raids, I suppose.'

'Maybe, but the Allied raids are still knocking hell out of all our cities. So it can't be that effective.'

'It's effective wherever it appears. If the Nazis had a couple of thousand of them, they could drive the Allies out of the skies.'

'Yes but they haven't thousands of them, have they? And how can they get enough before the Allies and the Russians finish the job?'

'I suppose the Allies don't want to take any chances. No one thought the V1 and V2 rockets could be produced in effective numbers but they were.'

Scowling, Hausmann took the cigarette Meyer offered him. 'I still think they've no right to ask us to get involved again. Don't they remember what happened in Nurnbach?'

'I don't suppose they give a damn about Nurnbach'.

'And yet you're still thinking of taking it on?' When Meyer shrugged his lean shoulders, Hausmann stared at him angrily. 'Why?'

Meyer drew in smoke. 'God knows. Maybe I want to finish the job. Maybe I don't like the Nazis. Maybe I'm a bloody fool. Who's to say?'

'You are a bloody fool,' Hausmann said fiercely. 'Since we killed those two Gestapo bastards, there's been a manhunt on. If they captured us and found out who we were, they'd put us through hell before they killed us.'

As Meyer gave a semi-humorous grimace, there was a crash of plates from the kitchen. Embarrassed by his warning, Hausmann turned the accident to his advantage. 'Mama's having fun and games getting your meal ready. You'd better pretend to enjoy it when it comes.'

'I'll enjoy it,' Meyer said. He continued in the same tone of voice. 'No one'll blame you if you don't take part. You've got Freda and the kids to think about.'

Hausmann's bushy eyebrows came together in a heavy frown, 'Did I say I wouldn't take part?'

'No, but you called me a fool. You don't want to be a fool too, do you?'

Hausmann rose, picked up both empty glasses and took them to the cabinet. 'I suppose there's no chance of Lorenz being involved in this, is there?'

Meyer, knowing Lorenz was Anna Reinhardt's code-name, shook his head. 'No, after that affair in Nurnbach, even London and SOE know it would be suicide to send her over again.'

'At least thank God for that,' Hausmann muttered. Filling both glasses again, he handed one to Meyer, then sank back into his chair and picked up his cigarette. For a long moment he sat staring at his glass, his weatherbeaten face dark and brooding. Then he glanced up at Meyer. 'How soon does SOE want to know?'

Meyer gave his sardonic grin again. 'I don't think they've considered we might refuse. It's that sort of war. But there's nothing they can do if you say no. I think you should. You've done enough.'

Hausmann gave a grunt of irritation. 'Let me make up my own mind.' In the silence that followed the ticking of a clock could be heard. Hausmann broke it with a curse. 'I can't tell you tonight. Can I send you word tomorrow?'

'Yes. Send that schoolboy you've used before. Fake some message but put a tick or a cross somewhere. I'll know what they mean.'

Hausmann put up a warning hand as Freda gave a shout from the kitchen. 'Horst, your food's ready. I'm not setting up the dining room table. You'll have to have it in here.'

'Coming,' Meyer called. Lowering his voice he turned to Hausmann. 'I'd like you with me but I think you'll be a fool if you come.'

Hausmann scowled. 'Shut up and go and eat your dinner. Otherwise the old woman will know what you came for.'

Shining through a chink in the curtains, the moonlight was throwing a bar of cold light on the bedroom floor. Lying on his side in the big double bed, watching its slow movement, Hausmann was reminded of a sundial he had seen as a child. As a special treat his father had taken him on an outing to Herrenschee, Ludwig 11's extravaganza built in the style of the palace of Versailles and a sundial on a lawn had fascinated the young child more than anything else he had seen that day.

The golden days of youth, Hausmann thought. When one did not run but floated over the good earth. When the sun always shone, when the body was a joy to occupy, when one's life revolved around the simple things like food and play and Papa and Mama. When the grass was tall, the forests full of magic, and the evil in men was unknown.

Suddenly aware of the ache in his hip, Hausmann shifted his position carefully. Believing Freda was asleep he did not want to awaken her. Meyer had barely gone from the chalet when she had turned on him. 'Well, what did he want?'

He had shown surprise. 'He just wanted a chat, that was all. And something to eat.'

'Don't lie to me, Gunter Hausmann. There's been a message from England, hasn't there? They want you to do something else for them.'

'No, Mama. Horst just likes to talk to me sometimes. About how the war's going and things like that. Isn't it natural enough? We've been through a great deal together.'

'Far too much, if you ask me. And now there's something else, isn't there? I could tell it the moment he came in. Why are you lying to me?'

He wondered now why he had lied. She would have to know sooner or later. He must have been thinking about the stress she had lived under the last two years. It had aged her. Before the war no one had possessed a more placid nature. Now she jumped at the slightest sound and showed nervousness whenever a stranger entered the village. For a moment Hausmann felt hatred for those who had inflicted such burdens on her. Those bastards in England cared nothing about German wives and families. They used him and Meyer and others like them for their own purposes. When the war was over no credit would be given the German Resistance, as was already given to the French, the Norwegians and the others. It did not suit Allied propaganda to admit there were Germans who hated the Nazis more than they did.

Then Hausmann's spasm of resentment faded and died. The Allies were fighting a life and death struggle against a ruthless war machine. How could the private tribulations of a few enemy dissenters enter their equation? The real villains were those who had brainwashed Germany's citizens into believing their finer feelings were symptoms of weakness and only the hard of heart deserved to survive. Not for the first time in Hausmann's life, hatred of what the Nazis had done to his country made the Bavarian break out into a cold sweat.

Damning the nagging ache in his hip, he shifted his legs again. This time Freda's voice made him start. 'You're not sleeping, are you?'

From the clarity of her voice he knew immediately she had not been sleeping either. 'No, Mama. My hip's been keeping me awake.'

'You're lying to me again, Gunter. You've been thinking about the things Horst said to you. You can't keep things from me. I've lived with you too long.'

It was true, he thought. When you'd lived with someone for thirty years they were almost part of one's own brain.

'Go to sleep, Mama,' he begged. 'Stop thinking about Horst.'

'How can I stop thinking about him when you've been doing nothing else since he left. What does London want you to do this time?'

He knew now it was worse to keep her in ignoranc than to tell her the truth. Taking a deep breath, he tol her the full story.

She listened in frozen silence until he had finishec Then she turned towards him, her voice distressed an condemning. 'I knew it. They'll use you until you ar dead and no longer any use to them. And you are fool enough to want to do it, aren't you?'

'No,' he said, knowing this time he wasn't lying. 'I don't. I was hoping our work was over.'

'But you are still going to, aren't you? Isn't that why you haven't been able to sleep?'

'Mama, things aren't that simple. Have you ever thought that if I stay here I might be called up into the *Volksstrum*. So isn't it better I fight for a cause I believe in?'

She sounded both shocked and disbelieving. 'You were wounded in the last war and honourably discharged. So how can they call you up? You're just using it as an excuse.'

'I'm not, Mama. Germany is scraping the barrel these days. Even children of fourteen years are being drafted.'

'If it were to happen, it would be something you couldn't help. And it hasn't happened yet. Please God the war might end first. But this other thing is different. If you were caught you would be treated as a traitor.'

Hausmann turned and propped himself up on one elbow. 'Mama, try to understand. Horst and I have worked together for a long time now. He needs me, as I need him. How can I let him down now?'

In the darkness he could not see her expression, only the blur of her face above her white nightdress. He listened to her voice, burdened with urgency and fear. '*Liebschen*, Horst hasn't got a wife and family. You have grandchildren.' Hausmann winced as for a moment her voice faltered. 'Now Heinrich has been killed, you are the only man they have to talk to and learn from. Don't you realise how much they will lose if you are killed?'

No mention of her own loss, Hausmann thought. He loved her for that. 'Mama, it isn't that simple. There is the future to think about.'

'The future? What future is there if you are killed?'

'I mean the future of Germany, Mama.'

'Germany? What has Germany to do with it? All Germany has done for us is call up our only child and get him killed fighting other mother's sons! So what nonsense are you talking about Germany?'

Hausmann wished he could explain. 'So many of our own people have died fighting the Nazis, Mama. We can't let them down.'

'What others?'

'Canaris for one, Treschow, Leber, Von Trott, Moltke, Stauffenberg . . . it's a long list, Mama.'

'They were high-ranking officers or aristocrats, Gunter. Rich and powerful men who hated Hitler because of what he took from them. They didn't do it for Germany.'

'No, Mama. That's not true. They did it for Germany's good name. And there have been many poor people too who have opposed the Nazis. What about the members of the Abwehr who smuggled Jews into Switzerland? What about the White Rose Organisation? They were only kids at Munich University. But they still died fighting to save Germany.'

Freda went on as if she has not been listening. 'We're simple people, Gunter. We had nothing for them to take. So why do you want to make yourself a martyr?'

'They took our son, Mama. Our only son.'

In the sudden silence that fell in the bedroom Hausmann hated himself. Her voice sounded weary when she spoke again. 'What are you trying to say to me, Gunter?'

At last Hausmann found the word he was searching for. 'It's conscience, Mama. People who resist the Nazi are the conscience of Germany. And that's going to be so important when the war's over.'

'But you've always said the Allies don't care about our resistance. You and your friends won't get a mention

Stauffenberg and a few of the others might be remembered because they were aristocrats. But not simple people like us. So what is all this about conscience?'

Not for the first time Hausmann was finding that some feelings could not find expression in words. 'It's for the kids, Mama. Like our grandchildren. They're going to carry a stigma unless the world knows that some Germans detested all that the Nazis stood for. And the world will know. It might take many years but the truth will come out one day.'

'And so that's what you want to do? Risk your life again in the hope a few historians find out a few Bavarians didn't like Hitler?'

'Mama, don't put it that way. We're not trying to be martyrs. We just feel it's our duty to fight tyranny.'

'Your duty? Do you realise what the Nazis will do for you if you're captured. Do you think I don't know about the two Nazis you killed in Nurnbach.'

Hausmann gave a start. 'How did you find out about that?'

'I'm not a fool, Gunter. I knew you were in Nurnbach that night and I saw the proclamation offering a reward for the men who killed the Nazis. Do you think I can't put two and two together?'

Hausmann sighed. 'We had to save a girl's life, Mama. A very brave German girl.'

As he spoke he heard a sob. '*Mein Gott*, I'm frightened, I'm not brave like you. I'm terrified every time someone comes to the house. I think they're going to take you away and kill you.'

Those who knew Gunter Housmann would have been amazed at his gentleness as he took the trembling woman into his arms. 'I'm sorry, Mama. I know what all this is doing to you. But try to be brave a little longer. The war will be over soon and then it'll be like old times again.'

Her tears were wetting his face and chest. 'If you are dead it won't be like old times. What will my world be without you? I know I don't always show it but I love you, Gunter.'

Hausmann had not known tears since he was a child but he could feel them burning his eyes now. 'I love you too, Mama. Ever since that day we met at that party beside the lake. Do you remember it?'

She pressed close to him. 'Of course I remember. You were so big and strong and yet you were so shy.' A tremor ran through her. 'Take care, *Liebschen*. For me and the grandchildren.'

His arms tightened around her. 'I promise, Mama. I promise.'

It was a long time before Hausmann turned away to ease his aching leg. When he did he saw the bar of moonlight had left the floor and was now reaching across his side of the bed. Without knowing why, he felt a chill as it slid towards him and touched his face.

Chapter 9

Gabby tapped the arm of the driver. 'Over there! That'll do fine.'

The young American officer halted the jeep and gazed at the dark glass-fronted building on the opposite side of the promenade. 'What is it?'

Gabby's voice was slurred. 'What the hell do you think it is? It's a concert hall.'

A girl sitting at the back of the jeep gave a giggle. 'We can't go in there. They'd see us.'

'Who'd see us?' Gabby demanded. He jabbed a finger at the deserted promenade on which an icy mist was settling. 'Who's going to come along here tonight? It's below zero out there.'

The girl giggled again. 'But how're we going to get in?'

Gabby, who had his arm around a curvaceous blonde squeezed in alongside him, laughed scornfully, 'We'll get in. Leave that to me.'

The driver turned towards his rear passengers, two girls and a fellow American. 'What do you guys think? Shall we try it?'

The second officer shrugged. 'What can we lose? We've tried everywhere else.'

The driver switched off his engine and headlights. 'OK. Let's go.'

Gabby was already on the move, leaning across the blonde and throwing open the door. 'Come on, love. It's party time.'

Hesitating a moment, the girl shrugged up her Army greatcoat collar, then jumped from the jeep. Following her, Gabby grabbed her arm and the two of them ran across the frosted promenade. Behind the jeep Millburn's car and a large transport drew up. As Gabby waved invitingly at them, laughing officers and Army girls jumped out of all three vehicles and followed him. As they congregated under a wide covered canopy at the side of the building, Millburn found Gabby trying to open the huge entrance door. He grabbed the Welshman's arm. 'What the hell are you doing? This place has been closed for months. If anyone sees lights inside, they'll tell the police.'

Gabby, who had lascivious intentions on the big blonde alongside him, was too full of bourbon to worry about the police. Turning, he jerked a thumb at the icy, deserted promenade. 'Who's coming down here tonight? It's the safest place in town.'

Before Millburn could reply, there was a shout from one of the American officers. 'Hey, Gabby. How do we get into this goddamed place?'

Pulling away from Millburn, Gabby disappeared for a moment and then returned with a stone. Before Millburn could check him, he smashed the stone against a window. As the glass shattered, a shout went up and inebriated men began breaking off the remaining shards of glass with anything they could lay their hands on. In a couple of minutes the triumphant Gabby was able to clamber inside. Finding he could not open the main door, he returned to the window and with the aid of an American, pulled the blonde inside. She was followed by her laughing companions and then by their American escorts. Left outside, Newcombe glanced at Millburn. 'What do you think? Shall we play silly buggers too?'

Millburn shrugged. 'I've no choice. That navigator of mine is as pissed as a fart. If I'm not around he could end up in the Tower of London.'

As the two of them clambered inside, someone found the switches and the lights came on. Newcombe's voice rose above the laughter and cheers. 'Get those drapes drawn, you guys. Otherwise someone might spot the lights and tell the Air Raid wardens.'

As the men obeyed him, Millburn gazed round the large hall. Although seats for the audience were still in position, the large stage was empty except for a draped grand piano. As a tall American officer pulled off the cover, another officer, rummaging in a large cupboard at the side of the stage, gave a yell of excitement. 'Hey, you guys. Look what I've found!'

As men turned, they saw he was dragging out a set of drums. As cheers sounded, Newcombe grinned at Millburn. 'It looks as if we're in for quite a night. Shapiro used to play drums and Atkinson, the tall guy at the piano, is great on jive.'

With the curtains drawn, Americans were now producing bottles of spirits from their overcoats and tunics. With no glasses available they and the girls were forced to drink straight from the bottles and any inhibitions that had remained when the party arrived were soon swept away. As the pianist struck up and the beat of drums joined him, the decibel count soared as men and girls began jiving on the stage. Although the hall was unheated it was not long before tunics as well as greatcoats were being tossed aside.

Gabby was prominent among the dancers. Having drunk enough bourbon to float the Queen Mary, the little Welshman was kicking out his legs and throwing his big blonde about as if she were a featherweight. Millburn pointed him out to Newcombe. 'Look at the guy. Tanked up to the eyebrows. He'll bust a gut if he swings that girl over his shoulders just once more. Look at the size of her.'

Newcombe grinned. 'He's sure is one ball of fire.

Where did you find him?'

'I didn't find him,' Millburn grunted 'The bloody RAF dumped him on me.'

Newcombe's grin spread. 'Some guys get all the breaks.' Then his eyes fell on two spare girls standing near the piano. 'As we got the girls out, we can't leave 'em without partners. You're joining me, aren't you?'

Hesitating for a moment, Millburn followed him. In doing so he missed noticing that Gabby, at the other end of the stage, had ceased dancing and was arguing with the blonde. With his libido already primed by liquor, Gabby was finding the girl's generous proportions, amplified by her gyrations, were proving too much for him. 'Come on, love. Dancing's all right but we've got better things to do.'

The blonde, whose name was Martha, frowned. 'But I like dancing.'

'So do I, love. But it doesn't compare with some other things, does it?'

Martha stared at him. 'What other things?'

Gabby laid a finger alongside his nose. 'You like surprises, don't you? Then come with me and have one.'

Martha gave a hard laugh. 'I know what your surprise is. Do you think I'm stupid?'

At that moment a jiving couple collided with her and sent her spinning into Gabby's arms. As his hands closed around her tightly filled blouse, Gabby's libido became too much to bear. 'We're wasting time, love. Let's go into one of those rooms at the back. You'll love it. You will, honestly.'

She eyed him scornfully. 'You don't half think well of yourself, don't you? Who do you think you are? Robert Taylor?'

Gabby decided it was no time to be modest. 'You know what they call me on the station?'

'I can guess. Big head. Right?'

'Wrong. The girls call me the Swansea Stallion. They do, honestly.'

Her laugh was a mixture of scorn and curiosity. 'The Waafs call you that?'

'That's what I'm told. I suppose they're exaggerating but you know how these stories get around.'

Before she could answer another gyrating couple collided with them. This time Gabby held on to the girl. 'Let's go where it's quiet, love, so we can get to know one another.' He patted his trouser pocket, 'I've got half a bottle of whisky in here.'

Her expression changed. 'Oh, all right. I suppose it is gettin' too noisy in here.'

Eyes shining triumphantly, Gabby helped her down from the stage and towards a series of doors on the far side of the hall. Two were locked but the third one opened. Fumbling for a switch, Gabby found it and the light revealed a room full of covered furniture. The girl gave a shiver. 'God, it's cold. Too cold. We can't stay in here.'

Afraid he was going to lose his fish, Gabby tightened the line. 'It won't be in a moment, love.' He handed her the half bottle of whisky. 'Have a drink while I look around.'

Finding a large electric fire, he plugged it in. When to his surprise the fire began to glow, Gabby decided it was his night and drew the shivering Martha towards it. 'You'll be all right in a minute, love. Have another drink while I bring a few cushions over.'

It took him a few minutes to find cushions beneath the covers of the furniture and when he returned with them he found Martha stretched out on the carpet before the fire. As he dropped the cushions down alongside her, she handed the bottle up to him. Blinking when he saw it was now only half full but deciding it boded well for his plans, Gabby took a quick drink himself and then settled down beside her. 'Isn't this better than jiving?'

Stretching out on the cushions, she gave her hard laugh. 'It might be if you weren't shooting a line back there.'

Little knowing what was coming, Gabby leaned over her. 'What was that?'

'I said it might be if those Waafs of yours were tellin' the truth.'

Gabby grinned. 'Why should they lie?'

She stretched herself again. 'They'd better not be. Because I don't go for men who don't satisfy me.'

Gabby felt a sudden twinge of apprehension. Until that moment, with his vision impaired by drink and desire, he had taken in few details of her except that her vital statistics were to his taste and her face seemed reasonably attractive. Now, with the firelight full on her, he saw she was older than he had realised and there was an indefinable coarseness about her features. To his dismay Gabby felt himself sobering and his libido weakening. As she reached for the bottle again, he drew it hastily away. 'Don't you think you've had enough?'

Her voice sharpened. 'What the hell's that to do with you? I drink when I like. Give me the bottle.'

He had little choice but to obey. She took another long drink and then, with a contented sigh, sat up and drew off her blouse. Her eyes, emboldened by drink, stared up at him challengingly. 'Well, isn't that what you want?'

Gabby was no longer sure. 'You look great, love. Beautiful.'

She eyed him a moment, then began unbuttoning her khaki skirt. Wriggling out of it, she threw it over a nearby chair. Then she unfastened her bra and lowered its cups slowly. Her hard laugh jolted him. 'You should be doing this? Why aren't you?'

Gabby did not know himself. In spite of the chill in the

room he was sweating. 'It's nice seeing you do it, love' he muttered. 'It's like a strip tease.'

Her eyes were assessing him. 'Then why aren't you taking your clothes off?'

Gabby stirred himself and drew off his shirt. 'I suppose I was too busy watching you.'

Apparently satisfied by his answer, she lifted her hands and squeezed her huge bust provocatively. 'Then don't waste any more time. That booze has made me randy. Get your pants off.'

Gabby, used to the role of aggressor, was beginning to believe this was a terrible mistake. Reaching out, Martha tugged at his trousers. 'What are you waitin' for? Get a move on.'

For the first and only time in his life Gabby was wishing Millburn would burst in and save him. Stunned by the unexpectedness of it all, he allowed Martha to pull off his trousers and then drag at his underpants. As they went down to his knees, he heard her hard laugh. 'What's the matter with you? I thought you were a stallion. Here, take a hold of these.'

Without knowing how it happened, Gabby found himself lying flat on his back on the carpet, with Martha poised naked over him and his hands clasping her huge charms. Terrified of a failure that he felt sure would haunt him for life, he found some relief in the tactile feel of her breasts. She felt it too because a moment later she lifted up and then sank down again on his hips. 'That's more like it. Now close your eyes and think of England.'

Locked together in flagrante delicto, neither noticed they had forgotten to draw the curtains over the outer window or saw the astonished images of two policemen outside. One, a sergeant, turned to his younger colleague. 'I don't know about this one but them in the hall are Americans. So get to that phone along the promenade and tip off the Yank MPs. Tell 'em to get a move on.'

The younger man's eyes were glued to the naked form of Martha. 'Hadn't you better go, Sarge? They mightn't listen to me.'

The sergeant rose to his full height. 'Do yer think this lot'd tek any notice of you? It needs somewun of authority to handle 'em. Now you get off and tell them MPs what's goin' on.'

With a last look at the pulsating Martha, the dazed youngster climbed on his bicycle and started down the promenade. Watching him for a moment, the sergeant hitched up his coat collar and renewed his vigil at the window.

Back in the room Gabby was discovering what it was like to be a stallion. With one session over, he was reaching out for his clothes when Martha pushed him back and thrust a cigarette into his mouth. 'There's no hurry, lad. Let's enjoy ourselves while we can. By the sound of it, the party's still going strong back there.'

Gabby realised she was right. The sound coming through the closed door was twice as loud as before, convincing the Welshman his chances of rescue were lessening by the minute. 'I ought to get back, love. My pilot might be looking for me.'

'What'll your pilot want you for? You're not flying tonight, are you?' She handed him the bottle. 'Have another drink, duckie. It'll perk you up.'

Uncomfortably aware that his usual role was completely reversed, Gabby let the raw spirit run down his throat. As he drew on his cigarette again, she began sliding backward and forward over his hips. 'Isn't that nice,' she whispered. 'Doesn't it make you feel good?'

Before Gabby could answer her, she took the cigarette from him and pressed it out. Then she leaned forward until his face was between her breasts. As she swayed from side to side, he heard her hard laugh. 'You know what they say, don't you, duckie? You could become deaf and blind having this done to you.'

Struggling for breath, Gabby could believe her. She swayed back and forth a moment longer, then sat back with a chuckle. 'Aren't you a naughty boy doing these things to me?' Before Gabby could get his breath back her body began rising and falling again.

At the far window the sergeant had moved out of sight while the couple were talking but now was back gaping at the copulating couple. Still flat on his back, Gabby heard her cooing voice as her body rose and fell. 'The first one for you and this one for me. The next one for us both. Isn't that what they say, duckie?'

Gabby gave a yelp. 'We'll have to go to the others after this, love. We can't go on all night.'

She pushed him back. 'Two's nothing to a stallion, lad. And you are one, aren't you? That's what you told me.'

After that time began to slip away for Gabby. When her body ceased to rise and fall, he was allowed another cigarette but not allowed to sit up. By the time he was allowed his third cigarette he believed he had lost the strength to rise. 'We've got to join the others now, love. I've got to get back to camp.'

She patted his sweating face. 'All in good time, lad. Take a little rest if you want. But no, stay where you are. It's nice sitting like this, isn't it? Don't you find it cosy too?'

Gabby never dared to think afterwards what would have happened if the sound of engines and the screech of brakes outside had not made her turn and rise. As the music ceased in the hall and alarmed shouts sounded, she glanced down at the shattered Welshman. 'Someone's come. Maybe the police. Get yourself dressed.'

The dazed Gabby was dragging on his trousers when Millburn burst into the room. 'So this is where you are. Get your clothes on. The MPs are here.'

The night was throwing up too many horrors for Gabby. 'MPs?'

Millburn threw his shirt at him. 'Yes. And the police.' As shouts, screams and indignant voices could be heard in the hall, Millburn stared round the room. 'Is there another way out of here?'

Martha, miraculously back in her uniform, was trying a door at the far side of the room. Seeing it opened into a corridor, she called to Millburn and then ran out. The American grabbed Gabby's arm. 'Come on. We gotta get to my automobile before they find us.'

'My greatcoat's in the hall.' Gabby wailed.

Millburn dragged him towards the far door. 'Sod your greatcoat. Let's go.'

They reached the open door but not before a huge American MP blocked it. He had a truncheon in his hand and his grin was triumphant. 'I told the guys there'd be other ways out. You're under arrest, buster. Both of you.'

'You can't arrest us,' Millburn told him. 'We're British officers.'

'With that accent, buster? You're as British as my arse.'

Expecting other MPs to burst into the room from the hall, Millburn was sweating. 'What the hell is this uniform? Scotch mist?'

Although looking puzzled now, the MP was still truculent. 'I don't know what game you're playing, buster, but you're still coming with me. I guess your police will sort it out.'

Millburn took a firm grip of Gabby's arm. 'You're out of line, soldier. I'm ordering you out of the way.'

The MP took a firmer grip of his truncheon. 'You going to move me – sir?'

Millburn was breathing hard now. 'Move it, soldier. Now!'

Grinning, the MP drew out a whistle. Desperate, Millburn glanced round. Seeing a hardbacked chair, he grabbed it. An expression of unholy joy spread over the MP's face. 'You going to hit me with that – sir?'

Never one to avoid a fight when it was thrust on him, Millburn wasted no more words but swung the chair. In seconds the two men were rolling over the floor, kicking, cursing, and struggling. As Millburn's head rose from the mêlée for a moment, he let out a yell to Gabby. 'Run. Get to the automobile. Get going, you stupid . . .' His voice died as a huge fist landed on his mouth.

With the two men blocking the doorway, there was no way Gabby could obey Millburn. Instead, seeing the MP's truncheon fly from the man's hand, he grabbed it up and waited his moment. As the two men rolled towards him, he swung the baton down. His first blow brought a yell of pain from Millburn but his second blow knocked the helmet off the MP. Dodging the MP's attempt to kick him, Gabby landed his third blow on his close-cropped head. As the man grunted and fell back, Gabby yelled at Millburn and fled down the corridor.

Gabby's next memory was the icy touch of mist on his face and then falling into the seat of Millburn's car. Across the road sobered girls and officers, escorted by MPs and police, could be seen filing from the concert hall. Cursing, Millburn started his engine, and with a scream of tyres reversed the car. A moment later, with a couple of MPs running out on the road and yelling for him to stop, Millburn drove along the frozen promenade as if the devil himself were chasing him.

Chapter 10

Millburn swung his car into a darkened side street and switched off the engine. Listening for a moment but hearing no sounds of pursuit, he switched on the interior light and examined his face into the rear mirror. Cursing, he swung round on the subdued Gabby. 'I ought to kill you. I ought to smash in your skull and stick it on a flagpole. Maybe I still will.'

Gabby's restrained response was an indication of the shock he had received. 'I don't know what you're making such a fuss about. We got away, didn't we?'

Rage almost choked Millburn as he jabbed a finger at his face, already discoloured by heavy bruising. 'Don't you realise what this means, you moron? After what we did to that MP, there'll be a witchhunt out for us. And what chance am I going to have with a face like this?'

'That's silly, Millburn. They can't prove it was you just because your face is bruised. You could have got that anywhere.'

'Could I? Didn't you hear what that MP said. He knew I was a Yank. And how many Yanks are there in these parts in the RAF? They've only to ask Records and they'll zero right in on me.'

Gabby realised he was right. 'Supposing they do find you. It's only an MP's word against two officers. If we stick together he could end up the one in trouble.'

Rage choked Millburn again. 'You don't get it, do you? I'm on leave next week and hoping to see Carol. If they find me and there's an inquiry that'll be the end of it, no matter what happens. I might never get the chance to see her again.' The very thought threw more oil on Millburn's fury. 'I ought to kill you. I don't know why I haven't already.'

'It wasn't my fault the MPs latched on to us.'

'What do you mean – it wasn't your fault. If you hadn't been so eager to have your nookie that you forgot to pull the drapes over those windows the police might never have spotted us.'

Until now the fight and the headlong escape had been merciful to Gabby's memory. Now it all came back with a vengeance. 'It wasn't like that, Millburn. It was awful.'

Millburn started at him. 'What was awful?'

Gabby groaned. 'The things that happened in there. She wasn't like any other girl I've known.'

'You mean she didn't fall for that line of yours? She had you taped from the beginning?'

'No, Millburn. Just the opposite.' Gabby groaned again. 'It was awful. The worst thing that ever happened to me.'

Intrigued in spite of himself, the American started at him. 'What did she do? Make rude jokes about your performance?'

'Don't be stupid, Millburn. She raped me. There's no other word for it. Over and over.' Now he had begun to describe his ordeal, Gabby found he could not stop. 'It was horrible, Millburn. My back's still killing me.'

Millburn's roar of laughter made the small car rock on its suspension. 'If I'd have known that I'd have given her a medal. You've been asking for that for years, you randy little tom cat. Wait until I tell the boys.'

Gabby's eyes widened in horror. 'You wouldn't do that, Millburn. You couldn't. It would ruin me.'

Millburn switched off the interior light. 'If you've cost

me my leave, boyo, I'll tell every Waaf you've slept with. You'll be the joke of the year.'

Gabby was aghast. 'That's terrible, Millburn. I wouldn't do that to my worst enemy.' Then the Welshman remembered his role in the fight and rallied. 'What about that MP? If I hadn't clobbered him, where would you be now? In some guardroom or at the police station. What would have happened to your leave then?'

Millburn scowled. 'I could have handled him.'

Sensing he had found a vulnerable spot, Gabby went for it like a dog seizing a bone. 'Handle him? He was knocking hell out of you. Look at your face. I saved you, Millburn, and don't you forget it.'

'And why was I there in the first place? Because you had to have your nookie. It's a pity those policemen saw you. Or she might still be doing it to you.'

Thrown back on his heels again, Gabby shuddered. 'It's all right your joking about it, Millburn. I went through hell. It might have put me off women for the rest of my life.'

'Let's hope it has. Then the rest of us might be able to keep out of trouble.'

'I didn't ask for your help, Millburn. I never have.'

'That's a laugh. You've dropped me in the shit more times than I remember.'

'Go to hell,' Gabby muttered.

Millburn opened his mouth to reply, then closed it as if running out of invective. For a full minute neither spoke. Then Millburn drew out a packet of cigarettes, lit one, and exhaled smoke. About to return the packet to his greatcoat he glanced at the sullen Gabby and then thrust the packet at him. 'I suppose that girl got your cigarettes too?'

Gabby was on his dignity. 'I never said that.'

'You don't need to. Your women always get your cigarettes. Are you having one or not?'

About to refuse, Gabby decided it would be punishing

his nose to spite his face and took one. The smouldering silence returned until the Welshman could contain his curiosity no longer. 'What are you going to do now?'

'What do you mean, do now?'

'About your leave?'

'I can't go back to hospital, can I? They'd want to know right away what's happened to me, In any case I'm conspicuous there.'

'But won't the hospital want to know why you're missing?'

Millburn shook his head. 'I was due out this weekend in any case. I'll phone them and tell them I've gone back to the station.'

'Is that where you're going?'

'Where else can I go? I can't go AWOL or I'll be in even more trouble.'

'But isn't that where the MPs will come once they've checked with Records?'

Millburn's cigarette glowed resentfully in the darkness. 'You see the mess you've gotten me into?' Grim humour entered the American's voice. 'Mind you, I won't be alone at that court-martial, will I? Not when they establish you're the guy who persuaded those Army girls to play hookey and then clobbered an MP with his own truncheon.'

Gabby gave a grunt of alarm. 'You're not going to drag me into it, are you?'

'I don't need to, boyo. They'll get all the witnesses they want from that Army school.'

Gabby realised he was right. 'Then what are we going to do, Millburn? We can't just sit on our arses and wait for them to find us.'

Millburn sat silent for a moment, then, crushing out his cigarette, he reached for the starter. 'There's only one thing we can do. I'll come back to the station with you and first thing in the morning I'll go and see Pop Henderson.'

'The CO? You're kidding!'

'No, I'm not. The bastards are going to visit him sooner or later. So isn't it better to get our story in first?'

Gabby sounded more than doubtful. 'What will you tell him?'

Millburn allowed himself a painful grin. 'About a randy little Welshman who got his comeuppances on the floor of a Scarborough concert hall. He'll laugh so much he'll give us both an extra week's leave instead of punishing us.'

'You won't mention it, will you?' Gabby pleaded.

Millburn's face darkened. 'That's all you're thinking about, isn't it? Not my missing my leave and not seeing Carol.'

'But you can't compare the two, Millburn. I might never get over tonight. Don't make things worse for me.'

Millburn switched on the engine. 'You'd had it coming for years, you randy little sod. So don't expect any favours from me.' As the car pulled away Millburn issued his warning. 'Keep an eye for any police cars on our way back. If they catch us before I've seen the CO, I'm telling them everything.'

'You wouldn't do that, Millburn. You just couldn't.'

Millburn's reply brought another groan from the dismayed Welshman. 'You want a bet? I'm up to here with you, baby. If the police or the MPs catch us, what happened to you tonight will be in the RAF journal along with PO Prune and Sergeant Bullshit. You'll be immortalised, boyo.'

Chapter 11

The chatter and laughter from the bar below was growing louder, forcing Adams to turn up the radio. He glanced at Helga. 'I'm sorry about the noise. Does it bother you.'

She shook her head. 'Not at all. In any case it doesn't happen that often.'

'I don't know why they're so noisy tonight or why so many have come in. Perhaps it's someone's birthday.'

'Don't worry about it,' she said. 'It's good to hear them so happy.'

The couple were sitting before a small electric fire that Adams had brought her. The radio was an old set he had picked up in Highgate and had overhauled by the Station's wireless section. With Helga alone during the day, Adams had felt it would be company for her. What he had not anticipated was the pleasure she got from British programmes. 'After the German censured programmes in Norway, it's like another world, *kjaere*. All the things people are allowed to say. They can even poke fun at Churchill. I think I'd forgotten what freedom was like until I listened to your BBC.'

'Then you are glad you came over?'

She had thrown her arms around him. 'You still worry about that, don't you? My not wanting to leave my friends had nothing to do with my feelings for you. Of course I'm glad to be here.'

He had known it was her loyalty that had made her want to stay in Norway but, being Adams, he had needed constant reassurance. In return she had teased him with her own question. 'I could ask you the same. My coming has changed your life. While Valerie was in London you were living like a bachelor, doing what you pleased. Now you have to come and see me every night like a married man. Don't you find that tiresome?'

He had broken out laughing. 'Tiresome? What a word to use.'

Her eyes had twinkled. 'But you are living with a mistress, *kjaere*. A scarlet woman. Doesn't it embarrass you? After a week here everyone on the station must know about us.'

Adams had forgotten the exact words of his denial but in his heart he knew the situation did make him uncomfortable. A conservative where sexual behaviour was concerned, he could not believe his affair was not causing gossip on the station.

Some of his suspicions were undoubtedly valid. Richardson, his wife's ex-boyfriend, had frequently made innuendoes to his cronies when Adams had been in the Mess, and in the evenings, when Adams crossed the road to spend the night in the Black Swan he had often heard the amused whispers of the sentries.

He knew that his imagination was his enemy and that most of his friends – and they were many – were only too glad he had found some personal happiness at last. But imagination is as much a part of some men as idealism, and Adams suffered from both. To love a woman was to protect her, and, among other things, protection to Adams was to keep her free of scandal and gossip. Going to her room every night and staying until the morning virtually under the eyes of the entire station was not Adams' idea of protection. Not for the first time he wished he had been able to find her rooms in Highgate.

His gaze was on her now. She was curled up on a pillow beside his chair. The room itself was in darkness.

When listening to the radio in the evenings, she preferred to turn off the light and Adams himself found the glow of the fire cosy and relaxing.

There was a comedian on the radio and she was laughing at his jokes. Wearing a skirt and white polo-necked sweater that enhanced her shapely figure, with her long supple legs curled beneath her and the firelight illuminating her massed blonde hair, she made Adams think of an El Greco painting. Sensing his gaze, she turned to him. 'What is it, my love?'

Adams cleared his throat. 'I was thinking how beautiful you are.'

She laughed, then made a moué of pleasure. 'And I was always told Englishmen found it difficult to pass compliments.'

'They do,' Adams said. 'But sometimes a woman is so lovely they can't help it.'

She laughed again. 'You see. My teachers were wrong. My Englishman passes compliments all the time.' Pulling the pillow towards him, she laid her cheek on his knee. 'Sometimes I think this is a dream, my love. The two of us together and the war far away. It is happening, isn't it?'

Adams nodded. 'Yes. It's happening. Although I find it a miracle myself.'

'It is a miracle. When I heard the Gestapo had captured you I was sure I would never see you again. And yet here we are, a few weeks later, sitting together in an old English pub.' Her face lifted to him. 'What a funny world it is, *kjaere*. Don't you think so?'

Adams smiled down at her. 'Funny but nice.'

'You don't think that at all,' she accused. 'You think it's a cruel place. I've heard you say that.'

'That's true,' Adams admitted. He reached down and caressed her cheek. 'But it's not a cruel place tonight. Not for me anyway.'

She leaned her head against his hand. 'No. We are two

of the lucky ones. But it's not the same for millions more, is it, my love?'

Adams had noticed before how quickly her mood could change. Was it because sadness is always close to happiness, he thought. Or was it her Scandinavian temperament?

There was applause on the radio as the programme ended. In the short silence that followed, the sounds of merriment in the bar were heard more clearly. Her voice barely carried to him. 'I find this war of yours so different to the war we have known in Norway.'

He gazed down at her. 'How do you mean?'

'Those boys down there. I see them going to Highgate to see their girlfriends. Or playing football on the airfield. Or coming over to the pub for a drink. And yet within hours they could be over Germany fighting for their lives.'

'They're standing down at the moment.' Adams told her.

'I know that. But in normal times their lives must be hell. Among friends at one moment and among enemies the next. Day after day after day. It's the way Pavlov destroyed the temperaments of his dogs, by being kind to them one moment and cruel the next. Far better to be in discomfort and danger all the time, as we were on the high viddas.'

Adams, who had often had the same thoughts himself, made a sudden decision. 'Why don't you come down to the bar and meet them?'

Her mood changed again as her voice teased him 'What? Meet the Scarlet Woman? Won't you be uncomfortable?'

Adams wondered if his complex nature was rebelling at his previous embarrassment and challenging it head on. Rising, he pulled her to her feet. 'They'll love you. One or two of the drunken ones might mak a pass at you, of course, but you won't mind that, will you?'

Laughing, she planted a kiss on him. 'No woman minds that, *kjaere*. But are you quite sure you want to do this?'

'Why not? Anyway, you've met some of my friends already.'

'Only one or two, my love. And one was a woman.'

With his decision made, Adams showed impatience. 'Let's go while the place is full. I want to show you off.'

Laughing, she touched up her face and hair and then followed him down the stairs. As he approached the smoke-filled bar Adams wondered if Richardson and his cronies would be there. He knew it was unlikely. Joe Kearns allowed no rank distinctions in his pub and Richardson was not one to rub shoulders with other ranks. Nevertheless, to his annoyance, Adams felt his heart beating faster as he led the girl into the packed bar where a perspiring Maisie and Kearns were struggling to cope with the orders thrown at them.

For a few seconds only a couple of Waafs in the doorway noticed them and the chatter and laughter continued unabated. Then, as Adams steered the girl towards the bar, the noise ceased as if a switch had been thrown. As men moved aside for the couple to reach the bar, a single wolf whistle sounded, followed immediately by a ripple of half-embarrassed laughter. As Adams swung round, Helga caught his arm and whispered in his ear. 'No, *kjaere*. It is nothing. Keep quiet.'

Swallowing his annoyance, Adams guided her forward. Ahead of him two young officers were propping up the bar, oblivious of the scene behind them. Adams tapped one of them on the shoulder. 'Hello, Tomlinson. Can you find room for me and the lady?'

The two young officers spun round. Tomlinson was a

pilot officer with a cheerful, freckled face and a mop of fair, curly hair. His companion, a navigator, was a smaller man with a dark moustache. Both men showed surprise at seeing the couple. Tomlinson, his cheeks flushed by drink, was the first to speak. 'Hello, sir. Sorry, I didn't see you. Can I get you both a drink?'

Adams was about to refuse, then thought again. 'That's nice of you, Tomlinson. Let me introduce my friend . . .' For a moment he hesitated then went on hurriedly: 'Miss Lindstrum.'

Tomlinson held out his hand. 'Nice to meet you, Miss Helga Lindstrum.'

Adams turned to the navigator. 'And this is Pilot officer Mason. He's Tomlinson's observer. The one who always gets him lost.'

Tomlinson grinned cheerfully at his somewhat shy navigator. 'Every time. Even coming over to the pub. What're you going to have, Miss Lindstrom?' He glanced at the bar. 'Joe and Maisie usually keep something extra for the ladies.'

By this time Maisie had noticed the couple and, ignoring the orders thrown at her, was hurrying towards them. 'Hello, Frank. Hello, Miss. What can I get you?'

Helga indicated the glasses of the two men. 'Can I have what they're having?'

Tomlinson stared at her. 'Beer?'

'Yes, why not. I have often drunk beer back home.'

Slowed down by alcohol, Tomlinson had not taken notice of her name and accent before. Then the penny dropped. 'You're the Norwegian lady, aren't you? The one who worked over there with Mr Adams?'

She glanced at Adams. Reading her silent question, he nodded. 'I think it's safe to talk now.'

She was given no chance to confirm or deny Tomlinson's question. Turning to the curious onlookers, the young pilot let out a yell of excitement. 'Hey, you fellers. Com and see who's here. The lady's one of the Norwegians who helped us over Rosvik.'

As a loud cheer went up and men crowded in on all sides, Adams realised what the earlier silence had indicated. Some of the men, if not all, had known or suspected who Helga was and respect had done the rest. Now, with the truth out in the open and the barriers down, they could not wait to meet her. As the beer flowed, Adams introduced one excited young man after another to the laughing girl.

'Helga, this is Davidson. He was Red Six in Harvey's flight. You remember, the first one to land bombs on the mine? He's the squadron's chess player. To date, no one's beaten him. At least I don't think they have?'

Davidson, a good-looking young man with a sensitive face, grinned. 'I haven't played you recently, sir. They tell me you're practising.'

'That's right, Davidson. You'd better watch out. I'm improving by the day.' Adams turned again. 'Helga, this is Atkinson. He was seventh in line. Remember, he nearly hit the second bluff. He'd probably been on the booze the night before.'

Atkinson, dark-haired, stoutly built, gave a solemn shake of his head. 'Don't listen to him, Miss. I hardly ever touch the stuff. It's bad for the brain cells.'

'It is, Atkinson. That's why you can never read DROs. Who's next? Yes, Thomas. Thomas was in Millburn's flight, Helga. They had the nasty job of attacking the cruiser. Thomas is a Welshman, Helga. They're the ancient Britons with the funny sing-song voices who think they can play rugby.'

Thomas, built like a pocket battleship with a cleft chin and square face, pushed forward and took the girl's hand. 'You know, it's a funny thing, Miss. We beat 'em every year but they don't know it. That's because they can't count, you see.'

As a chorus of cat-calls sounded, Adams glanced round.

'Where are Millburn and Gabby? Aren't they here?'

A voice came from the back of the room. 'They went into Scarborough this afternoon, sir.'

'What about Von Breedenkamp?'

'He's on duty tonight.'

'Then what about Paddy Machin and Baldwin?'

A lean dishevelled figure, holding a pint of beer in one hand, emerged from the crowd of grinning men. 'Oi'm here, sur. Baldwin's gone into Highgate to see his girlfriend.'

Adams drew him forward. 'Helga, this is our resident Irishman, Flight Lieutenent Paddy Machin.'

Clearly well into his cups but with the courtesy of his kind, Machin drew himself together and lurched forward. 'Good evening, Miss. It's a pleasure to meet yer.' His inebriated eyes ran over the girl's figure as he shook hands with her. 'You won't mind my sayin' that you're a foine figure of a woman, will yer, Miss?'

She managed to keep her face straight. 'No, Mr Machin, I don't mind at all.'

Suppressing a belch, Machin turned to Adams. 'My congratulations, sur. No man could do better.'

Adams hastily changed the subject. 'We have to keep an eye on Paddy, Helga, in case he leaves any bombs under our beds.'

'Bombs?' she asked.

'Yes. He says he was a member of the IRA before he joined up. They're the terrorists who've been bombing us for years.'

Machin took a swig from his glass of beer. 'Aye, that's right, sur. And we'll be back at yer again when this shinnadeg is over. But one at a time, sur. One at a time.'

Helga was looking puzzled. 'I don't understand.'

Adams grinned. 'I'll explain later.' Making the last of his introductions, he led her towards the fireplace. 'You have seen these photographs, haven't you?'

'Yes.' Helga glanced round and saw that Maisie was

fully occupied again at the bar. 'I asked Maisie to tell me about them but she said she'd rather you did it when you had time.'

Adams nodded. 'I think she still finds it too painful.' He pointed at the photograph of a huge craggy-faced man wearing a flying suit. 'That was Gillibrand. The Canadian who died defending the airfield. I don't think Maisie's ever got over his death.'

She examined the photograph closely, then gave a faint shiver. 'It shouldn't be left up here to remind her every time she comes into the bar.'

'You try to take it down.' Adams said. 'She'd scratch your eyes out.' He moved across the fireplace and pointed at two photographs mounted in a single frame, one of a slender blonde girl and the other of a naval lieutenant. 'Those are your two countryman, Hilde and Eric Bergman.'

She moved closer. 'The ones you told me about in Norway?'

'That's right.' Adams pointed at another photograph alongside the frame. 'And that's Roy Grenville who led the attack on the Swartfjord. You'll know all about that raid, of course.'

She nodded. 'Oh, yes. It's a legend over there. Although the Germans tried to suppress it, the news spread like a fire. It did wonders for our resistance movement.'

'I'm glad because it was murderously expensive,' Adams said. His eyes returned to the photograph. 'But at least Grenville survived even if he is a prisoner of war.'

A burst of laughter behind them checked her question. A young recruit, who had taken a bet he could drink a pint of beer at one sitting, had choked halfway through and spilt beer all over his tunic. As the laughter died down she turned to Adams again. 'Didn't Hilde ever find out why Grenville had to kill her brother?'

'Oh, yes. She was told. But by then it was too late. Grenville had been shot down.'

'Where is she now?'

'Nobody knows. She went away and joined up. No one's heard of her since.'

Womanlike, she wanted a happy ending. 'Do you think they'll ever meet again?'

Before Adams could reply a shout from Joe Kearns sounded behind them. 'Time, ladies and gentlemen. Time, please.'

Seeing Adams hesitating, Helga asked her question again. 'It's too sad to end there. They will meet again, won't they?'

Never able to take much alcohol without the sentimentalist in him coming to the surface, Adams sighed. 'I've always hoped so. I suppose much depends what prison life has done to Grenville. Whether he's realised he had no choice or whether his guilt has grown worse.'

'You must all tell him. Explain it was an act of mercy. You must do that, *kjaere*.'

Adams gave a wry smile. 'If I ever meet him again, I probably will. But it won't do much good if Grenville still blames himself. He's that kind of a man.'

With backward glances at the couple by the fireplace, men were now filing out of the bar. As the last one disappeared, Joe Kearns called out to Adams. 'Would you and the lady like a last drink, Frank?'

Adams glanced at Helga, who shook her head. 'Thank you, Mr Kearns, but I think I've had enough.'

When Adams also declined, Maisie came bustling out to collect the empty glasses. 'You two should come in here more often. The lads were over the moon at meeting you, Miss.'

'Maisie's right,' Adams said as he led the girl upstairs. 'I've never seen the boys more enthusiastic. They loved meeting you.'

She laughed. 'Even though you introduced me as Miss Lindstrum?'

Adams showed embarrassment. 'I couldn't think of your married name. Did you ever give it to me? I could only remember your mentioning Rolf.'

'I don't know. Perhaps I didn't. But it doesn't matter.' Her voice teased him again. 'If your friends think I'm unmarried, perhaps you won't feel so embarrassed the next time you come over to see me.'

He frowned. 'That wasn't why I said it. I honestly didn't know your married name.'

'I know that, you silly man. I'm only – what do you call it? – pulling your leg. But my meeting so many of your friends might make you feel better now. Isn't it true?'

Adams lookd rueful as he switched on the fire. 'It wasn't the way you think. I just didn't like you being the object of gossip.'

'I know that, my love. But you'll never stop gossip. The secret is to ignore it.'

They were in bed before she spoke about the evening again. 'They're so young, aren't they?'

'You mean the aircrews?'

'Yes. Some are little more than schoolchildren.'

'Some could still be at school,' Adams said. 'Young Wells, Atkinson's navigator, is only nineteen.'

There was a short silence. Then: 'How long is the war going to last, Frank?'

'God knows,' Adams said. 'Some think it'll be over in a few months. But I wonder.'

'Will those young men have to fly again?'

'Oh, yes. This is just a refit. They'll be flying again in a week or two.'

'Will they be given something as dangerous as the osvik operation?'

There was a taint of bitterness in Adams' reply. 'I can't say. That depends what the war brings up. And on Davies, of course. I'm sure he'd like another major operation.'

'You don't like Davies, do you, Frank?'

As so many times before, Adams had to question his feelings towards the mercurial Air Commodore. 'I'm not sure. He's certainly a fine wartime leader. Perhaps it's just that I'm prejudiced against the breed.'

Her voice softened. 'I know, my love. You're a different kind of man.' Turning, she pressed herself closer to him. 'Try not to worry. Perhaps this time Davies will not find another dangerous target for your young friends. Perhaps the war will end before one is necessary.'

Adams wished he could believe it as his arms closed around her. 'Amen to that. Let's hope it does.'

Chapter 12

The following morning Henderson was frowning at a large requisition form on his desk when his assistant, Laura, appeared at the door. 'Squadron Leader Millburn is here to see you, sir. You remember he asked to see you earlier this morning.'

Henderson raised his head. 'Aye, so he did. All right, Laura. Send him in.'

Lowering his eyes to the form, the Scot did not immediately notice the American's appearance as he entered the office. It was only when Millburn reached his desk and saluted that Henderson glanced up and gave a start. 'Good God, man! What's happened to you?'

For once in his life Millburn was finding words hard to find. His bruises had come out during the night and he now sported a shiner of an eye, a cut lip, and a badly swollen chin. Henderson was looking solicitous. 'Those bruises have taken a time to come out, haven't they? I hadn't realised you'd had head injuries as well. They shouldn't be discharging you from hospital yet, Tommy. You look as if you ought still to be in bed.'

Realising his leave could be in jeopardy from another source, Millburn was quick to explain. 'It's not from my wound, sir. I got these bruises last night.'

The big Scot's expression changed. 'Last night? Don't tell me you've been in a brawl.'

Millburn chose his words carefully, 'Not exactly a brawl, sir. More a misunderstanding.'

Henderson's voice was wry as his eyes ran over the American's bruised face. 'It must have been a hell of a misunderstanding. Is that what you came to talk about?'

'Yes, sir. I felt you ought to know everything.'

Henderson frowned. 'It's that serious, is it? All right. You'd better sit down and get on with it.'

'I think I'd better stand, sir, if you don't mind.'

Irritable because of a quarrel he'd had that morning with his Equipment Officer about the stores he was ordering, Henderson was uncharacteristically brusque. 'All right. Stand if you want to. But get on with it. I'm busy this morning.'

Realising he had not chosen the best time to make his confession, Millburn braced himself and told his story, leaving out only the details of Gabby's sexual adventure. By the time he had finished Henderson was frowning heavily. 'You broke into a concert hall? For Christ's sake, Millburn, you're a senior RAF officer. Don't you realise what the local authority will make of this? At the least they'll want compensation. And what about the provost people, the police and the Army school? Once it comes out they'll all be baying fo our blood.'

Although feeling something of an apostate to his fellow Americans, Millburn felt the situation had to be clarified 'I don't think the RAF will be blamed for any damage sir. Apart from Gabby and myself, the rest of the guy were Americans.'

'Army or Air Force?'

'Air Force. Decent guys who were just looking for bit of fun. They belonged to Major Dent's squadron. Yo remember them, sir.'

Henderson remembered them very well. 'What are the doing up here?'

'Doing some low-level mountain practice in Scotlan They're the ones the Yank MPs will be reporting.

got away before they saw me. And Gabriel was in another room.'

'With a woman, I suppose?'

'Yeah, he was with a woman. That's why the MPs didn't see him.'

'Except this big MP who beat you up.' Henderson reminded him. 'The one Gabriel clobbered.'

'That's true, sir. But I don't think he'll remember much about Gabriel.'

'But you think he'll remember you?'

'Yeah, I'm afraid so, sir. He recognised my accent and that I was an American before we had our ding-dong.'

Henderson scowled. 'You've been a bloody fool, Millburn. You're a senior officer and you've behaved like a stupid school kid. Did you have a brainstorm? Or was it all Gabriel's idea?'

Millburn hoped he concealed his slight start. 'Gabriel, sir?'

'Yes, Gabriel. That business of the Army training school sounds like him. The wee bugger can't keep his hands off women. Am I right?'

Millburn stared blankly at the wall beyond Henderson where a poster informed all visitors to remember that Walls have Ears. 'No, sir. He was no more to blame than the rest of us.'

Behind his scowl, the Scot's eyes were twinkling. 'So why are you here? Are you hoping I'll cover up 'or you?'

Millburn swallowed. 'It's my furlough, sir. I don't want o lose it.'

'You could lose a lot more than leave, Millburn, if the rovosts get their teeth into you.'

'I know that, sir. I'll take all that's coming to me. But I vould like my furlough first. It's very important to me.'

Henderson, who knew far more about his men's private ffairs than they suspected, rocked back in his chair. 'It must be. I've never known you ask any favours before. Yet you're asking me to protect you from a serious civic misdemeanour. It's not like you, Millburn.'

The American looked rueful. He took a deep breath, then came to attention. 'I'm sorry, sir. I know I've no right to ask for help. Can I go now?'

Henderson gave a grunt and checked him. 'Hang on a minute. When do you go on leave?'

'On Sunday, sir. In three days' time.'

'And Gabriel?'

'The same, sir.'

'All right. This is the score. If there's no word from the provosts by then, I haven't heard anything about this shindig and you can both go as planned.' As Millburn began to thank him, the Scot held up a hand. 'But if they do contact me, I'll have to give them a hearing before I make any decisions. Fair enough?'

'Yeah, that's very fair. Thank you, sir.'

Henderson rocked back to his desk and the guilty requisition form. 'All right, Millburn. If I were you I'd stay near the station for the next three days and keep your fingers crossed.' As Millburn nodded and moved to the door, Henderson's afterthought checked him. 'I'd also have a word with that navigator of yours. Otherwise one of these days he's going to drop you so far into the brown stuff it's going to run right into your ears.'

Millburn fought back a grin and threw up a salute. 'I'll talk with him, sir.'

'You do that, Millburn. Now piss off so I can get some work done.'

Hausmann paused at the distant roll of thunder. As i reverberated among the wooded hills he relaxed and began pedalling along the road again. It could be small avalanche, he told himself. Brought on by th heavy snowfall they'd had this winter. Or was it a freak storm coming up?

Hoping warmer weather would help his arthritis, Hausmann couldn't wait for the spring. At the same time, he thought, there were some people like old Holdberg who argued it wasn't the heat or the cold that brought it on but changes in air pressure. If that were the case, there was no damned hope for him because there weren't many days in these parts when wind wasn't blowing from one direction or the other.

He found Meyer waiting in the shadow of an old barn at the far end of the village. He was greeted by a sardonic grin. 'So you've managed to ride. I was afraid I might have to put you on my crossbar.'

Hausmann scowled. 'Don't worry about me. I could still outlast you if I had to. Where's Anton?'

'We're meeting him at Penzburg. He was expecting more news from London at 21.00 hours, so said he'd meet us there.'

Hausmann indicated the uniforms the two of them were wearing. 'What do you think of our disguise?'

Meyer's wink showed his approval. 'Like Anton, I think someone's had a brainwave. With the Allies knocking hell out of our transport systems, just about the only men left in Germany who aren't in danger of being reported to the Politzie are railway engineers.'

Hausmann had to concede the point. 'I suppose you're right. But how is Anton going to carry his radio?'

'Anton's not coming,' Meyer announced.

Hausmann gave a start. 'What do you mean, not coming? He has to come. Or how can we get messages back to London?'

'SOE thinks it's too risky for three of us to be wandering about together, even if we are railway engineers. So Anton's been brushing up my Morse. I'm not brilliant but if I take my time I can get a message back. After all, SOE only wants to know the location of the 262 centre.'

'But what if something goes wrong? You can't repair a radio, can you? And how are you going to carry it? With an aerial sticking out of your handlebars?'

Meyer grinned at the older man's sarcasm. 'SOE were getting a special one to Anton today. That's why we're meeting him at Penzburg. He says the radio will be hidden at the bottom of our toolbox.'

'*Toolbox*?'

'Why not? Travelling engineers carry tools, don't they? And, as you say, we must have something to hide the radio in. Don't worry. It'll look natural enough. SOE are good at these things.'

'Sod SOE,' Hausmann muttered. 'They're too pat at telling us what to do. What happens if the thing breaks down?'

'Anton's shown me how to make minor adjustments. I should be able to cope.'

Hausmann was still looking sceptical. 'But do you know the right call signs and everything? We don't want to find the centre and then not be able to tell London where it is.'

'I'm going to transmit every twelve hours. Anton will be listening on the same wavelength and if I run into any trouble, he'll get back to us. It should work out all right.'

'Why didn't you tell me this before?' Hausmann demanded.

'Does it matter? It only means my transmitting instead of Anton. That's no big thing, is it? If London's right it should be safer.'

'You still should have told me,' Hausmann grumbled.

'Why? Wouldn't you have come if I had?'

When Hausmann only scowled at him, Anton's tone changed. 'How did Freda take it? Was she very upset?'

'Upset? She's terrified. She's scared to death the Gestapo catch us and find out about the two agents we killed.'

For the first time Meyer showed some hesitation. 'Then

maybe you shouldn't have come. If she's that upset she might break down and talk to somebody.'

'Freda? Talk? Don't be a bloody fool. She wouldn't talk to God himself if she thought he'd give us away.'

'Then you're still happy to come?'

Hausmann's sarcasm returned. 'Happy? Oh, Christ yes, I love shivering out here in the cold and making a fool of the Nazis.'

At that moment the road darkened as a large threatening cloud slid over the waning moon. Hausmann glanced up and nodded. 'That's all we need. A blizzard all the way to the railway station. Want a bet?'

Meyer laughed and slapped his thick shoulders. 'You're in great form tonight, laughing boy. That 262 factory won't have a chance with a bloodhound like you sniffing after it.'

In spite of himself, Hausmann had to grin. 'I suppose we're lucky in only having one train to track down. When's this shipment of prefabricated parts expected to reach Rostock?'

'On Saturday. Two days' time.'

'Have you any ideas how we can follow it?'

'I'm hoping SOE's contact in Rostock will help us there. Our first job is to get to Rostock.'

Hausmann nodded. 'What time's our train arrive at Penzburg?'

Meyer glanced at his watch. 'We've 98 minutes to collect the radio from Anton and hop aboard. Plenty of time if you don't crack up on the way.'

Hausmann slung a leg over his bicycle. 'I was cycling before you were born, laddie. You remember that.'

Meyer grinned, jumped into his saddle, and began pedalling away. 'Come on you old bastard. I'll race you to Penzburg.'

A minute later the dark road, contouring a hill, took them out of sight of the village. As they reached a second hill, thunder rolled again and large flakes of snow brushed Hausmann's face. Breathing hard as he pedalled uphill, the older man shouted at Meyer as the echoes reverberated round the hills. 'I hope you're not superstitious?'

Meyer's laugh came through the dying echoes. 'Me? I've been walking underneath ladders all my life.'

Hausmann gave a disapproving grunt as he drove on his pedals. 'That really cheers me up. Let's just hope you don't have to pay for your stupidity next week.'

Chapter 13

Gabby closed the door of the Confessional and stood with his back to it. He was breathing hard. 'They're here, Millburn.'

Millburn turned to him. 'Who's here?'

'The provosts. The bloody MPs.'

Millburn, alone with Adams in the large Nissen hut, gave a start. 'How do you know?'

'I saw their car outside the guardroom. There's an officer and a big sergeant.'

'Yours or ours?'

'The officer's ours. The sergeant's a Yank.'

Millburn glanced at Adams. 'So they have been in touch with Records.'

Adams, who as a friend of the two men had heard the whole story that morning, showed his concern. 'It seems that way. Unless one of the American officers they caught let it slip out that you were attached to us.'

Millburn had a vision of the unfriendly Simpson for a moment, then shook his head. 'They were a decent bunch of guys but in any case their captain would see they kept their mouths shut. No, it's my guess they or the police have made an enquiry through Records.'

There was a hiss from Gabby. 'What the hell's it matter how they found out? They're here. So what are we going to do?'

His tone brought a glare from Millburn. 'If the CO prefers their story to ours, there's nothing we can do.

You'll be for the high drop for breaking into public property and for clobbering an MP's skull with his own truncheon. I hope you get ten years.'

'And why did I clobber him, Millburn? I ought to have left him to beat the hell out of you.'

Seeing the way things were going, Adams broke in quickly. 'It might turn out better than you think. The CO won't want to lose two of his best men. Nor will Davies for that matter.' He made his appeal to Gabby. 'Why don't you sit down and have a cigarette?'

'But they might find us in here?' Gabby protested.

'If they want you, they'll find you wherever you are. So you're as well off here as anywhere else.'

Realising he was right, Gabby pushed himself away from the door. As he slumped down on a bench, he gave Millburn a look of dislike. 'If it wasn't for your face and your confession to Pop Henderson, they'd never be able to prove anything against us.'

'So now it's all my fault?' Millburn growled. 'Did anyone ever tell you what an ungrateful little bastard you are?'

While the recriminations were flying to and fro, Henderson was preparing to meet his visitors. He had already received a phone call from the guardroom and Laura, his well-endowed secretary, had entered his office to tell him a provost captain and a sergeant were outside requesting an interview. Motioning her to close the door, Henderson lowered his voice. 'What's the officer like?'

She made an eloquent gesture. 'All spit and polish, sir and very cold. You know the type.'

Henderson groaned. 'Too true, I do. All right. Keep 'em waiting a couple of minutes and then bring 'em in.

Smiling, Laura went out and closed the door. Picking up a piece of paper, Henderson started writing gibberish on it. After a couple of minutes Laura appeared again 'Are you ready to see the captain and the MP yet, sir?'

Henderson answered without looking up. 'Yes, all right, Sergeant. Send them in.'

The words had barely left his mouth before the office trembled under the impact of marching feet. Although his intention has been to play the 'you-wait-until-I'm-ready' game, Henderson was totally thrown by the military apparitions that halted before his desk. The Provost captain, who had removed his raincoat, was perfection from his highly polished shoes to his beautifully tailored uniform and Van Heusen shirt. The American MP resembled an oak tree wearing spotless gaiters, belt and a white helmet. As Henderson gaped at them, the captain shouted an order and both men whipped up salutes, the captain's forefinger striking his right temple with deadly accuracy, the MP giving the American salutation with the amiability of a karate chop.

As he was capless, Henderson decided to exercise his prerogative and reply to neither. 'Yes, Captain. What can I do for you.'

As stiff as a ramrod, the provost officer shot out his words like armour-piercing bullets. 'You are Group Captain Henderson, sir?'

The Scot nodded. 'I am. What do you want?'

'I'm Captain Dutton of the Provost Service, sir. I understand you have a Squadron-Leader Millburn on your establishment. An American.'

'I have. A fine young officer. What do you want with him?'

'There are serious charges against him, sir. He was one of a number of officers who broke into a concert hall in Scarborough last night. He and another man resisted arrest by attacking this American military policeman. We have since established that Millburn is stationed here.'

Henderson had been examining the provost's face as the man was talking. It was lean, cold, with thin lips and pale blue eyes. Deciding it was an unpleasant face,

Henderson gave a loud amused laugh. 'Squadron-Leader Millburn is a highly responsible flight commander, Captain. And you are accusing him of breaking and entering and then having a brawl with American MPs. I'm afraid someone's been pulling your leg.'

The captain glanced at the oak tree. 'Take off your helmet, Sergeant.'

The oak tree obliged, revealing a square, coarse face and a shaven head. Turning on Dutton's instructions, he showed Henderson a large lump behind his left ear. 'De little guy did that, sur, when the Yank was tryin' to rough me up.'

Henderson decided he did not like him either. 'What little guy?'

Dutton's cold voice took up the story. 'He is clearly a friend of Millburn. Perhaps his crewman. I don't have to stress how serious it is for an officer to strike a military policeman, sir? Or any other serviceman for that matter.'

It was a reminder that brought a scowl from Henderson. 'No, you don't, Captain. I was in the services before you wore long trousers. What do you want from me?'

'I would like to see Squadron-Leader Millburn, sir. If he is the officer we are looking for, he will bear marks of the fight he had with this MP. In that case we shall have no option but to prefer charges against him.'

'Don't you realise Millburn is an American volunteer who has been fighting for this country since the beginning of the war? He's worth a hundred MPs or concert halls.'

Not a muscle moved on the hard, cold face opposite him. 'Nothing is more important than military discipline sir. You must know that. Without it the services could no function.'

If there had been a battle in Henderson's mind before it was won at that moment. 'In other words you'd tak an ace pilot out of action for a trivial misdemeanour like this. Have you people lost all sense of priorities?'

'Do you call striking an Allied serviceman with a truncheon a trivial misdemeanour, sir?'

'Are you saying the sergeant did not strike this unknown officer first?'

Dutton glanced at the oak tree, who shook his shaven head. 'Naw. I just told de guy to come wiv me. Then both guys beat me up.'

Examining again the size of the oak tree, Henderson decided his respect for Millburn and Gabby had never been higher. 'I don't have any heavyweight boxers or wrestlers on this station, Captain. I'm afraid you've come to the wrong unit.'

'That is always possible, sir. But I would still like to see Squadron-Leader Millburn.'

Henderson took a deep breath. 'Well, you can't see him. Millburn's on leave.'

This time the cold eyes flickered. 'He can't be. He was in Scarborough last night.'

Henderson put on his severest frown. 'What are you doing, Captain Dutton? Calling me a liar?'

'Of course not, sir. But I find it hard to believe there are many more Americans serving in the RAF in this area.'

Henderson was beginning to enjoy himself. 'I don't think you know much about the RAF or about active service in general, Dutton. Perhaps you're too busy charging real airmen for trivial offences.'

The man's thin lips tightened at the gibe. 'I don't think that's called for, sir. It's not my fault Squadron-Leader Millburn made a fool of himself last night.'

Henderson never realised he could lie so glibly. 'Millburn didn't, Dutton. Millburn's up in Scotland, and for all I know he's taking part in the Highland Games. Now will you leave me, please? I've more important work to do.'

Dutton's cold face was a study in anger. 'Then may I see your unit records, sir? I must confirm Squadron-Leader Millburn was not in Scarborough last night.'

Henderson leaned forward. 'No, you can't see my bloody unit records. I've told you where Millburn was last night and that's all you're getting out of me. That's it, Captain Dutton. The interview is over.'

As the two men's eyes clashed, the silence for a few seconds was as loud as a clap of thunder. Then Dutton glanced at the sergeant, rapped out an order, and two salutes came up like the crack of whips. As Henderson picked up his pen and glanced down at the sheet of paper again, he heard Dutton's voice at the door. 'You do realise you will be hearing more about this, sir?'

Scribbling busily, Henderson saw the words 'Piss Off, You Little Bastard' forming on the paper before him. He heard his voice a moment later. 'I'm sure I will. Goodbye, Captain Dutton.'

The incensed footsteps had barely died away down the corridor before Henderson was on the telephone to the guardroom. 'Listen. The moment that provost captain's car has cleared the station, I want you to get in touch with Squadron Leader Millburn and send him to me. At the double!'

Millburn closed the Confessional door behind him, sighed, and leaned against it. Seeing the distress on his face, Gabby gave a groan. 'Well, what did the CO say?'

Millburn shook his head lugubriously. 'We're in deep trouble, kid. The deepest. We haven't to leave the station. The provosts are coming tomorrow to fetch us.'

Gabby's faced paled. 'That's terrible, Millburn. Terrible. What're we going to do?'

'What can we do? It'll be a court martial for sure. And maybe the glasshouse for you.'

'Glasshouse?'

'Yeah. For clobbering that MP. You'll be cashiered and given years in the jug. No question about it.'

As the horrified Gabby sank down on a bench, Millburn's bruised face suddenly broke into a grin of delight. 'It's OK, you little fart. Henderson told 'em we were away on leave last night. So we have to vanish from the station.'

The switch from despair to rejoicing was too much for the stunned Welshman. 'Stop clowning about, Millburn. What really happened?'

Millburn grinned at Adams. 'Henderson said we had to piss off before the provosts come back. So go and get your things packed if you want me to drive you to the station.'

Gabby was still floundering. 'But how can we go? Our leave doesn't start until next week.'

As Millburn threw his arms in the air, Adams came to his aid. 'The CO's told a lie for you, Gabby. That's why he wants you off the station quickly.' He turned to Millburn. 'He's taking a chance, isn't he? What about the unit records? Surely the provosts will get permission to look at them.'

Millburn nodded. 'Henderson said he was having a word with the Adjutant. He didn't say why but you can guess the rest.'

Adams gave a low whistle. 'He's taking a big risk for you. I hope you both appreciate it.'

Millburn nodded. He glanced at Gabby who, with the news registering at last, was looking like a cat with a bowl of cream. 'You hear that, boyo. If you ever let out what Pop's done for us, I'll see you off myself.'

With leave imminent, Gabby for once took no umbrage. 'Don't talk crap, Millburn. Just let's get out of here before someone changes their mind.'

Chapter 14

Millburn checked the name of the hotel and walked into the foyer. Seeing it was almost empty except for a couple of middle-aged ladies, he settled into a chair and picked up a newspaper from a table alongside him.

Although he appeared to be scanning the newspaper Millburn's mind was full of the girl he had arranged to meet there. Carol Manning, a pilot and a member of the ATA, had flown into Sutton Craddock the previous year. She had brought in the high altitude Mosquito that he and Gabby had later used to attack and capture the Junkers 86p that had been carrying out surveillance over Britain before Operation Thor. Although Millburn and Carol had only spent a few hours together before the girl had to return to her ferry pool, Millburn had asked if he could see her when his next leave was due. She had agreed and the two of them had been corresponding by letter ever since.

Millburn had phoned her from Sutton Craddock minutes after Henderson had given him clearance to go on leave and to his delight the duty officer at her ferry pool had found her and put her on the line.

'Hello. Is that Tommy?'

'Yeah. I'm lucky. I thought you might be flying today. Did you get my last letter?'

'Yes. I was going to reply to it tonight.'

'There's no need. Guess what?'

She had laughed. 'What?'

'I'm on leave from now. From today.'

'But I thought you weren't due until next week.'

'I'm not. I'll tell you all about it later. The thing is, did you get the leave you applied for?'

'Yes. From Monday. Two weeks.'

'Two weeks? Kid, that's wonderful. We're going to have the time of our lives. Can I see you before then?'

'Where are you phoning from?'

'I'm on the airfield but I'm leaving in a few minutes. If I can see you, I'll drive down right away. I've got enough gas coupons for the journey.'

'Do you mean today?'

'Yeah, why not? I can drive through the night if necessary.'

'Are you sure you want to do that?'

'Sure I'm sure. I want to see you. Are you flying tomorrow?'

'I think I might be. But not in the morning.'

'That's OK. I should be down by then. Give me a place and a time and I'll be there.'

She had given him the name of an hotel in Hatfield, the town close to her ferry pool. 'But are you sure you want to drive all night, Tommy? It's such hard work on the blacked-out roads.'

'Kid, I've been waiting to see you since I can't remember when.'

She had laughed again at his parody of a song popular at that time. 'Poor Tommy. How you must have suffered.'

'You can't imagine, baby. You be there at 10.00 hours tomorrow morning and leave the rest to me.'

'All right, Tommy. It will be good to see you again.'

Arriving at Hatfield earlier than he had expected, Millburn had had an early morning wash and brush up before making his way to the hotel. With another half hour to wait before Carol was due, the impatient American ordered a coffee and was trying to settle down to the newspaper when a woman's voice made him start. 'Excuse me, young man. May I speak to you for a moment?'

Glancing up, Millburn saw that one of the two middle-aged women who had been sitting at the far side of the foyer was now standing before him. Millburn rose to his feet. 'Yes, ma'am. What can I do for you?'

The woman was stout, white-haired, with a pleasant face and rosy complexion. She indicated the flash on Millburn's shoulder. 'You are an American, aren't you?'

'Yes, ma'am. I am.'

The woman indicated her companion who was smiling at them across the foyer. 'My name is Forsythe. Mrs Forsythe. My friend and I often meet here in the mornings for a cup of coffee and we couldn't help noticing that you were alone. So I was wondering if you would care to spend the rest of the day at my home. I know my husband would be delighted to meet you.'

While she was talking the woman was trying without any great success to keep her eyes off the American's face. Understanding her invitation now, Millburn managed a painful grin. 'It's OK, ma'am. I didn't get it in action.'

Mrs Forsythe displayed innocence. 'Didn't get what, young man?'

Millburn indicated his bruised and swollen face. 'These lumps and bruises. I got them clowning about. Not when I was flying.'

Mrs Forsythe showed well-bred surprise. 'Oh, yes, I see now. You've had an accident, have you? But that makes no difference. I would still like to offer you hospitality for the day.'

'Ma'am, it's kind of you and I'd love to come. I really would. But I'm meeting a friend here soon. A girl.'

The woman's eyes began to twinkle. 'Oh, I see. We thought you might be alone. Then you certainly won't want to spend the day with two old fogies like us.'

'Ma'am, I would have enjoyed it. I surely would and thank you for asking me. And thank your friend too.'

Millburn hid a grimace as he returned to his seat. If two old ladies could see his bruises right across the foyer, he must look like Boris Karloff's Frankenstein. Not for the first time Millburn, who had been counting the days to this meeting with Carol, wondered why fate had to be so goddammed perverse.

She arrived fifteen minutes early, a slim, blithe and attractive figure in her ATA uniform. Spotting him, she gave a wave and started happily across the foyer. Then she paused, gave a cry, and began running towards him. 'Tommy! What's happened?'

Millburn, who had jumped to his feet, put up a hasty hand. 'It's OK, honey. It's nothing. Honestly.'

Ignoring the presence of the two older women and the curious gaze of a youthful attendant, she clutched both of his arms in her distress. 'What happened, Tommy? Were you shot down? Have you had a crash?'

It took more than embarrassment to quell Millburn's sense of humour. 'I didn't like seeing you in this state, honey, but maybe I had it all wrong. Maybe I'm going to score this way.'

She bit her lip. 'It's not a joke, Tommy. Stop fooling about and tell me what happened.'

He drew her down into a chair alongside his own. 'It's nothing. You'll split your sides when I tell you what happened.'

She was smiling when he finished. 'So it was just another of those scrapes you and Gabby are always getting into? But isn't there a risk the military police might still trace you?'

'Not a chance. I've three weeks' furlough. These bruises will have gone by then. In any case, Henderson said I was on leave the night it happened.' Millburn's voice became impatient. 'Let's talk about us. How long have you got?'

His face fell at her answer. 'I have to be back by 11.30 at the latest. I've an Airspeed Oxford to deliver to a unit in Scotland.'

'An Oxford? I thought you only flew Mosquitoes from Hatfield?'

'We normally do. But this Oxford trainer flew in yesterday. The pilot was complaining of abdomen pains and when they got him to hospital they found it was appendicitis. So I've been told to deliver the Oxford to Scotland myself.'

'How will you get back?'

'By train I suppose.'

'Then I won't see you until tomorrow?'

'I'm afraid not. It might even be longer if I'm kept up there for any reason.'

Millburn frowned, then gave a start. 'Why don't I fly up with you?'

For a moment her attractive face lit up. Then she showed doubt. 'I don't know if they'll let you, Tommy. They're very strict about our taking passengers.'

'But I won't be your passenger. I'll be your navigator.'

Her smile, which brought twin dimples to her cheeks, had a way of making Millburn's heart give a double beat. 'I'm not sure they'll fall for that, Tommy.'

'Then what if I tell them I've got an ailing Scottish aunt and need an urgent lift to see her?'

She laughed. 'You're a terrible man, Tommy Millburn. I'm not sure I ought to go on seeing you.'

'I'm a terrible man, honey, because I can't take the idea of not seeing you for a couple more days. Let me come back to the pool with you and see what I can do. Have you eaten today?'

'No. I had to miss breakfast to get here in time.'

'I've had nothing either. So let's go and eat. Then I'l

go back with you and tell 'em my old aunt's on her death bed crying out to see her long-lost nephew.'

Her dimples returned. 'You're going to corrupt me. I know you are.'

Grinning, Millburn drew her to her feet. 'I sure hope so, honey. I sure hope so.' Taking her arm, giving a farewell wave at the two smiling women across the foyer, he led her happily outside into the busy street.

The Oxford was flying at 6000 feet above the Northamptonshire countryside. Below, occasional dark clouds kept obscuring the green and brown chequered fields. The met. report, given to the girl pilot before take off, had warned of a deep Atlantic depression approaching the British Isles. Although already bringing rain to Northern Ireland, it was not expected to reach England and Scotland until the late evening. Millburn, sitting in the starboard seat of the dual-controlled plane, was less optimistic. 'That report was way out, Carol. That low pressure belt's coming in faster than they thought.'

Carol, wearing a warm flying suit with a fur collar that enhanced her attractive face, glanced at him. 'Are you nervous, Tommy?'

Millburn grinned. 'I'm scared to death. Flying always terrifies me.'

'Don't you mean flying with a woman pilot terrifies you?'

'Don't put words into my mouth, honey. I just like my two feet on the ground, that's all.'

'I suppose that's why you joined the RAF.'

'Yeah. I liked the uniform and thought it would pull in the girls. I didn't reckon they'd make me fly.'

'So it must mean something for you to be flying with me today?'

Millburn grinned again. 'Now you're getting the score.'

Carol was thinking how easily Millburn had obtained

passage on the aircraft. His rank and status in 633 Squadron had made recourse to his fictitious aunt unnecessary. His only problem had been finding a spare flying suit and in the end he had been forced to make do with a borrowed pullover and a pair of overalls.

Sudden turbulence brought the girl's thoughts back to the present. As she steadied the Oxford into level flight again, Millburn gave her a look of approval. 'I take it you have flown one of these ships before?'

'Only a couple of times,' she told him. 'But that was over a year ago.'

'Then you're doing good. I did some initial training on them. How does this one handle?'

'Very well. Do you want to take over for a while?'

'No. I like being a passenger.' He glanced out of the perspex canopy. 'I take it you know your way up to Scotland?'

She threw him a look. 'No, I haven't a clue. That's why I'm always losing Mosquitoes when taking them up to the Banff Wing.'

Grinning at her sarcasm, Millburn settled back comfortably in his seat. 'Great. Then you don't need a navigator.'

Flattered that he seemed completely at ease with her piloting, she spent the next few minutes getting back the feel of the twin-engined aircraft. Painted yellow to warn other pilots they might be in the hands of a trainee, the Oxfords enabled crews to become familiar with multi-engined aircraft before they moved on to high-speed bombers.

Turbulence came again, rocking and jerking the crew against their seat straps. Millburn squinted down at the clouds that were beginning to hide the chequered fields. 'That's been a bum met. report, honey. They must have underestimated the wind. That depression's more than a hundred miles ahead of schedule.'

She glanced up through the canopy. Although the

winter sun was still visible, its brightness was already dimmed by a thin veil of cloud. 'It seems to be multi-layered as well. Do you think I ought to turn back?'

Millburn shrugged. 'You're the skipper, honey. It's your decision.'

She glanced at her fuel gauge. 'We've plenty of petrol. And there are plenty of airfields in Yorkshire if it gets really bad.'

Millburn grinned. 'I'm happy as long as you don't set me down at Sutton Craddock. Those MPs might be back.'

'Then I'll go on,' she said, wondering immediately if her decision was based on her wish to prove her mettle to him. 'If it's really bad when we cross the Humber, we can make another decision then.'

The turbulence came again, pitching the Oxford sideways and down before her airfoils gripped again. Millburn pointed a finger upwards. 'Why don't you take her up a few thousand feet? It might be quieter up there.'

'Do you think so?'

Millburn shrugged. 'It's worth a try, honey.'

With that the girl drew back on the control column and the engines took on a new note. Totally unaware that he was putting the girl into deadly danger by his advice, Millburn nodded his approval and sank back comfortably into his seat.

Chapter 15

The Oxford altimeter was reading 10,000 feet when Carol glanced at Millburn. He nodded. 'Yeah. Try it now.'

She eased the column forward and the engines' note sank. The sky was now clear with the sun warm through the canopy. As Millburn glanced around he noticed another aircraft on his starboard side. Flying in the opposite direction, it was little more than a speck but his battle-trained eyes sighted it before the girl. As the American watched it, it began to turn in a wide arc towards them.

Alongside him Carol noticed his attention. As she questioned him, he told her to bank to starboard. 'There's another ship back there. I want to take a look at it.'

She obeyed him and as the Oxford swung round the other aircraft came back into his vision. It was now as large as a wasp and growing larger by the moment. Millburn swung round on the girl. 'Have you a pair of binoculars?'

Reaching into a locker, she handed him a pair. He put them to his eyes, focused them, and then gave a violent start. 'Christ!'

The shock in his voice alarmed her. 'What is it, Tommy?'

He turned to the girl, keeping his voice controlled as possible. 'Give me the controls, kid. Quickly!'

'But why? What's happened?'

He knew he had to tell her. 'It's a Kraut aircraft, honey. A 110.'

Her face paled. 'But it can't be. They don't come over in daytime any more.'

There was no time to argue with her. Grabbing the control column, he jerked a thumb at the rear of the fuselage where two parachutes were stored. 'Get your chute and put it on. Now!'

For a moment she was paralysed by shock. Cursing, he leaned across and grabbed her arm. 'Go and get your parachute on! While you can!'

This time she obeyed, unloosening her straps and stumbling back to the parachute receptacles. Forced to keep the Oxford on as even a keel as possible while she was out of her seat, Millburn banked gently to starboard in an effort to see the 110 again. A few seconds later it appeared. It was no more than half a mile behind him now and as it banked to follow him he could see its details clearly, its clipped wings, long-range tanks, and radar aerial on its nose. A G-4 night fighter, his frantic brain told him. Therefore equipped with 20mm cannon and four machine guns. Enough speed and armament to blow the Oxford out of the sky in seconds.

He felt a tap on his shoulder and saw Carol standing beside him with two parachutes. He shook his head violently. 'No. Put yours on and jump. Now!'

Her pale lips moved. He had to strain to hear her protest. But you must come too'.

There was no time to be kind with words. He indicated his overalls. 'I've no harness on these. But you have and so you can jump. So do it now, for Christ's sake.'

To his horror she threw both parachutes down and dropped back into her seat. 'Then I'm not going.'

Millburn had never known such a turmoil of fear and frustration. His voice rose into a shout. 'God damn you, you've got to. You'll die if you don't. Get back and jump!'

Although her face was ashen with fear, she was fastening on her seat straps again. Beside her Millburn knew there was no longer time to argue. The 110 was less than a quarter of a mile behind, close enough for its pilot to be lining up his sights. Seeing Carol was strapped in again, Millburn swung the Oxford violently to port and put down her nose almost vertically, cursing himself at the same time for suggesting his present height.

As the Oxford plunged down and built up speed Millburn felt her airfoils juddering and knew she would never withstand a power dive to the cover of the clouds below. For a moment he wondered what stresses she would take. Then, as the shuddering grew worse, he heaved on the control column and gave the Oxford full rudder. As the plane came out of her dive and swung crazily to port, Millburn winced as he heard the popping of sprung rivets in the bowed wings. But the aircraft held together and a moment later Millburn saw the 110 flash past his starboard beam. The unexpected manoeuvre of the trainer plus the higher speed of the 110 had combined to deceive the German pilot and he had overshot his target.

Millburn could see him below, climbing like a hawk that had missed its prey on its first pass but had no intention of repeating the mistake. In the few seconds left to him, Millburn made his appeal again. 'You can still get out, honey. Please go. Please!'

Although huddled down in her seat, her face ashen with fear, she still shook her head. Frantic now, Millburn reached out and grabbed her arm. 'You're only makin things worse for me. Can't you see that?'

He had to strain to hear her words. 'I'm sorry, Tommy But I can't go without you. I just can't.'

The Oxford lurched violently as Millburn tried t

unfasten her safety straps. Unable to reach them, he hardly knew what he was saying in his fear for her. 'You stupid little bitch. Jump while you can. Please!'

When she shook her head again, Millburn knew argument was futile. Cursing, rolling the Oxford to gain visibility, he saw the 110 had reached their altitude again and was in hot pursuit. Although he had both his throttles full forward, Millburn knew it would be only seconds before the 110 was in range again. With the Oxford's top speed only 190mph, the odds were no better than a contest between a hawk and a pigeon. As the gap between the two aircraft shrank at frightening speed, Millburn knew he was in a fight he could not win. Nevertheless, as the German aircraft closed within range, the American swung the Oxford over and did as tight a turn as the groaning aircraft was capable in the hope the faster aircraft could not match it.

Earth and sky swung dizzyingly around. Unable to see the 110, Millburn shouted at the girl, 'Can you see him?'

He saw Carol shake her head. Holding the control column hard back, Millburn searched the spinning sky. For a moment he caught sight of the 110. To his surprise it seemed to be circling in its own orbit above them but then it disappeared as the Oxford swung round on its desperate spiral. Puzzled now, Millburn watched for it to appear again and this time he saw the German aircraft was rocking its wings.

Carol noticed it at the same moment and turned her pale face to Millburn. 'What's he doing? Is he signalling to us?'

Wondering if it were a trick, Millburn continued his spiral while watching the 110. Seeing it was still signalling when it could have dived down and opened fire on them, Millburn knew he had little option but to investigate the German pilot's intentions. With great care, ready to dive away if the 110 made the slightest aggressive move, he brought the Oxford back on an even keel again and held his breath.

To his amazement the 110 made no attempt to gain the firing position behind him. Instead it kept before him and within his vision, slowly sinking until it was flying alongside him. With every nerve in his body tingling and alert, Millburn watched it close to within 50 metres of his starboard wingtip. As its wings rocked again, Millburn heard Carol's gasp of astonishment. 'The pilot's waving at us, Tommy. What does it mean?'

Millburn felt as if every muscle in his body had suddenly gone lax. 'It means he's sparing us, honey.'

The 110 was now close enough for Millburn to see the pilot's face. As the German waved to him, Millburn waved back and then blew a kiss. The American imagined he saw the other pilot grin before the 110 waggled its wings again, broke station, and dived away eastward.

Millburn's relief was heartfelt. 'You lovely, beautiful guy. I hope they give you the Iron Cross and make you Chancellor.'

Carol, dazed from the encounter, was still trying to understand. 'What happened, Tommy? Why did he spare us?'

Millburn turned to her. 'He saw from our yellow markings that we're a trainer and so knew we were unarmed.' He glanced back down the fuselage. 'If we'd been in one of those upper turret jobs, it might have been different. But we weren't and so he let us go.'

She was still trying to come to terms with their escape. 'I didn't know German pilots could be merciful like that.'

'They aren't all Nazis, honey. We met one of the decent guys.' Millburn's tone changed as he saw the colour returning to her cheeks. 'Why didn't you do as I told you? If he'd opened fire you wouldn't be getting your leave next week or ever.'

'How could I leave you when you couldn't escape? Would you have left me?'

Conditioned by the dangers of combat to recover quickly, Millburn was now his old self again. 'Only one thing would have kept me back, honey.'

'What's that?'

'I'd have been scared that Kraut pilot fell for you and took you back with him to Germany.'

She managed a laugh, which pleased him. 'Nothing affect you, does it, Tommy?'

Millburn's expression changed. 'Don't you believe it, honey. I was scared to death five minutes ago.'

She was still finding it hard to believe they had escaped. 'Why do you think that 110 was over here? He must know it's almost suicide these days, particularly in daylight. Do you think he was lost?'

'I don't know, honey. But I sure hope he makes it home. That's one guy that deserves to.' He gazed down at the clouds below. 'But whether he was lost or not, he hasn't helped me to find my sick old aunt.'

Following his eyes, she saw what he meant. During the last few minutes of frantic activity the Oxford had gone right off course and all that could be seen below was a thick plain of cloud. Glancing at the compass, she saw that they were heading due west, right into the advancing depression. As the Oxford swung to starboard she knew Millburn had noticed the error and corrected it. 'How far off course do you think we are?' she asked.

He shrugged. 'Who can say? We could have covered a lot of ground while we were playing hide and seek. I think you'd better get on the radio and try to get a fix.'

She obeyed him but could hear nothing but static. 'I can't get through. I think the radio's faulty.'

Millburn took the earphones from her but with no more success. 'It's unserviceable all right. Aren't your radios checked before you fly?'

'They should be,' she told him. 'Perhaps because the Oxford's not one of our regular deliveries it's been overlooked.'

Keeping his opinion of the slack servicing to himself, Millburn returned the earphones. 'It's all happening, honey. Let's go down and see what's under those clouds.' As he put the Oxford's nose down, he glanced at her, 'Do you want to take over?'

She gave a faint shudder. 'No, thanks. I've had all the flying I want today.'

The altimeter reading began to fall. 7000 feet, 6000 feet, 5000 feet . . . At 4000 feet cloud began to brush against the canopy. First in whisps, then it closed in like dense fog, muffling the roar of the engines. 3500 feet, 3000 feet . . . At 2500 feet, flying on instruments, Millburn glanced at her. 'See anything yet?'

'No. But I shouldn't go much lower. We might be ove the higher Pennines.'

He lowered the aircraft another 500 feet and the levelled off. With the heavy cloud pressing in fron all sides she lost the sensation of speed and felt sh was floating in a grey limbo. She heard his voice embellished with humour to keep up her spirits. 'W might have to make it one of these Yorkshire airfield after all. Let's just hope we don't run into the provo guys. They mightn't like it if I knock off their helme with our undercarriage.'

'We don't know we're over Yorkshire, do we?' sh said. 'We could be anywhere.'

He grinned at her. 'The British Isles aren't that bi We gotta be somewhere.'

Unless we're over the sea, she thought, but bit t words back.

They flew for another five minutes before he turned her. 'We'll have to go lower and find this cloud base. O gas won't last for ever.'

Knowing he was right, she gave a jerky nod. 'Yes. Go ahead.'

She felt her muscles tighten as the Oxford nose lowered again. For a full minute she saw nothing but grey mist pressing against the windshield. Then suddenly it fell away and she had a momentary glimpse of a rocky, mist-shrouded hill rising sharply before them before the cloud closed back again. Her cry was sharp with alarm. 'Get her up, Tommy! Quickly!'

His low curse told her he had seen the hill too. The engines roared their protest and the cockpit floor pressed had against her feet as the Oxford fought for height. Millburn took her up a thousand feet, then turned to the girl. 'We must be over the Pennines. Right?'

The shock from the near collision made her voice unsteady. 'We could be. I don't know.'

He reached out a hand. 'Hand me the map and let me ake a look.'

It was a full minute before he handed it back to her. 'I'm going further east. We'll hit flatter land there.'

She managed a smile. 'They say it's very flat in Holland.'

He grinned back, delighted by her spirit. 'As you say, oney, it's flat in Holland. Let's make a pact and never y without a fit radio again. OK?'

Her reply was fervent. 'Never. That's something you n be sure of.'

A moment later the Oxford banked on its new course d droned on into the blinding cloud.

Chapter 16

Hausmann, muffled up in his railway engineer's coat, scarf, and cap, paused outside the cafe window. 'This must be it.'

Meyer, equally heavily dressed against the cold, glanced at the name above the shop door. '*Ja*. That's the name he gave us. Do you think he'll have got the details through yet?'

Hausmann gave an involuntary shiver as a gust o wind blustered down the ice bound street. 'Schultz sai Thursday. And it is 14.00 hours.'

Meyer shugged. 'Then let's try. We don't want anothe night in this godforsaken place if we can help it. For on thing it's too dangerous.'

Hausmann nodded and pushed the door open. As h entered, he saw a dozen or more elderly and disable workmen sitting at tables, drinking ersatz coffee ar smoking evil smelling cigarettes. The smell of new baked bread mingled uncomfortably with the stench stale sweat and damp clothes.

A stout woman emerged from a door behind t counter and eyed Hausmann sullenly. 'Yes. What you want?'

'We want sandwiches to take away.' Hausmann tc her. 'A friend of ours, Schultz, told us you bake the b bread in town!'

Only the woman's left eyelid flickered. 'Schultz right. I do. Have you got coupons?'

While the other two were talking, Meyer was eyeing the seated workmen. Only three had turned when the door opened and all had now resumed their conversation. Satisfied, Meyer listened to Hausmann's question. 'How large are your rolls?'

As the woman slapped a roll of coarse brown bread on the counter, Hausmann turned to Meyer. 'Will three be enough for you?'

When Meyer nodded, the proprietor gave a grunt of disgust. 'Three? You'll get five between you and like it. You're lucky to get anything with the Ruskies knocking hell out of our armies and grabbing all the food in sight. Give me your coupons.'

A moment later she vanished behind the rear door. Grinning, Meyer edged up to Hausmann and whispered in his ear. 'She doesn't bother to hide her feelings, loes she?'

Hausmann shrugged. 'With everyone else thinking the ame, it's probably her best cover.'

The woman returned five minutes later with five rolls vrapped in a piece of brown paper. As she took payment, er left eyelid flickered again. 'Give Schultz my regards. 'ell him to keep on recommending me. I need all the usiness I can get.'

Thanking her, the two men left the café and hurried up e street. On the opposite side stood a ruined church and a attered block of flats. Rostock, the home of the Heinkel rcraft industry and also a large shipbuilding centre, had ng been a target for Allied bombing. Today it was ermany's chief base of supply for her eastern armies, w struggling without success to hold back the vengeful issians.

A tram passed the two men, disgorged its passengers rty metres ahead, and jolted on. Shabbily dressed omen and a few old men hurried past them. As usmann slipped on a patch of ice on the pavement, he gave a shiver. 'The Russians must be bringing their weather with them.'

Meyer grinned. 'Is there a better weapon?'

They walked another fifty metres before reaching a side street. Seeing it led to a small park, Hausmann pushed Meyer down the street towards it. They entered an opening where once there had been a metal gate and started down a frozen gravel path. On their right forty or more children between the ages of twelve and sixteen were being drilled by a crippled sergeant on a snow-covered field. Meyer's expression was a mixture of disgust and pity. 'Poor little bastards. Fodder for the Russians to gobble up.'

Hausmann, who had not yet forgiven the SOE fo giving them the mission, showed equal disgust. 'An London and Washington are worried about a new fighter when all the Nazis have left are old men and school kids This lot will probably be going to Rendulic on the Eas Prussian front.'

'Isn't he the bastard who has set up flying courts-marti to shoot every soldier picked up outside his unit area?

'That's the man. That's what Germany is down to, th very dregs. Any time now the *volkssturm* around he will be absorbed into the army. So we'd better get th job done soon or they'll be picking us up with the rest Hausmann pointed at a small pavilion that overlook the field. 'Let's go in there and see what news Schul has for us.'

To both men's relief, the pavilion was empty. A lo wall offered some relief from the icy wind. Dropping a seat, Hausmann began opening the rolls. On breaki open the third one, he gave a grunt of satisfaction a showed Meyer a tiny cylinder of greaseproof pap Glancing round to make certain he was not overlook he unrolled the paper and found a tiny printed messa inside. Seeing him fumbling for his spectacles, Me snatched the paper from him. As he read it, Hausmann peered over his shoulder. 'What's it say?'

'We've got three days.' Meyer told him.

Hausmann looked thoughtful. 'Three days. Where do we meet up with the train?'

'He's given us a siding and a time when we can board it. Apparently its security crew changes there.'

'Where is this siding?'

Meyer, who was looking puzzled, handed the message back to him. 'Seventy miles down the line. I don't get it. Why does its crew need to change after only seventy miles?'

Hausmann, who had his spectacles on now and was reading the message, nodded on finishing it. 'You're forgetting about air attacks. It's too dangerous for trains to run in daytime. They'll be stopping in tunnels during the day and moving only at night. That's what takes so much time.'

Meyer realised he was right. 'So what's our next move?'

'We get moving right away.' Rising stiffly, Hausmann gazed up at the lowering grey sky. 'We don't know if it's going to snow again. If it does, we might have problems getting there.'

The Oxford had been flying blind on instruments for over fifteen minutes before Millburn put her nose down again. Carol felt her nerves tightening like taut strings as the altimeter crept lower and lower and still the dense cloud blinded them. Afraid a hill would suddenly loom up and crush them, she felt her eyes watering with the strain. Beside her Millburn, equally tense, was muttering his opinion of the met. officer who had sanctioned her flight.

The altimeter reading was down to 1400 feet before the cloud suddenly thinned and revealed a treeless landscape of stone hedges and sodden fields. After an exclamation of relief, Millburn turned to her with a wry grin, 'Recognise it?'

She shook her head. 'It could be anywhere. Perhaps if you flew on to the coastline we could take our bearings there.'

He glanced at the fuel gauge, then at the misted fields that were sweeping below them. 'It's not our day, honey. I reckon the weather's bringing fog with it. If we leave it too long we might find zero visibility right down to the deck.'

She felt fresh alarm. 'Then what's our alternative?'

'We can land her and wait until conditions improve.'

'Land her? Where?'

He grinned. 'When we find a field big enough.'

'Isn't it a bit risky?'

'Not as risky as flying around until our gas runs out.'

She knew he was right. 'Then let's get it over. How big a field do you want?'

He pretended to look surprised. 'Me? Are you letting me land her?'

'Who else? It's your idea.'

As he laughed, she studied the fields sliding below them. As they swept over a shallow hill, she saw a long stretch of grassland, fenced off on three sides by stone hedges and bounded at its southern end by a copse of leafless trees. She pointed down. 'Do you think that's large enough?'

She saw he was already considering it. Flying its full length, he began circling back. From the intense scrutiny he was giving it she witnessed the professionalism that his sense of humour was inclined to hide.

He circled the field three times before turning to her. 'I think it'll do. What about the wind direction? You think it's still from the west?'

His question flattered her. 'I think so. I felt we had a slight drift when we first came down.'

'So did I. But only slight. I'd like a stronger wind.'

With that he swung the Oxford eastwards. She felt a rumble as the undercarriage lowered. His hand reached out and tapped her arm. 'Tighten your straps. We don't know how hard or soft the field is.'

Her heart was bumping hard as the Oxford completed its turn and headed back for the nearest stone hedge. As it came sweeping towards them, she had the feeling she was floating as the aircraft flaps went down. A moment later Millburn throttled back and she could hear the shrill whine of the airfoils. As the nose began to rise, she could no longer see the stone hedge but it was visible through her side window, rugged and uncompromising. As the Oxford sank towards it, she felt certain they were too low and it took all her control not to shout a warning to Millburn.

A moment later the hedge passed below her, so near she could see the stains of moss on its uneven stones. For the briefest of seconds the Oxford shuddered, making her believe one of its wheels had touched the hedge. Then the aircraft's nose rose higher, the engines cut right out, and she held her breath.

The few seconds that followed seemed endless before the jolt as the wheels touched the ground. As the Oxford jerked forward she thought for a moment that it was about to turn over. Then its tail dropped and it began bouncing across the rough field. As Millburn applied the brakes, she saw the opposite hedge advancing towards them at alarming speed. Aware of the danger, Millburn braked harder, waited a few seconds longer, and then swung the Oxford to port. Although one wing dipped almost to the ground, the aircraft skidded a few more metres and then came to rest.

She let out her breath. 'That was wonderful. Marvellous. I couldn't have done that in a hundred years.'

Relieved himself, he grinned at her. 'Don't give me that. I think you're one of these sly Englishwomen who make men feel better than they are.'

'You were wonderful,' she said again. 'I thought at least the aircraft would receive some damage.'

'No, she seems fine although we might need a trailer to get her away.' Unfastening his straps, Millburn peered through the windshield, 'I guess we got down just in time. That fog is getting worse.'

She saw he was right. Fog, settling over the wet fields, was aiding the weather to bring the winter afternoon to an early end. 'What do you think we should do now?'

He eased himself from his seat. 'I'd better find a phone and let your people know you're safe. We'll also need somewhere to stay the night.'

'I'll come with you,' she said.

'No. You stay here with the kite. You don't want someone taking souvenirs from her. What's your airfield number?'

She gave it to him. 'Do you want coffee before you go? My flask's still full?'

'No. Keep it 'till I get back. I'll be as quick as I can.'

She watched him jump down from the Oxford, blow her a kiss, and then disappear into the fog that was creeping over the field. Left alone, finding herself shivering, she knew the events of the afternoon were catching up with her. Pouring herself a cup of coffee, she lit a cigarette and waited for Millburn to return.

It was nearly 30 minutes before he climbed back into the Oxford. 'No luck, honey. I couldn't find a phone anywhere.'

'But what about houses or farms?'

'I found one cottage but couldn't make anyone hear. In any case they hadn't a phone connection.'

'Only one cottage? Surely there must be others around.'

'If there are, I couldn't find 'em. And I couldn't spend too long looking or I'd never have found you again. Fog's making visibility nearly zero out there.'

Glancing through the canopy, she saw he was right. Although the stone hedge was no more than 30 metres away, she could no longer see it. 'So what do we do now?' she asked as she poured him a cup of coffee.

His shrug was almost apologetic. 'I guess we'll have to doss down here for the night and look for civilisation in the morning.'

She gave a shiver. 'It's going to be a cold night without blankets.'

'We've got blankets, honey. Or at least the next best thing.' At her look of surprise, he turned and pointed at the two parachutes still lying on the floor. 'Silk. Metres and metres of it. It ought to keep the cold out.'

'Of course. I hadn't thought of that.' She reached into a locker and drew out a half bottle of whisky. 'Our emergency rations. I'd say this qualifies as an emergency, wouldn't you?' She poured a generous dram into a cup of coffee and handed it to him. 'Drink it down. You look chilled to the bone.'

The darkness was closing in fast. The cigarettes they lit glowed and illuminated their faces. In the silence that followed she felt a tension that had not been present before. She broke it with a question. 'You've never spoken about your life in the States, Tommy. What you did before the war? Won't you tell me about it?'

His cigarette glowed again. 'What's the point, honey?'

'I want to know more about you. What your family is like. What school you went to. Why you entered the war before America came in. Everything.'

'Everything? That's a tall order.'

'You know what I mean. Start with your school days. Were you a nice little boy or a little hooligan? I want to know.'

'I was a hooligan, honey. Short breeches, hairy knees, and a turnip for a head.'

'I don't believe you. Stop being silly and tell me the truth.'

Slowly, sometimes with great difficulty and sometimes with the help of the whisky, she drew his past from him. How his father had been a drunkard and left him and his brother to keep the home together. How his mother had died when he was sixteen and he had wandered from El Paso to work in Texan oilfields and Oregon timber forests. By the time she poured them the last of the coffee, she knew more about Millburn than any of his squadron colleagues.

'There's one thing you haven't told me,' she said. 'You haven't explained why you joined the RAF nearly two years before America entered the war.'

Although total darkness had long fallen, the tone of his voice told her he was smiling. 'That's easy, honey. Flying excited me and the RAF were giving free lessons. So Canada it was.'

'I don't believe you. I believe you'd heard what Germany was doing and felt you had to do your part to stop her. It's no use denying it,' she went on, 'I know I'm right.'

He laughed. 'Sure you're right. I'm a proper little saint with a halo big enough to light up this cabin. Only we're sitting here in the dark. Doesn't that mean something?'

Knowing this was one truth she would never extract from him she changed the subject. 'You must be cold in only your uniform and overalls. Don't you want to unpack a parachute?'

'Not yet. I want to hear your life story.'

'There isn't much to tell, Tommy. I haven't had an exciting life like you.'

'Come on, honey. Play fair. I've told you about mine.'

He listened without comment while she told him about her childhood life in Essex, the exclusive school she and her sister had attended, and then the family disaster when her father's stockbroker business had collapsed along with the Wall Street crash of the late 1920s. 'My mother couldn't take it. She had an affair with an architect and divorced my father in 1936.'

'Whom did you live with?'

'My father. How he managed with two girls I'll never know.' She anticipated his next question. 'He's still alive. He has a small place in Worthing.'

'How did you learn to fly?'

'An uncle of mine paid for it just before the war broke out. I'd been mad on flying since I was a child and after things went wrong at home, he took pity on me and paid for lessons at Croydon.' Her voice turned rueful. 'Not that it helped to unite the family. For some reason it made my sister jealous, even although Tom gave her an equal amount of money, and things were never the same between us. She married in 1943 and now lives up in Scotland. Although I write her every now and then I never get a letter back.'

He pressed her hand, then switched on the cabin light. 'Can you believe it? We've been talking for over two hours. Aren't you tired?'

She realised that she was. 'A little.'

'Then why don't we make up the beds? Tomorrow could be a hard day.'

When she made no reply, he picked up a parachute and pulled on the ripcord. As silk billowed out, he began folding it into a makeshift bed. 'It's going to be a hard mattress,' he said. 'But your flying suit ought to soften it a little.'

While he was working on the second parachute, she

went outside. The fog was icy and dense now and she was shivering when she climbed back into the Oxford. To her surprise she saw there were two makeshift beds on the wooden floor and not the single one she had expected. 'Is that OK?' he asked.

She nodded jerkily. 'Yes, thank you. That's fine.'

He excused himself and when he returned he was shivering too. 'God, it's charpy out there. I hope you're going to be warm enough.'

When she made no reply, he waited until she had crawled between the folds of silk, then made towards the cockpit switch. 'Is it OK to douse the light?'

She nodded and the cabin went dark. She heard him fumbling along the fuselage towards her, then the hiss of silk as he covered himself. 'You OK, honey?'

'Yes, thank you.'

'Then goodnight.'

'Goodnight,' she whispered.

She closed her eyes and then it happened. The 110 was sweeping towards them again but this time with murderous intent. As it swung behind them she saw lines of white-hot tracer snapping past the canopy. The tracer swung towards her and she saw a wing tearing apart as if it were linen. Knowing the tracer would smash into her cringing body at any moment she gave a cry and tried to tear away from her seat. But the straps held her tightly and she knew she was facing death when a familiar voice broke the nightmare. 'It's all right, honey. It's all right.'

She realised it was not the seat straps that were holding her but his arms. Her heart was hammering as if it would burst. 'Oh God, Tommy. I was so frightened. I was terrified. I thought we were going to die.'

'I know, honey. It was a hell of a thing. It was sure to give you nightmares.'

Sobbing, she clung to him. 'Thank God you were with me. I'd have died of fright if you hadn't been.'

'No, you wouldn't. You're a brave girl. Look how you acted back there. I thought you were wonderful.'

'No, I was scared. I was terrified.'

'It's not how scared you are, honey. It's how you act when you're scared. And you were terrific.' His arms slackened as he moved to sit up. 'Do you want a cigarette or another shot of whisky?'

With tremors still racking her body, there was only one thing she wanted. 'Don't leave me, Tommy. Not yet. I didn't think we were going to be together like this. I felt sure we were going to die.'

He sank back. She had never imagined his voice could be so gentle as he drew her towards him. 'I'm not leaving you. You just lie here and relax. It's all over now.'

She could feel his body heat warming her and his breath on her face. As her nerves began to slacken, her nightmare faded away. She snuggled closer to him. 'Where did you say we're going next week?'

'Somewhere in Devon. One of the guys in the squadron has offered me his parents' cottage there. They've gone to stay with some friends for a month. Will that be OK?'

'Yes,' she said quietly. 'It'll be OK.'

He lifted his head. 'You sure? I respect you, kid. I want you to know that. So, if you like, I could stay in the local pub. We could still see each other every day. There'll be a local pub, won't there?'

Without knowing why, she suddenly felt her eyes fill with tears. 'Yes, I'm sure there'll be a pub. But it won't be necessary.'

'Are you sure, honey?'

It was his doubt that allowed her to break free from her upbringing and background. Leaning forward, she kissed him. 'I'm very sure, Tommy. So just hold me and don't worry about it any more.'

Hesitantly at first but aided by her, he removed her flying suit and the two of them made love. In the dying throbs of her orgasm she heard her sobbing voice. 'I'd meant to wait until later, Tommy. I really did. But it seemed right tonight. It seemed so right.'

He did not release her as some men do. Instead his arms stayed around her and she lay within them while outside a rising wind sighed and rocked the Oxford and rain began to patter on the cabin roof.

Chapter 17

To the two men crouched among bushes on the heathland, the hoot of the distant train was a bleak and hostile sound. It brought a swift response from Meyer. 'That has to be it. It's right on time.'

Hausmann nodded at a small railway siding some forty metres away from which a couple of shaded lights were visible. 'Let's just hope Schultz is right and it stops there. We're going to look a couple of stupid buggers if it goes straight past.'

The siding stood on only one side of the rail track, the opposite side being snow covered heathland. Meyer pulled aside a branch to get a better look at it. 'If there is a security crew inside, they're keeping quiet, aren't they?'

The disturbance, which had shaken the entire bush and sent particles of snow down his neck, brought a curse from Hausmann. 'It's two o'clock in the morning. What do you expect 'em to be doing? Playing football or having a sing song? There's a guard all right. Or what would that Army transport be doing there?'

Meyer's eyes moved to the narrow road that ran from the siding to the dark horizon. A car and a large covered transport were standing by the side of the station. 'Let's hope you're right and they've still got sleep in their eyes when we board the train.'

'Amen to that.' Hausmann grunted. 'Have you got that knife ready to cut the tarpaulin ropes?'

Meyer nodded and the two men sank back among

the wet bushes. In the silence that followed they could hear a singing in the wires that ran alongside the rail track. The hoot of the train came again and this time Hausmann imagined he could pick out the rhythmical pounding of its steam engine. Or was it his heart? he wondered. Neither he nor Meyer needed telling this was one of the truly dangerous moments of their mission. For a week, in a country so near defeat it was mobilising its very children, their uniforms, forged papers and good luck had seen them through. But during that time they had been passive actors. Now they were moving to the very front of the stage. If either the train's crew or its security guard spotted them furtively trying to board a wagon, it was inconceivable they could pass as railway engineers trying to hitch a lift.

Even at this late hour Hausmann wondered whether they ought to have played it more boldly and, acting the role of two stranded railway engineers, requested a lift from the siding staff. Had the train been carrying general freight, the risk might have been worth taking. But with the wagons loaded with secret cargo, interrogation would inevitably have followed, and even if their lies and their papers had withstood the test, the tool box with its hidden radio would not. After that, with the Gestapo eager to find the killers of its two agents, death by firing squad would be a mercy.

Not that their present choice was that much better, Hausmann thought. If they were seen and caught, they would be under suspicion from the onset. But at least success or failure was in their own hands and not in the hands of the suspicious guards.

With his senses fine tuned by danger, Hausmann could feel the ground trembling as the freight train covered the last mile to the siding. With its platform less than 50 metres in length, both men were praying the train was large. Working on the psychology that the arrogan

German Army took priority over civilians, the Bavarians had decided the locomotive would run on past the siding, leaving the flak crew an easy step down to the platform while the locomotive crew would have to climb down and trudge back. Accordingly the two men had positioned themselves 40 metres past the siding and on the opposite side of the track.

There was a final hoot and then Hausmann saw the train, a massive black hulk in the darkness, throwing out sparks and a plume of white smoke. Meyer's voice sounded hoarse. 'I think we're lucky. It looks a long train.'

Hausmann found his throat would not allow speech. He could hear the train's brakes now, a metallic screeching that jagged the nerves. As the long, black hulk with its shaded headlight began slowing down, a sudden oblong of light fell on the platform as a door opened. At the same time lights switched on at either end of the siding. Hausmann gripped Meyer's arm. 'There they are. Security guards and flak crews.'

Uniformed men, some yawning, were now emerging from the offices. Hausmann was counting them when the locomotive slid in front and hid them from sight. To his enormous relief, the massive hulk kept moving on although its brakes were still screeching. As it reached them, a wave of hot, oily air swept over the two men. Then the locomotive was past, grinding to a halt another 30 metres along the track and leaving the flak wagon at its rear alongside the platform.

Meyer was rising when Hausmann caught his arm. 'No, wait. Give the old crew time to climb down.'

Although the long line of wagons hid the crews from the two men and the train was panting like a living thing, they could hear voices and orders coming from the station. Hausmann was about to rise when he saw a flicker of light at the far end of the train. He pushed

Meyer back. 'Someone's lighting a cigarette. Perhaps a guard.'

A few seconds later there was the crunching sound of boots on cinders as an armed soldier came walking down the track. He passed within ten feet of the crouching men, close enough for Hausmann to see his features as he drew on his cigarette. As he reached the locomotive, he paused, doused his forbidden cigarette in a shower of sparks, and then disappeared. Taking a deep breath, Hausmann grabbed Meyer's arm. 'Now!'

Snatching up the tool box, Meyer ran for the nearest wagon, with Hausmann hurrying after him. When the older man reached the wagon he found Meyer slashing through the ropes that kept the end of the tarpaulin cover in place. Jumping on to a steel step, he motioned for Hausmann to hand up the tool box. Then he reached down for the older man. 'Come on! Hurry!'

Hausmann swung his good leg on to the step and with Meyer's aid climbed over the metal surround into the black interior of the wagon. Struggling for breath, he saw Meyer's silhouette as the younger man struggled to lash down the tarpaulin again. A minute later Meyer dropped beside him, his whisper hoarse from tension. 'That's the best I can do.'

Listening, the two men could hear shouts and orders coming from both the siding and the flak wagon. To Hausmann they had an urgency that suggested the train had a strict timetable to keep. As if to endorse his belief, a shrill whistle sounded and a few seconds later, with a loud hiss of steam and a jerk of couplings, the train began to move again.

With the tarpaulin back in place, the darkness was intense. Taking the cigarette Meyer offered him, Hausmann was acutely aware of the trembling of his hands as he accepted a light. As Meyer lit his own cigarette, Hausmann caught a glimpse of his relieved grin. 'We made it. For moment I thought that hip of yours was going to foul things up.'

Hausmann's reply was testy with strain. 'Never mind my hip. When we've finished our cigarettes I want to see what's inside this wagon.'

Five minutes later Meyer struck another match and the two men saw three huge crates strapped to the metal floor, one extending almost the full length of the huge wagon. Code numbers were painted on each crate. Meyer glanced at Hausmann. 'Shall we take a look inside?'

Hausmann nodded and pulled a jemmy from the tool box. Prising back a plank of the large crate and easing aside some protective wrapping, the two men saw a section of a huge aluminium artefact. 'What do you think?' Meyer asked, striking another match. 'Is it part of a 262?'

Hausmann frowned. 'I'm no aviation expert. But at least it looks like the part of some aircraft. So we could be on the right track.'

'Maybe if we looked at the entire thing we'd get a better idea?'

Hausmann shook his head. 'No. We still wouldn't be sure. And they might see the crate's been tampered with. Let's get the plank back and see what happens later.'

Completing the task, the two men sank down into darkness again. Feeling an icy draught he had not noticed before, Meyer was about to look for its source when a brilliant light lit up the tarpaulin, followed by a heavy explosion. A second explosion followed a couple of seconds later. Hausmann cursed. 'That's all we need. An air raid.'

Meyer felt his way to the end of the wagon and peered beneath the repaired tarpaulin. In the distance he could see vivid flashes intermingled with jets of flame lancing into the sky. 'Whatever it is they're bombing, it's got flak batteries defending it. Who's doing the bombing? The Allies or the Russians?'

Hausmann joined him. 'It could be the Russians. Let's hope they don't spot this train.'

The faster pounding of the engine suggested its driver and engineer had the same thought. Soon the two men were compelled to hang on to the side of the wagon as it swung from side to side. As the explosions and gunfire fell behind, it seemed the danger was past when a huge explosion almost threw the wagon off its rails. 'One of them must have spotted our smoke,' Meyer yelled. 'We're in for it now.'

In the locomotive ahead the driver and his fireman were desperately aware of their danger. The driver, his sweating face glistening in the glow of the fire box, pushed his regulator to its quadrant limit. The huge pistons below him pounded back and forth and the engine's iron lungs gasped out steam like a living creature fighting for survival.

Two more bombs fell alongside the train, not as close as the first but near enough to send a shudder down its entire length. By this time its flak wagon was in action, pumping up 20mm shells into a black sky. The din forced Hausmann to yell into Meyer's ear. 'Thank God it's too dark for them to strafe us.'

Meyer yelled back as the wagons lurched perilously round a bend in the track. 'There'll be no need for strafing if this driver doesn't slow down. He'll have us off the rails in—'

A massive screech of steel wheels drowned his voice. As the two men clung to the wagon rim to avoid being hurled forward, huge sparks shone through the tarpaulin cover. As the screech of braked wheels diminished, the stench of steam and soot filled the wagon. 'What's happened?' Meyer shouted. 'Have we been hit?'

A huge jolt, followed by the clang of couplings, cut off Hausmann's reply. The silence that followed, broken only by the harsh panting of the locomotive, seemed deafening. Fumbling his way back to the loosened tarpaulin, Meyer peered outside. For a moment he could see nothing but total darkness. Then pin points of light at the rear of the train appeared and he heard distant, hollow-sounding voices. 'We're in a tunnel, Gunter. That's why the driver was in such a hurry.'

Hausmann was at his side now. 'Keep your voice down. There might be echoes in here.'

The voices were growing louder and the torches brighter. Hastily tightening the tarpaulin ropes, the two men waited in an agony of suspense as footsteps reached their wagon and paused. A man gave an order in an arrogant and authoritative voice. 'Run to the end of the tunnel and report to the driver the moment the aircraft have gone. Tell him we must arrive no later than 04.00 hours.'

Footsteps running towards the locomotive sounded a moment later. As the authoritative voice conversed with a second soldier, Hausmann saw a torch beam run across the tarpaulin. For a moment it rested on the refastened ropes and Hausmann felt his heart stop. Then it swung away and he breathed again.

Running footsteps and a breathless voice sounded a minute later. 'The driver says the planes have gone, Herr Hauptmann. We can board the train again.'

The tunnel darkened as the torches receded to the flak wagon. As couplings clanged again and the train jolted forward, Hausmann turned to Meyer. 'It seems they've got a deadline. I wonder why.'

Chapter 18

A jolt and the noise of brakes brought the half-frozen Hausmann out of his stupor. Nudging Meyer, he tried to rise, only to find his legs were too numbed to move. As he rubbed them to restore circulation, Meyer climbed to his feet and released the tarpaulin again. 'I can see some lights ahead. But don't ask me what they are.' He struck a match, glanced at his watch, and gave a start. '03.50 hours. This must be it.'

Hausmann felt his heart spasm and then begin pounding. They had come this far unscathed but what happened now? How could they clear the wagon without being seen? As his mind, depressed by the cold, told him it had been madness to embark on such a mission, Meyer moved to the opposite side of the wagon and began cutting through the ropes there. As he lifted a flap of the tarpaulin, he gave an excited exclamation. 'I think we might be lucky. I can't see any lights on this side.'

Hausmann stumbled to his feet. 'Are you sure?'

'Yes. I also don't think we're coming into a sid ing. There seems to be open country on both sides o the track.'

'Both sides? But that doesn't make sense.'

Meyer drew back. 'Look for yourself.'

Hausmann peered from both sides of the wagon befor being convinced. 'But then why are we stopping? An what are those lights?'

Meyer began working on the tarpaulin ropes agai

'Let's first get out without being seen. Then we'll worry what the lights are.'

The train was perceptibly slowing now. As Hausmann took another look down the track, he gave a start. 'The lights are moving. What the hell are they?'

Meyer pushed him to the other side of the wagon. 'Get ready to climb out the moment the train stops.'

The couplings clanged a minute later. As the wagon jolted to a halt, both men could hear the roar of heavy engines. With no time to investigate, knowing they might have only seconds left, Meyer drew the tarpaulin right back. Seeing no torch lights, he threw a leg over the wagon rim and climbed out. As he steadied himself on a step, he held his hand out for the tool box. Grabbing it, he jumped down and laid it alongside the track. Then he leapt back on the wagon and steered Hausmann's outstretched foot to the step before jumping down himself. Hearing voices through the sound of engines, he hissed a warning to Hausmann. 'Hurry up, for God's sake! Jump!'

With his good leg on the step, Hausmann closed his eyes and obeyed. The pain that shot through his hip on landing made him gasp. Ignoring his distress, Meyer grabbed his arm, and with the tool box in one hand nade Hausmann run towards a clump of trees. There oth men dropped, sobbing for breath.

It was a full thirty seconds before Hausmann could peak. 'Thanks for the help. I needed it.'

Meyer motioned at the wagons. Spotlights were now hining on them and men could be seen climbing on to eir steps and stripping off the tarpaulins. 'Just in time,' e breathed.

As a spotlight moved and brightened the trees around em, Meyer drew the curious Hausmann back. 'We can't ay here.' He nodded at a wooded hill on the opposite side the track. 'If we climb that hill, we'll be on the other de of the train and be able to see what's going on.'

Although Hausmann winced at the prospect of the climb, he saw the logic. 'All right, but watch out for sentries or guns crews. They might have some posted out here.'

Taking care, the two men kept within a screen of bushes and trees until they judged themselves a safe distance from the train and the activity all around it. Then they crossed the track and started up the hill. With the need to keep a close watch out for sentries or gun posts and the need to give Hausmann a rest, it was twenty minutes before they reached a hill shoulder that led them back towards the train. As they moved carefully around it, Hausmann saw that there was a second shallow hill opposite with a col linking the wooded heights.

The night breeze, more noticeable on the hill, kept bringing to the men the sound of gear changes and revving engines. The sounds grew louder as they forced their way through a patch of thick scrub. A few seconds later the snow-covered hillside around them dropped away and the train and its lights lay below.

Hausmann was the first to speak. 'The clever bastards. You see what they're doing?'

Meyer saw only too well. The moving lights were spotlights fixed on mobile cranes. As the two men watched, a crane lifted a large crate from a wagon and trundled with it to the col that linked the two hills. To the watching men's amazement, a lightened entrance was visible on its western face. As the crane drove through the lights, its spotlight was snuffed out as if by a giant's forefinger and thumb.

Meyer's voice betrayed his respect of the feat. 'They must have tunnelled right into the col. But surely they can't have an assembly plant in there. It would have to be an enormous mining project. Perhaps it's just a storage place for the parts.'

'They've done similar things before to escape th

bombing,' Hausmann reminded him. 'Germany's fast becoming a nation of moles.'

'I know that but it would have to be enormous excavation to make room for an assembly plant.'

Glancing at the wide darkened col, Hausmann had to agree. 'Let's hope it isn't, because no air raid's going to penetrate that amount of earth.'

'So what's our next move?' Meyer asked.

A gust of wind struck the ridge at that moment, sending a shiver through Hausmann. Warmed up for the first time that night by his climb up the hill, he could now feel the icy wind penetrating his sweat-soaked clothes. 'I don't see we can do anything until daylight. Until then let's find a place out of this damned wind.'

They found shelter of a kind in a thick copse of trees and bushes on the inside shoulder of the hill. Although out of sight of the train, they could still hear the throb of engines as the cranes continued their unloading.

Although they cleared the snow and made themselves a shallow bed of small branches and twigs, the bitter cold and stress ensured neither man could sleep. For another hour the throb of engines continued, then it faded and died away. At the same time Hausmann heard the hiss of steam and the rumble of a moving train. Glancing at his watch he saw it was 06.20 hours.

The first grey light of dawn began to penetrate the copse n hour later. Opening the tool box, Hausmann pulled out roll he had kept from the previous day and shared it with Meyer. The younger man tried to make a joke of it. 'No uit juice or coffee? A hell of a host you'd make.'

They had a cigarette and then Hausmann painfully tried rise. 'We'd better get back and see what else we can nd. Help me up, will you? This damned cold's gone ght to my hip.'

Grey light was now filtering through the trees although e clouds were down almost to the hill tops. Knowing they were now in greater danger of being seen, the two men took extra care in rounding the hill shoulder. As they approached their vantage point of the previous night, they could hear the muffled sound of machinery, the scream of electric drills, and an occasional high pitched sound they could not identify. ‘They’re assembling something in there all right,’ Hausmann said. ‘But are they 262s?’

A couple of minutes later Meyer, a few metres ahead of Hausmann, gave a sudden exclamation. ‘You’re not going to believe this?’

‘What?’

‘Come and look.’

Moving cautiously from tree to tree, Hausmann saw the col coming into sight below, followed a few seconds later by the railway track. But that was all. No train, no cranes, and most of all no road from the rail track to the col. Only a stretch of virgin snow dotted here and there with leafless bushes.

‘I said they were clever, didn’t I?’ Hausmann muttered.

Meyer’s jest was to cover his astonishment. ‘We didn’ dream it all last night, did we?’

Hausmann shook his head. ‘No, we didn’t dream it It’s all timing and camouflage. They run the trains onl at night and schedule them so that the unloading ca be done before daylight. Then they drive off the trai and cover the crane tracks with camouflage netting s that from the air there’s nothing to suggest anythin is unloaded here.’ As he glanced at the col, his voic turned rich with satisfaction. ‘The beauty of it is, th isn’t a col as we thought last night. It’s a bloody hug assembly plant made to look like one. So it can be bombe after all.’

Following his pointed finger, Meyer saw he w right. Built to look like a high col between the tw hills, the assembly plant had a roof covered in wh camouflage netting with brown patches here and there to simulate bushes.

Nor had the Germans forgotten the entrance through which the cranes had passed the previous night. With its huge doors now closed, its green and brown camouflage would make it appear totally innocuous from the air.

Meyer's eyes moved back to the plant's white roof. 'I suppose in the spring and summer they'll change the camouflage to look like grass and vegetation.' Then his voice changed. 'You're right. If it had been the real thing, bombs would never have gone through it. But a factory roof can't be anything like as strong.'

Hasumann was having second thoughts now. 'But do we want it bombed? We don't know yet what they're doing in there.'

Meyer looked surprised. 'If these were 262 parts that came in last night, then surely it's 262s they're building.'

'We aren't sure yet they are 262 parts,' Hausmann reminded him. 'And even if they are, how do they get he finished aircraft out? Once they're assembled they can hardly be taken away by train.'

Meyer realised he was right. 'Then what's our next move?'

Hausmann was trying to see what lay at the other end f the false col but distance and the hills on either side id his view. He sighed. 'There's only one thing we can o. We'll have to look at the other end of the factory or hatever it is.'

Meyer gave his sardonic grin. 'You're a glutton for unishment, aren't you?'

Hausmann sighed again. 'You're right. I'm out of my ind. Come on. Let's get it over.'

With the overcast sky lightening, they were forced to ke every inch of cover they could find, and with the es obstructing their view Hausmann was denied the sight he wanted until they emerged into a clearing on the reverse hillside. There he grabbed Meyer's arm. 'That's it! That's the answer!'

Meyer followed his excited eyes. A straight broad road ran past the end of the valley, bisecting the hill and another shallow hill range to the east. The younger man looked puzzled. 'I don't follow you.'

Giving no reply, Hausmann led him back down the hillside until they could see the false col again. There Meyer showed disappointment. The rear looked much like the entrance, a high vertical surface camouflaged with green paint. Seeing Hausmann's satisfied expression, Meyer became impatient. 'What are you looking so pleased about? Are you saying they use the road to cart the finished aircraft away?'

Hausmann shook his head. 'No. That would be too slow. They'd be seen and attacked. It's much clevere than that. They fly the aircraft from it.'

Meyer started, then looked sceptical. 'Could they do that?'

'Of course they could. They've been flying fighters of the autobahns for a year now.'

Realising he could be right, Meyer gazed back at th assembly plant. 'If they're doing that, doesn't it sugges they're only assembling small fighters in there?'

'Not necessarily. From all we've been told these 262 aren't much bigger than ordinary fighters and don forget they have much greater engine power to use take off.'

'But you are guessing this, aren't you? Perhaps yc were right before and it's not 262s they're assembling

Hausmann scowled. 'That's why we have to see wh comes out.'

Meyer stared at him. 'You do realise we haven't hac decent meal for twenty-four hours. And it might be da before we see what they're building?'

In spite of his impatient temperament, Hausmann could be as dogged as a bulldog once he got a scent of his objective. 'We know they're working day and night, and if it is an assembly line there'll be parts from earlier consignments moving along it. With the Luftwaffe screaming for more aircraft, my guess is they'll be wheeling new machines out as fast as they can.'

Hausmann was proved right ninety minutes later. Hearing a deep rumbling, the two men broke cover from the trees and saw the end of the artificial col opening like the doors of an aircraft hangar. At the same time Hausmann noticed an object with a horizontal mesh screen rise from the hill opposite and begin revolving to and fro. He pointed it out to Meyer. 'They've thought of everything. That's a radar aerial checking there aren't any enemy aircraft around to spot the plant.'

Below, a dozen men had appeared and were dragging camouflage nets from the ground outside the massive doors. Soon a wide stretch of green tarmac came into view. When the nets were finally rolled back, a tractor appeared pulling an aircraft behind it. As a long slim shape came into full view with engines that carried no propellers, Hausmann gave a grunt of triumph. 'A 262! must be. We've found the bastards.'

As they watched, mechanics began swarming round ie aircraft's two engines and before long a high-pitching hine turned into a thunder of sound that sent a cloud starlings exploding into the lowering sky. Hausmann odded. 'An engine test. They must test 'em inside too. iat's the screaming sound we kept hearing during e night.'

Meyer drew Hausmann back among the trees. 'What you think I should do? Send a message from here? Or iit until we're further away?'

Hausmann hesitated for only a moment. 'Get it off now ile we can. We're on high ground, which ought to help.' Then, as Meyer turned for the tool box, Hausmann gave a violent start. 'Wait a minute. Where is this place? What co-ordinates can you give them?'

Meyer had to grin at his discomfort. 'While you were snoring your head off last night, we passed through a couple of stations. Because of the Russian advance, the names had been removed so I couldn't get any help there. But later on we passed a big lake and after we left it behind it took us only twenty minutes to get here. So I reckon we're approximately that number of miles south of it.'

Hausmann frowned at the younger man. 'I suppose you'll rub that in for the rest of the trip.'

Meyer grinned. 'What do you think? If I hadn't kept awake what would I tell them?' That we'd found the 262 assembly plant somewhere in north-eastern Germany?'

Scowling, Hausmann pointed at the tool box. 'Stop crowing and get on with the transmission. The sooner we send it the quicker we can find some food and shelter.

Finding a fallen tree trunk, Meyer sat the tool box on it, took out the tools, and removed the false bottom. Taking out an aerial he strung it between two trees. Then he handed a metal winder to Hausmann, who gave it a puzzled stare. 'What's this for?'

Meyer took it back and inserted it in a hole at the side of the box. 'You turn it to provide the current. Slowly and steadily while I transmit.'

While Hausmann knelt down in the snow and turned the handle, Meyer put on a pair of headphones and began tapping the transmission key. When he tapped his call sign for five minutes without a response, Hausmann, whose awkward posture was hurting his hip, gave a growl of frustration. 'Maybe the bloody thing isn't powerful enough.'

Meyer shook his head. 'It's supposed to be. And they're supposed to be on watch twenty-four hours a day. Perhaps the aerial isn't at the right angle.'

He made adjustments to it and began tapping again. This time he gave a start. 'It's faint but I think they're acknowledging.'

'Are you sure?'

Meyer tapped his key again, listened, and then nodded. 'Yes. It's them.'

'It had better be,' Hausmann muttered. 'If you're much longer the Nazis'll get a fix on us.'

In his hesitant Morse, Meyer tapped out his code and his message. When he ceased at last, Hausmann flexed his aching arm. 'Did they get it all?'

Meyer removed his earphones. 'Yes. They acknowledged.'

Hausmann relaxed. 'Thank God for that. Now let's get the hell out of here in case a D/F station picked up your ransmission.'

Meyer collected the aerial and handle and replaced hem in the tool box. As he picked the box up, Hausmann hook his head. 'No. Get rid of it.'

'But we're supposed to transmit every twelve hours to et London know we're safe.'

'Sod London. Get rid of it. It's a time bomb if we're rrested.' Hausmann pointed at a clump of snow-covered ushes nearby. 'Bury it in there.'

Meyer hesitated, then, accepting Hausmann's argu- ent, he hid the box deep in the bush and replaced the ow. As he straightened, he gave the older man a rueful imace. 'Where the hell do we go now?'

Hausmann pointed in the direction of the road. 'Maybe e can hitch a lift. Or find a town.'

'Or get picked up by the SD or some zealous bastard o wants to show what a patriot he is.'

Hausmann shrugged. 'It's a chance we've got to take. less you've any better ideas.'

'No. You're right. Let's try the road but keep a sharp tch for gun posts.'

Unable to descend the hill from their present point as they would be in full view of the garrison below, they had to retrace their steps uphill until they judged the hillside covered them. Letting Meyer with his sharper vision lead, Hausmann followed him through the bushes and trees until his patience and stamina ran out. 'That's enough. We must be out of sight of the bastards by this time.'

Agreeing, Meyer turned towards the eastern hillside. As they reached a clearing the road could be seen sweeping past at the base of the hill.

Meyer was scanning the clearing below. 'There's no cover until we reach the trees again. Do you want to risk it or climb the hill to the top and go down the far side?'

Weariness and pain were sapping Hausmann's patience. 'No. We have to get down, so let's get on with it.'

Giving him a look, Meyer led him down. A snow covered knoll rose from the snow a few metres tc their right. Both men eyed it suspiciously, but fron their viewpoint they could see no sign of life. As the hurried past it, Hausmann caught his foot on a hidde root. As he stumbled and swore, a sudden yell behind hir stiffened every muscle in his body. 'You two! Halt!'

Hausmann slowly turned. A young Army office muffled up in greatcoat and field cap, was standin six metres behind him with a Luger in his hand. H shout came again. 'Who are you? What are you doin up here?'

The shock stunned both men. Then Hausmann hea his hoarse voice. 'We're a couple of railway engineer lieutenant.'

'Railway engineers! Up here on this hill? Are y trying to make a fool of me?'

Hausmann spoke to Meyer from the side of his mou 'Run for it while I go for his gun.'

'Look behind him,' Meyer whispered back.

It was then Hausmann saw the flak post. It was si

30 metres away, half hidden by dwarf trees that grew at one side of the knoll, with the barrels of its pom-poms merging with the dark branches. Hausmann could also see one of its crew aiming a machine gun at them. From afar he heard the Army officer's question. 'I ask you again. What are you doing here?'

When neither man could think of an answer, the officer inclined his head to the gun post. 'Berger and Stein! Take these two men down to the guardroom and tell the Commandant where we found them. If they try to escape on the way, don't hesitate to shoot them.'

Two muffled figures rose from the flak post, rifles at the ready. With a nightmare coming true, both men were tempted to end it there and then by making a suicidal bid for freedom. Instead the survival instinct that all men possess betrayed them. Turning, urged on by their guards, they began tramping down the hill although their frantic minds told them they were almost certainly beginning a journey into hell.

Chapter 19

Staines gave a chuckle as he entered the High Elms library and saw Davies and Adams standing by the table. 'Hiya, Davies. I'm disappointed. I thought you were going t join the USAAF. We need gunners like you.'

Davies smiled as he saluted. It was the first time he ha seen Staines since the two of them had flown to Augsbur and Davies found it pleasing. Although his relations wit the big American had always been cordial there was a extra element in Staines's humour today and Davies kne what it was. The bond of shared danger. The discover of the other's courage. A special relationship that we beyond simple friendship. The two men had a person as well as professional respect for one another now.

There was less patience in the American's voice wh he acknowledged Simms' salute. 'I hope this ne you've got for me is good news, Simms. Because I' had a hell of a job getting away this afternoon.'

In situations such as these, Simms had a way with h that could charm the birds from the trees. 'I'm dee sorry, sir. At any other time we would have come strai to your headquarters. But as I'll explain in a moment is very difficult for me to leave High Elms today.'

Staines dismissed his apology with a grunt. 'C What's your news? I'm assuming it has to do w the 262s?'

'Of course, sir. We've had an interesting report fr our agents.'

'Good news or bad?'

'From your point of view, I think it is good news.'

Before Staines could question him further, Simms indicated a large map of Germany that was stretched out on the long mahogany table. 'If you will come over here, sir, I'll explain everything we have heard so far.'

When Simms had finished, the irritation had disappeared from the big American's face. 'You call that interesting news, Simms? I'd say it's sensational news if it's accurate.'

Simms nodded his greying head. 'We believe it is, sir, although my agents could only carry a small radio, which meant we had to set up a receiving station as far forward as our advance in Europe would allow. Even so, my station believes they gathered all the main facts.'

Staines's elation faded as he noticed Simms' expression. 'Then what's your problem?'

'Purely a departmental one, sir. We're a little concerned because we haven't heard from our agents since yesterday morning and they were ordered to contact us every twelve hours. That is why I'm tied to High Elms today.'

Davies broke in here. 'Are you suggesting they've been captured, sir?'

'We hope not, Davies, but it's always possible. As you will gather, the assembly plant is in a very isolated place, so it will have been difficult for our men to be inconspicuous.'

Davies glanced at Adams and read his thoughts. Anna would be devastated if her friends had become prisoners of the Gestapo. But were her friends involved, Davies wondered? Simms had given nothing away when the question had been asked by Anna earlier and Davies was only too aware that protocol strictly forbade any prying into the affairs of SOE and military Intelligence. For this reason Davies was amazed to hear his own voice breaking that protocol. 'Can you tell me if those two friends of Anna were used in this operation, sir?'

At his side, Davies heard Adams' deep sigh of appreciation. But the Air Commodore's eyes were fixed on the tall, slim figure of Simms that had visibly stiffened at the question. Although his controlled features barely changed expression, his glance and words brought a chill factor to the library. 'As you must know, Davies, my department never gives away information about its intelligence operations. So I am afraid I cannot answer that question.'

Although there were only ten years between the two men, in the years of their highly successful partnership Davies had come to see the man in an almost paternal light and it hurt him to see the offence he had caused. But Davies was not thought of as a thrusting bantamcock among his contemporaries for nothing. 'I asked because of Anna, sir. She has been a wonderful friend to this country and risked her life for us more times than I can remember. So it would be a small reward if we could take this worry from her.'

Adams, holding his breath throughout this exchange, thought at first Davies' offence was proving too great for forgiveness. Then he saw the elderly Brigadier relax and felt the chill leave the room. 'Believe me, Davies, I do understand her concern but I would ask you all to wait for a more appropriate time. Then perhaps I can help her.'

Satisfied and relieved, Davies drew back. Adams, whose sentiments for Davies had never reached such heights before, had a desire to slap him on the back. Instead he heard Staines's impatient voice. 'Whoever these guys are, they seem to have done a great job. So what's our next move?'

His manner mild again, Simms turned back to the American. 'Unless we hear more from our agents, I'm afraid the rest is up to you, General, and whether feel it worthwhile to send out a force of B17s on this information. But I do warn you the target might be hard to find. From what we hear, the security and camouflage are exceptionally good.'

Staines pulled an airship from his cigar case and injected it into his mouth, a sure sign his cordiality had returned. He grinned at Davies as he lit it, although to the Air Commodore's relief he made no comment. Instead he turned back to Simms. 'Yeah, it's my pigeon now. I'll first need to have a recce done. When I get back I'll have a word with our reconnaissance guys.'

'I could speak to Benson if you like, sir,' Davies offered. 'As you know, they're specialists at reconnaissance and photography.'

Staines inhaled, then released a cloud of blue smoke. 'Yeah, that's a thought. Some of 'em fly Mosquitoes, don't they?' When Davies nodded, the American went on. 'I guess Mosquitoes would have the best chance of survival if any of these 262s are flying around there. OK, Davies. Thanks. Only tell Benson they mustn't alert the bastards. I don't want a swarm of these super ships waiting for my boys when they make their attack.'

Simm's quiet warning brought a sudden hush to the room. 'There's one point you'll have to consider, General. If my agents have been captured the enemy may already be alerted.'

Staines stared at him. 'You mean they'll talk?'

'Everyone talks under torture, General. The only difference is that some hold out longer than others.'

Adams knew he was sharing the same thoughts as Davies. If Simms had used Anna's friends and the Gestapo discovered their identity, the word torture would take on a new meaning. He watched Staines remove the cigar from his mouth and walk over to the french windows, where he stared out at the gloom that was already shortening the winter afternoon.

A full thirty seconds passed before he gave a grunt of frustration. 'We've got to stop these 262s, Simms, or in the springtime they'll slaughter my boys. If it wasn't for this damned weather I'd take a chance and send my ships out tomorrow. But our weather men say the clouds go up to heaven over Germany and there's no hope of improvement for a week or longer. So my B17s can't do a damned thing even if the Krauts do learn we're on to them.'

Alongside Adams, Davies suddenly gave a start and half opened his mouth. Alarmed at what he might be about to say, Adams held his breath but to his relief it was Simms who answered the American. 'We can't confirm yet that our agents have been captured, General. That's something I won't be able to tell you for another day or two. In the meantime we are quite entitled to believe the enemy knows nothing about our discovery.'

The gentle, half-hidden admonition brought a sudden laugh from Staines. 'You're right, Simms. What am I bellyaching about? I wanted to know where the assembly point was and you've found it, which is a hell of an achievement.' Returning to the table, the American picked up his cap, then glanced at Davies. 'You'll let me have those plates if Benson gets lucky, won't you, Davies?'

'Of course, sir. Right away.'

Staines glanced at his watch. 'OK, guys. I have to ge along. Keep in touch and thanks again for all you've done I'm grateful.'

Simms waited until his footsteps died away befor glancing at Davies. 'I hadn't realised he cared about hi crews so much. It does him credit.'

Davies nodded. 'Let's hope your agents haven't bee captured. Then he might get a clear run at the target whe the weather breaks.' He picked up his own cap and turne to Adams. 'Come on, Frank. I must get back to Group

Both men saluted the Brigadier and made for the doo

As they reached it, Simms' quiet voice halted them. 'I shouldn't do this, Davies, but I found the case you made for Anna a valid one. So I am breaking my directives by telling you that the two agents I had to use were her friends.'

Adams could not remember what reply Davies gave. He only remembered the Air Commodore's comment when they were seated in the back of his staff car. 'It's a filthy war, Frank. And it's getting filthier by the day.'

Millburn, carrying two mugs of tea, shouldered open the kitchen door of the cottage. 'How's this for service? Two mugs of mother's ruin.'

Carol, seated on a settee drawn up before the fireplace, gave a cry of warning as he stepped forward. 'The beam! Look out!'

It was too late. There was a thud as the tall American's head struck the low lintel of the door. Suppressing a curse, Millburn managed a grin instead. 'Who did they build these places for? Pygmies?'

Carol watched him place a steaming mug on the fireside kerb alongside her. 'You're spoiling me. Do you know that?'

'I know, honey. But I like spoiling you.'

'I like it too. But you mustn't keep on doing it or I'll get lazy.'

'So what? Holidays are times to get lazy.'

'But you've been spoiling me ever since we got here.'

'So what? They aren't giving us that long together, are they? So what's a week of spoiling?'

When the girl made no reply, Millburn set his mug on table and sank down beside her with a sigh of contentment. 'You know, this is the life, honey. I think I'll retire from the Air Force and become a market gardener.'

Carol smiled as his arm went around her. 'For how long? A week? A month?'

He nuzzled her ear. 'That depends on you, honey. If you stick around I reckon I could grow carrots and potatoes with the best of them.'

She shook her head. 'You might think so now. But you'd soon get bored. I know you would.'

He turned her face towards him. 'Hey, you're serious, aren't you? What is it? Have I said something wrong?'

She pressed her face against his pullover to hide her expression. 'No, of course you haven't.'

'Then what is it?'

She tried to laugh. 'I'm just being silly, that's all.'

'How silly? Funny silly or stupid silly?'

'Stupid silly. You just reminded me that our holiday was half over.'

'Is that it? But we've still got seven full days and nights left.'

'I know that. But it's half gone. From now on I'll be counting the days.'

He put a hand beneath her chin and lifted her face. 'That's not the way to look at it. You've got to live each day as it comes.'

'Yes, I know that. I told you I was being silly, didn't I?'

He kissed her, then glanced at a clock on the mantel piece. 'Will the pub be open?'

She followed his gaze. 'Yes.'

He pulled her to her feet. 'Then come on. You nee cheering up.'

She shook her head. 'It was just one of those moments It's gone now.'

'Let's make sure and put it to rest. Go and g your coat.'

Two minutes later they were walking down a narro lane flanked by ancient cottages. As they rounded corner a pub appeared, opposite a mist-covered hillsid

Millburn exhaling a cloud of vapour. 'It's charpy, as you Limies say.'

She hugged his arm. 'You should have put your greatcoat on.'

They reached the pub a moment later. Warm air greeted them as they opened the door to the bar. Although the bar was almost empty, Carol saw a log fire was burning in the huge fireplace. She pushed Millburn towards a leather-covered bench that ran alongside it. 'Let's sit over there.'

He nodded. 'Yeah, it looks cosy. What will you have?'

'The usual,' she said.

'Wouldn't you like something to warm you up?'

'No, beer's fine. In any case spirits are hard to get these days.'

Millburn approached the bar where three old countrymen were chatting. All three of them nodded at the tall American and one removed his pipe. 'Mornin', Yank.'

Millburn, who had met the men on earlier forays to the pub, nodded back. 'Morning. Can I get you guys a drink?'

At this all pipes were removed and glasses pushed towards a middle-aged woman serving at the bar. Millburn turned to her. 'Morning, Lillie. It's a chilly morning out there.'

The woman, who had surreptitiously touched up her hair at the entry of the good-looking American, gave him her best smile. 'It is, Squadron-Leader. What can I get you?'

Millburn motioned at the three waiting glasses. 'Fill up these guys' drinks and give me a pint as well.' Then he winked and lowered his voice. 'You wouldn't have something a bit warmer for my friend, would you?'

The woman glanced at Carol and smiled. 'I think I might, sir. Just this once, mind.'

Millburn grinned. 'Just this once, Lillie.'

He paid her, raised his glass to the three old countrymen, and returned to the fireplace, where he handed Carol a glass of whisky. Her cheeks dimpled as she took it from him. 'You're a terrible man, Tommy Millburn. You've got that barmaid eating out of your hand, haven't you?'

Millburn looked hurt as he dropped on the bench alongside her. 'I just asked her nicely for a whisky, that's all. You guys just don't know how to go about these things.'

'Don't give me that, Tommy. You couldn't stop flirting with women if you tried.'

He grinned. 'I can't help flirting with you. You know something, kid? You turn the winter into summer. I could have sworn the sun was shining when we were walking here.'

'Is that why the mist's down to the chimney pots and your breath was steaming?'

'That wasn't the cold, honey. That was passion.'

She laughed, then lowered her voice. 'Then you want to watch your passion. It could be dangerous on days like this.'

He laughed. 'That's more like my girl. You could be right at that.' His tone changed as his eyes moved from the log fire to the oaken beams of the bar that were ornamented by brass implements of a bygone age. 'You know, this is something we don't have in the States.'

'You mean pubs?'

'Yeah. We've nothing like 'em. Drinking places but not pubs.'

'Is there such a difference?'

'Difference? Like chalk and cheese. These country pubs have such an atmosphere of age and tranquility. Somehow it gets to you. All our boys say the same. It's one of the things we'll miss like hell when the war's over.'

Her eyes were on his face. He was displaying a side she had suspected but not seen before. 'So you do appreciate tranquility, do you, Tommy?'

He gazed at her, then laughed as if remembering his role. 'Don't we all at times?'

'Not all. And some try to hide it. I wonder why?'

He lifted an eyebrow, then took a sip of beer. 'Don't look at me, honey.'

'But you do and you shouldn't. No one should be ashamed of being serious sometimes. Or of loving old, traditional things. I'm afraid I do.'

He shrugged. 'So what? It's no crime.'

'Then you don't mind if I'm serious sometimes? Like I was back in the cottage?'

He laughed. 'Me? I like all your funny ways.'

'Are you sure? I was afraid you might think I was too serious. After all, you are on leave and I shouldn't do anything to spoil things for you.'

Ignoring the old men at the bar, he took her hand. 'You just be what you want to be, kid. I wouldn't have it any other way.'

She was anxious now that he should understand. 'It's not that I'm not particularly serious by nature. It's just that this war seems to be making the world into such a crazy place. Do you know what I was thinking when you were at the bar?' As he shook his head, she went on: 'I was thinking about the happiness I'm having here. How quiet and peaceful and lovely it is sitting with you here in this pub or lying beside you in the cottage. And yet not that many miles away people are worrying themselves insane or dying in agony. Thousands and thousands of them, every day and every night. And somehow I can't equate the two. I find it hard to believe they can both exist in the same world. Does that make any sense to you?'

He lit a cigarette before replying. 'No, it doesn't make any sense. Frank Adams and Ian Moore, our old Squadron

Commander, often used to talk this way when Moore was still with us. But I guess I've always tried to keep my mind on the job in hand and to get what I could out of life outside it.'

'But you have thought about such things?'

She could feel his reluctance to make the confession. 'Yes, I guess I have. But not so you'd notice.'

She pressed his arm. 'I'm glad. So am I forgiven?'

'Forgiven for what?' When she made no reply, Millburn's laugh lightened the mood. 'I guess I will put in for that job as market gardener, honey. Gabby can look after the pigs.'

'Pigs? Market gardeners don't keep pigs, do they?'

'This one will. I gotta give Gabby something to moan about.'

As they both laughed and a log threw up sparks in the fire and the old men's soft country voices embraced her like a comforting blanket, she knew she would never be happier in her life and wished the moment would last forever.

Chapter 20

The Commandant motioned at the officer who appeared in the doorway. ‘Come in, Lerner. I want you to hear this.’

The man walked forward and stood behind the Commandant’s desk. Wearing the uniform of an SS Polizei officer, he was a handsome man with cold eyes, a clean shaven face, and a schlager scar down one cheek.

The seated Commandant was as untidy as the SS officer was neat. Stout in build, wearing a badly fitting uniform, Uwe Rosler looked less like a soldier than a practising engineer, which in fact he had once been. His face, heavy-jowled and lined, gazed up at Lerner.

‘These two men were discovered on the southern hillside this morning. I want you to hear their story and then tell me what you make of it.’

As the SS Polizei officer nodded, the Commandant turned back to the figures of Hausmann and Meyer standing in front of his desk with two armed soldiers guarding them. He pointed at Hausmann. ‘You seem to be the spokesman. Tell this officer what you have told me.’

Seeing the cold gaze of Lerner settle on him, Hausmann could feel his heart beating so fast it made him breathless. Before he could speak, Lerner barked a question. ‘Who do you claim to be?’

Hausmann took a deep breath to steady his heart. ‘As you see from our uniforms, sir, we are railway engineers. My name is Overbeck. My friend is Muller.’

'Railway engineers? Caught hiding on the hillside above this factory?'

'We weren't hiding, sir.'

'Then what were you doing? Building a railway up there?'

Hausmann, who had racked his brains for a reasonable excuse, was forced into the only lie he could think of, lame though it was. 'We were curious about the factory, sir. It seemed so ingenious that we wanted to see what it looked like from above.'

Lerner's educated voice was rich with sarcasm. 'So it was just curiosity?'

'Yes, sir. I'm afraid it was.'

Lerner glanced down at the Commandant. 'You have made enquiries about them to the railway authorities, sir?'

Rosler nodded. 'Yes, but I've been warned it might take some time to get an answer. Records have been badly disrupted by the bombing.'

'Are their papers in order?'

'Yes, they seem to be.'

'I'd like to see them.'

Rosler opened a drawer and offered the documents tc him. The Polizei officer scanned them and then threw them without comment on the desk. His cold eyes returnec to Hausmann. 'If you are railway engineers, what were you doing here in the first place.'

For that question Hausmann was ready. 'We wer going to Rostock. The Russians have been raiding th town heavily of late and our job was to help restor communications.'

'Then why the hell weren't you in Rostock?'

'Because of the bombing of railways we had to tak lifts in trucks and Army lorries. The last one droppe us off a mile down the road. That was when we sa an airplane appear and take off. We could see it w different to other aircraft and that's what made us curious about this plant.'

Beside him Hausmann could feel the silent approval of Meyer. It sounded a thin story but its very improbability could be its strength, particularly as little could be disproved except their status as railway engineers. And from what the Commandant had said, disproving that role might prove difficult.

Hausmann was feeling the faintest stirring of hope as Lerner's sarcastic voice attacked him again. 'So you both forgot all about your duties in Rostock and climbed the hill to survey a secret establishment. That in itself would be a crime if it were true. But it isn't true, is it? Every word you speak is a lie.'

'No, sir, it's true. I know we shouldn't have done it but the aircraft looked so revolutionary we couldn't help being curious. We thought it might still win the war for us.'

Hausmann wondered if his last comment had gone too far as Lerner turned to the Commandant. 'I want these men putting under close arrest, sir, until I've made further enquiries.'

Before the Commandant could answer Lerner barked another question at Hausmann. 'You are Bavarians, aren't you?'

Knowing their accents made it pointless to lie, Hausmann nodded. Lerner turned back to Rosler. 'You may not know this, Herr Commandant, but before last Christmas two Gestapo agents were killed in Nurnbach by a couple of Bavarians. They were helping a British agent to escape. It is possible these are the two men. So I want photographs taking of them which will be circulated around Nurnbach. If they are recognised the Gestapo will be more than grateful to us.'

Hausmann felt himself turn ice cold at the words. Rosler hesitated for a moment, then told the guards to take the men out of the office. He then turned to Lerner. 'I understand your suspicions but you do realise the value the High Command puts on railway engineers? With transport an absolutely critical factor at this time, their value in keeping the railways running is beyond price. I'm mentioning this because their papers do seem in order and we could land a black mark by keeping them here if their story is true.'

Lerner was thinking how these bloody engineers always stuck together. 'Do you believe it is, sir? Two men hiding in a wood overlooking one of the most secret projects in the Fatherland!'

Rosler's frown betrayed hesitation. 'They weren't hiding, Lerner. They were coming openly down the hill when they were seen.'

'They had to come down if they were to escape. The question is, why were they up there in the first place? They say their orders were to proceed at all speed to Rostock.'

'I know that but engineers are a curious breed and curiosity can make men do stupid things. I found that their most convincing argument. After all they weren't carrying a radio or any other suspicious equipment.'

'Of course they weren't. They'd have hidden it before coming out in the open.' Seeing the senior officer's hesitation, Lerner's contempt came to the surface. 'I don't understand you, sir. You surely don't think we should release them and risk the enemy learning all about your establishment here?'

Rosler's hesitation turned into irritation. 'No one's suggesting that, for God's sake. But I need more evidence before we treat them as out and out spies. Call them back, will you?'

Thirty seconds later Hausmann and Meyer were lined up in front of the desk again. Before the Commandant could address them, Lerner's aggressive voice made them both start. 'What did you do with your radio?'

Meyer was the first to find his voice. 'We didn't have a radio, sir. Why should we have one?'

Lerner took a threatening step forward. 'Did you bury it? Tell me.'

'No, sir. We didn't have a radio.'

Lerner swung round on the Commandant. 'I'd like you to detail a party to search the wood for a portable transmitter, sir. There'll be one somewhere.'

Rosler sighed. 'All right.' His eyes turned on the two prisoners. 'I'm holding you both under arrest until our investigations are completed. For your sakes I hope your story is true.' He glanced back at Lerner. 'I'll leave them in your hands for the moment. You can ask Driest in the factory to lend you a few men to carry out the search.'

The two Bavarians were pushed roughly down a corridor and into a large office full of blueprints and photographic equipment. After three photographs were taken of each man, they were marched to a room containing a lathe, a bench, and other items of industrial equipment. As the door closed behind them and a key urned in a lock, Meyer turned to Hausmann. 'If they ind . . .'

Before he could finish his sentence Hausmann's hand closed over his mouth. His urgent gestures told the ounger man of his fears the room might be bugged. When Meyer nodded his understanding, Hausmann released his rip and gave a loud, accusing laugh. 'You see now what uriosity can get you into? I told you, didn't I, they'd be s suspicious as hell if anyone was seen near the place.'

Meyer did his best to further the subterfuge. 'I suppose was bloody stupid of me. But planes have always ascinated me and that one looked out of this world.'

Little more was said between the two men. As cell ter cell of their shocked minds came to realise the full nplications of their capture, they could only pray that eir buried radio went undetected and the photographs failed to find harmful witnesses in Nurnbach. If either possibility betrayed them, they knew the Gestapo would take unthinkable revenge. Sitting in the unheated room, with the bitter cold of the oncoming night sinking into them, both men knew it was the darkest moment of their lives.

Staines rose from his desk as Simms, Davies, Henderson and Adams entered his office. Although his gravelly voice gave nothing away the perceptive Adams sensed his curiosity as he returned the salutes he was given. 'You guys want coffee? Or tea?'

When all four men shook their heads, Staines nodded at the uniformed girl who was waiting by the door. 'OK, Janet. You can go now.'

Staines waited until the door closed behind the girl before turning to his visitors. 'You guys are lucky to catch me. I was supposed to see Swartz this morning but he cancelled the meeting at the last minute.' His curiosity came to the surface as his eyes settled on the refined face of Simms. 'I'm taking it this visit means you've got more news for me?'

Simms nodded. 'We wouldn't have requested the interview if we hadn't, General. I'm afraid it isn't good news, however. I have reason to believe our two agents are now in enemy hands.'

Staines frowned. 'You're sure of that.'

'As sure as one can reasonably be, sir. If they had escaped we would have had a message from them by this time.'

One of Staines's big hands, resting on his desk, was curled into a granite ball. 'Goddam it, it is bad news. What happens now? Will they talk?'

'I'm afraid so. Sooner or later. The Gestapo will see to that.'

'How soon?' Staines demanded.

Simms lifted his slim shoulders. ‘I can’t say. As yet it’s possible the enemy hasn’t established their guilt. They were disguised as railway engineers and railway engineers have a privileged place in Germany these days. But it can only be a matter of time before their disguise is discovered.’

Staines swore again. ‘And I can’t get my B17s off the ground because of the weather. I’ve had to cancel two missions already this week. And the met. guys say there’s no chance of clear weather for at least four or five days.’

Adams was watching Davies’ face in the short silence that followed. He had received a testy phone call from Henderson at six-thirty that morning. ‘Frank, Davies has just been on the blower. He wants the two of us to be ready at 08.00 to go with him to Staines’ headquarters. Apparently he and Simms have made an appointment to see him.’

‘It’s a bit sudden, isn’t it?’ Adams said. ‘Haven’t you any idea what he wants?’

Henderson was clearly displeased by the early call. ‘Sometimes I think the little bugger never goes to sleep. No, I haven’t a clue what it’s about. All I know is his staff car will be at the guardroom at 08.00 prompt. So be on time.’

Simms had been with Davies when the staff car arrived at Sutton Craddock. Although in his blunt Scots way Henderson had asked outright the purpose of the journey and Adams had put out feelings more subtly, neither of the senior officers would give anything away and so the half-hour journey had passed either in generalities or uncomfortable silence. At the same time Adams, who over the years had grown to know Davies’ moods, sensed an anticipation in him that Simms did not seem to share.

It was Davies who broke the short silence that followed. ‘I take it you got the photographs I sent you, sir?’

Staines nodded. 'Yeah. Benson did a good job there. Had they any problems with the 262s?'

'Apparently not, sir. Of course Benson didn't let Jerry know what their target was. They followed the line to Gustrow before circling back.'

'So what'll happen to the agents now?' Staines asked

Simms answered him. 'They'll almost certainly be sent to Saindau.'

'Saindau?' Staines enquired.

Simms explained the significance of the camp. 'It's where the enemy sends his own people, the ones he considered traitors to the Third Reich. It's virtually an extermination camp, although the Gestapo make sure its inhabitants don't die quickly.'

Remembering his own brief experience with the Gestapo, Adams was thinking of Anna's torment if she heard the news. His thoughts were broken as Staines cursed, rose to his feet, and walked across to the window. 'So every minute counts. If we don't get there before those guys talk, they'll put a net of those 262s in the sky. If it wasn't for this damned weather I'd have a hundred B17s over there at this moment. But look at it. The goddam clouds are almost down to the deck.'

Davies' cough brought Adams' eyes back to his face. 'That's the reason I wanted to see you today, sir. I know you want to destroy this plant with your own aircraft and I understand why. But have you thought that a squadron of light bombers flying at low level could do just as efficient a job? Moreover, by flying low they could avoid the plant's radar system, which apparently it has.'

Staines gave a start, then swung round. 'What are you offering, Davies? To use your own squadron?'

Before Davies could answer there was a stifled gasp from Henderson. 'You can't do that, sir. Do you realise how far it is?'

Davies turned to him. 'It's no further than Bavari

Jock, and we've been there twice in daylight. Moreover we can fly from France this time.'

With no previous indication that his squadron might be used, Henderson was almost speechless. 'There weren't any 262s around then. If those two agents talk, there'll be a screen of them over the target. And what about the weather? Everyone but weather Spitfires are grounded at the moment.'

Davies was showing patience with the Scot, a sure sign to Adams that he knew the scale of his offer. 'I agree the weather's bad at the moment, Jock. But the met. boys say there'll be a higher cloud base in the next day or two. Not more than a thousand feet or two but that could be an advantage. It'll stop enemy aircraft from spotting them.'

'It'll also give the EAs' cover,' Henderson protested. 'You can't give the boys this job, sir. Not so soon after Crisis and Thor.'

'Why not? They've just had a good rest and their kites are refitted. They ought to be a fine shape for it.'

It was then Henderson made his mistake. 'I think you're asking too much of them, sir. I think their flight commanders will think the same.'

Red spots suddenly burned in Davies' cheeks. The Scot's suggestion that his prized squadron would resent and even baulk at the operation was offence enough. To say it in front of a high-ranking American officer was too much. 'Our squadron was formed for special missions, Henderson. And so far it has carried them out to the letter. If I approve this mission and get authority from High Command, they'll carry it out with similar loyalty and dedication. Do I make myself clear?'

For a moment the breathless Adams thought that Henderson would turn on his heels and walk out of the office. Instead his bitter eyes stayed on Davies' angry face. 'Yes, sir. You've made yourself very clear.'

Davies stared at the Scot for a full five seconds before

turning to Staines. 'I'm offering to use my squadron for this operation, General. Do you accept my offer?'

Staines, whose weatherbeaten face had shown some embarrassment during the exchange of words, seemed to be sharing hope and hesitation in equal measure. 'I'd sure like to, Davies. But as it's our ships that have taken the beating from these 262s, isn't it our pigeon?'

Davies' voice was still terse from his exchange with Henderson. 'No. We're fighting the same war. If that plant goes on turning out these 262s, we'll start running into them sooner or later. If we go, we'll have to go soon or the agents will talk or Jerry will guess their reason for being there. Either way he might increase the plant's defences.'

Adams held his breath as Staines hesitated. Then, with an almost apologetic glance at Henderson, the big American's shoulders lifted. 'How can I say no when they're savaging my boys like this? But we gotta help you in some way. What about a wing of Mustangs? If the weather relents a little, they can give you some cover. OK?'

'Will that be Major Dent's Mustangs? The ones that escorted us to Copenhagen?'

'Yeah. The same. They respect your boys so I know they'll do a good job.'

'Then we accept. How soon can they be ready?'

'Soon enough. Give us twenty-four hours if you can But we'll make it in twelve if we have to.'

Davies nodded. 'Then we'd better decide our tactic now so we're ready when the weather lifts. Have you th photographs, sir? I want to show them to Henderson.'

Staines crossed over the room to a safe. Unlocking i he pulled out a file of photographs and laid the print out on his desk. Davies motioned Adams and Henderso forward and pointed at the saddle between the two hill 'That's our target. Notice there are no tracks from th railway. They must eliminate them before daybreak. Clever, isn't it?'

Adams had seen the prints when Benson had flown them into Sutton Craddock but on Davies' instruction had forwarded them immediately to High Elms. As a consequence Henderson, although knowing the location of the target, had not seen the plant itself. He gazed at Simms in disbelief. 'That's the assembly plant? Are you sure?'

Simms nodded. 'Yes. It's the target my agents identified. If you examine the prints carefully you'll see the near side of the saddle is too perpendicular to be a natural part of a hillside.'

Henderson saw he was right. He also made it clear he still disapproved the use of his squadron. 'Even so, that camouflage is going to make it terribly difficult to identify from aircraft flying at nearly 300mph. These prints are taken from an oblique angle, which show up the flat side of the plant. It'll look as natural as hell from above.'

'They'll identify like the Benson boys did,' Davies snapped. 'By flying at low level along the railway track.'

'But how will they spot it? At speed it'll look like ınother cluster of hills.'

Red spots were back in Davies' cheeks. Recognising he danger signals, Simms broke in smoothly. 'We got o-ordinates from our agents before they went off the ir, Henderson. They were given to Benson and no doubt ıey'll be given to you.'

Henderson was anything but convinced. 'Surveillance ying is one thing. Combat flying is another. I wouldn't ke the job of finding that target in this weather.'

Only one thing toned down Davies' temper. The ıowledge, which he had no intention of imparting Henderson, that Benson had notched up two failed tempts before their Mosquitoes had located the plant.

'Come on, Jock. You're not saying your squadron, recognised specialists in low level flying, can't do what Benson does?'

The Scot was in no mood for flattery. 'Who do you intend putting in charge, sir? You can't use Harvey again.'

'I know perfectly well I can't use Harvey again. Millburn will be the squadron commander.'

'Millburn's on leave, sir.'

'Then get him back. He's not in America, is he?'

'No, of course he's not.' Henderson paused, then took a deep breath. 'I've grave doubts about this operation, sir. I would like that doubt recorded.'

'All right,' Davies snapped. 'I'll see it is.' When the Scot made no further comment, Davies turned to Staines. 'With your permission, sir, we'll get back to Sutton Craddock now, get our specialist officers together, and start work on the details. I want to be ready to brief my boys at short notice. May I take it you'll alert your Mustang wing and put them in touch with us?'

Staines nodded. 'I'll see to it personally.' As Davies picked up his greatcoat, the American's eyes moved on to Henderson. 'I sure appreciate what you guys are doing and hope it turns out OK for you. I want you to know that.'

Henderson, who had already donned his greatcoat, gave a brief nod and saluted. Giving him a scowl, Davies answered for him. 'We'll do our best, sir. You can rely on that.' With that he saluted the American and led his subdued party from the office.

Chapter 21

Adams had a phone call in his office at 09.00 hours the following morning.

'That you, Frank? It's me, your namesake – Frank Harvey. How's it going?'

'Hello, Frank. What can I do for you?'

'Can you see me this morning?'

'Where? Here?'

'Preferably not. Can you get away for a couple of hours? I could drive up to Selby, so you'd only have a short ride. You can get a car or transport, can't you?'

'Yes, I suppose so. But is it urgent? Couldn't we meet later, say this evening?'

Harvey sounded disappointed. 'I suppose it's possible. Only I'm down to give a lecture to a bunch of sprog pilots tonight. What's your problem? Surely the boys aren't flying today.'

Adams hesitated. 'No, it's not that.'

'Then what is it? Look, supposing I drive up as far s Pickering. You can be there in fifteen minutes. Even ess if you get a jildi on. And I won't keep you more ıan a few minutes. You can manage that, can't you?'

It was the final sentence that decided Adams. Asking vours was never Harvey's way and for the tough orkshireman to have gone this far meant the matter d importance for him. 'I'll see what I can do, Frank. here are you now?'

'I'm phoning from a neighbour's bungalow. We've

scrubbed flying for the day.'

Adams picked up a pencil. 'All right. Give me the number and I'll phone you back in a couple of minutes.'

Writing the number down, he replaced the receiver and stood wondering if he dared take a couple of hours off. As things stood at the moment, his presence was not required. He had spent the entire afternoon and evening the previous day discussing with Davies, Henderson, and specialist officers the problems connected with the squadron's forthcoming operation and he believed they had exhausted its every aspect and contingency. Certainly Davies if not Henderson had seemed satisfied when the Air Commodore had finally driven off. Nor had the weather improved, so there was no risk of a sudden emergency being called, certainly not that morning.

But Davies was notorious for his sudden bursts of enthusiasm and changes of plan and the knowledge the two agents might talk (if they hadn't already) would be uppermost in his mind. If there was the slightest chance of an early take-off, Adams knew Davies would grab it with both hands. Already he had given high priority orders to Henderson tha all personnel had to be kept within call until furthe notice and the squadron's Mosquitoes must be mad combat-ready at the earliest possible moment, an orde that had kept cursing engineers and mechanics workin throughout the night.

At the same time, in spite of Harvey being a clos friend, Adams was not certain he wanted to see hi that morning. Harvey's unusual urgency had awakene a sudden suspicion why the Yorkshireman wanted private talk. If his guess was correct, Adams knew would be more than difficult to decide how much how little to reveal.

But friendship always had first call on Adams' list

priorities. Suppressing a sigh, he turned to Sue Spencer who was sorting through a pile of photographs at the far end of the Nissen hut. 'That was Harvey, Sue. He wants to know if I can see him in a pub in Pickering this morning. Can you hold the fort if I go?'

'Yes, of course. Nothing's likely to happen today, is it?'

Adams took another look out of the Confessional window before replying. Mechanics, working on Mosquitoes parked on their hard standings along the airfield perimeter, were miserable figures in the fine, driving rain that was sweeping the airfield. 'There'll certainly be no flying before noon,' he told the girl. 'And I don't need to leave yet. But there is just the chance Davies or Henderson might call me.'

'Can't I phone you if they do?'

'That's what I was thinking. I'll find out the pub's phone number and give it to you. I'll leave you to stall hem if it's anything urgent.'

She smiled. 'Don't worry. I'll think of something.'

Knowing he could rely totally on the girl's discretion, Adams picked up the receiver again and dialled. 'All ight, Frank. Only it'll have to be the Pickering pub. What's its name?'

'The Saracen's Head. Right in the centre of town.'

'All right. Ring me when you get there so I know hen to leave. And give me the phone number at the ame time so Sue can contact me if I'm wanted.'

Harvey sounded relieved. 'OK, I'll do that. And I'll ave a pint waiting for you.'

was only a few minutes past eleven when Adams ove into the Saracen's Head car park. He found rvey propping up the bar when he entered. The rkshireman's greatcoat was slung over a stool and he s chatting to the elderly bartender. Catching sight of

Adams he slid off his stool and held out a big welcoming hand. 'You've been quick, Frank. I hadn't expected you for another ten minutes.'

'I was able to borrow young Jenkin's MG,' Adams told him. 'It goes like the wind. I nearly took off on that long stretch coming into town.'

Harvey grinned. 'You were lucky. I thought you might have to use a 15cwt to get here.'

Adams shook his head as he discarded his own greatcoat and threw it on top of Harvey's. 'No. All the boys are under orders to stay within call, so there's plenty of transport available.'

Harvey gave a faint start. 'Within call?' Before Adams could reply, he pushed a pint of beer towards him and then motioned to an empty seat by the window. 'Let's go over there.'

Nodding at the bartender, he picked up the two greatcoats and led Adams towards the seat. The low conversation of three middle-aged women and two elderly men, the only occupants of the bar, died as his tall angular figure crossed the floor. He was wearing his working uniform with its faded blue serge, shiny elbows and row of ribbons. There was no vanity about Harvey nor had there ever been, yet to Adams the man's ver lack of it seemed to accentuate his virility and soldierl qualities. To Adams Harvey was an archetypal fightin man and although he had known the Yorkshireman fc years, Adams, who still regretted his age and fitness ha not allowed him to fly, had often felt a sense of inferiorit towards him.

He felt it now as the elderly men whispered to or another and the women eyed his ribbons and cragg features with interest. Harvey, noticing none of it, thre the greatcoats on a nearby chair and indicated Adams sit on the window seat alongside him. He lifted his gla: 'Cheers, Frank.'

Adams took a sip of his own beer. 'Cheers. How's Anna? Fit and well, I hope.'

Although Harvey gave a grimace, Adams had the feeling he was relieved at being given an opening to talk about Anna. 'She's not too good, Frank. She hasn't been for the last few days.'

Adams showed concern. 'She's not ill, is she?'

Harvey pulled out a packet of cigarettes and offered it to Adams. When Adams shook his head, the Yorkshireman lit one and sucked in smoke. 'No, I don't think it's anything physical. But she's not herself. She's been off her food and unable to sleep at nights ever since Davies asked her to attend that bloody meeting you had at the station.'

From the resentment that entered the Yorkshireman's voice, Adams knew now beyond any doubt why Harvey had requested the meeting. 'I'm sorry to hear it. But why did that upset her?'

Harvey scowled at him. 'C'mon, Frank. Don't play he innocent with me. I got it all out of her last night, lthough God knows it wasn't easy.'

Adams sighed. 'She didn't want you to know. She felt ou'd enough to worry about.'

'That's plain stupid. As I told her last night, I'd rather now the truth than believe she had something physically rong with her.' Harvey glanced round and saw the derly party were well out of earshot before continuing. Vhat's the score on this 262 affair? Has Simms used r two German friends or not?'

Adams frowned. 'That's something I can't talk about, ank. You must know that?'

Harvey gave a nod of satisfaction. 'Then you do know mething.' When Adams made no reply, his voice turned ustic. 'Why do you think I asked to see you outside the tion? I want to know if Simms is using these men or t. Anna deserves that, doesn't she?'

Unsure how much he ought to say, Adams prevaricated. 'They must mean a great deal to her.'

'A great deal? Christ, she cried for half an hour last night just at the thought of them being captured. They did save her life, you know.' The momentary, slight tremor in the Yorkshireman's voice said mountains to Adams. 'Not just her life. Think what the bastards would have done to her when they found out she was German. She's not the only one in debt to those men, Frank.'

Adams cleared his throat. 'Yes. I appreciate that. But she mustn't let it affect her so much.'

'Do you think I haven't told her that? It's no use. To Anna friends are friends and the thought they might have fallen into the hands of those Nazi bastards is getting he down. She knows what would happen to them if it wa found out they'd killed two Gestapo agents. You shoul see her, Frank. She's even losing weight.'

Adams was thinking that men who did not know th tough Yorkshireman might be puzzled at his concer for a girl's speculative fears. The truth was, no ma practised loyalty and commitment to friends more tha Harvey. Which meant that no man was better equippe to understand her distress.

Adams took a deep breath. 'I know how worried sh is. She asked me to speak to Davies to see if he coul persuade Simms not to use them.'

'Did you?'

'Yes. Davies took it well and later broke all protoc by asking Simms if he had. I know that because I w present.'

'What did Simms say?'

'He wouldn't answer at first but before we left relented and said yes, he had used the two men.'

Harvey's craggy face set. 'The bastard!'

'I thought the same at the time but as they were best men I suppose he had to use them.'

Harvey's eyes were probing his face. 'You said "were". What did that mean?'

Adams felt there was little point now in withholding the truth. 'Simms believes they have been captured. There hasn't been a transmission from them for over forty-eight hours.'

Harvey stared at him, then gave a low, bitter curse. 'So Anna was right on every count. In God's name, what sort of people are Simms and his kind?'

Adams, who had always found Simms a sympathetic officer, was looking troubled. 'It can't have been an easy decision for him to make. But the two men did find the assembly plant and transmitted back its position before they were captured. So I suppose in one way Simms was right to use them.'

The Yorkshireman was in no mood to be charitable. 'What's happened to you these days? I thought you were he man who always tried to put human beings and their eelings first.'

'Be fair to Simms, Frank. Staines asked for help to ave the lives of his crews and Simms tried to provide t as best he could. Knowing what the two men did in Nurnbach, he must have found it a painful choice.'

Harvey's gesture suggested he hadn't been listening. So I have to tell Anna the Gestapo have got them. Can ou imagine how she'll feel?'

'Do you have to tell her?' Adams asked.

Harvey sucked in smoke again. 'I can't lie to Anna. I ver could. She sees through me right away. Anyway, sn't she a right to know?'

'Simms doesn't think they'll be punished or executed t. He believes they'll be sent to Saindau, a concen-tion camp about twenty miles from the assembly ant.'

Harvey gave a harsh laugh. 'That's going to comfort r no end, isn't it?' He lifted a hand to his throat, a gesture that was almost punitive. 'You know something, Frank. I'm up to here with this bloody war. Combat is one thing. Deceit and torture is something else.'

Adams nodded. 'I know. It's getting filthier by the day. Soon none of us will know what we're fighting for.'

Harvey made another gesture of disgust as he raised his glass. As he drank deeply, Adams noticed one of the elderly men rise to visit the bar. In the irrelevant way Adams' mind sometimes shifted its focus in moments of emotion, he noticed the man had a pronounced limp.

Harvey set down his empty glass on the table. 'Where is this assembly plant anyway?'

As Adams told him, Harvey frowned. 'So what's the next move? Is Staines going to prang it? If he is, he'd better be quick or Jerry might start strengthening his defences, particularly if those poor sods are made to talk.'

'That's the problem. Staines can't get his heavies ove there in this weather.' Adams hesitated, then went on: 'S Davies has offered to use the squadron instead.'

Expecting a violent reaction from Harvey, Adams wa surprised to hear only a curse and then a bitter, triumphar laugh. 'I knew it! I bloody well knew it! I told Anna. Th little sod can't keep his fingers out of any pie. I suppos that's why you'd a problem getting away today?'

'Yes. Although we did our detailing planning ye terday, I couldn't be sure if Davies would have ar afterthoughts and come to the station.'

Harvey was shaking his head. 'God, what a ruthle little sod he is. He'll kill every man in the unit gain favour with the Top Brass. How is Henders taking it?'

'Not very well,' Adams confessed. 'In fact he a Davies had a bit of a ding-dong in Staines's office. Ap from the weather, Jock's worried about the range and 262s, even though Staines is giving us a Mustang esco

'Davies won't listen. He's been hoping to get into the act from the beginning. Who's to be the leader?'

'Millburn. He's on leave at the moment but the Adjutant was sending him a cable today.' The reminder made Adams glance at his watch. 'I'll have to get back myself, Frank. Davies is bound to contact the station sooner or later.'

Harvey checked him. 'Just one thing before you go. Why is Simms so sure these two agents will be sent to Saindau?'

'I understand it's a camp for dissident Germans.'

'So it'll be particularly brutal?'

Adams winced. 'I'm afraid so.'

Harvey said no more. Seeing the bleakness in his eyes, Adams' emotion suddenly broke to the surface. Don't tell Anna they've been captured. What possible good can it do?'

Harvey crushed out his cigarette. 'Stop worrying about t, Frank. It's my problem.'

Shaking his head, Adams said no more and picked p his overcoat. Harvey rose with him and gripped is hand. 'Good of you to come, Frank. Bring Helga the bungalow when you've a night off. I'd like to eet her.'

Adams found himself in the MG a couple of minutes ter. Still unused to the speedy little car, his mind as fully occupied with its eccentricities until he was lfway back to Sutton Craddock. It was only then began giving more thought to Harvey's questions d answers. No one was more protective than the rkshireman to his friends and colleagues; Adams d seen that demonstrated more times than he could nember. Then why, using Anna as his reason, had he uested so many details of the Germans' fate when he st know the extra distress it would inflict on her? The re Adams thought about it the more out of character it seemed. The puzzle was still niggling at him when he drove through the gates of Sutton Craddock and found to his relief that Davies had not yet requested his presence.

Chapter 22

A light sleeper, Millburn was awakened by the tap on the edroom window. Turning his head, he saw a small bird alancing on the window ledge. As he watched, he saw he bird lean forward and impatiently tap the glass again. This time Millburn could not hold back a chuckle.

The sound awoke Carol lying alongside him. With her usled fair hair half hiding her face, she gazed at him leepily. 'What is it, Tommy?'

Millburn grinned again. 'It's that robin you feed very morning. He's decided he's waited too long for is breakfast and wants you to do something about it.'

She lifted her head and saw the bird. 'It *is* him! Oh, n't he gorgeous?' She laughed. 'Do you think he's really ying to wake us up?'

'Of course he is. He's telling us it's past breakfast time d he's hungry.'

She snuggled towards him and ran a teasing finger wn his nose and chin. 'Wouldn't you like to feed him s morning?'

'Me? No. It's too nice and warm in bed. Anyway, he n't take food from me. He takes one look at me and htails off.'

That's just an excuse.'

No, it isn't. I'm too ugly for him. He likes people o're soft and warm and cuddly.'

Her finger ran down to his chest. 'Am I warm and dly, Tommy?'

He grinned. 'You're the cuddliest little transport pilot in the service.'

She pouted. 'That's not much of a compliment.'

'OK. You're the cuddliest pilot in the RAF. How's that?'

She prodded him in the ribs. 'I think you're horrible, Tommy Millburn. Why can't you say something nice and romantic?'

Laughing, he turned and drew her towards him. 'OK, honey. You're the greatest. The cuddliest, most curvaceous, most sexy woman a man could hold in his arms. How's that for starters?'

Her face was pressed against his chest and she could smell the masculine, bed-warmth smell of him. 'That's better,' she breathed. 'Go on.'

'You're gorgeous. I'm the luckiest man in the world.' Then his voice quietened. 'You're feeling better thi[s] morning, aren't you, kid?'

She nodded. 'Yes. I was stupid yesterday. You wer[e] right. We should enjoy each day as it comes. And w[e] have got six more days.' The thought sent a warm glo[w] through her and she pressed closer to him. 'Are you a[s] happy as I am, Tommy?'

'Me? Waking up seeing you instead of a moanin[g] Welshman? It's almost too much for a man to take.'

She snuggled closer to him. 'Do you think you can be[ar] it for six more days?'

'I'll try, honey. I'll really try.'

His arms were tightening around her and she cou[ld] feel his desire rising when there was another impatie[nt] tap-tap against the window. Millburn gave a gro[an.] 'Not again.'

The tap-tap was repeated. Although her desire w[as] growing with his own, she found laughter welling inside her. Afraid Millburn might take offence at su[ch] a moment, she tried to fight her giggles back, only the American to start laughing too. In seconds both were clinging to one another, convulsed with mirth.

It was a full thirty seconds before Millburn could speak. 'The little guy's jealous. He has to be.'

She wiped her eyes. 'If I don't feed him he'll keep it up all morning.'

'Yeah, I think you're right.' Millburn turned towards the robin eyeing them resentfully through the glass. 'You know what you are, buster? You're just a spoilsport.'

A sudden impulse made her lean over and kiss him. 'I love it, Tommy. I just love it.'

He eyed her quizzically. 'Who? That little spoilsport?'

'No. Your sense of humour. It's wonderful.' She kissed him again, then jumped out of bed. As she threw on a dressing gown, he eyed her ruefully. 'Has the little guy blown it for me?'

She shook her head. 'Just the opposite. I'm going to give him his breakfast and then I'm coming back to bed. Or would you rather come down and have breakfast too?'

Millburn gave his infectious grin. 'First things first, honey. That's what my Mammy used to say.'

'But you would like a cup of coffee?'

'That depends how long it takes. My libido says you've only got five minutes.'

Laughing, she ran to the door. 'Tell your libido he's got to learn patience. Keep the bed warm for me.'

Sinking back on his pillow, Millburn heard her run downstairs and into the kitchen. A few moments later the front door opened and the robin hopped from the windowledge and fluttered down. Shaking his head in amusement and disbelief, Millburn heard the girl talking to the bird before closing the door and returning to the kitchen to boil the kettle. Hearing the words of a popular song, Millburn thought for a moment the girl had switched on the radio but then realised she was singing. Listening to the happy sound, Millburn knew he had never felt more contented in his life.

Carol returned to the bedroom five minutes later with two mugs of coffee. Setting one on a cabinet alongside him, she sank down on the bed to drink her own. Millburn raised his head and shoulders. 'What's it like out there?'

She exhaled vapour. 'It's cold. Raw and grey and misty.'

Millburn sat up higher and realised she was right. 'The boys will be loving it. Plenty of time off to see their girlfriends.'

She nodded. 'Everyone will be grounded today.'

He took a sip of coffee. 'Except little spoilsport. I hope you tore a strip off him for breaking up our party.'

She laughed. 'I did.'

'And what did he say?'

'He said you shouldn't be thinking of such things sc early in a morning.'

'Let me talk to him tomorrow. A guy who puts hi stomach before his girl friend doesn't deserve that bi red chest.'

As she laughed again, his tone changed. 'Is you coffee hot?'

'Yes. Why? Isn't yours?'

'I wondered why it's taking you so long to drink it.

Her cheeks dimpled. 'Don't be so impatient.'

'It's not me, honey. It's my libido. It has a mind c its own.'

'If it has, you'd better give it a talking to, hadn you?'

'I've tried, honey. But it takes no notice of me. Wh don't you talk to it yourself before the bed goes cold'

Shaking her head at his banter, she set her mug on t cabinet beside his own and removed her dressing gow She was just lifting the blankets to help her slip benea them when they heard footsteps on the gravel path belc and then a rap on the door. Millburn gave a groan. 'Who is it now?'

She threw on her dressing gown again. 'It could be the postman. Or perhaps old Mrs Mellors bringing us another one of her pies?'

'I love Mrs Mellors,' Millburn said. 'And she's a sweetie for giving us home-made pies. But she's not good on her timing, is she?'

She blew him a kiss and then ran from the room. Sitting up, Millburn heard the front door being unlocked again and the sound of women's voices. Although unable to catch what they were saying, he decided the visitor must be Mrs Mellors and waited for Carol to run back up the stairs again.

Instead there was silence below. Puzzled, Millburn gave a shout. 'Carol! Who was it?'

It was then he heard her footsteps on the staircase. Not er earlier joyous scamper but a slower, more hesitant read. As she entered the bedroom and he saw her xpression, he gave a start. 'Honey, what is it? What appened down there?'

She was trying hard to control herself but her hand as trembling slightly as she handed him a small brown nvelope. 'It wasn't the postman or Mrs Mellors. It was girl with this cable for you. She let me sign for it.'

Frowning, Millburn tore open the envelope. Watching m apprehensively, Carol saw him wince and her heart nk. 'What is it, Tommy?' Then, as he made no reply: 's a recall to your station, isn't it?'

Millburn crushed the cable in his hand. 'Sonofabitch!' en he remembered himself. 'Yeah, I'm afraid it is, kid. ey want me back right away.'

Feeling as if all the strength had drained from her legs, sank down on the bed. 'But why? The weather's been d for a week. It's not likely to change tomorrow.'

'I don't know why. I'm as puzzled as you are.' Millburn

took a deep breath. 'Goddamm it. What a hell of a thing to happen.'

Suddenly she could hold her tears back no longer. 'How I hate this war, Tommy. It seems to be nothing else but goodbyes and miseries.'

He reached out and pulled her towards him. 'I'm sorry, kid. I know what this week means to you. I've never been happier in my life either. And they owed me a month's furlough. What in hell's going on?'

Although unintentional, his words added to her distress. 'It must be something urgent or they'd never call you back in this weather.'

He could feel her tears soaking through his pyjamas and tried to calm her fears. 'Not necessarily, honey. Davies is one of those dedicated guys who doesn't give a damn about his crews' furloughs. He could just be calling a conference and wants me to be there.'

Rebellion made her lift her tear-stained face. 'It's not fair. You need your leave. Can't you say you never received the cable?'

Millburn gave a rueful grin. 'Not now you've signed for it.'

She realised he was right and her voice turned lifeless. 'Then when will you leave?'

He grimaced. 'I guess I'll have to leave this morning.'

She knew she had to make it easier for him and began fishing in her dressing gown for a handkerchief. 'I'm sorry I'm behaving so badly. But it was such a shock.'

He took the handkerchief from her and dabbed gently at her eyes. 'I know that. I can't tell you how sorry I am. But there'll be another time, honey. The war can't last much longer.'

Her voice broke again. 'If it is an operation you will take care, won't you?'

'Me? I gotta take care. I fly with a little guy who gives me hell if I wander one degree off course.'

She had never needed his humour more. 'Then hurrah for Gabby. Remind me to give him a kiss when I next see him.'

He drew her towards him. 'You kiss the Swansea Stallion? He'd never stop bragging about it. In fact he'd be insufferable.'

They made love then but not as they would have made love fifteen minutes earlier, although their sadness added both an urgency and a tenderness to their embraces. When it was over they lay in silence, their breathing mingling, their arms still around one another. While the moment lasted she felt time was being merciful and holding back tomorrow. But when at last he gave a sigh she knew the remorseless clock was in motion again. 'I suppose I had better start getting ready, honey.'

He asked the question when he was packing his effects. 'You haven't said yet what you want to do. Will you stay on here to the end of the week? There's no reason why you should shorten your furlough.'

She was certain he knew the answer before putting the question. Until today the cottage had been a refuge of warmth and happiness. Tomorrow it would don its other face and make every room a cruel reminder of his absence. 'I'm going back to Hatfield, Tommy.'

His failure to argue with her told her he understood. 'Are you sure?'

'Yes. I'd rather be with my friends now.'

'Then I'll take you there before I go up north.'

'No. That would mean you'd have to drive through the night. I'll take a train.'

He put a finger under her chin and lifted her face. 'Listen. They know I've a long journey so won't expect me until tomorrow. If they do, it's too goddamed bad.'

As her eyes suddenly filled with tears, he cursed and shook his head. 'I'm sorry, kid. Desperately sorry. But let's make a date to come back here soon. OK?'

She brushed back her tears and smiled. 'OK, Tommy. Let's do that.'

They gave the key to Mrs Mellors and drove off an hour later. She watched the cottage until it disappeared round a corner in the road. As she turned back, she felt his hand grip her own. 'It won't go away, kid. It'll be there for our next date.'

Unable to trust herself, she kept the moment light. 'It had better be. I want to see my robin again.'

His wink was for her courage. 'He'll be there, honey, with his red breast puffed out and his little beak ready for action. Just you wait and see.'

Hausmann nudged Meyer as he heard a key turning in the lock. Chilled to the bone, covered with the only threadbare blanket provided, the two men were huddled together or a bare wooden bench. As the door swung open, Lerne appeared with two armed guards immediately behind him 'Good afternoon, Railwaymen. I hope you slept well las night and enjoyed your lunch today.'

Although his handsome face bore a smile, the mocker of his words made both Bavarians wonder if his men ha found the hidden radio. At the same time, Hausmann wa determined to play the wronged men to the bitter end an could only hope his chilled voice did not betray his fea 'You had no right to leave us in here with no beds an only one blanket. When you find out the mistake you hav made, we shall file a serious complaint against you.'

Lerner nodded and smiled again. 'You should hav been an actor, Herr Overbeck. In my opinion you wou have been a better actor than a spy.'

'We're not spies. How many times must we te you that?'

'You could tell me a thousand times and I still wou not believe you. Soon I shall have my proof and then tl farce will end.'

So the hidden radio had not yet been found! Hausmann felt a sudden stirring of hope. As it was clear no news had yet come in from Nurnbach, evidence of their guilt was still lacking.

The frustration the SS officer was feeling ran like a dark undercurrent beneath his next words. 'You are both fortunate that the Commandant here is a tolerant man. He does not want you punished until we can provide evidence of your guilt.' Seeing the expressions of the two men, Lerner's voice hardened. 'I must add that I do not share his tolerance. To me the security of the Fatherland takes priority over all else and the fact you have been clever so far in concealing your guilt would not save you from a firing squad if I had my way. Your movements in themselves tell me you are guilty.'

Hausmann cleared his throat. 'We're not, Major. We were just curious. Stupid, yes, but not guilty of anything more.'

Lerner's handsome face showed nothing but scorn. 'Trying to make a fool of me will not help your cause, Herr Overbeck. You can help yourself in only one way: by admitting your guilt and telling me what message you sent to the enemy.'

Hausmann shook his head. 'We didn't send a message to anyone, Major. How could we without a radio?'

Menace entered the SS officer's cultured voice. 'You will pay for every one of your lies, Overbeck. Believe me, you will pay most heavily. When I obtain the evidence our Commandant insists on, which cannot be long delayed, I shall take you myself to Saindau. Saindau, in case you do not know, is a camp that specialises in handling traitors of the Fatherland. When we have finished with you, you will curse your mothers for having borne you.'

When neither men spoke, Lerner addressed the two young guards. 'You will keep a close eye on these men both day and night. If either of them tries to escape by a suicide attempt, you will be held responsible.'

He turned back to the two Bavarians. 'You are probably hoping your message was received and your friends will be launching a raid against this establishment. If that is the case, you will find the result a grave disappointment. For I am recommending to the Commandant that he puts in an urgent request for extra defences.'

Alarmed by his words, Hausmann made a daring protest. 'Herr Major, is that wise? We're not spies and we never sent a radio message. So this plant is in no danger and you would be drawing guns from places where they are more needed.'

The man's cold eyes told Hausmann his warning hac registered. For a moment it seemed Lerner would walk forward and strike him for his audacity. Instead the SS officer spun round and left the room. One guard followec him outside, the other sat down on a bench at the far sid of the room.

As Hausmann released his breath, Meyer moved to hi side, his voice a mere whisper. 'That was brave of you Do you think he'll take the warning?'

Hausmann returned his whisper. 'It's just possible. don't think he and the Commandant like one anothe and as there still isn't any evidence against us, th Commandant might be afraid of crying wolf too soo Let's hope so.'

Meyer gave his sardonic grin. 'Let's hope we g the raid soon. I'd a damn sight rather die here than Saindau.'

Hausmann nodded. 'It'll depend on the weather.' Tur ing, he addressed the young soldier who was watchi them in some fascination. 'What's the weather like c there, soldier?'

The youngster seemed uncertain whether to talk them or not. Hausmann smiled at him. 'Don't wor

We're not spies as the major seems to think. We're railway engineers and we're wondering if we're going to have weather problems getting to Rostock once your Commandant finds out the truth.'

His words appeared to reassure the youngster although his voice had a doubtful ring. 'It's clear now. But it snowed heavily during the night and this morning.'

Hausmann had difficulty in not giving Meyer a triumphant glance. 'Does that mean the trains are running?'

The young soldier frowned. 'I don't think they could get through last night. But I think they're running now.'

Hausmann gave him a fatherly smile. 'That doesn't sound too bad. Thanks.' He added on his next words as if they were an afterthought. 'Don't worry about going to sleep later on if you feel tired. Neither of us are going to attempt suicide. The Major is making a silly mistake.'

The soldier muttered something and then lit a cigarette. Hausmann could read Meyer's thoughts as the two men exchanged glances. The heavy snowfall almost certainly explained why the radio had not been found. Could they hope their luck would last until the Allies were able to launch a strike against the plant? They could do nothing but pray as the slow hours dragged by.

Chapter 23

Davies was not looking pleased. 'Well, what is it?'

Harvey glanced at Henderson who was sharing his office with the testy Air Commodore. 'I did ask for an interview in private, sir.'

'For Christ's sake, this is the CO's office, Harvey. Are you asking me to kick him out?'

For once in his life, Harvey was looking embarrassed as he appealed to the Scot. 'I'm sorry, sir. But, as I say, I did ask for a private interview with the Air Commodore I hadn't known at the time he would be here today.'

Finding the situation not without humour, Henderso shrugged his wide shoulders and rose from his chair 'These things happen. Don't worry about it. I had to se the Armament Officer this morning. I can see him in th armoury just as well as in here.'

Harvey nodded his gratitude as the Scot left the office Davies' impatient bark came the moment the door wa closed. 'All right. You've got your private interview. No what do you want?'

Harvey took a deep breath. 'I've come to ask a favou sir. It has to do with Anna.'

Davies' tone modified at the mention of the Germa girl. 'Anna? What's her problem?'

'She's worried about her German friends. She's afra they might have fallen into the hands of the Gestapo.

Davies' eyebrows came together. 'German friend What are you talking about?'

'I'm talking about the two agents Brigadier Simms used in the Crisis operation. The ones that saved Anna when the Gestapo captured her. She's been worried from the beginning that Simms would use them and now she's under the impression they're prisoners.'

Davies had difficulty in hiding a start. 'Why does she think that?'

'She knows they are Simms' best agents. She went to Simms and asked him not to use them but as he wouldn't say yes or no she's convinced he has. Now she's afraid they might be prisoners and it's affecting her health. That's why I had to see you.'

Frowning heavily, Davies rose from his chair. He gazed from the window to check no one was outside and opened the office door to ensure the corridor was empty. Closing the door, he swung round on Harvey, his voice muted. 'Has Adams been talking to either of you about this?'

Hating lying though he did, Harvey had known Adams vould become a prime suspect once he saw Davies and s a consequence he had taken great care in preparing his ase. 'It's nothing to do with Adams, sir. Anna got this ear after you invited her here to discuss the 262 aircraft nd it's been bugging her ever since.'

Davies eyed the big Yorkshireman with dislike. 'You're aying it's my fault?'

As could happen when he was challenged, Harvey's eply was blunt to the point of rudeness. 'I didn't say it as anyone's fault. I'm just saying it was that interview at sparked off her fears for these men.'

Davies scowled at him, grunted something, then dropd back on his chair. 'I'm sorry she's not well but tell her t to be so sensitive. Tell her everything's going to plan.'

Hiding his dislike of Davies' evasion, Harvey shook s head. 'That won't be enough, sir. She's living in fear ey've been captured and she's terrified what the Gestapo ll do to them.'

Davies' scowl deepened. 'What the hell are you asking me to do, Harvey? Give her details of every operation we carry out? She knows we can't do that. She's a professional herself.'

'She's not asking anything, sir. I'm asking about these men for her.'

'Then you should bloody well know better. I can't talk about what agents Simms uses or what happens to them. If you need to know so urgently, you should ask him, not me.'

Harvey gave a contemptuous laugh. 'You think he'd tell me anything? I'd never get past first base. I asked to see you because of what Anna's done for this squadron. On top of that I've got something else to ask you.'

Davies gave a suspicious frown. 'What else?'

'It's related to these agents. Aren't I right in thinking you're going to brief the boys on an operation today?'

This time Davies could not hide his start. 'You *have* been speaking to Adams! Damn him. He's gone too fa this time.'

Harvey shook his head. 'I keep telling you Adam isn't involved. All your specialist officers know abou the briefing. I had a word with a couple of them whe I arrived at the station.'

The knowledge it was true about the specialist officer did nothing to appease Davies' short-fused tempe 'Harvey, you're no longer a member of this unit. Th means it's an offence to pry into its operations! I coul put you straight before a Board of Enquiry.'

Harvey cast off the threat with a shrug of his shoulder 'I'm concerned about Anna's health and state of min And, if you want it straight, so should you be after t risks she's taken for us.'

Red spots began appearing in Davies' cheeks. 'Wat that tongue of yours, Harvey. I've warned you about before.'

'If you'd come clean with me, sir, I would watch it. Isn't it true those men have been used and are now captured?'

'Damn it, stop asking me that. Talk to Brigadier Simms.'

'I don't need to talk to Brigadier Simms. From what you're doing I'm sure those men are prisoners.'

In spite of his anger, Davies was curious. 'What the hell does that mean?'

'Your operation's a dead giveaway. Even you wouldn't be sending the boys out in weather like this unless there was an emergency. I think the capture of the prisoners is the reason. Staines wants the plant to be hit before the men are made to talk but Staines can't use his B17s in this weather. So you've volunteered to do the job for him. Right?'

Secretly Davies had to concede the logic of the deduction. Then he recognised a basic flaw. 'How do you know they found the plant before they were captured? Adams has told you, hasn't he? You've presumed on his friendship.'

'I didn't need Adams,' Harvey lied. 'Your operation says it all. Why would you be sending the boys out in his weather unless time was at a premium? You know ie prisoners will be tortured and you need to hit the plant efore they talk. Otherwise Jerry will rush up heavier efences, perhaps using some of these 262s.'

The short but tense silence that followed suggested at Davies had conceded his case. His sullen question firmed it. 'What was the other thing you wanted to see e about?'

Harvey's tone changed. 'Anna says there's a concen- ation camp at Saindau where German dissidents are nt. She's convinced that the agents will be sent there r punishment. I want you to let me fly there and bomb at camp.'

Davies gave a violent start. 'You? Alone?'

Harvey gave a grim nod. 'If necessary, yes. I could do enough damage to give the inmates a chance to escape. But to make more certain of doing the job properly I'd like to take two other crews with me. Volunteers, of course.'

Davies' stare was a mixture of astonishment and grudging admiration. 'I took you off combat flying at Anna's request. So how can she agree to this?'

'Anna would never agree, so I haven't asked her. She'll be told when the job is done. Will you let me do it? If the agents have been captured, they'll probably be in Saindau already. So I'd want to be off at dawn tomorrow at the latest.'

The clock above Henderson's desk could be heard ticking as Davies' sparrow-like eyes examined the Yorkshireman's determined face. When his questio came it had undertones of respect. 'Do you know wha you're asking? Without a heavy escort you'd have onl a hundred to one chance of getting through.'

Harvey shook his head. 'I don't agree. I'd go all th way at ultra low level so I'd keep beneath their radar And in this weather even their Observer Corps woul have trouble spotting me.'

'They'd find you,' Davies said. 'And then you wouldn have a cat in hell's chance of either reaching the target o getting back home. Our people would think me crazy I asked them to authorise such a mission.'

'Not to save men's lives? Men who've risked ever thing for us.'

'Even if you reached the camp, there's no guarantee would save their lives.'

'Perhaps not but it might give them a chance to escap from the Gestapo.'

'But they're Germans, man. How the hell can I get aut orisation to risk precious planes and crews on Germans

'They're friends, sir. And they're men who saved Anna's life.'

The mention of Anna made Davies hesitate but only for a moment. 'I'd just be wasting my time, Harvey. I'm sorry but you must know that.'

'Then don't ask permission,' Harvey gritted. 'Authorise it yourself. We'll all stand by you if it gets you into trouble.'

Davies gave a harsh laugh. 'Trouble? They'd crucify me. And what good would that do to the squadron? It would be disbanded and split up in a week.'

'Would that be such a bad day to end it? At least we'd all finish up with our noses clean.'

Davies gave him a look. 'Would it make things any better for Anna if you killed yourself?' When Harvey scowled, Davies went on: 'As there's nothing any of us can do, take my advice and let her think the two men are safe. Say I told you that if you want to make it sound authentic.'

Harvey was breathing hard. 'So you won't let me go?'

'I've told you, it's bloody impossible. You can't be surprised. You must have known that before you came in.'

All Harvey's dislike of the man broke free at last. 'Aye, I did. I've always known you'd no heart. But I felt I had to make certain of it one last time.'

The red spots were back in Davies' cheek again. 'I'm sorry about Anna but this doesn't call for insults. I think you'd better go now before you say something you'll regret.'

Disappointment made the Yorkshireman throw all caution to the winds. 'I don't know how you sleep at nights, Davies. War's just a bloody game of chess to you, isn't it? Sacrifice a pawn here and another pawn there . . . it's all part of the game. Don't you ever stop to think what your pawns are? Don't you stop to think that they bleed and feel pain?'

It took no more to fire Davies' own hostility as he leapt to his feet. 'That's enough, Harvey. I've had a bellyful of your working class morality. If it wasn't for Anna, you'd have been in the guardhouse months ago.'

Harvey's contempt spilled out like a vitriolic acid. 'A hell of a lot you care about Anna. You've used her like you've used everyone else.'

'That's not true. She volunteered to help us.'

'That was because she wanted to help her friends, both here and in Germany. She cares about her friends, Davies. She doesn't abandon them when the going gets rough like you do.'

Davies' voice quivered. 'Harvey, for Anna's sake I'm giving you one last chance. One more insult and you're finished. Now get out and stay out.' As Harvey's craggy face showed contempt and he threw up a mockery o a salute, Davies' threat checked him at the door. 'And don't think I've forgotten all your past insubordination. If you get any ideas of taking a Mossie withou my orders, remember that every NCO and mechanic on the station will be told to ignore any orders yo give them.'

Harvey eyed him a moment, then cursed and slamme the door behind him. White-faced, Davies stared down a his hands and saw they were trembling.

Music from the radio was issuing from Millburn's bill as he pushed the door open. As he swung his suitcas inside, a complaining voice greeted him. 'So you're bac You've taken your time, haven't you?'

Turning, Millburn saw Gabby lying on the far bed wi a book alongside him. The American grinned. 'When d you get here?'

'Last night. Where the hell have you been?' Gabb

rose on his elbows and gazed at Millburn's unshaven face. 'You look pooped.'

Millburn swung his suitcase on his bed and unlocked it. 'I am pooped. I've been driving since yesterday afternoon.'

'Don't give me that, Millburn. You've been at it all night with that woman. Trying to make up for all the nights you're going to miss.'

Throwing off his greatcoat, Millburn scowled at him. 'That's all you ever think about, isn't it? I took Carol back to Hatfield before I started back. I thought they owed me that.'

Gabby's tone changed. 'What the hell's going on, Millburn? They can't want us for operations in this weather. Even the birds have given up flying.'

Millburn was transferring his clothes to his locker. 'Haven't you tried to find out?'

'Of course I've tried. But everyone is as baffled as I am. It seems the lads have been kept within call for the last two days.'

Millburn showed surprise. 'But not told anything?'

'Not a thing. There are more rumours flying about than warts on the SWO's backside but nobody knows anything for sure. Maybe you'll know more when you've seen Henderson.'

Millburn gave a start. 'Henderson? Has he asked for me?'

'He's been asking for you since 08.00 hours. I ran out of excuses trying to cover for you.'

'Why the hell didn't you tell me when I came in?'

'Give me a break. You've only been in here five minutes.'

Millburn moved over to a cracked mirror to examine his appearance. Gabby grinned. 'You look shagged out. Baggy eyes, sallow skin, the lot. And you need a shave.'

'I know I need a shave,' Millburn growled. 'How urgent did Henderson sound?'

'When?' Gabby grinned. 'The first time or the tenth?' When Millburn gave him a scowl, the Welshman went on: 'The last kid he sent to the billet said he was chewing nails. You could be in the shit, Millburn.'

Millburn showed disgust as he snatched up his great-coat. 'Why did they bring you back? Didn't they realise this was a chance for me to get a new navigator?'

Gabby took umbrage at that. 'You think I wanted to come back, Millburn? It's been like paradise without you. When you didn't arrive last night I thought maybe Carol had seen you off or you'd eloped with her. But no such luck.'

At the door Millburn's sense of humour returned. 'There's only one way to put things right. Remind me to do it after I've seen Henderson.'

Gabby looked suspicious. 'Put what right?'

Millburn grinned. 'Our situation. Remind me to cut your throat when I get back.' Before the scowling Gabby could find a suitable riposte, the door slammed shut.

Chapter 24

If the huge depression that was causing heavy mist and rain in the British Isles and dense cloud and snow over central Europe was frustrating Staines and Davies, it was ironically giving a reprieve to the two men whose confessions the airmen were fearing, Hausmann and Meyer. For two days soldiers and workers from the assembly plant, struggling to find the radio on the adjacent hill that Lerner felt certain was hidden there, found fresh falls of snow impeding their efforts. With Rosler refusing to allow physical interrogation of the two Bavarians until some evidence of their guilt was forthcoming, Lerner had asked him to provide more workers for the search, only to be told by Rosler that he had no intention of endangering his production schedules on what was looking more and more like a fool's errand.

The outcome was a private meeting between the two men in Rosler's office on the evening of the second day. It was held on Lerner's request and from the onset it was clear from the SS officer's tone that it was to be a meeting with no holds barred. 'Good evening, Herr Commandant. I am relieved that you have agreed to see me at last.'

Cigarette in his mouth, Rosler indicated him to close the door. 'I've been very busy, Major. I'm expecting a new shipment any night now and so I can't hold up my production line. What do you want?'

'You know what I want. The snow is hampering my search. I need more men to help me.'

Rosler sighed. 'I can't give you more men, Major. You've been told the reason half a dozen times. The truth is, if you don't find this radio soon, I shall have to take back the men you've got.'

Lerner's handsome face flushed angrily. 'You can't do that, sir. It's imperative these men are found guilty and punished.'

'What about those Nurnbach witnesses you were so keen on finding? Maybe you should concentrate more on them and forget about this radio.'

'Everything that can be done is being done there. But finding witnesses takes time.'

'Like finding this damned radio,' Rosler said dryly. 'Doesn't it ever occur to you that these men might be telling the truth and you're just wasting your time?'

'I am not wasting my time, sir. These men are agents of the enemy. Everything points to it. What about that enemy aircraft that flew past us yesterday? Do you believe that was just coincidence?'

Rosler saw his cigarette stub was short and lit another from it. 'We often have enemy aircraft fly over us. That's why we're working like hell to build enough of these 262s.'

'But this was a Mosquito. They're often used for reconnaissance and surveillance. And it wasn't overhead. It flew low, right along the railway track.'

'Of course it did. The snow clouds didn't allow it to do anything else.'

Although Lerner was unaware of it, the disgust on his handsome face was growing by the minute. 'I don't understand you, sir. Haven't you thought it might have been a response to a message these spies sent? That it was a preliminary reconnaissance sent out before a bombing raid?'

Rosler exhaled smoke. 'You seem obsessed by the danger of an air raid, Lerner. Don't you think our defences and our camouflage are adequate?'

'I never said that, sir. But camouflage is only a protection if the enemy is unaware of it. If he has been told about it, it becomes false security.'

'So we're back on our radio again. Hasn't it occurred to you that the enemy aircraft might have been making for Rostock?'

'Rostock?'

'Yes, Rostock. At the end of the railway line. The town where Heinkel aircraft are made. A place of great interest to Allied airmen as many of their air raids in the past have shown.'

For a second Lerner was taken aback. Then he shook his head. 'This aircraft flew not a hundred yards past the plant entrance. Surely you can't believe that was coincidence.'

'No, it wasn't coincidence. It was simply a good pilot doing what all good pilots do in atrocious weather. Follow railway lines. This one would take him right to Rostock.' Rosler's lined face mocked the SS officer. 'Now that you're attached to us, Lerner, you really ought to learn more about aircraft and their ways.'

In another dimension Lerner was raining savage blows on the ex-engineer. How dare you mock me, you stupid, ignorant *swinehund!* Somehow he kept his anger from his expression but it was betrayed by his reply. 'Have you thought that I could say the same to you about security? All my experience tells me these two men are guilty of espionage. Yet you refuse to let me interrogate them or take them to Saindau where I know they will confess their guilt.'

Rosler was showing distaste. 'I'm old fashioned enough to believe men are innocent until they're proven guilty. You haven't provided me with an ounce of proof yet.'

Frustration made Lerner go too far. 'Sir, you are harbouring two traitors. Germans who are seeking the downfall of the Third Reich. Don't you realise what could happen to you when I get my evidence and the facts are known?'

Rosler leaned forward across his desk. 'Are you threatening me, Major?'

Lerner took a deep, steadying breath. 'I'm warning you of the danger you are in. Men are being shot in Germany today for discussing even the possibility of defeat, much less for protecting traitors. Yet you not only protect these two men but refuse to take the precaution of strengthening our defences.'

Rosler shook his head. 'Wrong. I have made enquiries and been told that because of the disastrous situation on the Russian front no guns can be provided until I have positive proof our cover has been blown.'

Lerner gave an eager, triumphant laugh. 'Then you were given the answer. You have to let me interrogate these two men and obtain their confession. Then you will get your guns.'

'You mean torture them, don't you?'

Lerner shrugged his well tailored shoulders. 'I said interrogate. You don't need to witness it if you prefer not to.'

Rosler could no longer hide his dislike of the man. 'Has anyone ever told you you're a disgrace to the German Army?'

Lerner's aristocratic face froze in disbelief. 'I beg your pardon?'

'You're not just a disgrace to the Army, you're also disgrace to the German people. You don't give a dam whether these men are guilty or innocent, do you, as lon as I let you get your hands on them.'

Lerner's fury was now on the surface. 'You've no rig to insult me in this way. I demand an apology.'

Rosler gave a grunt of disgust. 'You go on demandi it. While I'm the commandant of this plant, we rema civilised people. If you can prove these men guilty I have no option but to let you take them to Saindau, although I won't like it. But until you do, they stay under my protection. Is that clear?'

Lerner was still quivering with rage. 'You do realise what will happen to you when it is known you have protected enemy agents?'

Rosler sighed. 'Yes, yes. I know. The same as has happened to all men of conscience in your new Germany. You'll shoot or hang me. Until then don't waste any more of my time. While you're trying to destroy two Germans, I'm trying to build aircraft to protect eighty million Germans. Get out and ask yourself which one of us it the most useful.'

Giving Rosler a look of pure venom, Lerner drew to his full height, clicked his heels and then marched stiffly from the office. Grinning wryly, coughing, lighting yet another cigarette, Rosler picked up his telephone and spoke to his chief engineer. 'That you, Driest? I've had word another shipment is on its way. Depending on weather and air raids, it could be here tomorrow night. So be ready for it. Yes, that's all.'

There was a sulphurous smell in the Operations Room that afternoon when the crews began filing in. The stoves had been lit only an hour before and as always were giving off invisible fumes before the coke was fully alight. Men oughed, cursed, and fouled the acrid air even more by lighting cigarettes.

As more aircrews filed in and the benches began to ll, the buzz of speculation grew louder. With clouds ill down almost to treetop level, men had been puzzled nough when they had received orders to stay within call f the station. To hear then of the arrival of Davies and e told over the Tannoy that all aircrews had to muster the Operations Room at 15.00 hours, men had to turn the Station's old sweats to make sense of it all.

In the mordant way of servicemen, the old sweats were only too happy to oblige. If an operation was forthcoming, it could only be one of Davies' 'specials'. In other words a mission so urgent that the normal rules that kept aircraft safely on the ground would be ignored.

As a consequence there was some apprehensive mutterings mixed in with the general speculation. Recent recruits or transfers found their mouths' dry and their hearts beating faster. Some tried to keep their minds occupied by reading the battle slogans on the walls, giving such admonitions as: 'Always watch the Hun in the Sun', 'Remember your Cockpit Drill', 'It's the One you don't see who gets You.' Others lifted their eyes to the ceiling where dangling scale models of enemy and Allied aircraft swung gently in the rising cigarette smoke and tried to remember their recognition lessons. But none could keep his eyes for long off the illuminated map of Europe positioned at the back of the platform which the crews were facing.

It came as a relief even to the old sweats when the Station Warrant Officer, known by one and all as Ber the Bastard, strode into the room. Rumour had it tha this SWO's stentorian yell had once brought a dozen stunned blackbirds tumbling from a tree and the thud o his boots and his bellow sent the dangling model aircraf into combat. '*Attention*!'

There was a loud rumble of benches as the assemble crews jumped to their feet. A moment later Davies an Henderson appeared, followed by Millburn, Adams, an a dozen of the Station's specialist officers. Ignoring th steps at the side of the low platform, Davies jumpe on to it like a man half his age. Millburn followe him without effort but after a moment's hesitatio only one of his specialist officers followed, the res including Henderson and Adams, taking the safer rout Some joker among the audience gave an amused bo

It was followed by a nervous titter that ran through the assembly.

Furious with Davies for his gymnastics, Henderson glared at the rows of men. 'Be quiet. All of you. Air Commodore Davies is here to talk to you about an important operation he wants carried out. So sit down and listen carefully.' He glanced at Davies who was chatting to Millburn. 'They're all yours, sir.'

There was another rumble as the men returned to their benches. Then a silence that was almost palpable fell as Davies walked to the front of the platform. A consummate actor on such occasions, Davies believed his first task was to relax his young crews. Accordingly he gave them a grin. 'Don't look so worried. The job I've got for you is a piece of cake. In fact it's the very thing this squadron is trained and famous for.'

In the tense silence Machin's low whisper could be heard right across the room. 'Oi don't like the sound of that. Oi don't like that at all.'

Davies knew he could always rely on the Irishman. Did you say something, Machin?'

'Me, sur? No, I just coughed, that was all. It's these stoves, sur. They're awful smelly things.'

'That's odd. I thought you said you didn't like something.'

'I did, sur. I was talkin' about the stoves.'

'You should complain about them, Machin.'

'Oi will, sur. Oi will. Thank you, sur.'

Davies could feel the tension easing as muted laughter pread round the room. Satisfied, he glanced back at the lled benches. 'I was saying before Flight Lieutenant lachin coughed that the job in hand is one this squadron famous for. But before I go into details, tell me how any of you have heard about the new fighter Jerry has ought into service, the Messerchhmidtt 262.'

Nearly every hand in the room was raised. In the

professional world of the Royal Air Force, details and merits of new aircraft, whether products of friend or foe, were as eagerly discussed as the charms of the prettiest Waaf on the Station.

Davies nodded at the response. 'So, even if none of you has run into it yet, I can take it you know it is an entirely revolutionary aircraft. Until now you've been fortunate to fly one of the fastest and certainly the most versatile aircraft of the war. But now we have to accept that Jerry has one that is at least 150mph faster.' As some one gave a low whistle, Davies nodded again. 'Yes. 150mph. You can see from that how the Yanks are suffering. So far our heavies haven't run into them, perhaps because Jerry hasn't found a way yet of flying such a fast aircraft a night. But the Yanks are running into them almost daily and because their fighter escorts are outmatched, they'r losing B17s at an unacceptable rate.'

Low whispers could be heard in the attentive silenc that followed. Seeing from the expression on the youn faces that he had their full attention, Davies walked bac to the map of Europe and picked up a pointer. 'Ou Intelligence boys had some trouble locating the plan because Jerry has become an expert in camouflage bu a breakthrough was made a couple of days ago.' Davie lifted the pointer and laid it on the map. 'The plant i here, just off the railway line that runs to Rostock, whic is about seventy miles away.'

Muted gasps sounded here and there and Davies kne why. Rostock was almost as far away as Berlin, an although long range Mosquitoes had been doing th 'milk run' to that city for many months now, the raids were carried out at night and at high level. T fly so far in daylight at low level would require th highest degree of skill and concentration, and althou so far Davies had made no mention of a low level attac the present weather and his comment that the raid was be the kind the squadron famous for left little to the imagination. Seeing the dismay on some of the younger faces, Davies made light of the moment. 'Don't look so worried. You're not going out until the clouds lift to at least a thousand feet. Then by flying at low level you'll get double protection. Jerry's radar won't be able to pick you up and neither will his fighters. As I told you earlier, a piece of cake.'

A couple of low, sarcastic laughs sounded, which Davies ignored. 'In many ways you're lucky with your target. It's not situated in the middle of a town full of flak posts. It's on its own right out in the country. It's true it's well camouflaged but this can be to your advantage because Jerry might feel he doesn't need heavy defences. In which case it could turn out one of the easiest targets I've ever given you.'

Although it was clear that no one believed Davies' last sentence, there was a certain relaxing of tension in he room. A hand was raised from the front bench. 'What s this camouflage, sir?'

The questioner was a freckle-faced, fair-headed pilot. A South African, Von Breedenkamp was one of 633 Squadron's longer serving survivors and the commander f B Flight. Nodding at the question, Davies motioned o the rear of the platform and a moment later a sergeant came into sight carrying an easel and a blackboard. Moving to the blackboard which held a sketch of the plant and its surrounding features, Davies laid a finger n the camouflaged target. When he finished his explanation, murmurs of astonishment were running round the sembly. Davies grinned. 'Clever, isn't it? Made to look ke a saddle between two hills.'

Another hand rose. 'But how will we find it, sir?'

'We've already found it, lad. And we've got photoaphs and co-ordinates. Mr Adams will show you all e photographs and the navigation officer will see that all navigators are given the co-ordinates, although, as I expect you will be going out in line astern, your navigation problems shouldn't be too exacting. But all navigators must keep a separate log in case any of you are dispersed and have to find your own way home.'

'Who is our Squadron Commander, sir?' Van Breedenkamp asked.

Davies glanced at the back of the platform where Millburn was sitting with Adams and the other specialist officers. 'Squadron Leader Millburn will be your commander. Have you any more questions before I pass you over to him for your battle orders and tactics?'

Adams, always a fascinated observer at briefings, was watching the reaction of the crews on hearing of their new leader. Although Millburn had acted the role in France the actions there had only called for a few aircraft at a time. To lead the entire squadron on one of its major spectacular missions was a responsibility the American had never carried before.

Watching the young faces, Adams detected unease here and there, for the American had a reputation for taking chances that more cautious men avoided. Nevertheless Millburn was universally popular and his skill and courage admired by all. So by and large, Adams decided, the reaction was favourable.

Davies was turning and about to wave the American forward when a voice sounded at the rear of the assembly. 'May I ask a question, sir?'

Davies eyed the speaker warily. Wilkinson, a navigator was a bright young man who had foregone his scholarship to Oxford to join the RAF. As a result Wilkinson's questions tended to have a wider orbit than some of his colleagues. Davies hesitated, then gave a grudging nod. 'Yes. Go on.'

Wilkinson stood up. 'I've been under the impression that our raids have forced Jerry to disperse his factor and build his aircraft all over Europe, sir. Then how does it happen there's a single main plant for such an exceptional aircraft as the 262?'

Davies was secretly punishing himself for being so generous with the navigator. With the end of the European war in sight, British politicians, knowing they would soon need all the foreign trade they could get to repair their economy, were anxious the general public should not be prejudiced against Sweden. As a consequence Davies was under strict orders not to mention the Scandinavian connection.

Nevertheless his sharp brain was equal to it. 'That's because it is exceptional, Wilkinson. I understand Jerry has only a few engineers qualified to work on it and so he has little option but to keep them all together. Thank God he does because it gives us a chance to end the threat in one go. All right?'

For a moment it seemed Wilkinson was going to question his answer. Then, to Davies' relief, he nodded and sat down. 'Thank you, sir.'

Waiting for no more awkward questions, Davies motioned Millburn forward. 'Take it over, Squadron Commander.'

Millburn moved forward and took his place. 'OK, boys. This is the drill. We'll be carrying 250 GPs, 25lb incendiaries, and wing rockets. The 250 GPs will be fused with ten second delays. I can't tell you yet how many 250s because that will depend on the fuel we'll need. That's something our specialist officers will work out. But I can tell you we'll be carrying full tanks of ammunition just in case any of those 262s show up.'

The ammunition Millburn was referring to was 20mm cannon shells. Because of the many tasks 633 Squadron was called upon in its special service role, the makers, de Havilland, had fitted the squadron's Mosquitoes with two short barrelled cannon as well as two Brownings, which still allowed their bomb bays to carry almost a full quota of bombs. The only Mosquitoes in service that had this adaptation, it meant that once 663's crews had released their bombs, they had an aircraft that was a match for any fighter the enemy could put into the sky. At least they had been until the advent of this new 262, Adams was thinking. Millburn's voice drew back his attention.

'Our first leg is to an old German airfield near Voziers in France, where we'll refuel and take on drop tanks. We'll go there in two sections. I'll lead Red Section and Van Breedenkamp will lead Blue Section. For once we won't need to worry about Jerry's flak ships and coastal defences. The Army and Navy have seen to that, so we shall fly straight there. Although Jerry's monitors are still working, we shan't need to fly there at low level because at that point they won't know where we're heading. It's only after we leave Voziers that we'll stay right down to the deck.'

A hand rose. 'Excuse me, skipper, but aren't we getting an escort?'

'You are, Atkinson, and a good one at that. Remember the guys who escorted us to Copenhagen when we dropped pisspots on that Jerry band?' As comments and laugh ran round the room, Millburn grinned. 'Yeah, we've go the same guys. Major Dent's Mustangs. They're going t give us top cover.'

There had been a time when RAF crews would hav groaned to hear their escort would not be a British b after the wholehearted support given them by America on earlier missions, they were showing nothing but reli they were not flying the dangerous mission alone.

Half a dozen hands rose after Millburn's announceme however. The American pointed at Van Breedenkamp the front bench. 'Yes, Van?'

'I'm puzzled about the escort, skipper. If the Yar are giving us top cover, won't Jerry's monitors pick th up? And in that case, what's the point of our keeping on the deck?'

Millburn nodded. 'That was a problem but we think we've cracked it. Dent is flying a dog leg from Voziers so Jerry will think he's making for a target further south. Instead he'll swing north at Wolfsburg and rendezvous with us over the target. It'll take good timing but support fighters like Dent's outfit are used to that kind of thing.'

As whispered comments broke out, Millburn motioned for silence. 'You'll get our route from the navigation officer later but I can tell you now it'll avoid all heavily defended centres like Kassel and Hannover. Your major problem will be to avoid high buildings and power cables. Unless Jerry's Observer Corps is right on the ball we ought to escape all heavy flak but watch out for LMGs. Don't, repeat don't, use your radio to tip off the guys behind you. The key to this operation is surprise, so radio silence will be kept all the way to the target. Major signals will be given by flares. OK so far?'

When no one spoke, Millburn went on: 'Our first job to find the rail track from Berlin to Rostock. We'll then ving north and follow it to the target. We're hoping to entify the target on our first run but if we miss it, I'll t you know and we'll circle back. That could be tricky space yourself well out to avoid collisions.'

A hand rose. 'What about those bombs, skipper? Won't ose time delays be dangerous?'

Millburn grinned. His relaxed answer, which brought disapproving frown from Davies, made Adams smile, it was not unknown for the Air Commodore to use ity language himself at times. 'You mean they could w up under our own arses? Yeah, they could so 'll orbit just under the cloud base and each crew l make his attack only after the previous bomb has ploded.'

What do we do if we run into these 262s, skipper?'

It was Atkinson again. 'Won't they be keeping a close watch on their own factory?'

The sudden silence that fell told the watching Adams the thought was in everyone's minds. Knowing the answer could save lives, he listened in fascination to Millburn's reply. 'What do you do when a 190 drops on your tail at an angle, Atkinson?'

'I turn into him, skipper. I increase his curve of pursuit.'

'That's right. It forces him to turn even more steeply to follow you and if you're lucky he blacks out. That's what you do with these 262s. Turn inside them and because of their higher speed they'll either overshoot you or find the g force too much for them.'

There was a malicious chuckle from Machin. 'You're doin' a foine job, skipper. In a minute you'll have me believin' I'm lucky not to be flyin' one of those nasty German thingummybobs.'

Millburn grinned back. 'You are, Paddy. Those Heinie are all crying in their beer at their tough luck.' He turne back to the laughing crews. 'That's all you need take i at the moment. You'll see the target photographs an get more detailed gen from the specialist officers in moment.'

With that, glancing at Davies, Millburn walked bac and sat down alongside Adams. Unsure whether not Davies approved of the American's informalit Henderson tried to read his expression but failed. H tone when he took Millburn's place on the platfor unconsciously betrayed his distaste of the operation. 'T code-name for the operation is Defiant. Your call sign w be Foxhound and the Station's William Tell. Major Den will be Hawkeye. After lunch I want you to air test yo aircraft. Then you go on stand-by until the weather m give us the green light. As we don't know when that w be, you'll stay on the Station until further orders.'

As groans sounded and a hand shot up, the Scot anticipated the forthcoming question. 'I know, Machin. You're worried about the beer. I'm worried about it too. I don't want half of you pie-eyed when the green light comes on. So you'll only get four bottles apiece today. Have them this evening and then get to bed early in case the weather relents tomorrow. If it doesn't we'll go through the same drill the next day. Now you can come up and talk to your specialist officers.'

As benches rumbled and men came forward, Adams was having the thoughts he always had before a major operation: that the informality of the briefing, a hallmark of 633 Squadron, gave an unreality to the occasion. The truth behind the humour and banter was pitiless: in a day or two some or even many of those young vital men approaching the platform would be gone for ever.

He did not have long to ponder on the morbid thought. A minute later men were crowding around him and like the rest of his colleagues Adams was too busy handing out photographs and information to remember what the bitter fruits of his labours might be.

Chapter 25

While 633 Squadron's aircrew were being briefed, a grim scene was being enacted a few hundred miles away. At the very moment that Davies did his gymnastic act and leapt on the platform, Lerner was entering the room where Hausmann and Meyer were prisoners. As the soldie guarding them snapped to attention, a second armec guard followed Lerner and stood behind him. The S officer's cold eyes settled on Hausmann and Meyer who half frozen with cold, were finding it difficult to move.

'Get up, you scum. At once.'

Neither man needed telling the news was bad. Lerner' voice and the look of triumph in his cold eyes said it al 'So you are both innocent railway engineers. Just a littl curious about this factory. Do you both still stick to th lie or has the last two days brought you to your senses

Somehow Hausmann found his voice. 'We are railwa engineers, Major. Just as we have told you.'

Lerner's laugh brought goosepimples to the old Bavarian. 'As I said before, Herr Overbeck, you wou have been a better actor than a spy. But now your da of acting are over. Look what we have found.'

Turning, Lerner said something to one of the guar A moment later the man walked forward and laid a to box on the bare floor before the two men. Feeling Mey start, Hausmann gripped his arm but not before Lerner h noticed the younger man's dismay. 'I see you recognise Herr Muller.'

Recovering quickly, Meyer shook his head. 'I've never seen it before. What is it? A tool box?'

Lerner smiled. 'Very perceptive, Herr Muller.' He turned to Hausmann. 'And you, Herr Overbeck? Is it a surprise to you too?'

It was all too obvious now that Lerner was enjoying his cat and mouse game. Although certain now that all hope had gone, a dogged streak in Hausmann decided to play it to the end. 'I don't know what you mean, a surprise. Why should a tool box be a surprise? But I haven't seen it before, if that's what you mean.'

'You have no idea what's inside it?'

'No, why should I have? Tools, I suppose.'

'Just tools, Herr Overbeck? Nothing more?'

Hausmann was wondering how his voice could be so steady when his heart was thumping so hard. 'What else would be in a tool box?'

'If you will be patient a moment, Herr Overbeck, I will show you.' Bending down, Lerner opened the box, lifted out the tool tray, and exposed the miniature radio beneath it. His handsome, quizzical face lifted to the two men. 'Now isn't that clever? A radio to give away our secrets to the enemy. Found hidden on the hillside where you were found two days ago.' Suddenly there was menace in the mocking voice. 'And yet you both tell me you have never seen it before.'

As both men shook their heads, Lerner straightened and turned to one of the sentries. 'Give me your rifle.'

The soldier hesitated, then handed it to the SS officer. Lerner turned to the two Bavarians. 'Come forward, both of you.'

Fear was flooding through Hausmann now and from Meyer's pallor he knew the younger man was equally afraid. As they moved forward, unsteady from cold and fear, Lerner balanced the rifle in his hands. 'Which of you was the radio operator?'

Hausmann's voice was little more than a hoarse whisper. 'Neither of us. We don't know what you're talking about.'

A moment later he felt his cheek had been crushed in as Lerner swung up the butt of the rifle. As the Bavarian reeled against the wall and clung to it to support himself, he heard Lerner's voice through sickening waves of pain. 'Don't you mock me, you filthy traitor, or the next time I'll smash your head in.'

As Hausmann's tongue felt blood and broken teeth, he saw Lerner turn to Meyer. 'Your turn, Herr Muller. Never mind who was the radio operator. What was the message you sent about this plant?'

Meyer's courage proved equal to the test. 'Neither of us sent anything, Major. We were just curious about the airplane and the building. That was all.'

Lightning fast, Lerner drove the butt of the rifle into Meyer's unprotected stomach. With a strangled gasp, Meyer doubled up and fell to the floor, retching and fighting for breath.

Breathing hard, Lerner stood back and eyed the two stricken men. 'If you were not Germans, that radio would be enough to have you executed on the spot. But you are Germans, which means you have committed the filthy crime of being traitors to the Fatherland. You have sent our enemies the site of this plant, something I always believed. I am also certain now that you are the men who killed the two Gestapo agents in Nurnbach. So there will be no more nonsense about keeping you here until you are proven guilty. In a few hours I shall take you to Saindau and if you do not believe in hell at the moment, you will believe it once you pass through Saindau's gates.'

When neither prisoner tried to speak, Lerner turned to the two white-faced young soldiers. 'Keep an eye on them for the rest of the day. Remember my warning about them trying to commit suicide. They have more reason to try now, so don't let them out of your sight for a minute. If you do and I lose them, I shall have you shot.'

With that he left the room. Although his head was still swimming and blood was trickling from his mouth, Hausmann managed to cross the floor to Meyer. 'How are you feeling?'

With the older man's help Meyer sat painfully upright. 'I think I'm all right. I don't think I've any broken ribs.' His whisper rasped in Hausmann's ear. 'When is that damned raid coming? If they don't send it soon that bastard will get the place surrounded by guns. And I'd rather die here than in Saindau.'

Hausmann gave a warning glance at the one armed guard who had stayed behind in the room and was eyeing them with some sympathy. 'So would I,' he whispered. 'So I'm keeping my fingers crossed and saying a prayer or two in the bargain.'

Meyer managed his old sardonic smile. 'I never knew you were the praying kind.'

Hausmann tried to grin but found it too painful. 'I'm not but a gambler like you ought to know that a smart man always hedges his bets.'

Adams heard the tap on the Confessional door as he was locking one of his two safes. 'Frank! Can I see you for a minute.'

Recognising Millburn's voice, Adams called back. 'Come in, Tommy. The door's not locked.'

Millburn, wearing a rain-stained mackintosh, appeared a moment later. He glanced down the Nissen hut before turning to Adams. 'Sue's not here?'

'No. She's had a long day. I let her go half an hour ago.'

Millburn nodded, then grimaced as he took off his cap and shook the rain from it. 'Did somebody say we were flying tomorrow?'

Adams nodded. 'It doesn't seem likely, does it? Although the Met. people think things will improve in the next twenty-four hours.'

'That'll still be too late for a morning take-off. We can't leave it any later or the light'll be going when we get there. It's going to be tough enough to pick out those rail sidings even in broad daylight.'

Adams knew it was true. 'I agree. Gabby will have to be right on his toes.'

'Don't I know it? That's why I've come to ask you a favour, Frank. Do you mind if I borrow the photographs of those rail sidings for the night?'

Adams hesitated. 'I'm supposed to keep them all under lock and key, Tommy. That was Davies' last order to me. He's afraid someone might lose or misplace one and cause a security leak. He's taking it so seriously he told me to post a guard outside tonight. I'm only allowed to give them back to navigators just before take-off.'

'Yeah, I know that. I've never known him keep his cards so close to his chest. But, as you say, it's going to be all too easy to louse up this job. So it would help if Gabby and I could have a longer look at them. We wouldn't leave them for a second. They'd stay with us in the billet all night and I'd return them to you first thing in the morning. Cross my heart.'

With Millburn one of the most confident pilots on the squadron, Adams was finding it unusual for him to make such a request. It was his suspicion that the likeable American was feeling the heavy responsibility of his promotion that swung the scales in Millburn's favour. Returning to his safe, Adams pulled out a file of prints. 'I've a set of these for every navigator,' he told Millburn. 'You can take this set if you want but I must have it back in the morning.'

'You will,' Millburn promised.

As he was about to pass over the file, Adams paused

'Hang on.' Searching around the Confession, he spotted a canvas bag. Slipping the file into the bag and zipping it up, he handed it to the American. 'That won't look conspicuous if one of the guards sees you leaving here.'

Millburn's good looking face expressed his appreciation. 'You're a good guy, Frank. We'll look after them.' Then his grin returned. 'If Davies finds out, we'll say we cracked open the safe and stole 'em.'

Adams laughed. 'I don't think he'd believe that, do you?'

'Sure he would. He'd believe anything about Americans. And what about Gabby? You couldn't blame him if he believed that shifty little guy used to be a cracksman, could you?'

Smiling, Adams continued to keep the tone light. 'It's a good job Gabby didn't hear that. Or he'd make sure you never find that plant.'

Millburn grinned. 'Yeah, that's true. I'd better butter up the little fart until the job's done.' As Adams turned to lock up the safe again, Millburn's tone changed. 'What are your private views on this job, Frank?'

Adams turned back. For some time, without knowing why, he'd had the feeling the American had other reasons for the visit than just the photographs. Wondering if this was it, Adams had to think for a moment. 'Like Jock Henderson, I don't like it. That long flight at low level will be a hell of a strain. On the other hand, if the plant is destroyed, who knows how many American lives it might save?'

Millburn lit a cigarette. 'Yeah, that's the part I like. From all I've heard our guys have been taking a hell of pasting from these 262s.'

Adams, used to seeing Millburn in RAF uniform, gave start at this reminder of his American nationality. 'I hadn't thought of that. Of course. You couldn't have had more satisfying operation.'

Millburn exhaled smoke. 'Yeah. That part's OK. But I don't like the rest of it.'

'The rest of it?' Adams asked.

'Yeah. Harvey came to see me after the briefing and told me the things Davies has kept quiet about and why he's in such a godammed hurry to get us off the ground. Harvey says you know all about it.'

Adams probed carefully. 'Know about what?'

'These two German guys who located the plant before they were captured. It seems Anna is worrying herself silly about what the Nazis will do to them.'

Adams tried to be non-committal. 'What did Harvey want?'

'After we prang the plant, he wants me and a few other guys to fly on and bomb this concentration camp. Saindau. He said he'd asked Davies to let him go himsel but Davies wouldn't hear of it.'

Giving up all pretence of ignorance, Adams showe astonishment. 'Harvey tried to go himself?'

'Yeah, but Davies said he was crazy even to think o it. So Frank tried to persuade me to take a few Mossie there after we've pranged the plant. He says it's only few miles away.'

Adams was finding it hard to believe what he wa hearing. 'What did you say?'

'What could I say? When he told me what those S bastards will do to those poor sods. I guess I wanted go. But how can I go when I'm the guy in charge of th mission?'

There was little wonder that Millburn was finding h responsibility a heavy burden, Adams thought. 'Have y told anyone else?'

Millburn showed some embarrassment. 'I guess t thing affected me so much I did mention it to Gab and a few others.'

'Who?'

'A few of the old gang who Gabby brought round to the billet for a poker game. Machin, Larkin and Van Breedenkamp. They're OK. They won't talk.'

'Do you know if Frank asked Davies to send the entire squadron?' Adams asked.

'No,. Just volunteers, but Davies wouldn't hear of it. Apparently they had a hell of a quarrel because Davies said it was pointless asking for authorisation.'

Adams nodded. 'It would be pointless. Concentration camps have never come into the bombing syllabus. I've often wondered why.'

Millburn exhaled smoke again. 'Yeah. From what Harvey told me we ought to have been bombing 'em from the word go. Why the hell haven't we?' The American paused, then he looked straight into Adams' troubled face. 'You're a guy with feelings, Frank. Everyone knows that. So tell me what you'd do in my shoes. Give it to me straight.'

Adams took a deep breath. 'I'd feel like you do because know the hell those men will suffer in Saindau. But I wouldn't go against orders in case my crews suffered for it.'

'You're sure of that? Dead to rights sure?'

Adams' eyes did not drop. 'Yes. Completely sure. Your first duty is to your men.'

Millburn stared at him for a long moment. Then Adams sensed the tension in him suddenly slacken. 'You've helped me, Frank. More than you know. I'm grateful.'

Adams cleared his throat. 'It sometimes helps to talk, doesn't it?'

'Yeah. It has tonight.' Before Adams could think of anything else to say, Millburn changed the subject. How's Helga getting on? Is she OK in the pub?'

Relieved to be on less emotional ground, Adams smiled. 'Yes, she loves it there.'

'You're a lucky guy to have her so close.'

'I know I am. By the way, I was sorry you had to be

called back from leave. That was rotten luck. How did your friend take it?'

'Carol? She was disappointed but took it well. I can't say I did. I called hell out of Davies all the way back to base.'

'I don't blame you. So would I.'

'Yeah, I hadn't expected a recall, particularly in this weather.' At that moment Millburn gave a start and began fumbling in his pocket. 'That reminds me, Frank. Do me a favour. See Carol gets this just in case Gabby gets us lost over there, will you?'

Adams found himself staring at an envelope with the girl's name and address written on it. 'Yes, of course.' His eyes lifted to the American. 'But Gabby's not likely to get you lost, is he?'

'Gabby? Oh, Christ no. He's a little fart but he's a good navigator.' As Adams slipped the envelope into his inside pocket, Millburn grinned as if a sudden thought was amusing him. 'Tell me something, Frank. If Helga was here and another Thor operation came up, would you volunteer like you did the last time?'

Puzzled by the question, Adams gave it a few seconds of thought, then shook his head. 'I don't think I would. No, I'm pretty sure I wouldn't. But why do you ask?'

For a man who was an extrovert, Millburn's laugh sounded almost embarrassed. 'I haven't a goddamned clue. It was just one of those crazy thoughts a man gets.' Then, before Adams could question him further, he turned and picked up the canvas bag. 'Frank, I'm keeping you from going over to Helga. Thanks for the photographs. I'll see you get them back in the morning.'

With that he picked up his cap and left the Confessional. Frowning, Adams stood listening until his footsteps died away before turning back to lock his two safes.

* * *

Helga shook her blonde head. 'You're too sensitive, *kjaere*. He was talking about you, not himself.'

Adams shook his head. 'I don't think so. I'd the feeling his entire conversation was leading up to it. It's something he's never experienced before and he needed to talk about it.'

The two of them were seated at a table in the Black Swan that same evening. Although the Station communications were cut and all personnel kept inside on standby, Adams' living out quarters were considered close enough to the airfield to warrant a dispensation. In other circumstances, because Adams was Adams, he would have refused the privilege, but his conversation with Millburn had triggered off all kinds of speculation in his sensitive mind and he had felt a strong need to discuss them with Helga. If Adams needed an excuse for his apostasy, the girl's sacrifices in Norway for the Allied cause had provided it.

In their room he had given her full details of the forthcoming operation and the reason for its urgency. At the same time, because Adams was often ashamed of his sensitivity, he had not mentioned the very thing that had induced him to break security, his conversation with Millburn. Now, seated with her at a table in the bar downstairs with two beers inside him, Adams was finding the walls of his reticence were crumbling.

With its usual RAF clientele absent, the inn was quiet although there were a few locals enjoying a drink at the bar. Judging them out of earshot, Adams felt it safe to talk.

'It wasn't a bit like Millburn. He's always been the happy go lucky type. I'm not saying he hasn't felt fear before – he's too intelligent for that – but he's always hidden it by making fun of every tight squeeze he's been in. But tonight it was a different Millburn.'

'Of course it was, *kjaere*. He has been given responsibility. That changes us all.'

'I know that,' Adams said. 'But there was something else too.'

'Of course there was. There was this horrible thing about the two Germans. That was enough to make any man question his orders. But, as you said, there is nothing he can do.'

Adams nodded. 'It helped him to be told that. He needed a second opinion. But it was the things he didn't say that are concerning me?'

Her blue eyes were travelling over his face. 'What things?'

After mentioning Millburn's letter, Adams told her about the American's question made just before he left the Confessional. 'It seemed such an odd thing to ask.'

Her hand moved across the table and rested on top of his own. 'Is that true, *kjaere*? Wouldn't you volunteer a second time?'

Adams shook his head. 'No. I suppose I was hurt by Valerie and wanted to take a slap at the world. You inferred something like that to me in Norway. But I wouldn't be such a fool again.'

Her hand tightened on his. 'Tell me why.'

Adams gave her a humorous scowl. 'You know why.

Her voice was full of innocence. 'But I don't, *kjaere* Please tell me.'

Adams' scowl deepened. 'It's because I hate you that's why. Now are you satisfied?'

She simulated shock. Then her attractive laugh ran out and made two elderly men at the bar glance round At the same moment Maisie, a buxom figure in sweate and skirt, shouted from the counter to ask if the coup wanted another drink. Helga shook her head but Adan acknowledged her invitation. 'I'll have another pint in few minutes, Maisie. But don't come over. I'll fetch it myself when I'm ready.'

When he turned back to Helga, she was smiling. 'My poor Englishman. I do tease you, don't I?'

'You do,' Adams muttered. 'I ought to put you over my knee and spank you.'

Her eyes rounded. 'Really. Is that a promise?' Then her expression and her mood changed. 'I'm sorry, my love. I shouldn't be teasing you at a time like this. You are worried about the American. You think he has fallen in love for the first time in his life. Isn't that true?'

'Yes, I think he has. Until now his affairs have meant nothing to him. But this seems to be the real thing.'

'And so you are worried it will affect his flying? Perhaps even his leadership?'

Adams showed surprise at her perception. 'I don't know about his leadership. But it must affect him in one way or another. Before this he would plunge into danger with hardly a second thought. Now he might first think about the girl and the future. I think that's what his question meant.' Adams gave an apologetic grin. 'When you love someone you've gained a hostage to fate. Wasn't that said by somebody once?'

'But won't it be a good thing if he is more cautious?'

Adams shook his head. 'It doesn't always work that way. In flying it's sometimes the reckless pilot who gets away with it. The cautious ones are sometimes the first to go. And as he's the squadron commander, that could affect the other crews and the entire operation.'

A shiver ran through the girl, reminding Adams how quickly her moods could change. 'You mustn't think that way. Or you could cause it to happen.'

Unseen by the girl, Adams winced. With a tendency towards superstition as sensitive people are prone to be, he wished Helga had not said that. Telling himself he was a fool who made war an even worse ordeal by exaggerating the problems of others, Adams rose to get himself another beer.

Chapter 26

Hausmann had never known fear like this in his life. His stomach was knotted into a rigid ball, his heart was leaping about in his chest as if about to burst, sweat was pouring from him, and he felt he would urinate at any moment.

For a while the screaming from the adjacent cell ceased, making Hausmann lift his head. Perhaps Meyer had died. Lying on the icy brick floor where Lerner and his guards had thrown him, Hausmann prayed that he had. Let his agony be over, dear Jesus. Let him have escaped from this world of devils and fiends from hell.

But the screaming began again a minute later. Astonishingly it rose a full octave higher than before, making Hausmann wonder how human vocal cords and arteries could sustain such agony. As he clapped his hands to his ears, bitterness thrust his faith aside. What divine power could allow its creations to suffer like this? Where is the mercy we are promised? If it is true that man is born in the image of God, then what is God if he resembles man in all his acts of wickedness?

The screaming ceased again but this time the silence was more menacing than the cries themselves. Listening, Hausmann heard a dragging sound outside and a moment later the cell door was thrown open. Believing his own time had come, Hausmann lifted his head and saw the unconscious figure of Meyer being thrown into the cell.

Lerner, flanked by two burly uniformed men, was

standing in the doorway. His cultured voice added to Hausmann's nightmare. 'I hope you have enjoyed the last half hour, Herr Overbeck. I did think of letting you see the entertainment but that might have prepared you for it. Better that it is left to your imagination, I think.'

Glancing at the unconscious, quivering Meyer, his prison garb bloodstained and one of his hands lacerated and bleeding, Hausmann felt a massive surge of hatred. His mind screamed at Lerner. You sadistic devil. Where do they find creatures like you? Do they drag the sewers or the cesspits? Do they breed you in some devil's brothel? Hausmann wanted to shout his loathing to the very stars but found his throat was too strangled by fear.

Instead he heard Lerner's voice again. 'You look frightened, Herr Overbeck. I'm not surprised. You have a great deal to be frightened about. Your fellow spy has found that out already.'

Somehow Hausmann found his voice. 'Get it over, for God's sake.'

Lerner glanced at one of his accomplices, who grinned 'All in good time, Herr Overbeck. We like our guests to have time to ponder on their treachery.'

Hausmann climbed painfully to his feet. 'What's the point of all this? Why don't you kill us and have done with it?'

Lerner lifted an eyebrow. 'Kill you? We're not going to kill you, Herr Overbeck. We shall not even permanently cripple you yet, although from the pain you suffer you will find that hard to believe. After this first lesson we shall release you among your fellow traitors. Among them you will wait for your second lesson which might come at any time. That one might cripple you. It will certainly be more painful than the first. By the time we do kill you, you will be quite sure it does not pay to be a traitor.'

Hausmann shook his head to clear it. 'You're insane

People like you are turning Germany into a sadistic madhouse.'

Lerner smiled. 'No, Herr Overbeck, I am not insane. I am a patriot who knows that fear is the only certain way to keep men obedient to their orders and to their Fuhrer. Even if I were to release you today, I doubt you would betray the Fatherland again.'

A treacherous cell in Hausmann's mind was wondering if it were true, if he would risk facing this hell again. 'If you are so sure, then why do you keep all these men here?'

Lerner smiled again. 'The answer to that is very simple, Herr Overbeck. I don't think that traitors of the Fatherland deserve a second chance. They betray our soldiers who are fighting so heroically to hold back the Bolsheviks and they betray our womenfolk who are facing the terror flyers so bravely. That is why I am going to make you and your friend wish to God you had not sold your soul to the enemy for a few pieces of silver.'

Nodding at his accomplices, he withdrew, followed a few seconds later by the two men. As a key turned in the lock, Hausmann crossed the bare cell and knelt over Meyer who was doubled up like a foetus. As Hausmann gently lifted his sweat-soaked head, Meyer's eyes opened. For a moment there was raw terror in them. Then he recognised Hausmann and tried to speak.

'It's all right,' Hausmann said gently. 'They've gone.'

Meyer's body was still quivering, reminding Hausmann of a deer he had once found after the animal had been truck by a car. 'Are you in pain?' Hausmann asked.

Meyer tried to speak but failed. Thinking his ashen face ooked ten years older than before his ordeal, Hausmann ut his ear to the man's lips. This time he heard a hoarse hisper. 'What do you think?'

Hausmann's swollen face managed a grin. 'It was a upid question, wasn't it? What did they do to you?'

He regretted the question a moment as Meyer's body spasmed in memory. As Hausmann gazed down at him, the younger man rallied and shook his head. Puzzled, Hausmann bent over him again. 'What did you say?'

Meyer's cracked lips struggled for words. It was long seconds before Hausmann caught his hoarse whisper. 'Better . . . you don't . . . know.'

A fresh wave of fear swept over Hausmann. He tried to hide it from the stricken Meyer. 'Did you hear what Lerner said? Tomorrow we'll be joining the other inmates. It might not be so bad then.'

Meyer was trying to straighten his abused body. As he gasped with the effort, Hausmann helped him to sit upright. 'Did you tell them about our broadcast message?'

Meyer's breathing was coming easier now although he was clearly in a great deal of pain. 'They never asked. They know we must have sent it.'

So it was the infliction of pain for its own sake, Hausmann thought. His hatred of Lerner grew. Meyer's shaking hand touched his arm. 'Do you think Lerner will go back to the plant?'

Hausmann shook his head. 'I don't know. Didn't he say anything to you?'

'No. But I suppose he might.' Meyer's cracked whisper was a prayer from the soul. 'Oh, God, let him be there when the Allies raid it. I'd die happy if he were blown to hell.'

Little was said between them after that. In an effort to keep Meyer warm, Hausmann held his still shuddering body close to his own. As the long minutes passed and Hausmann kept hearing footsteps in the corridor outside it was clear why he was being kept waiting. Every sound made his stomach knot and his mouth turn dry, every footstep clutched at his chest with burning fingers.

In an attempt to aid him, his mind recalled visions of

his home and Freda. The alpine meadows, the wooded hills, the dawn chorus of birds, Freda's scolding voice when he was late for supper . . . For a few moments Hausmann found escape in the memories, although the yearning they brought was an agony in itself. He turned to Freda for solace, for her warm arms and comforting body, but then remembered her pleas on their last night together. How would she manage without him in a Germany that would be in ruins when the war was lost? In his wish to help destroy the evil that was occupying his country, had he not betrayed the woman who loved and needed him so much?

When at last the cell door opened and he was dragged outside, Hausmann knew beyond any doubt that the clergy's talk of hell in the hereafter was hopelessly misdirected. Hell with all its pain, its insoluble dilemmas, and its self-recriminations was right here on earth.

Millburn was right about the following day. Although the clouds were a few hundred feet higher when crews were called for breakfast, a steady drizzle was still denying he visibility the mission required. Davies' voice over Henderson's red telephone gave vent to the small Air Commodore's frustration. 'What a bastard it is, Jock. You'd think the weather was on Jerry's side.'

'They say the devil looks after his own, sir. Maybe ey're right.'

Davies' snort showed what he thought of the Scot's phorisms. 'We have to go tomorrow, Jock. Or Jerry ight make the target impregnable.'

Henderson was having none of that. 'We can't go until e weather's suitable, sir. You know that's out of the estion.'

The Scot missed hearing Davies' muttered curse. top making obstacles, Jock. The Met. boys think e clouds are lifting and should be OK tomorrow.

So air-test your kites again and see the boys have an early night.'

Henderson's sigh was pregnant with disapproval. 'Very well, sir. Will you be here tomorrow?'

'Of course I will. And so will General Staines.'

After a start, Henderson remembered the Operations Room was still wired up to the American's headquarters. 'What time will you arrive, sir?'

'As I'm hoping the boys will have an early start, we're coming tonight. The General is picking me up on his way. So arrange for our accommodation, will you? We're hoping to arrive around 21.00 hours.'

Sighing, Henderson replaced the receiver and spoke to the Adjutant about arranging accommodation. He then phoned A Flight office and left a message that Millburn had to report to him at his first opportunity.

Millburn was in his office five minutes later. 'You wanted to see me, sir?'

Motioning him to sit down, Henderson told him the text of Davies' orders. Millburn showed surprise. 'General Staines?'

Henderson nodded. 'As it could affect his B17s so much, I suppose he's keen to find out the kind of job we do. He'll also be able to monitor his two squadrons of Mustangs.' When Millburn made no further comment, the Scot went on: 'So I want all kites air-tested again before dusk. I'm also going to arrange with Adams that the boys have a chance to see those photographs again. With Staines so deeply involved we can't afford a cock-up. Are you happy with everything so far?'

Like Harvey before him, Millburn was not one to hide his reservations. 'I'm not happy about the weather, sir. If the clouds are down to the deck over there or it's snowing we could be in deep trouble.'

'I know that, Millburn. So there'll be two weather kites out there taking a look at the conditions before you take-off. If they give us a negative report, I shall abort the operation.'

'Davies won't like that,' Millburn ventured.

Henderson scowled. 'Davies will have to lump it. I'm not sending the boys into a death trap for anyone or anybody. But let's proceed on the assumption the Met. boys are right. Get the kites air tested, run over the operation with the boys again, and don't let 'em stay up too late. Apart from anything else, with Davies and Staines here I don't want them fooling and clowning about past midnight. Let Staines think we're a straight-up-and down, well-behaved unit.'

Millburn grinned. 'Which of course we are, sir.'

'Right,' Henderson snapped.

Millburn gave the Scot a salute and then returned to A Flight office where Gabby was waiting for him. 'Well. What did he say?'

Hearing the question, other members of A Flight began crowding round. Millburn dropped into a chair and pushed back his cap. 'It's on tomorrow morning providing the weather improves. And the latest forecasts say it will.'

A disturbed buzz of voices sounded. The squadron had lown many foul weather sorties but never in weather as ad as this. Gabby showed his disgust. 'They're all talking load of cock. It'll never clear by the morning.'

Millburn shrugged. 'Maybe and maybe not. But you ot have to be ready in case. So directly after lunch ou'll air-test your kites again. Then, at 14.00 hours, you uys and B Flight will meet me in the Operations Room nd we'll run over the photographs and the operation gain. For everybody's sake, I want nothing to go wrong morrow.'

As men nodded and drifted away, Gabby's eyes folwed them. They don't look too happy, do they?' He inned at the American maliciously. 'Maybe they're not ppy you're leading them.'

For once the American's humour failed him. 'More likely they're worried about your navigation. I want you to stare at those photographs until your eyes pop. It's vital we don't over-shoot this plant. If there are 262s around we mightn't get a second chance at it.'

'I spent half the night looking at the bloody things,' Gabby complained.

Millburn rose from his chair. 'You're lucky you didn't spend all the night. I'm going over to B Flight office. In the meantime you get over to A-Apple and make sure she is getting a full maintenance check. I want her ready for air-testing by 13.30 hours.'

Chapter 27

Millburn had never known a longer day. Unable to phone Carol because the Station's communications were cut, he managed to fill in his time during daylight by air-testing A-Apple and running over the operation again with his crews. After dinner he felt every contingency had been covered and there was nothing to do now but wait. Restless, he walked around the airfield perimeter where the Mosquitoes were parked and tried to estimate the state of the weather. The sky was still heavily overcast but the rain had ceased and he imagined the cloud base had lifted since the afternoon. Unsure whether he was pleased or disappointed, he finally found himself in the Mess.

Many of his crews were in there, drinking sparingly of the four beers that for a second day were their ration. Seeing Adams sitting at a table talking to a young pilot, he crossed over to him. 'Mind if I join you, Frank?'

As Adams nodded, the young officer jumped to his eet. Millburn waved him back. 'It's OK, Jenkins. You an stay.'

Jenkins, a recent recruit, was looking flushed. 'It's all ght, sir. I was just leaving.'

Millburn shrugged. 'OK. Whatever you say.' As the oungster hurried away towards the bar, the American azed after him. 'What's wrong with him. He's not scared f me, is he?'

Adams, who'd had more than his usual ration of cohol, gave him a benign grin. 'You're the leader, laddie. One of the old sweats the newcomers talk about with bated breath. Can't you recognise hero worship when you see it?'

Millburn muttered something, then recovered himself. 'Can I get you a drink?'

Adams waved his pipe at a half glass of beer on the table. 'No. That's my lot. But I'll get you one if you like.'

Millburn waved him back into his chair. 'Not just now. I had a couple earlier on. In any case I suppose I ought to set a good example.'

Adams smiled. 'Leadership does have its price. Just the same, I wouldn't think the boys would hold another beer against you.'

Millburn made no reply. His eyes were wandering around the Mess. On the surface 633 Squadron was its usual self before an operation. Sangster and Jones were playing darts; Davidson had found a chess player in Dobbs, a new transfer; Tomlinson and Mason were playing snooker; and four of the old sweats, Gabby Machin, Baldwin and Larkin were playing their usual cutthroat game of poker. It would be the same in the Fligh Offices, Millburn knew. As usual before an operation men were trying to control their nerves according to thei temperaments.

Yet Millburn sensed a difference. Tight nerves usuall betrayed themselves by excessive behaviour. Shouts o triumph were heard when games were won, argument were more frequent, singing was louder and more def ant.

There was none of that around him tonight. The pian was silent and even the shouts of Gabby or Machin whe they won a jackpot lacked their usual boisterousness.

Millburn glanced back to Adams. 'Aren't you goir over to Helga?'

Adams shook his head. 'No. Davies might want

see me when he gets here. In any case I'd feel a bit uncomfortable visiting the pub when none of you can go out.'

Millburn shrugged. 'You're too sensitive. The boys wouldn't give it a second thought.'

Adams smiled. 'You're probably right. They probably wouldn't even notice. But I've told Henderson I'm staying so it's too late to change my mind now.'

In the short silence that fell Millburn found himself listening again to the comparative quietness of the Mess. Unable to resist the impulse any longer, he put his question to Adams. 'You're the psychologist, Frank. So tell me what's wrong tonight. Is it because I've been made the leader? Is the operation bugging them? Or is it all just my goddammed imagination?'

Adams' reply told him immediately that the Intelligence Officer was also conscious of the muted atmosphere. 'It's neither, Tommy. Or at least I don't think so.'

'Then what is it?'

Adams packed his pipe before answering. 'It's the war, Tommy. It's something Harvey and I once talked about ust before the invasion. Only it's far worse now.'

'War? I don't follow you.'

Adams pressed down the tobacco in his pipe. 'The end f the war's too close, Tommy. That's the problem. A year go, even six months ago, men had come to terms with ying. So each operation was just another job. But it's ifferent now. Men are starting to reassess their chances f surviving. Harvey put it to me very well. He said at ne time a man could accept each day of life as a gift. ow, paradoxically, each day is a threat.'

Millburn was listening very intently. 'Harvey felt at?'

Adams nodded. 'Yes. Even tough old Harvey felt it. is it strange the rest of the boys feel it too? After all, it's quite a time since they had a major operation of this kind. Some of them might have started to believe they'd flown the last one.'

Millburn was looking more relaxed. 'So you don't think it's because of me?'

'Good heavens no. They all admire you. No, it's the war. Every risky operation is getting harder for the boys to take now there's now a good chance of getting back to their families and their girl friends again.'

Although Millburn's expression did not change, something moved in his eyes and not for the first time Adams cursed alcohol for giving him a careless tongue. Disgusted with himself, he rose. 'Let me get you that beer, Tommy. The bar will close early tonight.'

Millburn shook his head. 'No. I've a few things to do before I turn in. But thanks for the chat.' He gave his humorous grin. 'It's good to hear you don't think the boys are scared of my leadership.'

To counter his earlier gaffe, Adams was almost too effusive. 'Good God, no. They've enormous respect for you. Don't even think that, Tommy.'

Millburn laughed and clapped him on the shoulder. 'OK. I won't. I'll tell myself the boys can't wait to follow me in the morning.' Before Adams could reply the American rose. 'See you at breakfast, Frank.'

Adams watched him cross the Mess floor, acknowledging with humour every comment made to him. As he vanished through the far door, Adams knew one thing beyond any doubt. If he had to live the war again he would make very sure he never fell in love until it ended.

Sutton Craddock broke into life at 03.15 hours the following morning when the teletype bell in the Operations Room rang. It awoke the dozing Duty Officer who grabbed his telephone and began alerting the relevant officers, the CO, the Squadron Commander, the

Intelligence Officer, the Engineering Officer . . . as each call was made the Duty Officer ticked the name off his list.

In no time the Tannoy began rasping out orders. Cursing mechanics emerged from their billets or dispersal huts into the icy blackness of a February morning and began setting storm lanterns around their individual Mosquitoes. As NCOs yelled orders, men bruised their chilled hands on spanners and aircraft panels. Truck engines started up and dimmed headlights began moving round the airfield perimeter. Tractors began trundling long trolleys of bombs towards the waiting Mosquitoes where armourers were feeding belts and tanks of ammunition into the aircrafts' Brownings and Hispano cannon. Soon there was a cough and then a roar as a fitter put the first of his Merlins under test.

While all this organised chaos was under way, the aircrews were having their breakfasts. When men saw eggs, a scarce commodity in 1945, appearing on their plates, mordant jokes were aimed at the latest transfers, or it was believed crews were given eggs only before a particularly dangerous operation. Gabby, never in a good mood after an early call, scowled at the yellow orb on his late. 'That's a bloody good start. You'd think they'd be more tactful, wouldn't you?'

Machin, sitting beside him, held out his plate. 'Aye, you would at that. So just pass it over and it'll take the bad ck away from yer, so it will.'

There was a laugh and a shout further down the table as e Welshman indignantly snatched his plate away. 'Don't aste it on the IRA, Gabby. Give it to me.'

A second voice mocked the speaker. 'What's wrong th you, Jones? Don't you think your luck's bad enough is morning? Or didn't you notice the weather when you me over here?'

Other men began to join in at the mention of the

weather. Gabby, who was sitting opposite Millburn, was in the right mood to share their complaints. 'I think they should scrub it,' he announced. 'It could be pissing down or snowing over in Jerryland.' He glanced at Millburn who was sitting opposite him. 'What do you think, boyo?'

The American was frowning. 'Belt up, Gabby.'

Gabby took immediate umbrage. 'What's wrong with you? You've been looking lower than a bullfrog's arse ever since you got up this morning. Have you had a Dear John letter from that Transport pilot or something?'

Even Gabby knew he had gone too far from the look Millburn gave him. As the chatter and murmurs abruptly died, the American rose to his feet. 'That's all the moaning I'm taking from you guys today. The mission's on and we're going to make the best of it. So get your breakfast over and then hightail it to A Flight Office. I want you al assembled there after I've had a last word with the CC That'll be in fifteen minutes, so you'd better not wast any more time bellyaching about the weather.' With tha Millburn turned and made for the Mess door.

With every man in the room knowing the complain had only been the crews' time-honoured way of facing hazardous mission, the usually good-natured American reprimand was a shock. No one spoke a word until h reached the Mess door and disappeared outside. On then did a low buzz of surprise and conjecture run rour the tables.

The eastern horizon was growing lighter as Millburn ma for the CO's office. Glancing up at the heavy sky, saw the weather men had been right. The drizzle h ceased and the cloud base had lifted another thousa feet. It was still foul weather, Millburn thought as an i breeze chilled his face. But if it grew no worse over Continent, they had a chance of getting through.

He allowed himself no more speculation. He had always had faith in his luck: today was not a time to lose it. Pushing away doubts, Millburn ran up the steps into the Administration Block where he knew Henderson, Davies, Simms and Staines were waiting for him.

It was the harsh bellow of the Station Tannoy ordering transports to the Flight Offices that woke Helga. Throwing on her dressing gown, she ran to the bedroom window. As she watched the shifting lights, there was a tap on the door. 'Miss. Can I come in?'

Helga turned. 'Yes, of course.'

Maisie, wearing a mackintosh over her nightdress, ame to her side. 'You're sure you don't mind, Miss? nly I often watch from here when the room's empty. heir engines wake me up and then I want to see them ke off.' She glanced back at the window. 'I wonder here they're going.'

Knowing it wasn't a question that expected an answer, elga only shook her head. As they stood watching, aisie gave an involuntary shiver. Turning to her bed, elga threw a blanket over the girl and draped one over rself. She smiled as the girl thanked her. 'If we're going watch until they take off we might as well be warm.'

Lights were being extinguished on the airfield as darkness began to dissolve. Dim figures were now sible fussing around the picketed Mosquitoes. Merlin er Merlin was firing and trucks could be seen running und the airfield perimeter. As they stopped alongside picketed aircraft, Maisie pointed at the men who mbed from them. 'Those are the crews. The pilots navigators. See them?'

Helga nodded, then turned to her. 'You care for those s, don't you?'

Maisie looked surprised at the question. 'Of course I They're my friends.'

Without being quite sure why, Helga found the simple statement moving. 'I'm told they all look forward to seeing you when they return.'

Maisie smiled. 'I try to be at the gate. The boys all wave back to me.'

'I know. I think it's rather lovely.'

The blast of engines was shuddering the icy air now as Mosquitoes began to move clockwise round the airfield. 'The wind's blowing from Bishop's Wood,' Maisie explained. 'So they'll start their take off from this end.'

At that moment the flarepath lights blazed on, two dazzling lines of yellow lights that reflected back from the thick cloud above. Maisie gazed at the reflection anxiously. 'It must be something urgent or they wouldn' be sent out in weather like this. I wonder what it is.'

The first Mosquito, its recognition lights flashing, ha now reached the flarepath and was swinging on to i As it paused and the pilot blipped his engines, Helg thought of a runner taking deep breaths as he waited fc the starter's pistol.

It came in the guise of a green Very flare arching fro the Control Tower. The Mosquito's engine thundered a it began moving down the flarepath. Faster and faster, i wheels throwing out spray, its tail rising . . . faster a faster, its wheels lifting and then falling under its hea bomb load. Then, just as it seemed it would disappear in the dark mass of Bishops Wood, Helga saw its recogniti lights rising and banking to port.

One by one the rest of the Mosquitoes followed. they circled above to formate, Helga could hear the pu old windows rattling under the thunder of their engin

Then they were gone and the flarepath lights w out with them, leaving both girls blinded for a mome Maisie's voice sounded a little unsteady as she remo the blanket and laid it on the bed. 'Thanks, Miss. It kind of you to let me in.'

'Don't be silly,' Helga said. 'I found it fascinating too. I wonder when they'll be back.'

Maisie moved to the door. 'Frank'll probably know. If he tells you, will you tip me off? Joe wants me to go into Highgate and I don't want to be missing when the boys fly in.' Helga caught a slight catch in her voice as she went on: 'I know they're a crack squadron but even so it's awful weather to be sent out. So I've got the feeling this could be a bad trip for them.'

Helga felt chilled by her words. She nodded impulsively. 'I'll let you know. Just keep it to yourself, that's all.'

'Of course I will. Thanks, Miss.'

Feeling tired as if the scene across the way had exhausted her, Helga slipped back into bed when the girl had gone. It was a decision she was soon to regret. In the half-sleep that followed, her dreams were full of a girl standing at a gate waving a scarf. But the aircraft she was waving at were not sleek Mosquitoes. They were things of skeleton spars and blazing engines that were sliding and tumbling out of a cloud-shrouded sky.

Chapter 28

Davies glared at the sergeant. 'They must be there by this time. You haven't been sleeping, have you?'

The flushed wireless operator shook his head. 'No, sir. So far there's been no word from Voziers.'

Davies swung round on Henderson. 'Then what the hel are they doing? Millburn hasn't got 'em lost, has he?'

Suppressing a sigh, Henderson glanced up at th electric clock on the Operations Room wall. 'They'r not due there for another fifteen minutes, sir.'

Taken aback, Davies recovered well. 'Millburn coul have kept us in touch, couldn't he?'

'He wasn't asked to transmit on the way to Vozier sir. I expect he's thinking the less Jerry picks up on th radio the better.'

Davies' grunt could have meant anything. 'I want know the moment Voziers tells us they've arrived. So se this lad puts a phone message to the Mess.' A pause ar then the small Air Commodore added a reluctant cave 'I suppose I'd better keep Staines and Simms in the until we get nearer the target?'

Henderson nodded. 'I should, sir. Now the Gener has got his confirmation message, there shouldn't any more for him until his boys link up with us over t target. That'll be a long wait and this place isn't heat up yet.'

Adams, the other officer present in the Operatic Room, knew Henderson was referring to a messa received from Voziers ten minutes ago stating Dent's two squadrons of Mustangs had arrived safely. After acknowledging the message, Staines had retired to the Mess on Davies' invitation.

Davies was nodding disparagingly. 'I suppose you're right. Simms wouldn't mind. He keeps his office like a refrigerator. But the Yanks shiver every time the damned wind blows.' Feeling better after his final bleat, Davies had a last word with the wireless operator and then hurried away.

Giving a groan, Henderson turned to Adams when the far door swung shut. 'He doesn't change, does he? He'll be like a dog with fleas until the action starts. Thank God Staines is here. Otherwise he'd be making our lives a misery today.'

Adams was amused to see the sergeant wireless operator, whom the Scot had forgotten, was hurting himself trying not to laugh. 'It's his temperament, I suppose. But I agree, it is wearing.'

Henderson gave a snort. 'Wearing? Do you realise he goes wandering all over the Station while he's waiting, finding fault with everybody and everything. Why the hell doesn't he just arrive around ETA time?'

With no answer to that, Adams raised the collar of his greatcoat. Henderson nodded. 'It is charpy, isn't it. Let's have some coffee.'

Hearing his words, the sergeant was just reaching out for an internal phone when he checked and pressed his headphones tighter to his ears. As the two officers gazed at him, he began scribbling a W/T message on a pad. Thirty seconds later he handed a sheet of paper to Henderson. 'It's Voziers, sir. Foxhound has arrived safely.'

The Scot scanned the message, then nodded. 'Acknowledge and ask what the weather's like.'

As the sergeant tapped his Morse key, the two officers waited for the reply. It came a minute later. 'They say the cloud base is 1900 feet, sir. And it's not raining.'

Henderson betrayed his disappointment the operation could not be aborted with a muttered curse. Then, recovering himself, he nodded at the sergeant. 'All right. Phone the Mess now and tell the Air Commodore.' Then, as an afterthought. 'And ask them to send that coffee over.'

As the sergeant obeyed, Henderson turned to Adams. His voice was wry, resigned. 'That's it, then. For better or worse, the damned thing's on. All we can do now is keep our fingers crossed and hope those 262s don't spoil the party.'

The Mosquitoes, flying in line astern, were skimming over the lake like as many flat stones, their slipstreams ruffling the grey water. In A-Apple at point Millburn switched on his fire-and-safe button and tested his guns. As the aircraft shuddered under the recoil of its machine guns and cannon, Millburn tapped Gabby's knee. Nodding, Gabby pulled the Very pistol from its clip and fired it through the flare chute. Behind, Mosquito after Mosquito swung momentarily out of line and spat flame as every pilot tested his guns.

Ahead, tall trees were bordering the shoreline. Easing back on his control column, Millburn sent A-Apple flying over them like a leaping horse. Behind him, like a long piece of string being flipped by some giant hand, the following aircraft cleared the trees and then sank down again over a muddy ploughed field.

So far so good, Millburn was thinking. The flight t Voziers had been incident free and left him time to se Dent, the commander of the Mustang Squadrons who ha arrived sixteen minutes earlier.

Dent was a stocky affable New Yorker who ha an excellent relationship with his men. He knew c Millburn not only because of Millburn's participatio in the Copenhagen frolic but because of the stories his men had brought back from Scarborough. 'You're the guy who's got that crazy navigator, aren't you? The one who organised the party?'

Millburn nodded. 'Yeah. I'm saddled with him. He's having coffee with your boys at the moment. Keep an eye on him or he'll be organising a thrash with local talent. He's got some weird ideas about French women, has my little Welshman.'

Dent grinned. 'My boys said you got into a fracas with an MP that night. What exactly happened?'

Millburn told him, not leaving out Gabby's encounter with Martha. When he finished, Dent was wiping his eyes. 'That's a hell of a story. I must tell it to the boys.'

'Yeah, but don't let Gabby know. Or he'll land us up somewhere in Russia. He's kind of sensitive about that night.'

Dent laughed again. 'I'm not surprised. It can't be too good for his image.'

It had been a brief but pleasant encounter. Ten minutes later, when the Mustangs were re-fuelled, Dent came over to have a last word with Millburn. 'That's it, Foxhound Leader. We're moving out.'

They shook hands. 'We'll see you over the target,' Dent said.

'Yeah. Have a good trip, as the Limies say.'

'You too. Good luck.'

Five minutes later the Mustangs were climbing into the grey, heavy sky. Gabby, renewed by coffee, watched them critically. 'Let's hope they don't get lost. Or don't bugger things up by giving themselves away to Jerry's monitors.'

Touchy about his kinsmen, Millburn gave a scowl. 'Why should they?'

Gabby's smug expression had never made him look more like a gremlin. 'We can't all be the best, boyo.'

Millburn eyed him suspiciously. 'What's happened since we got here? You were like a dog with a sore arse before. You didn't get the Yanks to lace your coffee, did you?'

Gabby showed indignation. 'You've a dirty mind, Millburn. You always have had.'

Millburn's tone changed. 'Now you listen, boyo. If you've had even one shot, you go back for more coffee. I need you bright-eyed and bushy-tailed for the next few hours. Understand?'

A professional in spite of his ways, Gabby knew the time for banter was over. 'I didn't have any booze, Millburn. Honestly. I want to get the job done as much as you do.'

'I'm glad to hear it. Remember all the time to keep an eye on our fuel situation. I'm hoping we've enough but this low level flying can play hell with fuel reserves.'

Before leaving Sutton Craddock, Millburn had been involved in an argument about fuel. In accordance with standard practice, fuel load for the Mosquitoes had been balanced against the weight of the bombs and rockets they were carrying and although allowance had been made for the extra fuel that the long, low-level flight would consume, Millburn had asked for extra gallons in case an emergency should arise.

With specialist officers bringing out charts to prove their figures, it had not been an easy argument to win. But Millburn's reputation for being able to charm Waafs and Air Commodores in equal measure had eventually been vindicated and the extra gallons had been pumped into the Mosquitoes' tanks. Although Millburn could not know it yet, he was to thank God for his foresight before the mission was over.

His thoughts were broken by a tap on his shoulder. 'Electric cables, Millburn!'

Millburn had already seen them, thin murderous lines

slung across the road A-Apple was following. Waggling his wings, he leap-frogged over them and sank down again on the road. A minute later Gabby nodded to him. All the Mosquitoes had crossed them safely.

An Army convoy appeared below. Mile after mile of trucks carrying Allied troops to the front. Soldiers waved rifles as the trucks flowed beneath them like a strip of movie film. Tanks appeared, mastodons waddling along to their destiny. Six minutes later the landscape seemed to clear of troops but Millburn knew it was a great illusion. They had reached the juncture of the two conflicting armies where men and machines took shelter behind and under every natural obstacle. Fountains of earth and smoke as far as the eye could see betrayed the desperate battle raging there.

A wide stretch of water appeared. The Rhine! Not a man in the 16 Mosquitoes did not feel his nerves tighten as his aircraft skimmed the sullen, steel-grey water. No escape now if his engines failed. From that moment on every hand would be against him. They were entering beleaguered Germany itself.

Black bursts of smoke in the sky around them brought home the message. German gunners on the eastern shore waiting for the Allies to attempt a crossing had time to see the aircraft and line up their guns. Millburn waggled his wings again and the following aircraft spread out to port and starboard. No men were better trained than 633 Squadron to handle the problems of low level flight. By giving the gunners widely dispersed targets, fewer guns could be registered on each aircraft.

They shot over the dug-in guns without loss and squatted down on a road again. With the prospect of heavy cloud all the way to the target, the Navigation Officer and his staff had consulted Gabby and agreed that map reading would make his task easier. Accordingly a route had been drawn from Voziers to the target that missed all areas of dense flak and Gabby had been given roads and navigation points to help keep A-Apple on track.

One of the major identification points began streaming beneath the Mosquitoes a few minutes later. 'The autobahn to Limburg and Cologne,' Gabby announced. 'We're on track, Millburn.'

With the broad and smooth highway offering only bridges as obstacles, Millburn was able to relax for the moment. 'When do we leave it?'

'Thirty miles beyond Koblenz,' Gabby told him. 'But watch the flak there. They might think that's our target.'

Both men knew that the highly efficient German Observer Corps, while unable to follow their route as radar could have done, would certainly have alerted its local posts to be on the look out. While in general these posts would find it difficult to predict the aircrafts' route, a long run along an autobahn would certainly ensure that flak gunners ahead would be stripping the tarpaulins off their guns in the hope the aircraft would sweep towards them.

Millburn had no intention of making this mistake 'We'll turn to port before we reach Koblenz,' he tolc Gabby. 'It'll throw you off track a little, so keep an ey on your compass and map.'

A skyline of buildings and smoking chimneys appeare four and a half minutes later. Nodding at Gabby, Milbur swung a few degrees to port, leaving the autobahn behinc A few puffs of black smoke burst around the Mosquitoe but they were out of range within seconds.

Millburn swung back on his original compass cours The transverse Limburg–Cologne autobahn flashe beneath him. Gabby jabbed a finger ahead. 'We' cross the Frankfurt–Dortmund autobahn in a few minute We want the small town alongside it, Siegen. That'll g us back on track.'

Like a line of cavalry, the Mosquitoes raced o

Starlings and crows, grubbing for seeds and worms in the wet fields, scattered like black confetti at the scream of engines and airfoils. Farmhouses swept past, cattle bolted, startled farm hands ran for shelter. A train, puffing out dense smoke, was seen running alongside a narrow road. As the aircraft screamed on, patches of snow began to appear in hollows and on shallow hillsides.

The transverse Frankfurt–Dortmund autobahn swept below. A small town appeared. Gabby gave a shout of triumph. 'That's it. Siegen. We're back on track again, Millburn.'

All the crews, old sweats and transfers alike, knew from experience that the heavily protected massive industrial heartland of Germany lay only a few miles north. But their route took them round its fringe and although a few 37s around Siegen opened fire on them, their speed and low altitude carried them past.

Fields, narrow roads, villages, and woodlands returned, then the dangerous corridor between Brilon and Kassel. The strain of low level flying was beginning to be felt now. Pilots could feel their eyes aching and burning, yet few dared rub them. With trees leaping at them, with telegraph and electric cables looking as thin as cotton in the poor light, the loss of vision for half a second could mean disaster.

The strain was no less severe for the navigators. Not only were they needed to warn their pilots of perilous obstacles, they had to keep a close watch on the cloud base above. While it was true the dense ceiling hid them from high flying fighters, it could also shield fighters from detection until they pounced with guns blazing. With the feared 262s never out of mind, navigators found their necks aching with strain as their eyes moved unceasingly from ground to sky.

With Millburn feeling the strain himself, he knew there would be no question of the squadron flying back the way it had come. The alarm would have gone out to every fighter base by that time and the squadron's route would have been plotted in its entirety by the enemy Observer Corps. The Mosquitoes would have to try to turn the dense clouds into an ally by hiding in them on their way back to base.

With eyes aching and nerves as tight as violin strings, men lost all track of time as the long flight continued. Snow was appearing everywhere now as the Mosquitoes penetrated deeper into Germany, firstly on hills, then in thin sheets on the fields. With its tendency to hide or change the shape of the things it covered, Gabby was finding it more and more difficult to keep A-Apple on track.

Even so, as he flashed over the Hannover–Kassel autobahn, Millburn had every reason to feel satisfied with the mission so far. It was only when they crossed the Hannover–Magdeburg autobahn further east that the first tragedy occurred. As they swung starboard to miss the town of Braunschweig, twin forks of tracer stabbed upwards from a clump of trees. They missed A-Apple, drilled holes in Machin's fuselage, but caught Red Three flown by Drummond right in the cockpit. With Drummond mortally wounded, Hill, his navigator, tried in vain to grab the control column.

But at zero height, the effort was futile. With both engines still under full power, C-Charlie went headlong into a second clump of trees and exploded.

With the fatalism aircrews developed, few men made comment on the loss as the remaining fifteen Mosquitoes raced on, although friends of the two men held their own silent requiem. In A-Apple a grim-faced Millburn asked Gabby how much longer it was to their ETA.

Gabby consulted his watch. 'Twenty-five minutes.'

'We should hit the Berlin–Rostock railway soon shouldn't we?'

'Yes. Maybe in twelve minutes.'

'Then be ready to check the sidings with your photographs. We can't afford a cock-up now.'

Gabby muttered something but pulled the photographs from his wallet. Eleven minutes later he gave a shout of triumph. 'There it is, Millburn! The railway!'

Millburn spotted the telegraph poles and the rail line a second later, running at fifty degrees north of their flight path. He managed a wink at Gabby. 'Well done, boyo. Tip the boys off we're nearly there.'

Gabby already had the Very pistol in his hand. A moment later, as a green flare curled out from A-Apple, weary crews felt their heartbeats quicken as they swung north to follow Millburn along the snow covered track.

Snow tumbled from telegraph posts as the Mosquitoes thundered past. Birds resting on the wires turned and fled in terror. But navigators were no longer sharing their vigilance with the ground below. Their heads were back and their bloodshot eyes were searching the dense layer of cloud that had never felt more threatening. The same question was in every man's mind. Would the infamous 262s be waiting to guard their birthplace? In minutes now, men knew they would receive the answer.

Chapter 29

The Operations Room was silent except for the drumming of Davies' right hand on the W/T bench. First his thumb followed by his remaining four fingers, then the little finger and the other digits in reverse. Adams could see Henderson watching them and guessed what the Scot was feeling. To ease the tension Adams felt any comment was better than the drumming of those fingers. He made it to no one in particular. 'Things must be going well for the boys,' he said.

Davies swung round. 'Why do you think that?'

Realising it was a stupid remark, Adams was embarrassed by the lameness of his reply. 'There's been no wireless message. So I'm assuming it's good news.'

'For God's sake, you know better than that, Frank. Even if they came under attack, they're not supposed to break radio silence unless it means calling off the operation.'

Duly rebuffed, Adams was saved from a reply by a guarded hint from Henderson. 'Their ETA's still 90 minutes off. So we've a long wait ahead of us.'

Davies' tight nerves were making him touchy to any remark that morning. 'What does that mean, Jock?'

Henderson looked aggrieved. 'It doesn't mean anything, sir. Just that there's a long time to go yet.'

'I know there's a long time to go. So why do you keep harping on it?'

With nerves at this pitch, Adams knew it was going to be a trying day. When Henderson made no reply, Davies swung back to the W/T bench and began drumming his fingers again. Giving Adams a look of resignation, Henderson lit a cigarette. With Staines and Simms waiting in the Mess, the Scot had hoped once Davies knew the squadron had landed safely in France, he would feel obliged to rejoin the two senior officers. Instead it appeared he intended staying beside the W/T operator until the bitter end.

As it happened the tension was broken ten minutes later. All three officers turned as the far door opened and an MP approached Davies and saluted him. 'Excuse me, sir, but Mrs Harvey wants to see you.'

Davies gave a start, then showed anger. 'I can't see anyone today, for Christ's sake. Didn't the SWO tell her so?'

'Yes, sir. But she said it was very important and that you'd see her if we spoke to you. As she knows you, the SWO felt he had better check with you first.'

Davies swung round on the two curious officers. 'Do either of you know anything about this?'

Although suspicion had jumped like an electric shock hrough Adams, both he and Henderson shook their heads. Davies turned back to the MP. 'Where is she now?'

'Outside, sir. With the MP on guard at the door.'

Davies muttered a curse, then jerked his head. 'All ight. Let her in.'

The MP saluted, did a smart half turn, and marched rom the room. Davies was looking disturbed and angry. What the hell's she doing here today?'

A moment later Anna came hurrying down the bench-lled room. Wearing no hat, looking distressed and mbarrassed, she still impressed the susceptible Adams ith her rare beauty. Even her movements, urgent though ey were, remained graceful as she hurried past the rows f benches towards the three curious officers.

Her voice was breathless as she acknowledged them

and then addressed Davies. 'Arthur, I'm sorry about this. But I had to see you.'

Davies was not one to hide his feelings when service matters were involved. 'You couldn't have picked a worse time, Anna. We're right in the middle of an important operation.'

'I know that, Arthur, but that's the reason I had to see you.' She glanced round at Henderson and the sergeant wireless operator. 'Can I see you in private for a moment? Please, Arthur. It's terribly important.'

'Damn it, Anna, I can't leave here. It'll have to wait.'

Adams took his life in his hands. 'There is a small lobby alongside the platform, sir.'

The look Davies gave Adams threatened a summary court martial. Then, as Anna laid a pleading hand on his arm, he jerked his head resentfully. 'Come on then. You've got five minutes.'

As he led her towards the platform, the girl glanced at Adams. 'Can Frank come too, please?'

Although clearly baffled by her behaviour, Davies gave Adams a nod and the Intelligence Officer followed them into a small lobby with a table and chairs that adjoined the platform. There Davies faced her. 'All right. What the hell's all this about?'

Her lovely face was very pale and Adams saw she was trembling. He took a chair to her. 'Take your time,' he said quietly.

Davies glared at him. 'We haven't got time.' He swung back to the girl. 'What's your problem, Anna? Has that husband of yours got into trouble again?'

Shaking her head, she sank down on the chair. 'It's nothing to do with Frank, Arthur. All he has done is brought me here and that was only because I begged him to. I've come about those two German friends of mine.'

Davies gave a violent start. 'German friends? What German friends?'

'You know whom I mean, Arthur. The ones who've been captured by the Nazis.'

For a moment Davies tried to bluster. 'I don't know what you're talking about.'

She nodded. 'I realise it's all highly secret. But I know Brigadier Simms used them and I know they've been captured. You practically told Frank so when he came to see you.'

Her mention of Harvey gave Davies a target for his anger. 'So he *is* behind this? I should have known.'

All her distress was surfacing now. 'No. Frank didn't want to bring me. He said it was hopeless. But I had to try one last time.' Suddenly her grey eyes were brimming with tears as she pleaded with him. 'Arthur, won't you ask your men to bomb that concentration camp after they've completed the main raid? It's only a few miles further down the line and it could mean the difference between heaven and hell for those men.'

Davies' voice was harsh with resentment. 'For God's sake, Anna, you should know better than to ask this. I have to get authorisation for the operations my men carry out and there never was a cat in hell's chance of my getting permission to bomb a concentration camp. I told all this to Harvey. He should never have brought you here.'

The tears were running down her lovely face now. 'But, Arthur, have you any idea what will happen to those men? Or even what might be happening to them at this moment? Do you know the kind of tortures they keep for German dissidents?'

For a half second Davies hesitated. 'I know the Gestapo and the SS are brutes, if that's what you mean.'

Her bitter laugh was for his innocence. 'Brutes! Listen to what they do to our people, Arthur. Just listen.'

Davies started to interrupt her, then went silent. As she talked, Adams saw his expression changing. When she finished, Davies looked more shocked than Adams had ever seen him. He turned to Adams. 'Is all this true?'

Adams, who had gone ice cold himself at the horror of it, nodded. 'Yes. We get reports through our intelligence service. But even so there were things I hadn't been told.'

Davies turned back to the girl. 'All right. The SS are devils. Inhuman fiends. But isn't this why we're fighting the war? To wipe them out?'

She shook her head passionately. 'I hoped you were. It was why I have always done my best to help you. But when has Arthur Harris, the Air Council, or the American Air Staff ordered raids on concentration camps or their railways? Not once in four years.'

Davies was frowning. 'Surely our job has been to cripple the enemy's industry and defeat his armed forces. When that's done the Nazis can no longer murder innocent people.'

'But in the meantime millions have been murdered, Arthur. It would not have taken many aircraft to attack these camps or the railways that run to them. Just the bombing of a few camps might have changed the entire Nazi policy and saved all those people from pain and loss. Why is it, Arthur? Why have the Allies forsaken the very people they are supposed to be defending?'

Adams had seldom seen Davies on the defensiv but he was on the defensive now. 'We don't mak national policy, Anna. We're just the people who carr out orders.'

'I know that and I understand how difficult it would b for you to organise a special raid. But this is a differe situation. Your men have only to fly on a few more mil and hundreds of men who hate the Nazis more than yc can ever do might be freed.'

'For how long?' Davies asked.

The girl's sudden passion sent a shiver down Adam

spine. 'Does it matter how long? People like you have never known what it feels like to be mocked and humiliated. To suffer agony without hope of release. At least these men would be able to fight and die with dignity.'

To Adams' amazement he saw there were beads of sweat on Davies' forehead. 'But they would still die.'

'Not necessarily. Saindau isn't that far from the Russian advance. Some might reach the Russians. But die or not, they would know the world cared for the sacrifices they have made. They would not die in torment with their hearts full of bitterness.'

Davies' silence lasted only a moment. 'Anna, do you realise what you're asking? My boys will be tired out before they reach their target. Then they might have to face flak and air attack. How could I ask any survivors to fly deeper into Germany? The cost might be appalling.'

Exhausted by her passion, the girl gave a sob of distress. 'Do you believe I haven't thought about that? Mein Gott, some of these boys are friends of mine too. But if they knew what was going on in that camp, I think many of them would volunteer.'

Davies would not have been a military man had he not pressed home his advantage, although his tone was gentler now. 'But they don't know, do they, Anna? And here's no opportunity now for us to tell them.'

It was then Adams heard his own voice. 'Millburn knows, sir. And some of the senior crews.'

Davies spun round. 'What did you say?'

'Millburn came to see me last night. He said Harvey had old him everything and asked if he would raid the camp fter the assembly plant was destroyed. He found it such burden that he had spoken to his close friends.'

Davies' teeth could be heard gritting together. 'Harvey id that? Gave away top-secret information! Christ! What id Millburn say?'

'He asked for my views, sir.'

'And what were they?'

Adams avoided Anna's eyes. 'I told him his responsibility had to be towards his men.' Then, as Davies seemed to relax. Adams took a deep breath. 'But having listened to Anna, sir, I think my views have changed.'

Anna gave a gasp of surprise. Davies' expression turned into a mixture of resentment and curiosity. 'Why is that?'

'I think Anna's right, sir. I've never understood why those hellish camps have gone unscathed, particularly as the war was supposed to be about freedom and the liberation of the oppressed. I suppose it's because wars by definition destroy ideals. After a few years of slaughtering one another, we hate our enemy so much we forget why we're doing it. But Anna has just reminded us.'

Davies was eyeing Adams with dislike. 'So you believe I should risk the lives of my boys, perhaps all of them, for two Germans?'

'Not two sir. Saindau is full of German dissidents.'

'All right. A hundred. A thousand. Are you prepared to explain to the boys' mothers that we sent them to their deaths to liberate a campful of Germans?'

Adams winced. 'I know it's a hard choice.'

'Hard? It's a hellish one and a choice I don't want to make. There's something else too. If I give my boys this unauthorised order, it won't just mean my going before a Board of Inquiry. I might be able to live with that but it would almost certainly mean the disbanding of the squadron, the finest pound for pound military unit this country has ever produced. I've too many enemies and there's too much jealousy around for it to survive. That's what the cost could be, Frank.'

Adams knew he was probably right. 'But could we have a better reason for paying it, sir? On our last operation we chose to save lives rather than to take them. Wouldn't history appreciate that choice one day? Until then I think I could live with that kind of disgrace.'

Davies' growl betrayed what he thought of history and justice. 'Do you think that's the way Records would show it? Or the way history would think of us? We'd be stigmatised and remembered as the squadron who disobeyed orders. No more, no less.'

With no argument left, Adams fell silent as Davies turned back to the girl. 'I understand how you feel about these men. I'd probably feel the same in your shoes. But the truth is, I couldn't help you even if I wanted to. You see, to gain maximum performance out of our aircraft, we give them only enough fuel to cover the journey. So even if Saindau is only twenty miles from the plant, I couldn't send the boys or by the time the action was over they'd all run out of fuel. I'm sorry, Anna. I truly am.'

Later, when the outcome and cost of it was known, Adams with his bedevilled conscience was never certain he had been right to correct Davies. But at the time, with Anna's lovely face showing despair, the protest leapt to his lips. 'That isn't correct, sir. Not knowing what kind of opposition he might meet over the target, Millburn persuaded his advisers to give the aircraft extra fuel.'

Davies looked as if he had receive a blow in the face. 'Are you just saying that, Adams?'

'No, sir. Millburn told me just before take-off. They will have enough fuel if you authorise the attack.'

With his last card trumped, Davies turned away from Anna and stood motionless by the small window. Showing renewed hope, Anna rose and went to his side. 'Doesn't that say something to you, Arthur? That perhaps was meant to be. I've never asked for any reward when worked for you but I am asking one now. Please give my friends their freedom.'

It was a plea that made Adams' eyes burn. With one side of Davies' face visible, he could see a muscle working in the small officer's cheek. In the silence that followed Adams could hear an order being shouted in one of the aircraft hangars. Then Davies gave a long, deep sigh. 'All right, Anna. You've won. I'll send the order. After that you might say a prayer or two because I think we're going to need all the help we can get.'

With that he turned and left the lobby. As if totally exhausted by her efforts, Anna stood for a moment supporting herself at the table. Then, with a sob, she turned and threw herself into Adams' arms.

Chapter 30

Gabby heard the signal as A-Apple was skirting a small town that lay alongside the rail track. 'It's William Tell,' he shouted at Millburn.

The American looked puzzled. 'What's the message?'

Gabby was listening intently. When the message had ended, he turned to Millburn. 'They say we've permission to attack the second target when we've destroyed the first. Our rockets must be kept for it.' Gabby was looking shaken. 'That means the concentration camp, doesn't it?'

'Yes, it must. Does William Tell want a reply?'

'No. We've to keep radio silence until our attack on the plant. Then you have to ask for volunteers.'

Before Millburn could reply, the Morse came again. Gabby nodded at Millburn's question. 'Yes. It's the same message. They're making sure we get it. What the hell's happened, Millburn? Why do they suddenly want an attack on the camp?'

Millburn was looking disturbed himself. 'I don't know unless Harvey's managed to talk Davies round.'

'How the hell can we be expected to attack two targets? We don't know how tough the first one's going to be yet.'

Thinking the same thing, Millburn was trying to analyse his own feelings. Shocked by Harvey's revelations, he was feeling a certain grim relief that he and the squadron had a chance to bring some aid to Saindau's victims.

At the same time he could not quell the thought that his chance of surviving the mission had been considerably reduced by the message. Although it was a thought any sane man would have, Millburn was not used to such morbid contemplations and its persistence worried him.

In an effort to escape it, his thoughts turned to the squadron. Machin, Larkin and Van Breedenkamp probably understood the message but what would the rest of the crews be making of it? Unable to talk to them yet, Millburn could only hope their bewilderment die not affect their performance when they reached the primary target.

With the small town left behind them, the Mosquitoes were back on track, their slipstreams and the blast of their engines tumbling snow off wires and telegraph poles. With no dangerous obstacles ahead, Gabby turned back to Millburn. 'What are you going to do, Millburn?'

Fatigue and his mixed feelings made the American irritable. 'What do you mean, what am I going to do?'

'Davies' message mentions volunteers. That must mean we don't have to raid Saindau if we don't want to. So how do you feel about it?'

'I don't know yet. I'll have to see what happens over the plant.'

'That means you're going to do it if you can!' Gabby looked indignant. 'Shouldn't you consult me first? I'm i the bloody kite too, aren't I?'

'You think I can forget it? Quit the bellyaching an watch out for flak posts. Every station we pass will b sending signals ahead. So keep your eyes peeled.'

Although he scowled, Gabby knew it was true. Th telegraph wires below them would be singing wit warning messages as the Mosquitoes raced past. Proof o this came only a minute after Millburn gave his warnin As A-Apple swept over a rail crossing, tracer leapt u from a mobile gun carrier standing on the road. Carryin multiple pom-poms the carrier drilled holes in Millburn's port wing tip and forced Machin and the machines behind him to swerve dangerously to starboard. With more than one aircraft forced to take sharp evasive action to avoid collision, it was a full minute before the squadron was in formation again.

It was an incident that gave every man a warning. With their route locked to the rail track, it meant the assembly plant would be getting messages every few seconds that the Mosquitoes were heading towards them. Whether its flak defences were light or heavy, there was no doubt their gunners would be on full alert.

'How much longer to our ETA?' Millburn asked.

'Ten minutes, give a minute or two either way,' Gabby told him. Then: 'Let's hope the Yanks haven't got lost or we could be in the shit.'

Millburn was about to reply tartly, then thought better. With the target sweeping nearer, any arguments or distractions, however small, could be dangerous or even fatal. He himself was secretly hoping their rendezvous vith the Mustangs was not delayed. Although it was ıot uncommon during the air war for aircraft to find heir target or keep their rendezvous within minutes of heir scheduled ETAs, Millburn knew the unusually bad veather might cause problems today. Bearing it in mind, e gave Gabby a mild reply. 'We don't want them yet. 'o give us high cover they'll have to climb from low evel to the cloud base. That's high enough for radar to etect them.'

Gabby gave him a scornful glance. 'Will it matter? very station along the line must be tipping off the plant this time.'

Knowing he was right, Millburn was wondering if it d been a mistake to plot the last 80 miles of their route ng the railway. Better perhaps to have dog-legged and acked from the west. Then he shrugged. It was too late now to change the plan and in any case there had been the poor weather and fuel consumption to think about. For better or worse, the die was cast.

As they approached another small town, the black bursts of 37mm shells began exploding ahead of them. Waggling his wings, Millburn led the formation round the town outskirts before circling back to the track. No damage had been done but the warning had been given. They were expected.

Beside Millburn Gabby was examining his photographs with increased care. Another siding and rail crossing came and went and then he tapped Millburn's knee. 'Only a couple of miles, Millburn, if those Benson boys are right.'

The American felt his muscles tighten. In less than a minute they would all know if the agents had talked or if the enemy had guessed the reason for their presence and reinforced the assembly plant's defences. With no message yet from Dent's Mustangs, Millburn was only too aware his squadron was defenceless against a high level attack, and with their priceless new fighter's birthplace under threat, the Germans might have recalled any number of 262s to defend it. Yet the tyranny of low-level flight allowed him only the briefest of glances at the threatening clouds above.

A sudden yell from Gabby scattered his thoughts 'There it is! At one o'clock.'

Millburn followed the Welshman's pointing finge Ahead two shallow wooded hills were rising from th snow-covered plain. With no siding or branch line visible, they looked as innocent as any of the lo hills they had recently seen. 'Are you sure?' Millbur shouted back.

Clearly unsure the moment he had spoken, Gabb watched the hills intently as A-Apple raced towar them. As the Mosquito shot past, Millburn caught glimpse of the saddle between the two hills. Although was snow covered like the hills around it, the flatness of its side facing the track was its betrayal. Without waiting for Gabby's triumphant shout, Millburn hauled back on his control column and switched on his R/T. 'Foxhound Leader to Squadron. There is your target. Orbit with me under cloud base.'

Relieved of the massive strain of low level flight, pilot after pilot climbed after A-Apple and went into orbit over the wooded hills. While Gabby inspected the target with binoculars, Millburn gave his orders. 'OK, guys, let's get the job done. Red One, you know your target, so make your attack. Red Two follow after his bombs explode. Go.'

B-Bertie, flown by Machin, dipped a wing and went plunging down. As it headed for the saddle and its bomb door opened, hell suddenly broke loose. Vicious lines of tracer coned on the diving aircraft and a bracket of red-cored explosions burst around it, throwing it off course towards the southern hill. As Machin tried to swing the Mosquito back, more tracer stabbed up from the trees, forcing him to turn south and miss his target.

The Irishman's apologetic voice came over the R/T moment later. 'Sorry, Foxhound Leader. Oi wasn't xpecting the welcome. Oi'll come round and try again.'

Millburn, who had grabbed the binoculars from Gabby, as staring down at a huge black vehicle that had ppeared near the side of the rail track. Covered earlier a white camouflaged net, its crews had clearly been ld not to betray their position until the Mosquitoes clared their intentions. Now the attack had commenced, armoured flak wagon, almost certainly brought to the ant by train, was ready and spoiling for a fight.

Nor was it alone. In addition to the LMGs on the lsides that had forced Machin off course, two gun sts had become visible on the roof of the assembly nt. Moreover, 37mm flak bursts rising from the far side of the plant hinted another flak wagon was stationed there, no doubt brought up on the road that ran past it. The soft target Davies had hoped for was bristling with fire power.

Millburn cancelled Machin's intention. 'No, Red One. Formate behind me for a moment. Attention, Red Two. Make your attack now.'

Red Two, manned by Tomlinson and Mason, dipped a wing and dived down. As they headed towards the saddle, pom-pom shells and tracer shot out from the flak wagon like the quills of a porcupine. For a moment it seemed Tomlinson would reach the plant but suddenly a 37mm shell hit his port wing. As fuel tanks exploded, B-Bertie suddenly became a fiery comet that plunged towards the northern hillside. A few second later a massive explosion lit up the trees and the clouds above. Tomlinson's cheeky, freckled face would bring laughter and gaiety to the Mess no longer.

With the plant guarded on every side, Millburn pushed aside his misgivings and lifted his face mask. 'Foxhound Leader to Red One. You know the score, Paddy. You take the north side of the bastard and I'll take the south. Us a bomb, not your rockets. The rest of you guys stay i orbit and keep an eye open for bandits. OK, Red One Let's go.'

The two Mosquitoes broke formation and plunge down, A-Apple banking to starboard and B-Bertie t port. Levelling off less than 200 feet above the groun flying on a near collision course, they headed back fo the flak wagon that was pumping out shells at the aircra orbiting above.

The manoeuvre was one Ian Moore had original introduced to the squadron and which had since be used by Harvey and Millburn himself. Flak wagons wi their massive fire power and thick armour were in gene a suicide target for aircraft if a single aircraft was us against them. But if an attack was pressed from two sides simultaneously their firepower could be proportionately reduced.

But they were still a highly dangerous target, as Millburn knew only too well. For the pilot and his navigator the worst part of the attack came in the long seconds it took their aircraft to circle round and head back to face the fury of the wagon's guns. It gave men time to feel their fear, the rapid beating of their hearts, the throb of blood in their temples. It also gave them time to think about the loved ones they might never see again.

Although Millburn had known normal fear many times in the past, he had never suffered crippling thoughts of this nature before. As A-Apple devoured the half mile or so of track that lay between him and the flak wagon, and its crews, realising their danger, frantically depressed heir guns, Millburn felt sweat pouring from him.

Then, from the corner of his eye, he caught sight of Gabby preparing to open the bomb doors. Although ooking pale and drawn, the tough little Welshman had ever spoken a word of complaint when Millburn had rdered the attack on the flak wagon, although he had nown its perils. Nor was he complaining now although is fate was entirely in the hands of his pilot.

A-Apple quivered as its bomb doors opened. In spite f his fear, Gabby was carrying out his every task. he example gave Millburn victory over his nerves and eared his mind. 'Fuse No. 1 bomb,' he shouted.

The flak wagon was now in range of A-Apple's nnon but Millburn dared not fire in case his shells ruck Machin attacking from the other side. Instead gritted his teeth and flew obliquely into the sheets LMG fire that the flak wagon was hurling at him. the other side, Machin was having to face the gon's 37mm shells. As their aircraft shuddered under impact of shells and bullets, both pilots cursed the order that forbade them to use their long-range rockets.

Alongside Millburn, trying to make himself as small a target as possible, Gabby had the bomb release button in his hand. Waiting until the massive flak wagon was filling A-Apple's windshield and it seemed the two war machines would weld together, Millburn gave a yell. 'Now!'

Gabby pressed the button and a half second later Millburn hauled back on the control column. As A-Apple rocketed upwards Machin's Mosquito flashed past on its portside and released its own time-fused bomb. As the two aircraft went skyward like two launched rockets, vengefu shells from the wagon followed them.

But only for a few seconds. As the breathless crews i orbit gazed down, a huge cloud of smoke suddenly hid th wagon. Three seconds later a second explosion hurled th huge vehicle over on its side.

Shouts of relief and congratulations filled the a waves as Millburn and Machin climbed back in fo mation. Millburn's voice hushed them. 'Keep quie you guys, and listen. I want Blue Section to attac those gun posts on the hill sides. Red Section is resume attack on the target. So down you go, Re 3.'

As Blue Section went searching for the LMG gunpos and Larkin dipped a wing and dived towards the camo flaged plant, Millburn and Gabby had time to breat again. Millburn addressed his R/T. 'Well done, Padd Are you OK?'

A breathless voice answered him. 'Oi think so, Fo hunter Leader. But Oi think I could do with a drop o' good stuff.'

Reaction brought a laugh from Millburn. 'You'll some when we get back, Paddy. I'll buy it myself.'

Gabby, his colour returning, gave Millburn a gla

'You never buy me drinks afterwards, do you? You just take me for granted.'

Grateful to the Welshman and also knowing he was always irritable after a close engagement, Millburn punched his arm. 'You're part of the family, boyo. You're supposed to buy drinks, not scrounge them.'

'Family? That'll be the day when I'm related to a colonial, Millburn.'

Before Millburn could reply, an American voice sounded in his earphones. 'Hiya, Foxhunter Leader. Hawkeye Leader here. Sorry we're a few minutes late but we had a brush with 190s on the way.'

Glanced west, Millburn saw in the distance a couple of dozen small shapes climbing up to the cloud base. 'Hello, Hawkeye Leader. We're sure glad to see you. Did you have any losses?'

'Yeah, a few. But we're OK now. Have you seen any bandits yet?'

'No. But they're expected. So you're welcome to he party.'

A chuckle came over the R/T. 'You're starting to ound like a Limie, Foxhunter Leader. Where do you vant us?'

Millburn spoke while watching the progress of Red 'hree. 'How about orbiting as near to us as you can? 'hen you'll be on hand if any bandits arrive.'

Although threatened by LMG fire, Red Three had ıanaged to reach the plant and, as Millburn watched, arkin released two 250 bombs. A moment later there as a dismayed cry from the New Zealander's navigator. 'he roof must be reinforced, skipper.'

Millburn was thinking nothing could have emphasised ore the value the Germans put on the 262 plant than e care that had gone into its construction. The two mbs, released from less than 300 feet, had skidded ɔng the roof instead of penetrating it and ended up on the northern hillside. As Larkin swung south to avoid the explosions, two huge bursts of smoke and flame sent trees and branches high into the air.

Expecting a fighter attack at any moment, Millburn's orders were urgent. 'Your turn, Red Four. Drop your eggs from 1500.'

With every crewman understanding the order, Thomas in F-Freddy broke formation and headed for the snow-covered roof, now disfigured by the skidding marks of the two failed bombs. Holding his breath, Millburn watched two black objects detach from the mosquito and drop into a nose down trajectory. Gabby's complaining voice sounded in his earphones. 'We should have brought armour-piercing eggs, Millburn. What're we going tc do if these don't break through?'

To the American's huge relief, the question provec unnecessary eight seconds later. Reaching a much highe velocity than the stores before it, Thomas's bombs struck the roof and disappeared. As Thomas let out a yell o triumph, the near end of the snow-covered roof liftec releasing a cloud of black smoke. A couple of second later a second explosion blew away one of the hug side doors.

Millburn's voice sounded over the shouts of exultatio that filled the air waves. 'Cool it, you guys. It's a bi factory. Hit the centre this time, Red Five.'

The words had barely left his mouth when an agonise cry came over the R/T. Excited by their success, starir back at the damage they had wrought, Thomas and h navigator had forgotten the flak wagon at the far end the factory. As they swept over the road, the wagon gunners had taken revenge. An explosive 20mm sh killed the navigator instantly and another struck Thoma right leg and blew it into gruesome fragments. F-Fred reeled like a wounded animal towards a nearby hill, th Thomas lost all control and the Mosquito spun down a exploded. Thomas would never see Wales beat England at Twickenham again.

Survivors from the bombing were pouring out from the plant, some milling black dots in the snow, others trying to find shelter up the hillsides. Gabby motioned down. 'What are you going to do about them?'

'Leave them,' Millburn said. 'Most of them will only be factory hands anyway.'

Extensive as the 262 plant was, its end was now only a matter of time. As Millburn's Blue Section took out more and more of the LMG posts, the remaining Mosquitoes were able to drop their bombs with precision. By the time Blue Section had joined in and dropped their quota of bombs, the last portion of the roof had gone and the entire edifice was a raging furnace. Even allowing for the renowned German power of recovery, it was certain that no more 262s would be built or assembled there.

As the last Mosquito climbed back into orbit, Dent's voice came over the R/T. 'That's a hell of a job, Foxhound Leader. Our bomber boys will feel a lot happier now.'

Hoping it were true, Millburn nodded at Gabby. 'OK. You can call up William Tell now. This is the message I want you to send . . .'

Chapter 31

Adams thought Davies looked like a delighted gnome as he swung round on Staines. 'They've done it! They've wiped the plant right out.'

Staines drove a huge fist into the palm of an equally large hand. 'Goddamn it, that's wonderful. You've got a hell of a squadron there, Davies. Congratulations.'

Adams, standing beside Anna who was sitting on a bench, saw Davies glance at her. Although the small Ai Commodore was at least 20 feet away, Adams could se his eyes were glowing with pride. 'More than that, every man of 'em has volunteered to fly on to Saindau.' A Staines shook his head in respect, Davies went on: 'It' a tradition. They always volunteer.'

Before Staines could reply, Henderson motioned a the slip of paper in Davies' hand. 'How many casu alties, sir?'

'Three, Jock.'

Henderson winced. 'Do we know their names?'

'Not yet. We'll have to wait for that.'

'Three already,' the Scot muttered. 'And they've st to reach that second target.' He made his request witho looking at Anna and Adams. 'Do they have to go, si They must be damn nearly exhausted by this time.'

Davies frowned. 'Don't complicate things, Jock. W agreed the plan, so let's stick to it.'

Henderson's voice was bitter. 'I never agreed it, sir don't agree with it now.'

For one with such a short fuse, Davies was unusually patient. 'They're not all going, Jock. Millburn says he is only taking his Red Section. He's sending Blue Section back under Van Breedenkamp.'

'That's still half our squadron, sir. If those 262s find them, it could be murder.'

Staines, whose eyes had been moving from one man to the other, approached the wireless operator. 'I want to send another message to Hawkeye, Sergeant. Give me a pencil and paper.'

As he scribbled on the paper, Anna gave a shudder nd glanced up at Adams. 'I shouldn't have asked, hould I, Frank? I haven't been fair to Arthur or any f your men.'

Speaking quietly, Adams tried to calm her. 'You did for your friends. I'm not sure I wouldn't have done the ıme thing.'

Her low question moved him. 'But what will I do if you se more men? I'll never be able to forgive myself.'

'Why don't you go and stay with Frank until this is ver,' Adams urged. 'I'll come and give you the news soon as it comes in.'

She shook her head. 'No. I'd be too restless. I prefer stay here.'

Staines was handing the slip of paper to Davies. The all Air Commodore looked both relieved and shocked he read it. 'But what about their fuel, sir?'

'They'll have enough,' Staines said. 'You said it's only ew more miles, didn't you?' When Davies nodded, ines went on: 'Then they should be OK. If they're , they can keep going and land in Russian occupied itory. From the way those Commies are advancing, y're not that far from Saindau.'

Davies hesitated. 'Of course, I hadn't thought of that. are you sure you want to do this, sir? You do realise involve you in an illegal operation?'

Staines's tough face looked as if it had been chiselled out of stone at that moment. 'I know the score, Davies. But I also know this whole goddamned operation was laid on for us and we like to pay our debts.' Turning, he thrust the slip of paper at the wireless operator. 'Send it, son. Right away.'

Millburn caught sight of the branch line three minutes after leaving the blazing factory. Black against the snow, it forked away from the Rostock line and headed into a white desolate landscape relieved only by occasional farm houses and trees.

Guessing the news of the recent raid would have reached Saindau, Millburn waited until the branch line was a mile behind him before he swung east. Although he felt the camp was unlikely to feel threatened, ther was no point in advertising an attack was coming.

Not that Millburn expected much opposition fror Saindau itself. With concentration camps having enjoye total immunity from air attacks throughout the war, it wa known that their defences were geared to keep prisone inside rather than to drive attackers away. But havir already lost three crews, Millburn was taking no chance His thoughts, like the thoughts of all the crews, we on the missing fighter attacks. Why hadn't the 26 appeared yet?

The remainder of Millburn's Red Section was forma ted behind him, with a dozen Mustangs flitting in and c of the snow-filled clouds above. Staines's message h been for the Mustangs to stay with the Mosquitoes matter what, but when Millburn had ordered the relucta Van Breedenkamp to take his Blue Section home, D had split his force and sent half of his Mustangs to esc them. Dent himself was staying with the attacking for

With a chance at last to talk unhurriedly to his cre Millburn lifted his face mask. 'Foxhound Leader to I

Section. We'll be attacking our second target in a few minutes, so listen carefully. This target is a Nazi concentration camp with some of its prisoners our own agents or sympathisers, so our job is to destroy the defences so they can escape.

'We'll first go into orbit to suss out the place,' he went on. 'When we've established the administration buildings and the guards' quarters, Red One and I, who still have bombs, will go down and use them. Then hopefully I'll be back to control operations but if anything happens to me, attack the enemy buildings in clockwise fashion. Use your rockets and cannon and don't spare any survivors this time because they'll be SS guards or Gestapo agents. Also remember if we leave many alive they might re-capture the prisoners.'

Although Milburn had deliberately avoided using the name Saindau, he knew enough had been said over the assembly plant to alert the German radio monitoring service. With his younger crews needing more information before the attack, he could only hope the job could be completed before enemy fighters were vectored owards them.

Beside him, Gabby was grinning. 'You're getting loodthirsty in your old age, aren't you?'

For once Milburn's humour was not forthcoming. 'If ou'd heard what those bastards do to their prisoners, ou'd want to get down there and tear 'em to pieces with our bare hands. So cut out the crap and help me to find aindau.'

While Millburn was issuing his orders, an example f the camp's inhumanity was being played out on its now-covered parade ground. For the third time that day e prisoners were being subjected to a roll-call. Clad nly in their thin striped prison uniforms and surrounded brutal guards and snarling dogs, they were being rced to stand to attention in a freezing wind while an SS sergeant slowly and sadistically called out their names. If any man fell – and weakened men kept falling – they were immediately dragged away and tossed into a concrete bunker to await execution.

Hausmann and Meyer were among the parade. After the agony of their torture the previous day, they had been thrown into a wooden hut occupied by living skeletons rather than men. With only a filthy threadbare blanket to keep out the bitter cold, they had endured a night of suffering, only for a brutal kapo to order them outside at dawn for the first roll-call. Unlike the other prisoners they were forbidden to wear boots, and after the second call two hours later both men's feet were blue and numbed. In spite of the message they gave one another, they knew it was only a matter of time before frost bite would add its torment to their suffering.

A prisoner a few paces away from Hausmann, young in years but old in suffering, gave a sudden groan and collapsed. At a shout from the SS sergeant, two guards ran along the ranks and dragged him away. Remembering his arthritic hip, Hausmann wondered how long it would be before he followed the man and then realised that since entering the camp he had not felt a single twinge from it. Like everything in life, he thought, pain was a relative thing.

Fifteen minutes passed and still the sadistic roll-call was no more than half way through. Just when he was feeling the icy wind had reached his very soul, Hausmann heard a sudden shout from the administration building and saw Lerner running towards the SS sergeant. He could not hear what passed between them but a moment later the sergeant bellowed out the names of Overbeck and Muller, who had to step in front of the parade.

As the two men shuffled forward, Lerner ran towards them, his handsome face a mask of fury. Without warning he struck Meyer across the face, sending him reeling

Before Hausmann could react, he also received a vicious blow on his heavily bruised jaw. Through an explosion of pain he heard Lerner's curses. 'You filthy scum. You treacherous lice-ridden animals. I knew it. I warned Rosler but he wouldn't listen. God, how you are going to pay for this.'

'Pay for what?' Meyer managed.

He received another vicious blow across the face. 'As if you didn't know. You, who told the enemy where the factory was. Let me tell you this, you scum. For every man your terror fliers have killed today, you are going to die a thousand deaths.'

Like Hausmann, Meyer felt there was nothing to lose now. 'So the plant has been attacked and destroyed?'

His collar was seized and he was pulled to within inches of Lerner's contorted face. 'Yes, it has, you filthy traitor. Thanks to you the Fatherland has lost a weapon that might have saved the lives of thousands of our women and children. So you tell me what kind of death a traitor like you deserves. Go on! Tell me!'

The man's fury was intimidating, giving him the strength to shake Meyer like a dog shaking a rabbit. You cannot, so I will. It is waiting for you in that building over there, where we have punished traitors like you before. It will not give you a quick and merciful death, if that is what you are hoping. It will make sure your agony lasts for days and I promise you that every second of those days you will curse the moment you sold out your country and your Fuhrer.'

Shoving Meyer away, Lerner waved two armed guards forward. As they grabbed the two Bavarians, the white-faced Meyer caught Hausmann's eye. His message needed no words. They must both seek a quick death.

Driven by kicks and rifle butts, they were sent stumbling across the parade ground to a brick building at its far end. As the door was thrown open, Hausmann had a glimpse of meat hooks attached to the far wall and the brown stains of blood beneath them. An intense shock struck the Bavarian, and then disbelief. This was not possible. It was a hideous nightmare. No human beings, however fanatical or depraved, could commit such acts on their fellow creatures.

A blow across his kidneys brought back the truth. A shove sent him stumbling across the bare concrete floor to a blood-stained bench that stood beneath the hooks. Beside him Lerner drew a Luger pistol from his belt and nodded at the two guards. Propping their rifles against the walls, the two men grabbed hold of Meyer while Lerner covered Hausmann with his pistol. Knowing they could wait no longer if they were to escape an agonising death, Hausmann was about to shout out to Meyer and to defy Lerner's pistol when a shadow flashed past the door, followed by a thunderous roar.

The blast of sound, followed by another a second later, startled both Lerner and the guards, all of whom spun round to identify the cause. The distraction was enough for the two desperate Bavarians. Meyer jumped down from the bench, while Hausmann, the nearest to the rifles, snatched one up and fired at Lerner before the officer could recover and shoot.

There was no time to see if Lerner was hit. One guard was already running at Hausmann. Unable to reload in time, Hausmann jabbed with the muzzle of the rifle and caught him full in the throat. Choking, the man collapsed. As the second guard rushed at Hausmann, Meyer tripped him. As the man stumbled and fell, Hausmann swung the rifle butt down on his skull. Feeling his thumping heart would burst from his weakened body at any moment, Hausmann swung round, half expecting to see Lerner covering them from the doorway.

But the SS Officer was lying on the floor with a hand clutched to his side. His other hand, however, still held the Luger and he was clearly making a massive effort to lift it and fire. As Hausmann cocked his rifle, Meyer, his voice unrecognisable, caught his arm. 'No, I want him.' Grabbing a bayonet from the second unconscious guard, Meyer ran across the concrete floor and drove the bayonet into the man's stomach. He was still driving it back and forth like a man possessed when Hausmann grabbed his arm. About to strike Hausmann and then recognising him, Meyer's eyes lost their madness and he lowered his ashamed head over the dying Lerner.

As an explosion sounded at the far side of the compound and guards fled for shelter, Hausmann saw through the open doorway that the skeletons on the parade ground were either fleeing in terror or dropping to their knees in thanksgiving. Turning back, he gave Meyer no time for penitence. 'It's an Allied air raid and might give us a chance to escape.' He indicated Lerner and the two unconscious guards. 'Take their boots and rifles, and then get blankets from the huts. Then pray those airmen do a good job on the guards.'

Still trembling from his violent act of revenge, Meyer began tugging off Lerner's polished boots. 'Do you think we can reach the Russians?'

Hausmann already had a pair of boots in his hand. 'We can only try. They can't be that far away, so if we get out of here we've got a fair chance.' Then, as he picked up the Luger, Hausmann took a deep, satisfying breath. 'At least we've got the rifles and the pistol. So whatever happens, no Nazi bastard is going to take us alive again.'

Gabby was the first to spot Saindau. 'Over there, Millburn. At one o'clock.'

Millburn saw the camp now, a square shaped compound set apart in the desolate countryside. 'Foxhound Leader to Red Section. Target in sight. Remember your orders.'

The compound grew larger by the moment as Millburn headed towards it. He could see the rail track again, running through a high brick entrance. But his eyes were drawn to a snow-covered square where a mass of tiny figures could be seen. Puzzled, he pointed them out to Gabby who picked up his binoculars. A moment later the Welshman gave a start. 'I think they're prisoners, Millburn. I can see uniformed men with dogs guarding them. Christ, there must be two hundred of them.' Gabby re-focused his glasses, and then turned to Millburn in astonishment. 'You're not going to believe this but the poor bastards are out there in just their prison uniforms. In this weather.'

Millburn nodded grimly. 'Didn't I tell you what to expect? Watch out when we reconnoitre the buildings. I want to know where the SS and the guards have their offices and billets.'

A-Apple swept over the compound a minute later. Peering down, Gabby saw that brick buildings lined two sides of the square, with a couple of dozen wooden huts forming a block on the third side. A sinister brick building with a smoking chimney occupied the fourth side with a water tower alongside it. The entire complex was ringe in depth by two barbed wire fences equipped with lights with armed guard towers every thirty or forty yards.

The arrival of the Mosquitoes was causing conster nation below. Guards were running for shelter and pris oner showing panic or rapture according to their physica and mental condition. Gabby, gazing through his binocu lars, sounded horrified. 'They're just skeletons, Millbur Don't they give them any food at all?'

Millburn was in no mood for speculation. 'Watc where those guards are taking shelter. That's where o bombs go, so make a note of them.'

Obeying, Gabby turned to Millburn a few secon later. 'They must live in the permanent buildings rour the edge of the camp. The prisoners are in the wooden huts.'

Millburn nodded. 'That's what I thought. So let's get round and begin our business.'

Behind A-Apple, the rest of Red Section were circling the compound, their crews expressing the same horror as Gabby. Machin's voice sounded, his Irish humour missing for once. 'Oi'm glad you brought me here, skipper. It's going to be a pleasure to drop my bomb on these people, so it is.'

Other crews were expressing the same sentiments. Millburn silenced them. 'Go into orbit until Machin and I have finished. Then you can take over.'

Although taken by total surprise by the Mosquitoes' appearance, two of the tower gun posts had begun firing. Nodding at Gabby, who opened A-Apple's bomb doors, Millburn swung round and made straight for the high brick entrance. As he shouted, Gabby pressed the bomb release. As A-Apple bounced, Millburn made for the next brick building and the next, Gabby dropping a bomb each time. Before the last of Millburn's 250 GPs had gone, explosion after explosion was hurling bricks and debris high into the air.

Dropping his last bomb, Millburn turned on a flak tower that was firing at him. Squinting through his illuminated reflector sight, the American fired a burst of cannon shells that slaughtered the SS guards and blew the tower into pieces. As Gabby let out a yell of triumph, Millburn drew back on his control column. 'OK, Paddy. Your turn now.'

The Irishman dived down with gusto and began his sequence of bombing. With their buildings blowing up around their ears the SS personnel were now trying to escape through the wire fences that the bombing had destroyed. Catching sight of their uniforms, Millburn swung back and dived on them. Seconds later his Brownings and 200mm cannon were cutting men down like scythes chopping down weeds. Knowing that the strafing of men was something Millburn normally disliked, Gabby was driven into silence by the American's passion. It was only when Millburn heard the clank of breech blocks and the whine of compressed air telling him that his ammunition was exhausted that he drew in his breath and climbed away. 'All right, you guys. Come down with your rockets now.'

In five minutes the camp was totally destroyed. All the brick buildings were in ruins, the barbed wire fences were down, and uniformed bodies lay everywhere. What few guards had escaped the storm and fled into the desolate countryside were being ruthlessly hunted by the avenging Mosquitoes. Watching from above, Millburn saw bands of prisoners collecting coats and boots from dead bodies and crossing the destroyed fences to freedom. He could only hope Anna's two friends were among them.

It had all been so easy, he was telling himself as he called his Red Section back. It could have been done to every camp in Germany. It might not have stopped the Nazi savagery, yet on the other hand it might have proved a salutary warning to the SS what the Allies felt about their barbarism and what their fate would be if the war was lost. At the worst, Millburn thought, it would have given countless men and women a chance of freedom and let persecuted minorities know they were not forgotten.

A sudden urgent shout over his R/T shattered his thoughts. 'Bandits, Foxhound Leader! 262s among them Watch your backs!'

The warning had barely died away before a slim bodied twin-engined aircraft with tapered wings streaked ove A-Apple and settled on the tail of M-Mother who, afte strafing Nazi guards, was about to rejoin Millburn' section. The 262's speed only allowed it to stay few seconds on M-Mother's tail but that was enough M-Mother staggered like a pheasant catching the full blas of a shotgun and blazed a trail of fire and flaming wreckage on a snow-covered field below. Almost at the same moment a Mustang with a wing shot away came spinning down and crashed near the stricken Saindau. Knowing his surviving crews would have heard Dent's warning, Millburn added his own urgent order. 'Foxhunter Leader to Red Section. Corkscrew and make for the clouds. At the double!'

Corkscrew was a complex manoeuvre that the highly trained crews of 633 Squadron had used successfully in the past. While every Mosquito covered the tail of the aircraft circling ahead of it, the entire formation climbed for cloud protection. With the 262s and other enemy fighters appearing at last and having height on them, Millburn knew it was the one manoeuvre that gave them a chance of survival.

What the American did not know was how lucky he had been so far. Although the German Observer Corps had sent in numerous messages about the Mosquitoes' outward route, a German fighter controller had believed their target was Rostock and had accordingly routed the 262s and other fighters to that city. Only when the assembly plant was raided had the controller realised his mistake but by then the 262s, whose high speed allowed them only a short range, had to find an airfield to refuel.

But now, having at last found the Mosquitoes that had destroyed their factory, they wanted revenge. With most of the Mosquitoes short on ammunition because of their hunger to punish the SS guards for their atrocities, it was likely the 262s would have gained that revenge had it not been for Dent's Mustangs who, at heavy cost to themselves, were keeping the main attacking force at bay.

But in spite of the Americans' bravery, it was impossible to keep every fighter from breaking through and Millburn's section found both 190s and 262s trying to prise open their formation. Knowing their fate if it were broken, Millburn and his crews fought grimly to preserve it while struggling to reach the clouds that could save them. But the clouds that earlier had seemed so low and threatening now seemed to reach to heaven itself as one fighter after another broke through Dent's cordon and swooped down with blazing guns.

Chapter 32

Davies peered anxiously over the wireless operator's shoulder. 'Is it from Foxhunter?'

'No, sir.' The sergeant finished taking down the message, then handed it to Davies. 'It's from Blue Section, sir. They say they've enough petrol so they're not landing at Voziers but coming straight back here.'

Davies glanced at the paper, then turned to Henderson. 'What the hell's Millburn doing? Why hasn't he sent us a signal since his section plastered Saindau?'

Henderson's face expressed his fears. Taking it as a look of reproach, Davies grew more irritable. 'For Christ's sake someone could contact us. What about Dent's Mustangs. They've got wirelesses too, haven't they?'

Although Davies' questions were not meant as a criticism of the Americans, the highly charged atmosphere of the Operations Room ensured that Staines was not pleased by them. 'My guys know their job, Davies. If they haven't reported in, there has to be a reason.'

Realising he had been misunderstood, Davies made amends. 'I wasn't criticising your boys, General. I just can't understand this damned silence.' Before Staines could reply, Davies turned back to the sergeant. 'Get hold of Voziers again. Ask if they've heard anything yet.'

As the sergeant began tapping his key, Davies glanced at Adams. 'Where's Anna gone?'

Adams stirred. 'She went off with the Brigadier, sir. I

think she was going to the Mess to tell Harvey the news about Saindau.'

Davies, so occupied with the fate of his squadron he was noticing little else, looked puzzled. 'Why did the Brigadier go?'

'He did tell us, sir. He said he had to get back to High Elms once the good news about the two operations came through.'

'Let's hope it is good news,' Davies muttered. 'It's not looking that way at the moment.'

A silence followed while the sergeant finished his transmission. As Morse sounded in his earphones, Davies leaned over his shoulder in an attempt to translate. Failing, his eyes followed the sergeant's pencil as it ran over his pad. Before the sergeant had time to tear off the sheet, Davies straightened and gave a groan. 'Not a word from Millburn. I don't understand it.'

Like everyone else in the room, Adams was thinking the explanation could be simple. Enemy fighters, with 262s among them, could have totally wiped out the small force of Mosquitoes. Davies' voice broke into his thoughts. 'I take it the Mustangs escorting Blue Section will go straight to your base, General, once they've crossed our coast?'

Staines nodded. 'Yeah. Those are their orders. But after all the help you've given us, they'll want to meet your boys face to face. So I suggest we throw a party for all you guys as soon as things settle down. It'll all be on us, drinks, girls, everything. What do you say, Davies?'

With two successful operations beneath his belt, there had been a time when Davies would have shown delight at this appreciation of his prized squadron. There was little of it in his expression now. 'It's good of you General, but we'd better wait until the operation details have gone through to our lords and masters. Celebrations might prove a bit optimistic then.'

Staines frowned. 'You still believe there'll be trouble over the Saindau raid.'

'I expect more than trouble, sir. I'm certain they'll call for a Board of Enquiry. But I want you to know that I shall put your involvement down to Allied co-operation, that you didn't agree with the raid but you committed your aircraft as a gesture of appreciation for our raid on the assembly plant.' Davies glanced at Henderson and Adams. 'I know my officers will bear witness to that.' As both junior officers nodded, Davies turned back to Staines. 'If we handle it that way, I can't see your Air Staff criticising your involvement in the Saindau raid.'

Staines was frowning heavily. 'Goddam it, Davies, I can't allow that. I did agree to it. I couldn't do much else after I heard what those Nazi bastards were doing in that camp. But are you sure your Air Staff are going to make such a fuss? After all, it was only a follow-up mission to the main target.'

Davies' voice was bitter. 'They will. Particularly if it turns out I've lost over half my squadron because of it. Those camps have been sacrosanct, General. God knows why but they have. And I've committed the mortal sin of attacking and destroying one.'

Staines appealed to Adams. 'You're in Intelligence Frank. Why haven't they been raided before?'

Adams cleared his throat. 'No one seems to know, sir. Some give a shortage of aircraft as the reason. Others that the distance of the camps from Britain would have meant unacceptable losses. But neither argument stands up since France and Belgium were liberated.'

Staines was examining his expression. 'You think it's political, don't you?'

Adams hesitated, then took the plunge. 'Frankly, I do. The politicians can't claim ignorance because Anthony Eden made mention of the camps to the House of Commons in 1942. And Jewish leaders on both sides of the Atlantic have been begging for years that something is done. The Allies argued that once their secret was known the Nazis would cease their extermination policy in fear of punishment but from all the reports we've had, they killed a million more people in 1944 than in 1943. Reports say that thousands of Jews are being killed every day in Auschwitz alone.'

Staines looked horrified. 'Thousands a day! In one camp?'

Adams nodded. 'It's organised genocide on a massive scale. So why no Allied aircraft have been used against the camps or the railway systems is a mystery, although we can all speculate.'

The shocked American turned to Davies. 'Did you know this?'

Davies shook his head. 'I knew they had concentration camps. But I'd no idea how brutal they were until Anna talked to us today.'

Staines's voice was bitter with self-reproach. 'You know what's wrong with us military goons, Davies? We don't think enough and we don't ask questions enough. Christ, this is a goddamed nightmare. So how can you get into the shit for taking one of these hell holes out? They ought to give you and your guys a medal for it.'

Davies was about to reply when a muffled voice in the sergeant's earphones brought all conversation to a halt The sergeant glanced up at the anxious Air Commodore 'It's Blue Section, sir. One of its aircraft has developed engine trouble and is asking the station to be ready.'

Davies turned to Henderson. 'Are your crash wagon on standby, Jock?'

Henderson looked affronted. 'They've been on standby for the last half hour, sir.'

Davies turned back to the sergeant. 'I'm going up to the Control Tower to see Blue Section in. If you get a message from Foxhunter, phone me immediately. Understand?'

As the sergeant nodded, Davies glanced at Staines. 'Are you coming up with us, sir, or do you want to get back to your HQ?'

'Hell, no. I want to know what's happened to my guys too.'

As Henderson moved to go with Davies, the Air Commodore turned to Adams. 'What do you want to do, Frank? See the boys in or wait for them in your Confessional?'

Anxious for news of Millburn, Adams accepted the offer. 'I'll come too, sir, if I may. It'll be some time before I can debrief the men.'

Davies shrugged. 'All right. Come on then.' Moving as if his age had caught up with him at last, the small Air Commodore pushed himself away from the bench and led his small party towards the Control Tower.

The urgent howl of a siren sent Helga running to her window. As the strident noise died away she heard a low humming in the distance. Gazing into the leaden afternoon sky she saw half a dozen black specks approaching the airfield. As they took definition and became aircraft, the engines of crash wagons and an ambulance standing on the field began to cough into life.

The roar of Merlins grew louder, disturbing half a dozen birds perched in the crabapple trees. As the Mosquitoes went into orbit over the airfield, Helga saw that one of them was trailing smoke from its port engine. From the attention the aircraft around it were paying, the sight made her think of a party of soldiers carrying a wounded comrade.

She saw that Maisie was at the gate now, a scarf in her hand. Like herself, the girl's anxious eyes were on the damaged Mosquito that was being given priority to land. As it swept over the inn, low enough for both girls to see patches on its wings and oxide stains from its exhausts, its smoking engine was coughing like a man with blood in his lungs. Then the coughing ceased and the only sound was the painful scream of airfoils. Before it settled down on the runway, crash wagons and the ambulance were already racing alongside it. As it touched down, its port wheel suddenly collapsed, dropping the wing and sending the aircraft into a vicious ground loop. Flames leapt from its damaged engine, threatening fuel tanks and its half-stunned crew.

But a crash wagon was on hand. As it skidded to a halt, asbestos-clad figures leapt out and in seconds foam was jetting over the wing and fuselage. As the half-stunned crew were helped from the cockpit and led away to the ambulance, Helga felt her taut muscles relax.

A green flare from the Control Tower gave permission for the remaining Mosquitoes to land. As each one swept over the inn, Maisie waved her scarf and received her acknowledgement in turn. Only when the last Mosquito had landed did Helga see the girl was crying bitterly.

She came up to Helga's room a minute later, her eyes swollen with tears. 'Did you see them?' When Helga nodded, the girl suddenly broke down and ran sobbing towards her. 'Only seven. Out of sixteen. Oh, Miss, isn't it awful?'

Arms around the girl's racking body, Helga tried to comfort her. 'There might be more coming later. Don't give up hope yet.'

Maisie was sobbing as if her heart would break. 'But why would they have split up like that? They don't normally.'

Helga sat her on the bed and tried to calm her. 'Try not to think the worst. There might be a good reason for it. Wait until Frank comes over. He'll be able to tell us what's happened.'

Her promise and sympathy gradually calmed the girl although tears were still trickling down her cheeks.

'You will do it, Miss? You will let me know soon as you can?'

Helga helped her to her feet. 'I promise. As soon as I find out from Frank. In the meantime try not to be too upset.' As the girl turned for the door, Helga's voice dropped conspiratorially. 'If I were you I'd sneak into the bar and have a stiff drink. Perhaps two.'

Maisie managed a smile. 'I think I will, Miss. I've never felt more like one in my life.'

Chapter 33

Watching the crash wagon completing its task and the ambulance speeding away with the two airmen, Staines gave a nod of approval. 'Slick work, Davies. I said you'd a class outfit here, didn't I?'

Although certain that Staines was trying to raise Davies' spirits, Adams was equally certain he was not being successful. The shrug Davies gave was subdued. 'I can't take credit for that, General. Airfield discipline is Henderson's baby.'

Unused to such compliments from Davies, Henderson might have shown some gratification if he had not been equally worried about his squadron. He glanced at Adams. 'I wonder if Van Breedenkamp has any idea what's happened to Millburn?'

Knowing it could be a hint for him to go and find out, Adams hesitated. 'I'd hardly think so. They separated after the raid on the plant, didn't they?' Then: 'But I'll go and ask him if you like.'

Henderson shook his head irritably. 'No. You're right. In any case he's sure to phone us here if he has any news.'

The long minutes dragged past. Down on the airfield the last of the Mosquitoes had taxied to its hard standing and was receiving attention from its mechanics. As two transports revved their engines and started along the perimeter track to pick up the weary crews, Adams knew he could not delay his departure any longer.

The ring of a telephone made all four officers start. As the duty Waaf picked up the receiver, Davies hurried to her side. 'Is it the Operations Room?'

The girl listened a moment, then shook her head. 'No, sir. It's a call for the Duty Officer.'

As the girl called over a fair-headed young flight lieutenant, Davies moved away with a sound that was suspiciously like a groan. 'For Christ's sake, what's happened to them? How can they all have bought it? It doesn't make any sense.'

Adams glanced at his watch. Henderson, who had been doing the same thing ever since the party entered the Control Tower, voiced his thoughts. 'They ought to have landed at Voziers thirty minutes ago. They're well out of fuel now.'

Although the thought was in everyone's mind, Henderson received a glare from Davies for expressing it. Feeling Millburn's letter in his pocket growing heavier by the moment, Adams decided he could delay the crews' de-briefing no longer. Excusing himself, he was a third of the way down the Control Towers' steps when he heard the telephone ring again. As it ceased he heard the Waaf's voice. 'It's the Operation Room for you, sir.'

With his heart suddenly pounding, Adams hurried back up the stairs to listen to Davies' high pitched voice. 'Yes, yes, lad, what is it? Voziers? Yes, of course I know. What do they say?'

The pause that followed seemed endless. Climbing back into the glass panelled tower, Adams saw Staines and Henderson looking like frozen statues as they watched the listening Davies. As he replaced the receiver, Davies stood a moment shaking his head as if stunned by the report.

It took Staines's irate, gravelly voice to break the silence. 'Come on, Davies, for Christ's sake. What was all that about?'

At that Davies pulled himself together, although the alarmed Adams saw his face was pale. 'I'm sorry, sir. But after all that's happened, it's hard to believe.'

'What's hard to believe? Come on, man. Get it out.'

Davies took a deep breath, then cleared his throat. 'Voziers say the men are safe. At least most of them are. But because of their fuel, they had to land in Belgium. That's caused the delay in communication.'

With everyone certain that a major tragedy had occurred, a sigh of relief sounded round the room. Henderson was first to speak, and in the irrelevant way his mind worked in moments of high drama, Adams found the Scot's reaction similar to that of an anxious parent, worried sick at one moment by his offsprings' truancy and then angry and scolding when they returned. 'I don't understand the crews' behaviour, sir. If they're all right, why in the hell didn't one of them get on to his blower and tell us so?'

'They couldn't,' Davies told him. 'Our boys used up most of their ammunition strafing Saindau and the Yanks used up most of theirs defending our boys when Jerry fighters intercepted them. So all of them had to fly back under strict radio silence to prevent another interception.'

Staines was shaking his head in disbelief. 'And I thought I'd lost a squadron. It's great news, Davies. We can throw that party now after all.'

Although showing relief himself, Adams had not missed the negative factor in Davies' statement. 'You said most of the crews are safe, sir. How many are missing?'

'Altogether four, and three of Major Dent's.'

'What about Millburn and Gabby?'

'They're all right. It was Millburn who got the message through to Voziers. I don't know who the missing men are yet.'

As Adams released his tight breath, Henderson drew up the balance sheet. 'So including B-Flight we've lost five crews altogether. Nearly a third of our strength. It hasn't been a cheap day, has it, sir?'

Seeing Davies' expression and knowing his fears for the squadron's future, Adams wished the Scot hadn't said that. 'No, it hasn't Jock. Not for us or the Americans. But it's a damn sight better than we thought five minutes ago.' Davies turned to Staines. 'I want to go down and speak to our Blue Section. Do you want to come, sir?'

Staines glanced at his watch, then shook his head. 'No, now I know Dent and most of his boys are OK, I'd better get back. I'll find out all the combat details from them later.'

The winter day was closing fast as the small party left the Control Tower. As Staines's staff car drew up alongside him, the American offered his hand all round. 'I'm indebted to you guys. If I can help you in the future, you've only to ask.' About to climb into the car, Staines turned and grinned at Davies. 'Let's have that party soon, Davies. If we play it right we'll get so pissed we'll tell those Brass Hats to go to hell.'

The three men stood a moment watching his car turn the corner to the guardroom and the station gates. Then, as Davies started forward again, a brusque voice checked him. 'Can you spare a minute, sir?'

Turning, Adams saw the tall figure of Harvey standing behind them, with Anna at his side. Davies frowned heavily. 'What is it this time? Can't you see I'm busy?'

Harvey stepped forward. 'I know that, sir. But this won't take a moment.'

Before Davies could say more, Anna's voice broke in. 'Please, Arthur. It's important to us both.'

Davies muttered something beneath his breath, then faced the Yorkshiremen. 'All right. What do you want?'

Displaying emotion was not Harvey's way and his blunt

Northern voice betrayed his embarrassment. 'I just want to shake hands with you. That's all.'

Davies jumped as if a dog had bitten his ankle. 'What?'

'I'd like to shake your hand, sir. For what you did today.'

Recovering, Davies eyed Anna suspiciously. 'This is your idea, isn't it?'

The girl shook her head. 'No, Arthur. I was as surprised as you are. But Frank thinks it was wonderful of you to authorise the raid on Saindau. He knows what it might cost you.'

Davies was not going to be won over as easily as that. 'You've got a bloody nerve, Harvey, after all the abuse you threw at me about that camp.'

Harvey's discomfort grew. 'I hadn't any choice but to ask you. Those men saved Anna's life last year. But I never thought you'd do it.' Looking more embarrassed than ever, the Yorkshireman held out his hand. 'Will you, sir?'

Adams, who had never known anything but dissension between the two men, was watching in fascination. As a shaded light clicked on at the Administrative Block entrance and drove back the growing dusk, he could have sworn there was the faintest hint of moisture in the small Air Commodore's eyes.

If it were true, Davies hid his emotion well. 'You always were a presumptuous sod, Harvey. But I suppose you can't help being what you are.' Frowning, pretending to begrudge the gesture, he hesitated and then thrust out his hand. 'All right, if that's what you want.'

A moment later he let out a howl. 'Damn it, you don't have to break it, do you?'

The startled Harvey hurriedly released his grip. 'I'm sorry, sir.'

'So you bloody well should be,' Davies snapped

nursing his hand. As Henderson and Adams fought back their hysteria, Anna stepped forward and kissed the Air Commodore's cheek. 'Thank you, Arthur. Thank you for everything.'

Before Davies could respond, she took Harvey's arm and drew him away. Davies stared after them indignantly. 'What the hell's the Service coming to? The bugger didn't even give me a salute.'

Adams thought afterwards that Henderson put it well. 'I think it was one of those cases when a handshake said much more than a salute, sir.'

Still embarrassed by the incident, Davies fell back on sarcasm. 'If we all started shaking each other's hand, Jock, the RAF would fall to pieces.' Before Henderson could reply, Davies turned to Adams. 'Come on, Frank. Van Breedenkamp's boys will have finished their tea and biscuits by this time. Let's go and find out what sort of a mess they made of that 262 plant.'

Adams left the bar and made for the hall telephone. After a couple of minutes of dialling and requesting numbers, he was both surprised and gratified to find himself in contact with Transport Command's station at Hatfield. 'Hello. Is it possible to speak with Miss Carol Manning? I'm afraid I don't know her rank.'

The speaker was cautious. 'Who are you, sir?'

'My name is Adams. Squadron Leader Adams.'

The voice changed in tone. 'Just a moment, sir. I'll see if she's available.'

A young voice sounded half a minute later. 'Hello. Who is that?'

'Is that Miss Carol Manning?'

'Yes.' Adams detected a quaver in the voice. 'Are you phoning about Squadron Leader Millburn?'

'Yes, I am.' As a sharp gasp sounded, Adams went on quickly: 'It's all right. Nothing's happened to him. It's just that he asked me to give you a letter. But as he'll be back at the station in the next day or two, I think he should give it to you himself if he still wants to. Is that all right?'

'Yes. But what's happened? Has he been on an operation?'

'I can't say anything about that. But I assure you he is safe and well and will be in contact with you in the next day or two.'

'You are telling the truth about him, aren't you? He is all right?'

Adams was thinking how young and vulnerable she sounded. 'Of course I am. You've absolutely nothing to worry about. I'll see he phones you the moment he gets back.'

At least there was one relieved and happy girl, Adams, thought as he made his way up the stairs. As he entered the bedroom he found Helga standing at the door. 'I thought earlier on it was you,' she told him. 'But when you went into the bar I believed I was mistaken until I heard you on the phone. What's been happening? And who were you phoning?'

Adams laughed as he kissed her. 'You sound just like a wife. Maisie saw me when I came in and I had to answer all her questions before I could get away. Then I had to phone Millburn's girl friend. I couldn't do it from the station because communications aren't restored yet.'

'Why had you to call her? Is Millburn one of those that are missing?'

'No, Millburn's all right. So are the majority of the others.'

Her face lit up. 'That's better news. Maisie must be thrilled. She was terribly upset this afternoon.'

'Yes. She's feeling better now.' Adams paused, then gave a grimace. 'Mind you, it has been quite a day.'

Sensing the emotion in him, she led him to a chair b

the fire. ‘Do you want to talk about it? Or aren’t you allowed to?’

Motioning her to sit beside him, Adams sank down. ‘I’m going to, whether I ought to or not. When he had finished speaking, she was looking both relieved and puzzled. ‘But if the two missions were successful, why might the squadron be disbanded?’

Adams could not disguise his bitterness. ‘Because we did the unforgivable. We bombed a concentration camp and perhaps saved hundreds of men from torture and death.’

Her eyes were huge. ‘I don’t understand. Why is that a crime?’

‘Ask our Air Staff. All we know is that it might mean disgrace for Davies and the end of the squadron. Ironical, isn’t it? The day we have heavy losses saving lives instead of taking them might be the day we are disbanded.’

Her spontaneous question could only have come from a woman. ‘If you are disbanded, would that mean all these special missions you have flown in the past would end?’

Adams nodded. ‘It might if a Board of Inquiry finds Davies guilty.’

‘But then wouldn’t that be a good thing for all those young men I met?’

Surprised by her question, Adams gave a wry laugh. I suppose you could say that. They might well have a better chance of survival if they no longer belong to a pecial service unit.’

She left her chair and sank on the carpet beside him, favourite posture of hers when they were alone. ‘Then why aren’t you feeling happy about it?’

It took a moment for Adams to answer that. ‘I suppose ’s because I’ve been part of the squadron for such a ng time.’

‘In other words you’re proud of it, aren’t you?’

There was reluctance in Adams’ admission. ‘Yes, I

suppose I am. I can't think of the times I've hated it when the boys haven't come back from an operation but there's the other side too. A man can't help but be proud of their achievements. It'll be hellish if it all ends up in disgrace.'

'But that's ridiculous, *kjaere*. The squadron's a household name all over Europe.'

'Even so, if Davies is disgraced and the squadron disbanded, it would be left under a stigma. People never believe there's smoke without fire.'

Knowing he was right, she laid her cheek against his knee. 'Perhaps it won't come to that. Perhaps Davies' superiors will understand it was a mission of mercy. After all, the German aircraft plant was destroyed. Surely that must be taken into account?'

Adams wondered. 'Perhaps. Perhaps not. But put tha aside for a moment. There's something I want to ask you.' As she lifted her oval face to him, Adams took heart. 'How would you like to be an innkeeper's mistress one day?'

She gave a laugh of surprise. 'Are you serious?'

'Very serious. While I was in the bar tonight, Joe sai he was definitely going to sell the pub once the war ended When I asked him if he'd give me first option, he said tha went without saying.'

'But what about your old job?'

'I can't go back to an office after living with th squadron all these years. I'd go out of my mind.'

'But what about Valerie? What would she say?'

'Valerie would never be an innkeeper's wife. In fa it could be the very thing that'll make her give me divorce.'

She was studying his face. 'But there is something el too, isn't there, *kjaere*? Something you haven't told me

She noticed he avoided the question when he replie 'You haven't answered me. Would you like to live he after the war? Be honest with me.'

She raised up and kissed him. 'Of course I would. I love this old pub already.'

'You are sure?' Adams insisted.

She put a finger on his lips. 'I'm very sure. I could be very happy here. So stop worrying about it. Just sit there and smoke your pipe while I go and see Maisie. I won't be long.'

Left alone in the room, Adams found he could not rest. Rising, he switched off the light and drew aside the blackout curtain. Pools of light from storm lanterns were visible round the airfield perimeter where mechanics were working on the surviving Mosquitoes. In the distance a truck engine was running and as Adams opened the window for a moment he could hear the faint music of a popular song coming from the men's Mess.

Evocative sounds, Adams thought. Sounds he had heard hundreds of times. Wartime sounds that he ought to be glad might soon be ended.

But he knew he would miss them and that worried the introspective Adams. War was filthy, disgusting, obscene. A disease of mankind. Then why in God's name did he want to settle himself down in a place that reeked with the atmosphere of combat and sacrifice? Was there something twisted in his psyche? After all, he had volunteered for two dangerous missions when there had been no call on him whatever to do so. Surely that must have some significance. Had he deceived himself all these years that he hated war when deep down he found its many elements exciting and fulfilling? The thought horrified Adams.

Steps on the stairs made him close the window and draw the curtain again. As Helga entered the room, illuminated only by the electric fire, she believed for moment Adams had retired to bed. Leaving the light switched off she moved forward, only then to see Adams standing by the window. 'What on earth are you doing there in the dark?'

Adams ignored her question. 'Is Maisie all right?'

'Oh, yes. She's much better.'

Adams returned to his chair. 'Good. I know how upset she gets when any of the boys go missing.'

She approached his chair, her voice soft and concerned, 'What's the matter, *kjaere*?'

Adams sounded almost defiant. 'Nothing's the matter.'

She hesitated, then sank down beside him again. In the silence they both heard the far off drone of an aircraft. Probably a weather ship going out to check enemy skies for tomorrow's operations, Adams thought. Then Helga broke the silence. 'Something has happened since I left the bedroom, hasn't it, *kjaere*?'

Adams hated his irritability. 'No, of course it hasn't. I'm just tired, that's all.'

'No, *kjaere*. It is something much deeper than that.' Lifting her face, she gazed up at him. 'I think you are wondering why you want to buy this inn.'

As he gave a violent start, she nodded. 'I'm right, aren' I? You are wondering why a man like yourself who hate war should want to buy a place that will remind you abou it every day of your life.'

Adams' voice was hoarse. 'How did you guess that?'

'Because I know you better than you know yourself my love. You can do nothing without questioning you motives.'

For a moment he wanted to hurt her. 'All right, if yo know me so well, why do I want to buy it? Why does man want to keep reminding himself of something unles it secretly attracts him?'

She gave a quiet laugh. 'There are times when you ca be such a silly man. Do you know that, Frank?'

'Often,' he said bitterly.

'But seldom as silly as tonight. You don't want th inn because you like war, *kjaere*. You want it becau you hate war so much.'

'That's pure nonsense.'

'No, it isn't. You know that people soon forget the horrors of war, just as they forget the sacrifices made for them. And so you want to remind them by displaying the photographs of the boys who had made those sacrifices. You want to show them the terrible cost of war. And you also want to honour your friends, the living and the dead.'

When Adams said nothing, she lifted a hand and turned his face towards her. 'I knew all this when you showed me the photographs in the bar,' she said. 'I could tell then how much you cared about those men.'

Adams made a grimace of disgust. 'You're making me sound like a sentimental fool.'

'You are sentimental, *kjaere*. You feel, you care, you are sensitive, and you are loyal. That is why I love you so much.'

Adams frowned. 'But surely men who hate war can't bear to be reminded of it.'

'Not the braves ones, *kjaere*. They know one should never forget what an evil it is or it might come again.'

Adams, who suddenly felt as if a window had cleared n his mind, took a deep breath. 'You're right. I do feel hat. We shouldn't forget. Those men gave so much of hemselves. They never counted the cost. All of them, he dead and the living. It would be a sin if all that were orgotten.'

She reached up and touched his face. 'They won't while ou are here, my love.'

With his mind clear now, Adams could not stop lking. 'There's another reason why I'd like to stay re. If the word gets around, some of those still alive ight come back.'

She knew he was thinking of Grenville and Hilde as ell as the rest of his friends. She took his hand and essed her cheek against it. 'It's settled, my love. You are going to have your wish.' Then, to lighten his mood, her tone changed. 'But when your friends come, I think I shall have to keep my eye on you. I have heard about the things you get up to in your Mess.'

Adams was visibly relaxing now. He began fishing for his pipe. 'Thank God you like these old inns.'

Her voice teased him. 'What would you have done if I didn't? Send me back to Norway?'

He smiled. 'Where else?'

She pouted. 'And I thought you loved me.'

He pulled out his tobacco pouch. 'You do realise we won't make much money.'

She lifted her shoulders. 'So?'

In the fireglow her face and blonde hair had the richness of an oil painting. Gazing down at her, Adams shook his head. 'What am I talking about? If you look half as beautiful as you look tonight, the men'll flock in just to gaze at you.'

Her eyes rounded humorously. 'That sounds very exciting.'

'Don't be a flirt,' Adams said.

'But I must flirt a little, *kjaere*, if we are to make a success of it.'

Adams tapped her cheek with his pipe. 'You flirt only with me. Let's have that clear from the beginning.'

Reaching up, she threw her arms around him and the laugh that delighted him lit up the darkened room. 'You know something, *kjaere*? I can't wait to becom an innkeeper's mistress.'